Gideon Rex

Philip Mazza

Also by Philip Mazza

From Under a Tree
Book One; The Harrow Saga

Shadow in the Flame
Book Two; The Harrow Saga

Children at the Gate
Book Three; The Harrow Saga

The Child of Fire
Book Four; The Harrow Saga
(Coming 2025)

The Neon Hive

The Quantum Gardener

At the End of it All

Beneath the Ashen Sky

I Know God is a Cat

The Road to Stillwater

The Never-Ending Road

The Cosmic Vending Machine

The Wicked Man Cometh

Gideon Rex

Philip Mazza

OMNI PUBLISHERS

Omni Publishers of New York
ISBN 979-8-9924526-4-8
Printed in the United States of America

First Printing: July 2025

From the Publisher: Readers will note a deliberate and distinctive prose style used in this novel. The author frequently employs a minimalist, almost unpunctuated style, often omitting commas, and using fragmented sentence structures. This choice is not accidental; it is designed to strip away artifice, immersing the reader directly into the raw, unmediated consciousness of the characters and the stark reality of their world. This unique rhythm compels a closer engagement with the text, reflecting the unvarnished truths and relentless forces at the story's heart.

To those who cling to the dying embers of this broken world, who dare to dream of a future even as the end may soon come.

If the One above, in grace or in grief, chooses to begin again, may you rise from the ashes of that divine reset, whenever it may come. May what follows be kinder. May it endure. But remember this: even in Eden, the serpent waits.

Prologue

I have seen the end of civilization.

It came in a blaze. In fire. Not in some righteous flood. No trumpets. No reckoning. No gods.

Just fire.

And then silence.

I remember the fields when they still held food and not dust. When men traded labor for grain and women sang into the wind like it meant something. That was before the black wagons. Before the voices on the loudspeakers spoke louder than the ones in your head. Before the drop of truth and the rise of the issue.

You don't understand, do you. I don't blame you. Who could. Born into this rot, suckled on plastic and praise. Every word fed to you like medicine. Like it might save you from the very man who brewed it.

No, you don't know the world before him. Before the one they called Rex.

Listen. I was there.

The boy had a name once. Gideon Stark. Carved out of steel and water, heir to the Mid-Con Food Amalgam, one of the largest food producers in the world. Not just born into power—birthed by it. Molded in its jaws. His father sat at tables the rest of us didn't know existed. Made decisions with the stroke of a pen that condemned thousands. But Gideon—he wasn't satisfied with that.

He wanted to be king.

The first time I saw him, he was standing on the hood of a truck in a dead town with no sign and no road, the sky hanging low and orange like it was sick of watching. He didn't shout. Didn't need to. His silence pulled men like gravity. I saw a man lay down his rifle and kneel in the dirt. I saw a woman lift her baby up like an offering.

Later, they said, Salve Rex.

And Gideon nodded.

"You know what I see when I look out there?" he asked me once.

We were in a high tower. The Spire. The kind of tower of stone and tinted glass and men with wires in their heads. I was there under pretenses—old connections, false clearances. Trying to see if there was still something human in him.

"I see mouths," he said.

"Is that what we are now?" I asked. "Mouths?"

He turned. That smile. Empty and full at once. "That's all they've ever been. But now I've made them honest."

People say he took control. Like it was something he did in a single day. Like lightning. No.

He slid into it. Like oil into water. Like a whisper in the wind.

He started with an issue. Never let it go. There was always one. Too much food. Too little. Refugee swarms. Poisoned rain. Crops failing. Crops thriving too much. Always a reason. Always a way to tighten the grip.

Then came the surrogation. You know what that means? Replacing what's real with what feels right. He made screens we all watched bleed lies until they became gospel. Showed faces on repeat until they became the only ones you remembered. He erased people. And when they were forgotten, they stayed forgotten.

Last came the supplication. He made the world kneel with their own legs. Gave them just enough to make them beg for more.

Food became currency. Currency became obedience. And obedience became survival.

I remember the Silencers first. Men in black coats, eyes red from the stimulants they took to keep them from dreaming. They didn't ask questions. Didn't scream. Just quieted things. Towns. Cities. Ideas. People.

Then the Droppers. Not soldiers—priests. They dropped messages. Chemicals. Both. Made people love what they feared and fear what they loved. Made them forget what came before and need what came next.

And the Echoers. Ah. Those were the worst. Not men. Not anymore. Walking speakers of the Word. You'd hear them humming in the woods, on dead streets. Salve Rex. Salve Rex. It would get inside you. Like hunger. But it became worse later. When they became servants to the Siren.

Someone asked me once, in the tunnels beneath the big city, while we were sorting sacks of synthetic flour: "Why do they follow him?"

I didn't have to think.

"Because it's easier than remembering what they lost."

He built a pyramid of power, did Gideon. Not of stone, but of need. Food at the top. Him at the top of food. Below that, the ones who could take it from you. Below that, the ones who could lie to you. And at the bottom, everyone else. Chewing. Starving. Praying. Not always in that order.

He stood at its apex like a monument to cruelty, and we worshipped him for it.

And he spoke to us. Not like a ruler. Like a god. With that voice. Flat. Slow. Made you lean in. Like maybe if you understood him, you wouldn't die today.

And we loved him.

I saw a man starve himself so his child could stay on the registry. Another fed his daughter rat meat. No choice. Told her it was from the Reserve. That it would be okay. When she suddenly died, he needed to explain it. He turned her in. What else could he do? Said the child was an enemy to the State. Asked that her name be struck from the registry.

Salve Rex, he whispered.

How could one so young be an enemy?

He stood there in the gray light with nothing in his hands. The world turned cold about him. The silence after. The ledger closed. The name gone. The father alone with his hunger.

Yes. I knew Gideon before all of it. Not well. But enough.

We were boys. Same school. I was a reader, they said. Smart, but not exceptional. He was different. He'd look through you like your thoughts were printed on your skin. Teachers didn't correct him. They deferred.

He once asked me if I thought people were good.

I said yes.

He said, "Then they deserve to starve."

I thought he was joking. He wasn't.

The wars came. Battles. Burnings. Sometimes whole cities. Sometimes just the books. Sometimes just the tongues.

Truth went extinct. I watched it die.

Then the Big Fire came. Green.

Some said he died, too. Died when the great fire came to the tower. Others say he merged with the systems. Became a signal, never-ending.

Me?

I think he still lives. Somewhere cold. Underground. Dreaming of new hungers. New ways to make the world need.

I'm not here to warn you. It's too late for that.

I'm here to witness. That's all I can do now.

Because when the fires stop burning and the wires go quiet and the food dries up and the people finally open their mouths and nothing comes out—they'll remember the name.

So, let me tell you about Gideon, the one they called Rex.

- Simon

1 The Amalgam Ascendant

Magnus Stark said to the boy, "The world is not kind. Never was. They say there was a time. A thinner world, draped in pleasantries. Smiles like paper lanterns, glowing hollow. Some speak of it still, but their teeth are few and their eyes gone milky with remembering. Such notions are now relegated to the realm of myth, whispered in hushed tones by the old and the foolish."

They walked the cut rows of MidCon, father and son, boots pressing down the hardpack between dying stalks and synthetic runnels. The sun sat low behind a wall of carbon haze, casting long iron shadows from the things in the field—metal men, their joints hissing soft steam, arms working in practiced rhythm. They moved without pause, without breath, without need. Fingers of alloy plucked wilted ears from browning stalks, bundled them in silence, stacked them high. Machines of old manufacture, patched with rust and wire, born from factories long silent.

The boy watched them. Their blank faces turned to no one. Their hands never slowed. It would be the last time he saw them there.

His father looked out across the rows.

"Too much upkeep, Gideon," he said. "Easier to have humans. Cheaper. You don't patch skin. You bury it. They work harder when their bellies cry."

Gideon didn't answer. He only watched the metal men, their backs bent in perfect submission as the wind stirred the dust around their feet.

Later, they went on to another field. The sun above them like something hung to punish. A pale eye. No warmth in it. Just heat. It beat down on the land with the slow force of judgment. Once the fields had moved like prayer. Wheat golden and clean. Now, only rows like scars. Marked and measured. Profit drawn in lines of absence. The sky leached of color. A wind flat and hot, pulling the reek of chemicals across the soil. Somewhere, a rig vented steam. The sound like a dying thing.

Ahead was a massive harvester. A great wheel of steel and iron that blocked the sun. The boy squinted at the machine, its blades whispering through the crop-like teeth through hide as it rolled, shredding heads of engineered lettuce with a wet crunch that turned the stomach. The machine's undercarriage glistened with moisture and grease, dripping in a slow rhythm that matched the thud of its treads. The engine growled low and constant, a mechanical hymn to utility, its breath thick and oily in the air, staining the lungs with every breath. Birds no longer came here. No insects. No worms in the dirt. Nothing but the machines and what they left behind: rutted rows, chemical husks, fields scraped down to the bone. Magnus Stark lit a smoke, watched it curl upward and vanish into the colorless sky like prayer unanswered. No rain, no mercy. Only the yield. The boy said nothing. He didn't have to. His face was all question, and the world all answer.

They stood there by the field of engineered lettuce, green in the way mold is green. More machines came, moving slowly and heavy, clanking their way through rows that bled when torn. An old man rode one like a condemned priest on a holy relic. His hands shaking on the controls, mouth sunken. He spat. Dust swallowed it whole. Magnus looked down at his son.

"Kindness," he said. "Gone like rain in a drought."

Gideon Stark, who would one day be called Rex, came up from a land that broke men like horses and didn't bother burying the bones. He was born under high ceilings and polished light, silver spoons laid out in tidy rows, but the world outside was ruled by the same hard sun and indifferent dirt that turned the rest of them mean and lean. His bloodline wound back through men who had carved the Food Amalgam out of the bones of old nations, and what they'd built was no company. It was a god. It breathed, it fed, it ruled. The Amalgam was in the grain and the water, in the mouths of children and the sweat of men. It fed a nation and would soon feed the world.

His mother was a pale ghost of a woman, half in this world and half-sunk in some quiet grief of her own. She sat often by the windows, thin hands folded like paper. Once, without looking at him, she said, "Our food feeds them, Gideon. But what feeds us?" Her voice was like the wind sliding under a door.

Gideon did not know the answer but would soon find one.

His father was a mountain. Broad and near silent, with eyes like glass pulled from deep water. His hunger was not for food nor warmth nor company but for dominion, and it spread in him like frost over windowpanes. He moved through the house as if it had been built for his shadow, each door opening before him, each voice going quiet. A king without a crown.

Gideon watched him. Watched how the man's hand closed around things. Not with love. With claim. From him, he learned that power was not bestowed—it was taken. Like a blade you lifted from a dead man's chest.

"Control," he told his son. "That's all there is."

Control the land. Control the seed. Control the hand that reached for bread and the mouth that dared to speak thanks. Nothing was sacred. Not love. Not mercy. Only the grip. Only the hold.

They stood out behind the barn where the boards were gray and split and the nails bled rust down the wood. The dry dirt blew in little eddies around their boots, and the sky hung low and hard as hammered tin. His father ground the nub of a cigar into the earth with the heel of his boot, slow and deliberate, and looked at him.

"You think the people love us, son?" he said.

Gideon said nothing. The wind worried at the hem of his coat. Somewhere a dog barked once and fell silent.

"They don't," his father said. "How can people eat our food and hate us? No. They fear us." He showed his teeth in a grin hard and joyless, a grin like a man who had seen the edge of the storm and stepped toward it. "They fear us because we control something they need. Fear's the only currency that doesn't lose its value."

The Stark compound stood like a wound in the land. High walls looped the estate like a noose. Inside, the grass was green, cut clean by machines. Villas sprawled in the sun. The air smelled of oil and citrus. Guards walked the parapets with rifles slung low, dead-eyed in the heat. Inside the walls, Gideon moved like a ghost through a dream built for him. But he knew the truth of things. He'd seen the lines. Seen the gaunt eyes of the workers bent under sun and hunger. The rations like slop ladled into stained tins. He'd seen men kneel for food. Women weep and wipe their mouths with the backs of their hands.

Gideon was not born to ignorance. His father saw to that. From the time the boy could stand on bowed legs, he was taught the ledger and the lash, taught that men were numbers and numbers were to be balanced or broken. "A man's life weighs no heavier than a bushel of wheat," his father told him. Gideon rode at his side into the fields where the laborers stooped double and coughed blood into the dust. He watched his father speak to them in the cold grammar of ownership. At night by firelight, the boy recited the rules of survival until the words fit into his mouth like his own teeth. In time, he grew tall and lean with a hard set to his jaw and a hollowness behind his eyes. A young man fashioned from profit and loss, tempered in the cold forge of his father's will.

One day, he stood by the fence and watched the workers shuffle forward in silence, a slow, broken tide of bodies moving through the dust. He turned to a guard. The man's arms were knotted with muscle, and his head shone in the sun like a forged slug of lead.

"They hate us . . ." Gideon started, ". . . don't they?"

The guard spat in the dirt and wiped his mouth with the back of his hand.

"Sir, hate don't matter when the belly's empty," he said.

They whispered where they could. In the dark corners of barracks and the stained stalls of latrines, in the muffled hours of smoke breaks, and under the low mechanical groan of the harvesters that never stopped. They said the Amalgam was stitched together with broken backs and drained spirits, that the fortune of the Starks was a thing bought not with ingenuity but with blood and silence and the spent years of men who had nothing left to give.

As a young man, Gideon seldom heard the whispers. The world he moved through was loud with labor and cruelty. He had little ear for anything else. When the words did reach him, they clattered harmlessly off the iron in him, no more than leaves blown against a wall. He would shake his head and laugh.

"Whining," he said. "The bitter song of the weak. Men too small to shape the world and too proud to be carried by it." His voice held a scorn, like his father. So clean and sharp it cut the speakers to silence.

He believed in the Amalgam. He walked among the machines with a kind of wonder. Watched the vats steaming and lines running thick with food, and he saw the bones of a new world rising from the ash of the old. The future will be costly, he thought. It should cost everything. He dreamed of the Amalgam swelling across the land, across the nation, across the world. He saw the growers and the millers and the haulers crushed like insects beneath the slow and endless turning of the wheels. He saw them all broken and brought under one hand. His hand. A kingdom of hunger ruled by one king.

He made his plans in the dark and quiet places of his mind. Plans to seize the fields and the factories both. To hold the seed and the harvest and the meal set down on every man's plate. To build a machine so great and so terrible that no man could live beyond its reach.

Gideon kept his thoughts to himself. Held his plans like a knife against his thigh, hidden from the world. Waiting. Waiting for the right time. After all, time didn't cost a damned thing.

His tutor, an elderly man named Silas, with hands that trembled from age or memory, once told him, "Progress has a price, Gideon. Always does. Pay it and you will be rewarded."

Gideon respected the old man. He sat with him in the gray hours and spoke of things he dared not share with others. The fear that he would fail. The fear that he would not.

There was a time when the heat held and the flies thickened, and Magnus killed a man beside the ration shed.

The worker had spoken, just spoken. Said the rations were getting smaller. His voice was calm. That was the mistake.

Magnus stepped forward and broke his jaw with the first hit. It made a sound like dropping meat in mud. The man folded. Tried to crawl. But Magnus kept on. Boot. Fist. Elbow. The dust turned dark beneath him. A tooth landed near someone's boot. No one moved.

When it was done, Magnus stood there, his chest rising, blood on his hands.

He took a bandana from the dead man's belt and wiped his knuckles slowly, deliberately, like brushing crumbs from a table. Then he tossed the cloth aside and walked off.

No one spoke. No one mourned. The line crept forward like cattle toward feed.

Later, Gideon sat with Silas in the dim room where the light fell in thin bands through the slats. "Why?" he said. "Why would my father do that?"

Silas watched the dust drifting in the shafts of sun. "Anger's a kind of fuel," he said. "Hot. Burns clean. Folks use it to move things in the world they got no other way to move."

Gideon shook his head. "How can something so wrong be so strong?"

Silas smiled without warmth. "World don't much care what you think is right. Only cares what you can carry and what you can't."

***

Gideon had learned from his father that power wasn't something granted, but something seized, held with the grip of a man who knew how to break others with the weight of his will. His father had taught him the old ways—how blunt force was sometimes the only way to ensure control was kept, how men had risen not through kindness, but through the calculated use of their fists, their words, their machines.

"A man who can't make the world bend to him is weak," his father had said more than once. "And weakness means someone else will make it bend for you."

Gideon had taken these lessons to heart. They were simple. Direct. Like the weight of his father's hand on his shoulder when the world seemed too large to hold.

Soon, he was walking the halls of the university. The weight of it lay heavy in the rooms like ash. Dead air and chalkdust. The droning of the professor like the call of something blind and old. Eyes upon him. But never knowing him. Never the cut of him. They spoke of nations and causes, of men who ruled by reason or song or the red ache of love. Children's talk. Gideon had seen the truth plain. What rose from the mire was not vision but violence. Not hope but hunger. The world was for those who took. However they took it.

When he sat in the university's lecture halls, he was never truly there. His mind was elsewhere, tracing the paths of power. He listened to the professors speak of strategy, of governance, of how leaders climbed their ladders. But it was all theory. Nothing like the dirt of the land, the grind of industry, the weight of control his father had shown him. He had been taught by his father to see through the veils of the world. He saw the game. And it wasn't played with words. It was played with things that moved in the dark—money, fear, and a well-placed hand on the throat of your enemy.

When the first term ended, he went home and crossed the long fields and found Silas sitting on the porch of his small shack with a cigarette burning down to the filter. Gideon dropped into the chair across from him and sat staring out at the dead rows of corn beyond the fence line.

"I hate that place," he said.

Silas took a drag from his cigarette and said nothing.

"The courses are worthless. The professors don't know a damn thing about the world. They talk and talk. None of it means anything."

Silas flicked the ash from his cigarette. "You're learning."

"Learning what? How to speak like a fool? How to live with your head in the clouds?"

Silas looked at him. "You don't have to like a thing to learn from it."

Gideon shook his head. "It's a fool's dream," he said. "They don't teach you anything real. Not like my father. Not like you."

Silas ground the cigarette out on the rail and dropped the spent butt into a jar among the others. "Wait," he said. "You may yet find something worth keeping."

And he did.

In the lab, he'd seen it and he knew. Power. Not the kind they wrote about in manifestos or whispered in parliamentary halls but the real thing. The wet, microbial truth of it. The folding of life's smallest codes into something sharp and wielded. Not just to feed the starved or bolster the sick. That was the lie. The dream they hung like bait from the hook. No. This was for control. Crops that withered unless you paid. Illness that walked only where profit pointed. The others in white coats didn't see it. Couldn't. Still clinging to notions of right and wrong like rusted dogma. But Gideon. He saw. He knew the game was older than ethics and deeper than guilt. There was no good. No evil. Just the scale of one man's reach. And he was ready. Hunger was a coin now. And he meant to mint it.

Hunger's a choice, he thought, his mind drifting as a professor's words fell like the steady drip of water onto stone. Only a few can choose who gets to eat.

When he could, he stayed on in the lab, and when the others had gone, he stayed still. The hum of the machines was a comfort to him. He worked in the half-light, the air thick with the smell of ozone and solvents. He pieced together the broken things. He ran tests no one had asked for. He sought the place where the rules broke down and the world revealed itself. He learned what could be learned. He learned everything

Because of this, he had few friends at the university. Most kept their distance. They watched him as if he were a shadow thrown by something larger. There was a darkness about him. They could not name it. But they knew it. He moved through the world like a man already departed, sent ahead of his own dying. He carried silence like a stone in his coat. Heavy. Known to him.

"You ever talk to Stark?" one student asked another.

"No. He doesn't talk to anyone."

"Yeah. Maybe he's got nothing useful to say."

They laughed.

His education was the kind measured not in grades but in reckonings.

His assigned courses at the university were strict and unforgiving, shaped by his father's hand, a curriculum of the old world and the new. Cicero. Sun Tzu. Clausewitz. The old voices. And the new.

He learned to speak so that men listened. And to listen so that men forgot they were speaking.

"You pay attention, son," his father told him.

"Yes sir. I will."

"You remember what you hear."

"I remember everything."

In one lecture, a professor asked him what he thought money was.

Gideon said, "It's not water. It doesn't flow."

"No?"

He shook his head. "It's a shadow. It moves with the man who casts it. And that man builds a wall with one hand and burns a bridge with the other."

One time, on another break, when Gideon was home from the university, he and his father sat at the table in the dim of the kitchen. The meat lay cold on the plates. Neither of them touched it. His father's eyes were like chipped granite.

"What's the first rule of war, son?"

Gideon stared straight ahead. "Know your enemy. And know how to starve him."

His father nodded once. A faint curl at the corner of his mouth. Nothing more. The silence afterward said the rest.

He excelled in the work. Journals thick as Bibles, their pages dense with the glyphs of synthetic biology and futures written in the script of the double helix. He read them all. He understood the old dance of genes and proteins, the silent calculus of life. Not in a way to mend them, to make them better, but to break them. He saw how a crop might be turned against its kin, how a field might feed one town and kill another. He knew the chemistry of blight, the mathematics of scarcity. He learned to speak the language of famine with fluency and precision. He dreamed of hunger not as a wound to be healed but a weapon to be sharpened. And he saw how it might be done.

He moved through the laboratory as a man might walk the nave of a church long since burned. The silence there was heavy. Machines murmured in their sleep. Blue light flickered on the walls. He had ceased long ago to think in terms of good and evil. There was only the work. The unlocking of patterns. The deciphering of codes older than men, written in blood and bone, and the green script of leaves.

He saw life not for its light nor its heat but for the cold rigging beneath. The joists and beams. The laced sinews of cause and end. He could look on a field and know how to make it yield or starve. He saw the seed's betrayal in the name of bounty. The helix twisted like wire round the throat of what was coming. He knew what others would not name. That hunger was not a curse but a craft. A thing men kept alive like fire. Not for warmth but for power.

The hour was late. The reason had fled. The air was sour with solvents and the slow rot of sleeplessness. Gideon stood over a tray of gene-sequenced corn, a priest at his altar. A young technician lingered at the sink, hands trembling around a cup of cold coffee.

"We can end it, you know," the technician said.

Gideon looked up. Skin pale beneath the lights. "End what?"

"Hunger," the tech said. "The famines. The empty plates. All of it. Gone."

Gideon blinked. "You talk like that's a good thing."

Gideon's eyes moved across the vials. Rows of them. Frozen, labeled, humming faintly.

"You don't think it is?" the tech said, setting down his mug.

"I think . . ." Gideon rubbed his jaw. "I think biotech like this is a kind of power. People don't just use power. They wield it. For whatever they want."

The tech nodded absently, not looking at him.

"Imagine what this could do," Gideon continued. "Plagues that find only one kind of blood. Fields that wither unless you pay for the cure. It's a blade. You know that, don't you?"

The tech turned then. No smile on his face. "I suppose anything's a weapon, if you're clever enough."

There was a silence between them.

"You ever think about that?" Gideon asked. "About where this goes? What this can become in ten years, twenty?"

The tech walked to a terminal. He keyed in a sequence without looking.

"Not really," he said.

"Don't you worry about some madman acting like a god? Using technology to wield power?"

The tech stared at Gideon. "We're not gods."

"No. Not yet."

The tech backed a step. "Jesus."

"Not yet," Gideon repeated.

And then he was quiet. The tech stood there in the sterile hum of the lab. The lights buzzed overhead. Outside, the wind keened against the windows like something shut out too long.

***

Upon graduation, Gideon came home and went to work at the Amalgam. His parents began showing their age. Fading. The house stood hollow and still. His mother lay in her bed with the covers pulled to her chin, her breathing faint in the gloom. The machines beside her pulsed and clicked. Keeping her alive. She had not risen in months. The world beyond the window might as well have been a world lost to time. Sometimes he would sit with her, her hand small and cold in his. She would stare at him with eyes blurred by fever and memory and say nothing at all.

His father moved through the halls like a shadow bent by the wind. The cane he leaned on might have grown from him like a branch from a dead tree. His back was bowed, his face drawn and gray. He paused often, steadying himself against the wall, the old strength gone from his limbs. He had lived a life shaped by labor and caution, the steady furrow drawn through a hard world. He made no room for folly and less for the dreams of his son.

Gideon watched him one evening as the sun bled out behind the fields, the old man standing in the doorway, the cane planted firm in the dust. "You ought to rest," Gideon said.

His father did not look at him. "Rest is for the weak and the dying."

"You can't do it all anymore."

The old man turned. Eyes like hammered iron under a sky going black. "The world doesn't give a damn what a man can do," he said, "Only what he's put here to do." He coughed, a dry rattle in his chest, and shuffled back inside, leaving Gideon alone in the failing light.

He pressed him for a lab. Wouldn't let it go. Said he needed space, a real place, something vast and wired to the teeth. Much larger than what they already had. Said the old work was dead. That this was new. Said he'd bend the marrow of men like wire, said the dirt would answer him, and the fields would speak his name. Said it was for the Amalgam. For what comes after. He talked like thunder, like judgment. Fire in his mouth, plague in his breath. The old man just stood there. Last scraps of light bleeding out across the land. The fields lay open, endless, their straight rows drawn like scars across the world. Like they'd been carved by God Himself and left to run out to the ends of the earth.

"What more do you need?" he said. "The land provides. Always has."

"If we don't move the Amalgam forward, the other producers will push us out."

"They can't push us out."

His father looked at him then, eyes narrowing as if trying to read something written in the air. "They think they know the land," he said. "But they don't. Them and their shiny machines, their fancy labs. They don't know a thing about the dirt, about the way it listens, the way it works with you. They're just selling promises to people who want to believe. They'll run their fields into the ground, Gideon. You'll see. They're too busy within their labs to notice the soil turning to dust beneath them." He paused, his hands rough against the wood of the porch. "They can't push us out. Not while we've got the land, and we've always got the land."

He had never touched anything born in a lab. He trusted the old powers. The soil and the iron and the grit in a man's hand. He believed in industry. In chemicals that burned the pests from the land and made it right. That was the law and the order of things. Anything else was heresy.

"You think this is the answer, Gideon?" he said, his voice failing at times. "It isn't. Why would I spend so much money for you to sit in a lab all day. It's reckless. A reckless tampering with forces best left alone."

The air between them was thick with the years and the things left unsaid, a slow war for the soul of the Amalgam. Gideon felt the hard hand of his father's caution, the old man's will clamped down on him like iron. He wanted to break free of it. To drive the Amalgam past the old ways, past mere survival. To make it into something else. A power that could shape the world anew.

The land was no longer just a field of grain. It was a weapon. A judgment.

He told Silas that night. "My father sees only the bottom line," Gideon said, his voice low and burning. "He's chained to the past. I see what's coming."

Silas stroked his graying beard, and the words came slow. Deliberate. "Your father's bound to the old ways," he said. "He's married to what's dead and don't know it. Clings to old things like they'll rise again. He don't see what's comin'. The future's a wild dog, Gideon. Hungry. It don't beg and it don't wait. Feed it what it wants and maybe it lets you be. But starve it and it'll come for you all the same. Remember that. You listen to me. The future don't honor the past. It replaces it. Always."

The words stayed there in the air. Gideon felt something stir inside him, some dark new thing uncoiling from its sleep. He knew the truth of it, knew it had been waiting in him all along.

The days slid by. He understood what must be done. One evening when the light drew long over the fields and the ground seemed to hum beneath his boots he went to his father. The old man sat in his chair, bowed by the years, the cane leaning against the frame. Gideon stood before him, his voice calm and sure. "Silas has shown me the way, Father," he said. "The world's changing. The Amalgam can be made into something different. We've fed the old beast long enough. It's time to feed the future. I need you to help me do that."

"Silas is an old fool," his father sneered. "You listen to that nonsense? I don't know why I've kept him around. A man like him can't see past his own shadow." His voice rose as if noise alone could smother the thought. "This past isn't some beast to be fed, Gideon. You don't feed the past. It feeds you." His eyes hardened, the long years carved deep in his face. "And what do you think will happen if you go on trusting this future of yours, eh? It'll eat you alive. Same as it's eaten better men. Crazy thinkers." He struck the cane against the floor, the sound sharp in the room, the fury in him sharper still.

Gideon left the chamber with his father's voice clawing at the dark behind him. The cane's crack rang on. He pitied the old man. A relic. Still, something cold turned in his gut. Not doubt in the cause. Only in the road ahead. The Amalgam had to change. The world would not be healed. It would have to burn.

But what Gideon didn't know was that his talk with Silas a few nights past would be the last of its kind. There'd be no farewell. No reckoning. Just the silence that follows when one man vanishes from the world of another, and the wind moves on like nothing was ever there at all.

The next morning, he went to visit the old man and found him on his porch. He was broken. Twisted in a way that spoke of violence. Skin torn, bruised, bleeding. The marks were cruel, as if the land itself had turned on him. No tool, no clear cause. Just the stillness after something awful. And in that stillness, something in Gideon began to turn.

Gideon stood over his mother's bed. The machines muttered their low song in the stillness, and her body lay there strung with wires like some broken marionette. Her chest rose and fell in fits. A life pared down to the barest terms. His hands trembled at his sides. In the hush of that sterile room, the fury in him gathered like dark weather over open plains.

"Silas is dead, Mother," he murmured, his voice low and rough. "Dead because of him." He slammed his fist against the wall, the sudden force making the air feel thicker, heavier. "I knew this would happen."

She barely stirred, her eyes flickering open for a moment, her voice a rasp as thin as paper. "Gideon . . ."

"Don't say my name like that," he snapped and stood, pacing the room, his voice rising. "You don't get to say my name anymore. You're not the one who has to live with this. Silas is gone.

And I know who's to blame." He stopped in front of her, glaring down as if she could offer him some kind of answer, some relief. "Father . . . that damn fool. He doesn't care about the future. All he cares about is his damn chemicals, his soil."

She closed her eyes again, the weight of his anger sinking deep into the silence. "Gideon . . . your Father only wants . . ."

"Don't you see," he said, fists clenched tight, his voice sharp with anger. "He's the reason Silas is dead. He's the reason I'm this way. He's the reason we're all this way." He stepped back, the room seeming too small, too tight, the walls pressing in. "He doesn't care. All he sees is the land, the earth like it's some goddamn altar to worship. And Silas . . . Silas just wanted to help. He wanted to make something better. Something that wasn't just about surviving. He would've helped me to change things, to fix things."

His mother sighed and turned her head away from him.

There was nothing but the quiet hum of the machines now, the sterile air heavy with unspoken words. Gideon sank into the chair by the bed, his shoulders slumping, exhaustion overtaking him. "Silas trusted me," he whispered. "And now he's gone. And I'm left with nothing but this."

***

Magnus Stark's death came swift as a storm, the kind of end that caught the breath in your throat. Some said it was a heart attack, the kind that eats at a man from the inside, fed by years of too much and not enough. Others spoke quieter. Their words heavy with suspicion—poison, untraceable, they said. A slow-acting death, administered with care. A son watching, waiting, eager to claim what was his. But no one knew for sure. In MidCon, truth had a way of slinking off into the shadows, leaving only rumors behind.

The house felt emptier than it ever had. Gideon entered the dim room where his mother lay, her face was pale, hollowed, eyes sunken with the sickness that had claimed so much of her. The air in the room smelled of medicine and dust.

He stood by the bed for a moment, watching her struggle for breath, hearing the machines drone on, before sitting down in the worn chair beside her. The silence between them was thick, but he knew better than to force words. She didn't need them. She'd never needed them much in the past.

"Change comes, Mother," he said, breaking the quiet at last. "Whether we like it or not."

Her eyes flicked to him, the old history strung up between them like a wire. He could feel her looking at him, still keen in her way though her body had long since turned against her.

"You think I don't know what you've done?" she said, her voice a shadow of its former strength, cracked and thin.

He leaned forward, elbows pressing into his knees, eyes locked onto hers. "What, Mother? What have I done?"

She coughed then, a sickly, hollow sound that made her whole frame shudder. After a moment, she spoke again, her breath wheezing in the quiet room. "You know what you've done. I don't have to tell you. One day it'll catch up with you. Just wait. It'll end and there'll be nothing left."

"It's all going to end, Mother. This . . . what's left of everything you've ever known. The way we live . . . it's soon going to be over. It's no longer enough anymore, don't you know." He sighed. "There's nothing left to hold on to but memories. And memories don't feed you."

She was still, her breath a shallow thing, the pause between them stretching longer. The room felt colder. The machines clicked and groaned, their presence more ominous than ever.

"You're an abomination," she muttered, barely audible, her eyes sinking shut, her words heavy with contempt. "A monster."

Gideon's jaw tightened, his lips pressing into a thin line. He looked at the machines again, the wires and tubes keeping her tethered to life, the same machines that had brought her to this state, that had replaced the life she once knew.

"We're all monsters, Mother," he said, his voice thick with something bitter. His gaze fell back to the machines keeping her alive, the pulsing heart of the room. "You know . . . machines wear out if not cared for."

Her eyes opened just a fraction, the weight of her gaze like stone, and for a moment, Gideon saw the woman who had raised him, fierce and unyielding in her strength. She breathed in shallow, broken gasps, her fingers twitching at the edge of the blankets. "Leave," she said, the word sharp and final, like a verdict. "And take your lies with you."

Gideon stood for a moment, his eyes lingering on her frail form, the hardness of her words settling like dust in the air. A slow, almost imperceptible smile tugged at the corners of his lips, something soft and sad in it. He leaned forward, his hand brushing the edge of her bed, and pressed a gentle kiss to her forehead.

"Your body is held hostage by time as much as your mind," he whispered.

He turned and walked out of the room, leaving her in the silence of her machines, and the door clicked shut behind him with a finality that felt more like an echo than a choice.

***

Gideon stood in his father's office, the weight of the place pressing down on him. The heavy oak desk, the leather chair worn by years of his father's sitting. The air still clung to the faint scent of cigars, stale smoke lingering in the corners. He looked around, his eyes tracing the familiar lines of the room as if something might reveal itself in the quiet.

"Did you see it coming?" he whispered to no one in the stale air. There was no answer, only the silence, thick and unmoving.

He moved behind the desk and ran his hand along the edge. The varnish cracked beneath his fingers. In the window's reflection, he saw the door was open, though he had closed it behind him. He turned.

His father stood there, or something that wore his father's shape—tall, broad, though the years had been stripped from him and he seemed carved from old sorrow. His suit was the same dark weave he was buried in, the tie knotted hard against his throat. His eyes were black, and they did not blink.

Gideon did not flinch. "You're dead," he said.

"I know," said Magnus.

The words came like stones falling into water. Gideon leaned back against the desk, arms crossed. "You here to tell me I made a mistake?"

His father stepped forward—the floorboards did not creak under him. "I know what you've done," he said. His voice was rough with earth as though it came from deeper down. "And the Almighty knows too."

Gideon tilted his head, studying the ghost. "If the Almighty has a problem, he can come down and tell me himself."

"You think this is courage." His father's face was empty of malice. "It's something else."

Gideon shrugged. "Maybe. Maybe it is. Doesn't matter much to me."

The ghost moved closer. The air grew colder, the breath tightening in Gideon's chest. Still, he held his ground. He could see the wounds on his father, blooms of black blood dried like tar— the wounds that had been covered by the embalmer. He wondered if the dead chose their scars or if they were forced to wear them forever.

"You've set things in motion you can't undo," his father said. "Blood answers to blood."

Gideon's mouth twisted in a grim line. "I answer to no one. Not anymore."

His father watched him with a silence that filled the room like rising water. The clock on the wall had stopped, the second hand frozen mid-tick. In the hallway beyond, the house murmured and settled, old bones in the walls.

"You are not afraid," his father said.

"No," Gideon said. "Not of you. Not of anyone. Not of your Almighty."

The ghost of his father seemed to lean back as if weighing him on some old balance. Then it nodded once, slowly, as though something long decided had only just now been admitted aloud.

"You will be," the ghost said. "Trust me. You will."

The office door swung wider on its hinges, and the thing that had been his father turned and walked through it. Gideon stayed where he was, his heart hammering in his ribs. He waited for the door to slam, for the ghost to scream, for some final terror to clutch at him. None came.

He was alone again.

He let out a breath he hadn't known he was holding and rubbed at his face with both hands. When he dropped them, he saw that they shook.

Gideon crossed the room to the liquor cabinet and pulled out a bottle of scotch, the same one his father used to sip from when the nights grew long and heavy. He poured himself a glass with hands that barely steadied and drank it down. The fire of it did little to settle him.

He looked back at the desk. The chair sat empty. The ghost was gone. He told himself it had been a trick of the mind. A trick of memory and grief. A man standing too long in the house of the dead.

Still.

He sat down hard in the leather chair, the smell of old smoke rising up around him like a second ghost. He leaned back and stared at the ceiling, at the yellowed plaster, the cracks that split it like river deltas.

Maybe he was going crazy. Maybe the Almighty had sent a messenger after all. He laughed low in his throat. A bitter sound.

"You hear that?" he said aloud to no one. "You'll have to do better."

The room answered him with silence.

He stayed there for some time, glass loose in his hand, the fire dying in the hearth, the darkness growing thick and whole around him. Somewhere deep in the belly of the house, a board gave a long sigh.

And Gideon wondered if madness was not a punishment but a gift.

Something to keep a man company when all the rest had fled.

Then the sound of footsteps and a voice.

"Sir," a servant said. "It's time."

2 In the Beginning

The hearse came up the winding lane, black cars strung behind it like beads on a mourner's thread, wheels hissing through the wet gravel. Fog hung low and heavy and parted slow. Silent. As if drawn back by some blind old god of the dead. The air was thick with sorrow, unmoved by the living, sour with age and memory. The world seemed to cinch in on itself, like it meant to bury more than the dead.

Gideon Stark stood at the gate in a long, dark coat, unmoving. His hand rested on the cracked leather grip of the wheelchair, and in it sat what remained of his mother. A thin shell. Skin like old parchment, the breath inside her borrowed and borrowed again. The frame that held her bristled with wires and plastic, tubes that shivered in the cold. Machines at war with the inevitable. A slow theft of everything she'd ever been. Somewhere beyond, the wind gave out a cry like a dog dying in the brush.

The mausoleum crouched in the rain, a black thing, squat and old, its stone washed gray and green by the years. Its door stood open, waiting to take what was owed. Behind it, the graveyard spilled out like an open ledger, rows of the dead leaning in quiet council, and past them the trees stood bare, their limbs hung with waterlogged leaves like spent paper offerings.

Six men came forward and lifted the casket. The wood was red and polished, the brass glistening. The men's boots slipped on the stone steps. One cursed under his breath. The thing gleamed faintly in the wet like it had no right to be pulled from the earth, a relic meant to stay buried.

The priest was thin and long and looked half-dead himself. His robe hung off him like a sack, and the rain had flattened what little hair he had against his skull. He held a swollen old book in both hands and read from it in a voice already giving up.

"We commit to the earth the body of Magnus Stark," he said. "Ashes to ashes. Dust to dust."

Gideon heard the words. But they meant nothing. He was not here for meaning. His eyes wandered the crowd, and he saw them—the real ones. Those in tailored, fashionable coats. Their shoes already ruined. Their faces fixed in solemn quiet like carved heads on a tomb. They watched him the way a man watches the weather.

Kenji Kuroda stood narrow and still, hands folded at the wrists like a man in church or a man weighing cost. The rain slid down his coat in fine streams, and his eyes, black as coal, moved with some small shimmer of thought not meant for the world. Gideon saw the algae farms of the Pacific, green as jade and just as quiet, the vats humming in endless procession. He saw the gilled creatures fed on light and pulse. Saw glass break. Water foul. Empire crumble.

Beside him stood Ivan Volkov. The man looked carved from the same stone they buried tsars in. His beard dripped, his greatcoat soaked through, eyes sunken and pale. Gideon thought of the rails that knotted up the steppes like stitches in a split hide. He saw grain towers. Rusted locks. The scent of fire drifting through wheat. Burn one field, he thought, and they'll burn them all.

Then Mei Liang. She stood like a shadow, no more than a slip of form beneath the rim of her wide-brimmed hat. The rain slid down its edge like silk unraveling. Her hands were hidden. Her eyes downcast. Gideon thought of the paddies and terraces, the silver rows of soy, the insect vats steaming like hell's kitchens. He thought of the drones, of slow rot working its way down into root and marrow.

And last came Ayo Okoye and Sami Ben Youssef. Stone-faced and watching, the water marked no expression on them. They owned the deserts and the savannahs. They moved pulse and millet and black protein through dead air. Gideon saw it all. The children bent under that sky. The treaties inked in promises and broken by morning. He saw what lay behind their stillness. There's a blade in every handshake, he thought. Every harvest bought with silence.

The priest closed the book with a soft wet clap like a dying fish flopping once at the bottom of a boat. The casket slid forward into the mouth of the mausoleum, and the great stone doors were swung shut with a sound like the grinding of a mountain's teeth, and there was a stillness then, a silence born not of reverence but of exhaustion.

They came to him one by one.

Kenji Kuroda first, his bow a shallow thing, his hand cool and dry.

"My condolences, Mr. Stark."

Gideon returned the bow with a courtly incline of his head. "Your presence honors my father's memory."

You are a weed grown too high, Kuroda. And I will cut you down to your roots.

Ivan Volkov lumbered forward, his hand like a slab of meat engulfing Gideon's, his breath steaming in the cold.

"He was a hard man," Volkov said, his voice like gravel stirred by floodwater. "The world needs such men."

"The world forgets them in time," Gideon said.

You will not be remembered, old bear. You will die in a ditch and no one will weep.

Mei Liang next, her hand light as the wing of a moth against his.

"Strength to your house," she said, her voice low and musical.

"And peace to yours," Gideon replied.

Your house will fall in silence, Liang. And no voice will be raised in its defense.

And last the Africans, Okoye and Ben Youssef, their smiles thin and formal, their eyes like stones plucked from a riverbed.

"You have lost much," Ayo said.

"We stand with you," Sami said.

"Grief is a teacher," Gideon said. "And I am a willing student."

You will learn, too, in time, the price of your arrogance. You will learn it in fire.

They turned away, and the black cars took them down the long road again, the mist swallowing them one by one, their tail lights winking out like dying stars.

Gideon stood alone with his mother and the dead and the rain.

He looked down at her in her chair, her head slumped sideways, her eyelids fluttering like broken shutters, and he thought that soon enough he would place her in that mausoleum too, her name etched in stone beside her husband's, the great Stark dynasty reduced to a pair of dates and a slab of cold stone.

An attendant came and turned the wheelchair and began to roll it down the path, the wheels leaving twin tracks in the mud.

The future stretched out before him, black and endless and terrible.

And he would walk it alone.

And he would own it all.

***

The rain hammered the glass in sheets. Thick gray light filled the office like smoke. The wide desk between Gideon Stark and the door. His father's desk. His father's chair. He sat heavy in it, the leather cracked and stinking of old sweat and power and death.

He waited. The ticking of the clock. Loud against the silence.

The door swung open without a knock.

Dorian Malgoth stood there, his bulk filling the doorway like some dark presence. His face, a map of scars, seemed carved from rock, each line a testament to the brutality that had shaped him. The shaved scalp gleamed with rain, and water ran in rivulets down his coat, the fabric soaked through, steaming in the cold air. His boots, caked with earth, left deep marks on the old floorboards, the scent of mud and metal and slaughter clinging to him like the ghosts of the dead.

Gideon knew this brute from a time when the man had worked the fields of MidCon, his hands raw and callused from the hard earth, his eyes always a shade too hard for a laborer. Before that, he had been a soldier, a hero in a war, but discharged from the armed forces for brutality, a thing that made the others fear him, but it was the jail term that had forged him. Ten years for beating men who had the misfortune of crossing him, a long decade spent in a cell where the shadows grew long and the days bled into each other. Now, he was Gideon's enforcer, the one who broke the bones and delivered the wrath, his loyalty unquestionable, his violence deliberate, a man who understood that in this world, strength was the only law that mattered.

Malgoth didn't move, didn't speak, just stood there, his eyes burning like embers from a long-dead fire. Gideon raised his eyes slowly, studying the man. He didn't smile.

"You have word," Gideon said.

"I have word," Malgoth replied. His voice low. Scraped raw. "All ready. All waiting."

"No trail," Gideon said.

"No trail," Malgoth shook his head. "No way back to the Amalgam. No way back to you."

The clock ticked between them. Slow and hard. Like a hammer on a nail.

Gideon studied him. The thick hands. The burned-out eyes. A man who had once been turned loose on the world and left it bloody.

"You're sure," Gideon said.

Malgoth simply nodded.

Gideon turned in the chair and looked out the tall window, the glass cold beneath his palm. The fields stretched endless before him, a churn of black mud swallowing all. Dead machines crouched under the storm like bloated corpses, rust creeping from their joints. The rain hammered the earth.

"They'll come looking," Gideon said, his voice flat, the words heavy with a slow, inevitable truth. "They'll tear it all down to find someone."

"They'll find nothing," Malgoth said, his voice low, certain as the crack of a rifle shot.

"You trust your men?" Gideon asked, his eyes narrowing on the man's hard, scarred face.

"I trust the leash," Malgoth answered. His eyes flicked briefly to the door, distant.

Gideon nodded slowly, his fingers tapping once on the desk, a single dry sound like a hammer striking stone. He let the quiet settle. "You'll wait for the signal," he said.

"I'll wait," Malgoth responded, his eyes unreadable, his body a coiled tension, ready to strike at the first command.

The clock ticked on. Rain ran in black rivers down the window.

"Nothing left standing," Gideon said.

Malgoth said nothing. His eyes said everything.

"You'll act when I say. Not before."

Malgoth nodded. Water beading and running off the scars on his face. The room smelled of damp cloth and old fear.

Gideon watched him. The man was a dog built to kill and bred too long in the wild. Now he wore a chain again, but you could still see the hunger in him.

"You'll have your time," Gideon said.

"I know," Malgoth said.

Gideon gave a small nod. Nothing more.

Malgoth turned. He paused at the door, his bulk filling it. He gave a nod back. Hard and final as the closing of a coffin lid. Then he was gone.

The door swung shut behind him with a soft snick.

Gideon leaned back. The chair groaned under his weight. The rain fell harder, washing the world in gray. He closed his eyes. He could feel it there. The old presence. The ghost that never left this room.

He smelled whiskey and oil and blood. The voice came low.

"You think you're the first," it said.

Gideon did not move.

"You think you can hide behind men like him," the voice said. "You think you can bleed the world and your hands stay clean."

He opened his eyes. The room unchanged. The desk empty. The rain endless.

"You wear my chair like you earned it," the voice said. "You wear my name like it was stitched to your skin."

Gideon rose. The bottle was still in the drawer. The old bottle. His father's bottle. He poured a drink and threw it back. Fire down the throat. The old medicine.

He poured another.

The ghost said nothing more. It didn't have to.

He crossed to the window and put one hand against the cold glass.

Outside, the fields rolled like a drowned world. In the distance, the towers of the Amalgam rose against the storm, black and jagged and blind.

The crops rotted in their furrows. The soil washed down into the rivers. The machines corroded where they stood. He thought of Malgoth waiting with his men. Black rain slicking their coats. Guns packed in oiled cloth. Names already spoken. Lives already broken. He thought of the children who would starve. The cities that would die inch by inch. The slow ruin of a thousand thin famines stitched into the earth.

It was nothing new.

The world had been dying for a long time.

He turned from the window. His hand left a smear on the glass.

He drained the second drink and slammed the glass down on the desk. The sound echoed hard in the empty office.

The ghost of Magnus Stark sat across from him. He could almost see the old man's grin. The black teeth. The black eyes. The black hunger.

"The Almighty knows," the voice said.

The Almighty always knows.

Gideon wiped his mouth with the back of his hand. The taste of whiskey and bile thick in his throat.

He moved to the desk. Sat again. He opened the ledger. The one his father had kept. The pages yellow and cracked. Ink smudged. Bleeding from the damp.

He turned to a clean page. Picked up the pen.

He wrote only a single word.

Ready.

He closed the ledger.

Outside, the rain kept falling. It would fall all night and all the next day and into the next. It would wash the blood away. It would bury the bones.

He sat alone behind the great desk. The world grinding on beyond the windows. The ghost breathing at his back.

And he did not pray.

And he did not ask forgiveness.

The Almighty knows.

The rain battered the roof and the glass and the broken fields beyond. The sound of it endless. Like the sea. Like the end of all things.

Gideon Stark sat in the dark and waited for the world to burn.

***

They came in the night. Gideon let them. They filed down into the chamber beneath the house. Where the stone was damp and the air held the stink of bleach and old soil. Glass vials lined the shelves and glimmered in the half-light like the eyes of things long dead. He stood among them without a word. The light struck his face and made a mask of it, but he did not turn away. They gathered in a circle. He spoke. It was his father's voice that came out. And the voices of fathers older still.

"This is what they've asked for," he said. "This is what we've earned."

He held up the seed, dry and shrunken. "It won't grow. None of it will."

He showed them stalks black and brittle. Mold creeping. Like rot through what grain remained. He cracked the vials open one by one and loosed the spores into the dark. The blight moved with purpose. It found the roots and the stems and the marrow of the harvest. And the fields lit like kindling. No sound to it. No screaming. Just fire.

"In the east," he said, "the rains have not stopped."

"In the west, the rivers are gone. The cattle die standing. Their ribs cut the air."

The others did not speak.

"The cities will riot," Gideon said. "They will starve. They will burn their own homes to stay warm. And the soldiers will shoot them for it."

And so, it was. In the cities, the glass shattered, and the shelves were stripped bare. The crowds surged. The rifles cracked. The blood ran out into the gutters. The rain carried it away.

Gideon watched it all from the high room. The windows blackened with smoke. His rivals sent envoys. He gave them nothing. The voice Amalgam spread over the earth like ice and the world shrank down to the shape of his closed fist.

The others waited for orders. He gave none. He waited.

Outside, the wind dragged its carcass through the fields. The air stank of ash and burnt meat. Thunder rolled far off like the tread of old gods. No rain came. The land was dead. The sky said nothing. And mercy was gone from the world.

Then Gideon raised his hand.

"Tell Malgoth," he said. "It's time."

***

The ground was wet with rain and something darker. The sky hung low, gray and glutted with the smoke of distant fires. Malgoth stood in the remains of the Pacific hatchery, boots sunk in silt and glass. The stink of rot came off the broken vats in heavy waves, and the fish lay bloated at his feet like cast-off organs from a failed god. His men moved behind him, silent, methodical, swinging steel into glass, prying open panels, setting flame to what would take. And elsewhere across the map, in places he'd marked with a dull knife on an old wall, others did the same.

He lit a cigarette with shaking fingers. Not from fear. His nerves were gone long before now. Worn out of him by prison years and battlefield nights. He smoked and watched the algae curl like burnt skin, green and slick and useless. A man had built this place. Fed millions with it. Lived in it like a priest in a shrine. Now the water was gone. The glass blown open like a lung shot. The sea beasts belly up in their own engineered filth.

A noise behind him. Boots in mud. Not one of his men. He turned.

A boy. Skinny. Thirteen, maybe. Shirt clinging to him in the rain. Eyes like he'd seen the end of the world and couldn't make peace with it.

"You come to eat?" Malgoth said.

The boy said nothing.

Malgoth took another drag. The fire in the cigarette hissed in the wind.

"There's nothing here. You can try the corpses if you want. I won't stop you."

The boy looked past him. To the jagged bones of the facility, half-submerged. A crane twisted like a snapped bird. He looked back.

"You did this?"

Malgoth spat into the mud.

"No. But I watched it burn."

The boy nodded. He walked toward the water, stepping over the fish with an almost religious reverence. He stopped and crouched by a pale thing, skin milky and blistered. Reached out and touched it. Drew his hand back fast.

"Hot."

"Chemical burn."

"Why?"

Malgoth shrugged. "Because it was time."

The boy looked at him again. "What's going to happen now?"

Malgoth dropped the cigarette and crushed it with his boot. "Now the world eats itself."

Wind tore across the water and sent the algae scudding across the surface. The smell was worse than death. A kind of manufactured decay. Malgoth turned and started walking back toward the road. The boy followed him.

They passed the body of a man face-down in the sand. His back broken. His head at an angle that nature hadn't intended.

"He was the boss," the boy said.

"Yes. Kuroda."

"Did he fight back?"

Malgoth stopped walking. Looked back.

"No. He tried to bargain. That was his mistake."

The boy looked down at the body.

"How many people have you killed?"

"Plenty."

"Does it feel bad?"

Malgoth walked on.

At the roadside, a rusted pickup leaned in the ditch. Malgoth opened the door, let the rainwater spill out. He climbed in. The boy stood there.

"Where you headed?"

"All over."

Malgoth lit another cigarette. The flame lit his face like a flash of memory.

"Everything's empty," the boy said. "The stores. The trucks."

Malgoth exhaled. "Then you know what it costs."

The boy stood quiet in the rain.

"What's your name?" Malgoth asked.

"Don't remember."

"Good."

He reached across and opened the passenger door.

"Get in."

The boy did. They sat in silence.

Somewhere in the distance, a tower collapsed. The sound came late, like thunder that forgot its place. Malgoth didn't turn toward it.

"There's more coming," he said.

"Worse than this?"

"Always."

He started the truck. The engine coughed and caught. The road ahead was washed out and full of things better left unnamed. He pulled onto it just the same.

In the mirror, the ocean hatchery disappeared behind them like a thing slipping beneath the surface for good. The dead man, the twisted steel, the bloated fish. All of it gone.

"You going to kill more people?" the boy asked.

"If they give me reason."

"What reason?"

Malgoth kept his eyes on the road. Smoke on the horizon. Fire farther still.

"Breathing's enough."

They drove on through the wasted dawn. The road ran gray and broken before them, and the land about them lay in ruin, and the sky was thin and cold. They came at last to a clutch of souls huddled about a fire in the lee of a toppled wall. The wind moved among them. They did not look up.

"Time to leave."

The boy looked at Malgoth. He said nothing. He opened the door and stepped out of the truck, and the door swung shut behind him with a sound that was small and final in the morning hush.

***

The smoke hung low across the plain, dull and unyielding as if the sky itself had sunk to earth. Ash curled in the windless air, the cinders of wheat and men. Malgoth stood at the edge of a burnt field with a rifle in one hand and a matchbox in the other. His coat flared in the scorched breeze, his boots black with soot. The sun was a copper disc behind the haze, disinterested, smeared across the sky like a bloodied coin.

He walked the perimeter of what had been a silo. The walls had folded inward like paper. Rodents skittered beneath the debris. Far off, a train lay keeled on its side, its cars cracked and split like old bones. Malgoth saw no movement. Not from the wreck. Not from the horizon. The land was done breathing.

He crouched beside a stump of what had once been irrigation piping. From a canvas satchel, he pulled a tin flask and unscrewed the lid with calloused fingers. He drank. The liquor tasted like gasoline. He poured the last of it on the blackened soil.

"To your empire, Volkov," he said aloud. "And to the flesh it fed."

The silence swallowed his voice. He stood again. His eyes scanned the endless flat of the steppes, broken only by ruined scaffolds and scattered husks of machines left to rust. This was the last of it. What had not burned had rotted. The wheat, the rice, the corn. Gone. The wind carried nothing but memory.

In the distance, several structures rose. Labs with biotech technology. Large structures with huge vats for food production. But there was one structure. Simple and low to the earth that caught his eye. Malgoth began walking. The soles of his boots made no sound against the cinders. He passed a rusted sign, the name of a township burned away to illegibility. He walked on.

The house was half-buried in ash, its windows shattered, its front door open like a mouth slack with death. Malgoth stepped inside.

He found Volkov hanging in the sitting room, a thick rope around the beam, his body spinning slowly in the stale air. The floor beneath him was dusted with plaster. His boots tapped faintly with each rotation.

Malgoth lit a cigarette. He sat down on the floorboards, cross-legged. The rifle leaned against his shoulder. He studied the dead man's face, its purple slackness. Volkov was a man of abundance. Full-throated laughter, cheeks red with vodka, hands always gesturing—broad hands that had once thrown dice in foreign casinos and signed death warrants in the same breath.

"You always thought you were safe out here, didn't you?" Malgoth said.

He smoked. The room was quiet but for the creak of the rope and the occasional settling of the ruined walls.

"Your fields," he said. "Nothing left but fire and salt. You fed the world, but you didn't know how the game was played. So, we came for your bones. Not even a proper funeral."

He stood and walked into the kitchen. Cabinets open, empty. A pot overturned in the sink. He opened the pantry and found a single can of pickled beets. He turned it in his hand and tossed it into the fire-blackened corner.

"You let it get away from you. The rails, the silos, the labs, the vats. You sat on a throne of bread and thought that meant anything."

He came back to the sitting room and stood under the body. He reached up and pushed against Volkov's chest so the corpse spun the other way.

"You knew I was coming. Maybe not me. But someone. You knew something would rise when your fields were dying."

He walked to the bookshelf, what remained of it. Pulled a half-burned ledger, the pages brittle and warped. Names. Schedules. Kilotons of grain routed through cities. Grain that no longer existed. All of it meaningless now.

Outside, the wind kicked up, carrying ash across the barren road. Malgoth stepped onto the porch and looked out. A figure stood near the edge of the property. A boy. Maybe. No. A young woman. Thin as a rail and shoeless. Her eyes were hollow.

"You alone?" Malgoth called out.

The young woman nodded.

"You hungry?"

She nodded again.

Malgoth reached into his coat and took out a tin. Opened it. Dry meat. He tossed a strip into the dirt at the young woman's feet. She looked at it and did not move.

"Pick it up," Malgoth said.

She bent and took the strip into her hand and bit down with the haste of the starving. Malgoth watched her. The bones showed clear beneath the skin. Her feet were blackened. Her jaw trembled as he chewed.

"You speak?" He asked.

"Yes."

"Where's your family?"

"Dead."

"How long?"

She shrugged.

Malgoth pulled the matchbox from his pocket and lit another cigarette. He exhaled through his nose.

"You seen others?"

"Not for days."

Malgoth nodded. "They won't come back. Not to this place. Nothing left for the taking."

He turned and went inside, came back with the pickled beets, and threw the can toward the young woman. She caught it and stared.

"Don't open it now. You'll throw it up."

She tucked it into a rag she'd tied around his waist. Malgoth knelt and scraped a line in the dirt with the barrel of his rifle.

"You cross this line, you do what I say. You don't, you walk. Starve if you want. But if you step over, you're mine."

The young woman looked at the line. Looked at the man.

"I can help you," she said.

Malgoth shook his head. "Maybe. Maybe not. But you got ears."

She crossed the line.

He rose. Put his hands on her shoulders and moved her back across like setting down a sack of grain. Then turned and walked.

He went on down the road. Volkov's corpse still twisting slow in the wind behind like some godless compass. He left the woman there. He'd see her again. When the snows came.

***

They came in the dark. No banners. No cause declared. Just the sound of boots and fire and the mechanical cough of guns. The city was quiet by then. Not dead, not yet. But quiet like a dog that knows what's coming. And Malgoth walked among them like a prophet of ruin.

The towers of Mei Liang's farms still stood, their glass facades pocked with bullet holes and streaked with soot. The lights had gone out days ago. The drones that once rose like flocks of iron birds now lay shattered in the dust, their wings broken, their tiny eyes staring at nothing. Wind swept through the empty streets, picking up ash and old wrappers, the debris of a civilization too proud to kneel until its spine was already broken.

"Strip away everything," Malgoth said. His voice was like dry leaves. "Leave nothing in the stacks."

The others moved quickly and without word. A dozen in number. Their eyes flat and empty, torches slung in gloved hands. Rags tied across their faces. The stench of mildew and rot lifting from the factory vents in such rank procession. Even the flies hung back from it. One climbed the scaffold, boots thudding dully against the rusted steel, and cut the copper lines clean as if they were string. Another dropped to his knees in the oil-slicked grime and tore the belly from a harvester drone, wires snapping wetly in his grip, the sound of it like meat coming off the bone.

"They fed their corner of the world," one said, holding a circuit board up to the failing light. "Thought they were gods."

"Gods don't burn," Malgoth answered.

The sky was low and yellow with haze. Somewhere in the distance, a fire still burned, but it wasn't one of theirs. The factory had gone up before they arrived, smoke pouring from its windows like the soul of something vast and wounded. Mei Liang had died in there. They said she lit the match herself. No one had seen her body, but there were bones in the ash, and a ring melted into a puddle that bore her family crest.

"Not a morsel of food here," someone laughed.

Malgoth was quiet. He walked the rows of dead crops like a man touring a cemetery. The vertical stacks, once lush with soy and chard and protein vines, were gray now, the plants wilted and coated in a fine powder of death. At his feet, the irrigation channels held stagnant water, milky and foul.

He came to a wall where a mural had once bloomed with painted hands planting seedlings beneath a sunlit sky. Now it was scorched, the faces smeared into grotesque shapes. He touched it with the flat of his hand. The concrete was still warm.

"She thought this place would last a hundred years," he said.

"She was wrong," a voice came.

Malgoth looked over his shoulder. A voice behind him. A man coming up slowly, dragging a broken leg like something half-dead. Rifle slung loose over one shoulder. Eyes gone yellow from sleeplessness, nothing left in them but the dull shine of someone who'd long since buried hope like a dog buries a bone it doesn't mean to dig up.

"Wrong," Malgoth said. "But not stupid. She built something mighty."

"So did Babel."

Malgoth's mouth moved, something close to a smile. "Keep the rifle," he said. "But aim it at me or my men and you'll learn what it means to vanish."

The man nodded once and limped off, the wet dragging sound of his boot like something being pulled from deep mud.

"Poor bastard," one of the men said.

Malgoth didn't answer at first. He watched the crippled figure go, a crooked line headed nowhere.

"Set him loose," he said. Then after a beat, "No. Set him free. Kill him. Make it quick. Take the rifle."

The sound came a minute later. A single shot. Then a thump like meat on wet earth.

Malgoth turned back to the others, the torches casting wild light on their faces.

"Tear down the south tower," he commanded. "No one's coming back."

The demolition team moved in with thermite charges. They worked fast. They knew the rhythm of endings.

The charges went off just before sundown. The explosion was brief, almost modest. The structure folded into itself with a groan like an old man falling to his knees. Dust rose into the sky, thick and colorless, and drifted over the city like a shroud.

"What now?" one of his men asked.

Malgoth didn't look at him.

"We continue on."

"But there's nothing left."

"That's not our concern."

They moved on, boots crunching over glass and bone. Dogs howled in the distance, feral and lean. In the silence left behind, the wind moved through the dead towers, playing mournful tunes on the ruined girders like a choir of ghosts.

Night came fast. The kind of night where stars don't shine and the sky feels too close. Malgoth set no fires, left no camp. He leaned against the husk of a delivery van and watched the darkness.

One of his men approached, older, broad-shouldered, eyes like flint.

"You think they'll come looking for her?"

Malgoth shook his head.

"They won't even say her name."

He looked back toward the ruin. Smoke still rose, slow and thin like the last breath of something holy.

The man nodded. "They'll come to us soon enough."

Malgoth didn't reply.

He already knew. They always came. When the shelves were bare. When the children cried. When the stomach turned in on itself. When there was no god to pray to but the man who held the grain.

And that man was not merciful.

***

Far to the south, the empire had withered. The sun rose with no master and fell with no witness. Dust rode the wind like ash from a fire long dead. Villages were swallowed. Roads vanished. And where once the sky trembled with wings, now it hung empty and gray. Ayo Okoye and Sami Ben Youssef, who had stood above all others, were gone. Their bodies lost in the sand.

Malgoth moved along the ridge in the early light, his boots black with the oils of dead machines. The land around him was cracked like scorched parchment, dotted with rusted towers that leaned as if ashamed. He paused beneath one of the great cisterns, its shell curled inward like a beetle on its back.

"They thought they could own this," he said aloud.

An old man, a servant of Okoye and Youssef, beside him, said nothing. He was lean and wrapped in rough cloth and bore the sun without complaint. His eyes were like pits in the stone. Malgoth glanced at him, then walked on.

"They built cities in the sand," Malgoth said. "Fed on what crawled. Thought they were kings."

The old man followed. A wind came from the west, and it brought a smell of old blood. They walked down a slope and into a basin where the remains of a refinery had collapsed into its own shadow. Metal lay warped across the earth. There were no voices. Not even the insects spoke now.

Malgoth stepped over a rib of scaffolding. "When I came here last, there were guards. I remember the way they looked at me. With the faces of men who believed they would never be undone."

He knelt in the dirt. A cracked mask lay there, half-buried, the filter clogged with grit. He turned it over, let it fall.

"They're in the sand now. Okoye. Youssef. The desert took them back. This place, too."

"Is it true what they say?" the old man asked.

"What's that?"

"That the insects turned on them."

Malgoth stood. "What else would they do."

They moved on. Through wreckage. Through silos torn open like fruit left for weeks in the sun. Through forgotten paths grown over with thorn and dryweed. They came upon a shack made of sheet metal and wire, half sunk into the slope of a dune. Malgoth pushed the door aside. Inside were bones and old paper.

"I told them," he said. "I told them it wouldn't last. You bend the wild long enough, it breaks you instead."

He sat. The old man stood in the doorway, the shadow of the shack cutting his body in half.

"You didn't know them," the old man said.

Malgoth smiled. "Were they cruel?"

"They were men. Men are enough."

Malgoth pulled a flask from his coat and drank. The heat was coming up now. Outside, the horizon shimmered like a thing trying to hide.

"I saw Youssef in Cairo," Malgoth said. "He wore silk in the middle of the riots. Spoke like he believed the words would build something around him. He had a way of saying your name like he already owned it. Okoye was worse. His eyes didn't blink. Not once. He gave the order to drain a whole valley of water just to keep a shipment on schedule. Said the people would adapt. Said survival was proof of loyalty."

The old man sat across from him. "Why? Why do all this?"

"Why not? It was broken."

"How was it broken?"

Malgoth said nothing. He closed the flask. There was a silence between them then, thick and old.

"They deserved it," he said at last.

"That's got nothing to do with it," said the old man. "The desert doesn't tally scores."

The wind passed over the shack and through it. The walls creaked like dying animals. Malgoth leaned forward.

"I seen what they did with the bugs," he said. "Cut them open. Wired them up. Fed the factories with their bile and spun gold from their eggs. It worked, for a time. You could smell it on the air. That chemical sweetness. They ran trains on their spines. Built hives so big they needed towers to cool the heat."

He shook his head.

"They never thought the swarm would remember. That it would feel pain. That it would come back. But it did. It always does."

Outside, the wind changed direction. Malgoth stood.

"Time to go."

The old man didn't move. "You hear them?"

"No."

"Exactly."

He rose slowly, joints stiff. They walked out into the white light of midday. The basin was quiet. No engines. No drums. No hum. Only the scouring silence of the wastes.

They came to the bodies in the sand. Okoye and Youssef. Their bones picked clean. Their coats torn to threads and left in knots. The insects had taken their flesh and moved on.

"Here they are," said Malgoth.

The old man crouched near them. "Did they know it was coming?"

"No. They thought they were the hand of God."

He drew a circle in the sand with his boot. "That's what power does. Makes you deaf. Makes you blind. Makes you dig your own grave and call it a throne."

The old man didn't answer. He stared at what was left of the two rulers, sun-bleached and forgotten.

"They say their last words were to each other," the old man murmured. "Whispers to no one."

Malgoth shrugged. "I doubt it. They probably screamed."

They moved on. The sun blazed. The sky was a dome of fire. Malgoth took off his coat and tied it to his pack.

"What's next?" asked the old man.

"More of this."

The old man sighed. "Is there anything left?"

Malgoth looked over his shoulder. "You. Me. That's enough."

They crested a dune and looked down into a valley where windmills spun slow. Broken. Malgoth narrowed his eyes. There was a sound now. A faint hum. Like wings.

"They're coming back," said the old man. "The bugs."

"No," Malgoth said. "They never left."

He unhooked the blade from his belt and drew it across the old man's neck. The blood fell red and bright on the sand.

"What are you doing?" he gasped, his last words.

"Letting them know I remember."

The hum grew louder.

***

Seasons passed. Two. Three. Maybe more. Hard to say. They ran together now. Ragged and without name. The heat came in waves like fever. The cold like punishment. Rain fell less and less. When it did it came down slow and burning. A sheen of oil that left welts on skin and turned soil to paste. The sky hung low and wrong-colored, the shade of old bruises and ash, and it did not change.

The sky rolled like iron above the plain. The light that found its way through was bitter and weak. A fine dust moved across the road in long, fingered spirals, never rising more than a few inches before falling back into itself. Gideon stood with his coat open, his hands deep in the pockets, his eyes fixed on the last of the silos that now leaned like old men about to confess. The land around them lay flat and wide and dead. Where once there were fields, there was now only a churned scab of ash and bone.

He heard the horse before he saw it. A slow gait. The hooves striking loose stone and then dirt. Then the man. Malgoth. Wrapped in black and gray, the wide brim of his hat pulled low.

His horse looked near spent. The foam on its neck had dried white. The skin hung from it like wet cloth.

Malgoth pulled the reins and looked down at Gideon.

"You're still here," he said.

"I am."

"I figured you'd be halfway to the coast by now. What's left of it."

Gideon didn't answer. Malgoth dismounted and let the reins fall. The horse didn't move.

"They're eating each other in the cities," Malgoth said. "Like dogs in a sack."

"I know. I lit the match."

Malgoth walked to the edge of the silo. He put a gloved hand on the rusting metal and pressed it like a man feeling for a heartbeat.

"I knew you had plans, Gideon. I just didn't think you'd finish the job."

"It was already finished. Just didn't know it yet."

Malgoth squatted, pulled a pouch from his coat, and tossed a few seeds into his palm. He let them fall to the dirt. They bounced once, twice, then stilled.

"Dead things," he said.

"They were dead before they left the packet."

"What comes next?"

Gideon turned. The wind caught his coat. His beard was speckled with dust, and his face looked as if it had been carved from the same stone that now lined the road.

"Order," he said.

"Order?"

"You can't build it with plenty. You build it with need."

Malgoth laughed, but it was short and it didn't reach his eyes.

"You sound like a priest. Or a butcher."

"Same thing now."

They stood in silence for a while. The wind rose, then dropped again. The silo groaned like something alive.

"You remember the labs that fat Volkov kept?" Gideon said.

"I do."

"They kept the vats warm even as the world turned cold. He thought it was hope. He thought he was feeding his little corner of the world."

"And you proved him wrong."

"I proved them all wrong. I showed them they were feeding a lie. They kept everyone fat enough not to look too close. Kept them from asking what was in the bread. What kind of meat they were eating."

"And now?"

"Now they ask."

"And starve."

Gideon nodded.

"And those who fed them?"

"They had their chance," Gideon smiled. "But they wouldn't listen to me. They wouldn't accept what I was offering.'

"Can't listen now."

"Can't do much of anything when all that's left are bones."

Malgoth walked back to his horse and touched its flank. It trembled under his hand. He hesitated.

"You're not a savior, Gideon."

"I don't want to be."

"You're not even a man anymore."

"I never was," he said. His eyes fixed on Malgoth. "You think I want a kingdom of ash and bone? You think I want to rule over graves?"

"You'll rule over what's left. Or someone worse will."

Malgoth studied him. A long look. The kind a man gives when he's measuring not your face but the thing behind it. The kind that cuts deep and doesn't bleed.

"Remember the woman I told you about in Volkov's territory?" Malgoth said.

"I do."

"She traded her shoes for a bottle of glucose. Her shoes, Gideon. Her fucking shoes."

"I remember."

"She died barefoot in the snow."

"I didn't kill her."

"No. You just made the world where it could happen."

Gideon stepped forward.

"And you were there to wrap her in a blanket she didn't feel. You tried to give her water. But she couldn't swallow. You said a prayer. And then you moved on."

Malgoth shook his head. "No prayer. But she had a name."

"They all did."

"And now?"

"Names won't help them."

"No. But food might."

Gideon smiled, but there was no joy in it.

"Then we'll grow some," he said. "Just enough, though. Keep them wanting."

"Grow? Out of what?"

"Necessity." Gideon looked down the road. The earth shimmered like an old coin rubbed thin. "You think they'll follow me?"

"They'll follow you because they're dying. And you're not."

"They'll eat me before they follow me."

Malgoth looked at him. "Then make them die at your feet. Or bend to their knees in worship."

"What about you?"

"I'll be by your side. Always. Waiting."

"Waiting for what?"

Malgoth looked up. The clouds were darker now. The rain would come soon, but it wouldn't matter.

"To see what you make of it." Malgoth walked a few paces and turned. "But sometimes I wonder."

"Wonder what?"

"Wonder what would happen if I left you."

"That's simple. Someone else would take your place."

Malgoth chuckled. "Of course. But that won't happen. I'm not going anywhere. So, what do we do next?"

"We watch the fire spread. Until there's nothing left to burn."

Malgoth mounted the horse. It groaned beneath him.

"You ever think," he said, "if maybe this world deserved to end?"

Gideon didn't move. His eyes focused on the horizon.

"It wasn't about what it deserved. It was about what it needed."

"And you decided?"

"I just removed the lie."

Malgoth turned the horse. The wind caught his coat now, pushed it back like wings.

"You may be right, Gideon. But God help us if you are."

"There is no God," Gideon said. "Just hunger. The currency of the future. We will feed who we want to."

Malgoth didn't reply. He rode off down the long straight road that led into the silence of what had been. Gideon watched until the man was nothing more than a smudge in the distance. Then he turned back to the silo. He opened the rusted door and stepped inside. The dark within was thick and close, warm with the scent of oil and the ancient breath of machinery long past its prime. He struck a match. It flared and died. He lit another.

And so it went, day after day. The world outside grew leaner, the people hungrier. Fields went untilled. Rivers ran dry. Many of the great cities emptied, their streets silent save for the wind and the cries of the starving. Millions perished, their bodies left unburied, their names forgotten in the dust. The roads cracked. The bridges sagged. The machines that once kept the world alive now sat idle, rusting in the sun, for there were too few hands left to tend them. The world's bones crumbled, its heart slowed, its breath stilled.

Yet, Gideon held dominion over all. He held the strings of food in his clenched fist, doling out life and death as he saw fit. The last of the people looked to him, their eyes hollow, their hope withered. He alone walked the empty halls of power, the keeper of the silo, the master of the feast and the famine. And the world bent to his will, until there was little left to bend.

But there was one place yet beyond his reach. Far off. Across the seas, beneath the southern sun. The Silent Land they called it. Australia. There, the wind carried word of Gideon, but the ground knew not his tread. It stood apart. Stern and unwilling. The last thing unbent. Yet the slow ruin reached even there. The ships ceased. The trade died. Famine moved like shadow over the scrub and saltlands. Towns withered. Cities crumbled. The dead lay in their homes and were not found.

And Gideon watched. Waited. He had time. Plenty.

3 A New Order

The men came on foot and by armored caravan. They came in tattered suits with collars wilted from sweat, in uniforms stripped of insignia, in cloaks and coats matted with travel. Some wore medals that meant nothing. Some had no name left. They came through the mud and smoke and silence.

The building was tall and dark and had no guards at the gate. No need for them. The guards were inside.

They were led into a long room that smelled of metal and ash and old books. The windows were high and narrow, and the rain bled down them in slow gray lines. At the end of the room stood a man. He did not turn when they entered. His back was to them. He was watching the rain.

The men did not speak at first. They stood like children summoned to the headmaster's office, their hands stiff at their sides, eyes flicking toward the floor.

At last, one of them—a man with a thin mustache and the look of someone who had once been proud of his voice—cleared his throat.

"We've come for food."

The man at the window nodded once. Still, he did not turn.

"Our people are dying," said another. "We need supplies. Whatever you can give. We're prepared to negotiate."

"You were here before," Gideon said. "You remember. When it first started. When your fields went black and the rains quit. You weren't ready then. And now you come saying you're ready to negotiate. You're not."

The men shifted.

"You've come to beg. You think you've come to trade. You've brought nothing. Then again, there's nothing left to bring. The ground is hollow. The oceans are poisoned. The skies don't answer anymore."

"We have what's left of our governments," one of them said.

Gideon turned then. He wore a coat of waxed canvas, the shoulders cracked. His beard was coarse and gray and trimmed to the jaw. His eyes were flat. Colorless.

"Your governments are bones," he said.

A silence followed. One of the men looked toward the doors as if wondering if they'd been locked behind him.

"We can offer you sovereignty," said a man from the back. "You'll have command over distribution routes. Military escort. Full support."

Gideon looked at him.

"What is the name of the last village your drones bombed? You know. To quell the riots."

The man blinked. "I—I don't know."

"No. You don't."

He walked toward them. His boots echoed softly on the concrete.

"I remember it. It was called Salmira. Eight hundred people. They had no weapons. They hadn't eaten in three days. Your men saw a fire in the hills and sent a charge."

"We didn't know—"

"You knew," Gideon said. "You just didn't care."

He stepped past them and they turned to follow his movement with their eyes.

"You come now because your cities have devoured themselves. Your people feast on the flesh of the dead. They call it salvation. In the hollows of your towers lie rot and brine. Still, your people call it prosperity. But your land is paved with steel and bones. With poison poured into the cracks."

He sat behind a wide table of black oak, the wood scorched in places. He folded his hands.

"I told you it would end like this," he said. "Months ago. When the rains stopped falling in the Centerlands. When the bees left the citrus groves. When the fish floated belly-up in the northern rivers. I told you."

"You did all that," came a voice from behind the group.

Gideon smiled. "I did what was necessary."

A man stepped forward. His skin was tight against his cheekbones, his uniform pressed but fraying at the cuffs.

"We're not here to argue the past. Our people are dying."

"And you are not," said Gideon.

The man faltered. "What—what does that mean?"

"It means you speak for them. But you are not them. You are not hungry."

A few heads turned. Another voice rose.

"You've made yourself a god with a grain silo. Is that what this is? A throne built on lentils and rice?"

Gideon smiled. Just the edge of it.

"No. I'm not a god," he said. "I'm the man who listened while the rest of you shouted."

He opened a drawer and drew out a map. It was hand-drawn, notes scribbled in margins. He set it on the table.

"I know where the water is," he said. "I know where the seed banks are hidden. I know where the soil still lives. I've spent so much time preparing for your ruin. And I didn't do it to save you."

The men stared. A slow anger building in their faces.

"You'd let millions die?"

Gideon tapped the map. "I already have."

He let the silence stretch, let the words settle.

"I know hunger empties the mind. It turns father against son. People are forced to eat bark and leather and things worse than either. And who watches it all? Men in suits. All the while, children starve under broken roofs. This is your mercy."

Another man stepped forward, his eyes dark with defiance.

"We come with open hands."

"No," said Gideon. "You come with nothing. You come now because you have run out of cruelty."

The men said nothing.

"The food will come," Gideon said. "But only when I allow it. Only where I direct it."

"You mean to rule."

"I mean to survive."

"What do you want?"

Gideon leaned back in the chair.

"Obedience," he said. "Total. Without question."

"You ask us to become your slaves."

"No," said Gideon. "I ask you to become servants of the living. And if that feels like slavery, then maybe you were never kings."

A man in a threadbare blue sash stepped forward. His accent was old-world, his hands trembling.

"Our stores were taken. Riots burned what granaries remained. We don't know who lives and who does not. But we can give you what remains of our fleet. The ports, the skiffs, the satellite links. You can have it all."

"Your security forces?"

"Yes."

Gideon nodded. "Good. That will be a start."

"And after that?"

"You'll bring me your governors. Your ministers. Brought here. One by one."

"And then?"

"I'll decide what to do with them."

There was a long pause.

"And if we refuse?"

Gideon stood.

"Then all your people will join the others," he said. "The ones whose names are lost to ash. The ones whose bones line the gutters of your cities. It is not a threat. It is a certainty."

No one answered. The men turned. Slowly. One by one. And they left the room.

***

The next day brought others.

A woman from the high steppes of the central continent. She came wrapped in wool and dust, her voice low and torn.

"They have eaten the dogs," she said. "And then each other. The grass has died. We found a child chewing her own fingers."

Gideon said nothing for a while.

"What do you offer?"

"The rivers," she said. "There are mines still. Solar fields. Old drones. We can find them. Our military forces. Everything."

He raised his head slowly. His eyes were like stones sunk in a dry bed. "What good are soldiers," he said, "to a field gone empty?"

"We can build," she said. "We have machines. Engineers."

He shook his head once as if brushing away a dream. "You have mouths," he said. "You have graves. You have broken statues and empty granaries. You have hands reaching out in the dark."

"What do you want then?" she cried.

"Everything," he smiled. "Your engines. Your weapons. The last shreds of your vanished empires. I want your silence. Your surrender. I want your people to come barefoot. Not with terms. Not with titles. No masks. No medals."

She stared at him.

"I want your dead named. One by one. I want the graves dug proper. I want you to remember who you were when the food was still good and the air still clean, and I want you to bury that person beside the others."

He looked past her, toward the place where the sun had begun to die behind the hills.

"I want you to learn the taste of the dirt before you ask for the seed. I want to see your hands torn by the same stones that bled mine. I want everything that's left in you when there's nothing left to give."

"I understand," she whimpered. "You want it all. Our nation's soul."

He turned to her. "I already have it."

***

By the end of the week, they came in caravans of limping power. Rigs stitched together from old hulls and rusted chassis. Some drawn by fuel-starved machines. Some pulled by animals. Others by men. A prince from the salt-licked ruins of his oil empire, wearing robes stained with brine and diesel. A banker-turned-minister out of the collapsed towers of what had once been Delhi, shoes wrapped in plastic and tape. A preacher from the southern belt, face blistered by sun, holding a cross in one hand and a ration tin in the other.

Each brought their stories. Their shame trailing behind them like smoke. They offered what they had: drones too brittle to fly, patents on old medicines, maps to vaults no longer guarded. They spoke of people starving in the high apartments, of mothers smothering their own to silence the crying. Some wept. Others grinned through cracked teeth.

And Gideon took it all. He listened. Made no promises. He scratched his ledgers with a bone-handled pen and muttered the names back to them like a priest reading sins aloud. The lists grew longer. The laws thinner. No code but his now. No appeal. Hunger was the only truth.

***

The knock was not loud. Not a battering. Not a warning. Just the sort of knock a man makes when he already owns the door.

Mara rose from the table where the children sat, eyes wide above their morning meal, hands frozen on cups of warm broth. The sun had just started to come through the slats of the shutter, laying pale bars across the stone floor. She opened the door without speaking.

Three men stood outside. Their uniforms were black and silent. No insignias, no names. Only the shimmer of weave under light, the dull sheen of weapons slung across their backs like tools. The one in front held a square of paper, thick and pale and official.

"This is a Declaration of Authority," he said.

Her husband, Abram, came to the doorway, pulling on a shirt. His face was unreadable. Years of judging men had trained every visible emotion out of it. He looked at the soldier, then the paper.

"I see."

"You've been remanded by order of Gideon, Protector of the Territories, Voice of Provision, Keeper of the Balance," the man said.

"No balance remains," Abram said.

The soldier did not answer. The other two moved in behind him.

"You'll come with us," the first man said.

Mara reached for Abram's hand. He took it. He turned to the children, who hadn't moved. The oldest, Thomas, stared at him with an understanding far too large for his years. The girl, Miren, clutched a doll to her chest as if it could speak sense into the world.

"I won't be gone long," Abram said, though it was a lie and they all knew it. "Keep each other safe. Stay near your mother."

"Where are you taking him?" Mara asked.

"Central Holding. Until review."

"Review by whom? There is no court anymore."

The soldier's eyes didn't blink. "There is Gideon."

Abram took a coat from the peg and slipped it on. He didn't look at Mara again. He didn't have to. He stepped past the man with the paper and onto the road where the black transport waited, no markings, engine quiet.

He did not ask for time. He did not resist. He had written too many sentences in his life to mistake the punctuation of this one.

Mara stood in the doorway long after they were gone. The broth cooled. The light moved. Somewhere down the hill, a drone whirred past on silent rotors. Its camera turned toward the house for a breath, then moved on.

That night, the children slept together on the floor. Mara sat at the window and watched the road. It did not bring him back.

***

In another house, a boy woke before dawn. He lay flat beneath the thin coverlet, the cold not yet pushed back by the sun. The silence in the house was thick. It had settled into the walls like dust, into the corners where laughter once lived, into the floorboards that no longer creaked with his father's step. He stared up at the ceiling. The red eye of the camera glowed dull above him, unblinking.

Across the hall, his mother's door stood shut. It had not opened in the night. Not for water. Not for the sound of his voice in dreams. He had not heard her cry since the men came. Not since they took his father in the dark like thieves.

"She don't cry no more," he whispered.

He wasn't sure if she did, not truly. If she wept at all now, it was the kind of weeping that came with no sound. The kind that stayed locked behind ribs. Where no one had to see.

He rose and dressed without a sound. The floor was cold beneath his feet. In the kitchen, the table stood set for three. The third chair remained empty as it had for seven days. His mother came in, her hair pulled back, her face drawn and pale.

She poured water into a tin cup and set it before him. She did not speak. The boy sipped, watching her hands as she moved about the room. They shook, but only a little.

Outside, the street was empty. The sky was the color of old bone. He heard the tread before he saw them. Two men, black coats, faces blank as slate. They did not hurry. Their boots left no mark in the dust.

His mother stood at the window, her hand pressed flat against the glass. The men passed without looking in. She let out a breath she had been holding.

"Do you remember," she said, her voice low, "what your father told you?"

He nodded. "To listen. To remember."

She knelt beside him, her eyes searching his. "Not to speak. Not unless you must."

He nodded again.

They ate in silence. The screens in the corners of the room flickered to life. A woman's face appeared. Isabella Krul'thor, the Oracle, as she was called. She was pale as chalk, her long silver hair falling like ash down her back. She moved like a specter among them. They did not use rope nor blade. Their trade was in words and they cut with them all the same. The broadcasts came without end. On every wallscreen. On every street. In every house.

Her voice drifted through the house, soft as wind over bone.

"Order is peace," she said. "Obedience is hope. The old world is gone. Let us not mourn what is past. Let us build what must come."

The boy watched the screen. His mother turned away.

After breakfast, he went to the door. The street was filling now. Neighbors moved with quiet purpose, eyes downcast. No one greeted anyone. The air carried the faint hum of the towers. Gideon's voice, everywhere and nowhere.

He walked to the edge of the square. There, beneath the statue of the old judge, a body had been left. Folded hands. Mouth sewn shut. The Droppers had come in the night.

A woman stood nearby, her face gray with grief. She did not approach the body. She stood with her arms crossed tight against her ribs and watched the wind tug at the dead man's coat.

The boy stood beside her.

"You knew him?" he asked.

She did not look at the boy. "He was my brother."

He looked at the body. The stitches were neat. The lips drawn together, no blood. "Why do they do it like that?"

She shook her head. "So we remember. So we don't forget."

He looked up at her. "Will you bury him?"

She glanced at the cameras mounted on the lampposts. "At dusk. When the Echoers have gone."

He nodded. He did not ask more.

A man passed them, his coat brushing the woman's sleeve. He did not stop. His eyes flicked to the body, then away.

The boy watched the man disappear down the street. "They don't look anymore."

The woman's voice was flat. "Looking is dangerous."

He thought of last night. Of the Silencers in the street. At their head, Malgoth, whose name bore weight like a chain dragged through blood. They did not hurry. There was no smoke, nor fire, nor clash of iron. Only the slow tread of men who had done this before and would do it again and would never speak of it.

Then he thought of his father, the way he had stood in the doorway, his shoulders straight, his eyes tired but unafraid. The Silencers had not spoken. They had only shown the red-sealed paper. His father had nodded, kissed his wife's hand, and gone with them.

The boy remembered the sound of the door closing. The silence after.

He turned from the square and walked toward the learning hall. The other children gathered in small groups, their voices hushed. A teacher stood at the entrance, her eyes rimmed with red.

Inside, the screens lined the walls. Gideon's voice filled the room.

"You are the future," he said. "You are the hope of the new world. Speak truth. Obey. Trust in order."

The teacher called the roll. Each child answered with a single word. Present.

At midday, the boy slipped away. He found his friend, Tomas, behind the old library. The building was locked, the windows boarded.

Tomas sat on the steps, knees drawn to his chest. "Did you see?"

The boy nodded. "They left him in the square."

Tomas's voice was barely a whisper. "My uncle. Last week. The Silencers came. My mother didn't cry. She just cleaned the room after."

They sat in silence. The wind rattled the boards on the library.

"Do you think they'll come for us?" Tomas asked.

The boy shrugged. "We don't do anything."

Tomas looked at him. "That's why."

A woman stepped from the dark. Nyx Gorgrath. The Wraith. Gaunt of face, the skin drawn tight across her cheekbones, eyes like tallymarks etched too deep, too long unreckoned. Her mouth curled in a sneer that seemed carved in, old as bone and just as permanent. She was tall and thin, wrapped in a black coat that moved when she moved and stilled when she stopped. The wide-brimmed hat cast her in a shadow that no lamp could lift.

"You boys lost?" she said, that grin cut into her like a wound that wouldn't heal.

They shook their heads.

She crouched, her coat pooling around her like spilled ink. "You know what happens to those who wander?"

Tomas swallowed. "No."

She smiled, thin and cold. "They get found."

She stood and walked away, her steps soundless. The boys watched her go, hearts pounding.

Tomas shivered. "I heard she never sleeps."

The boy stared at the spot where she had stood. "She doesn't need to."

They parted at the corner. The boy walked home, the sky heavy with the promise of rain. He found his mother in the garden, her hands buried in the earth.

He knelt beside her. "They came again."

She did not look at him. "I know."

He watched her fingers press seeds into the soil. "Why do you keep planting?"

She paused. "Because something must grow."

He looked at the dirt beneath his nails. "Will it?"

She pressed the earth flat. "If we remember how."

The screens flickered on. Gideon's voice filled the air.

"Obedience is peace. Peace is survival. Survival is hope."

The boy stood. "I don't like his voice."

His mother wiped her hands on her skirt. "It's not meant to be liked."

He looked at her. "What if we stopped listening?"

She smiled, a sad, small thing. "Then we'd be alone."

He thought of the empty chair at the table. The body in the square. The woman who would bury her brother at dusk.

He thought of the Wraith's eyes, cold and hollow.

He thought of the seeds in the earth.

That night, he dreamed of a world without voices. No screens, no broadcasts, no orders. Only the sound of wind in the grass and the hush of rain on stone. In the dream, his father stood beside him, silent but whole.

He woke before dawn. The silence pressed close. He rose and dressed. In the kitchen, his mother set the table for two. They ate in silence.

Outside, the Silencers passed. The boy stood straighter. He did not look at them. He remembered.

At dusk, he went to the square. The woman was there, her hands folded in her lap. The body was gone. The dust was smooth.

She looked at him. "You remember?"

He nodded.

She smiled, weary and grateful. "Good. Someone must."

He walked home in the dark, the silence deep as the grave.

And in the garden, the first shoots broke the earth.

***

The rain had stopped but the sky remained low, a lid pressed tight against the city. Water pooled in the gutters, reflecting the broken teeth of streetlights. Gideon walked along with Malgoth and armed soldiers, down the avenue, his boots leaving no sound on the slick pavement. The buildings on either side loomed, windowless, their brickwork stained and pitted as if the storm had scoured them clean of memory.

Ahead, the old courthouse stood. Its columns, once white, were gray with soot. The banners hung limp, their colors bled to the color of old wounds. Two men in black coats waited at the steps, rifles slung across their chests. They watched Gideon and the others approach. But the two men did not move.

He paused at the foot of the stairs, rainwater dripping from his coat. He looked up at the men. Their faces were blank, eyes glassy, as if they were carved from the same stone as the building behind them.

"You waiting for someone?" Gideon said.

The taller of the two blinked. "Council's inside. If that's your business."

Gideon nodded. "It is. And my friends are coming with me. Best if you let us pass."

The two men stepped aside and Gideon climbed the steps with Malgoth and the others. The doors opened before him, not by hand nor pulley nor trick of wind, but slow and soundless, as if the building had drawn breath and exhaled its defiance.

Inside the hall, his steps rang alone. The rotunda above him split and weeping. He crossed beneath it and entered the council chamber. Malgoth stood with his men along the walls, rifles at the ready. Watching. Silent.

They were all there. The councilors sat in their high-backed chairs, arranged in a crescent. Their robes were immaculate. Their faces pale and smooth as if scrubbed of expression. Each man and woman stared straight ahead, hands folded on the table.

Gideon stopped at the center of the room. He did not speak. He waited.

The chairman stood. Nervous. His voice was thin, brittle as old glass. "You have come to address the council."

Gideon looked at him. The man's eyes moved like things alive, hunting in the dark. Approval, maybe. Or mercy. Or some sign he'd not spoken into a void. He found nothing. He went on.

"We are prepared to hear your petition."

Gideon shook his head. "I have no petition."

A silence. The councilors shifted in their seats, robes whispering.

The chairman cleared his throat. "Then state your purpose."

Gideon stepped forward. "I have come to end it."

A ripple moved through the chamber, like wind through dry grass. One of the councilors—a woman with silver hair—leaned forward.

"End what, precisely?"

Gideon turned to her. "This. All of it. The charade. The hollow words. The pretense of order."

The chairman's hands trembled on the table. "Order is all we have left."

Gideon smiled, but there was no warmth in it. "You have nothing left."

He raised his hand. Not in threat, but in demonstration. The lights overhead flickered, then died. The room plunged into darkness, save for the pale glow of morning leaking through the high windows.

Someone gasped. Another began to rise, then sat back down as if remembering the rules.

Gideon's voice was quiet, but it filled the chamber. "You built your walls on oaths and fear. You thought them strong. But fear is a breakable thing. It shatters quite easily."

The chairman's voice was small. "We did what we must. For peace. For continuity."

Gideon shook his head. "You did what was easy. You traded truth for comfort. Now you have neither."

A councilor spoke, his voice trembling. "What do you want from us?"

"Nothing," Gideon said. "You have nothing to give."

He turned and walked to the doors at the end of the chamber. Laid his hand to the old wood. The hinges groaned. The doors opened inward like the jaws of some ancient thing. Beyond them, the city lay mute and gray and rimmed in ash. In the square, the people had gathered. They stood without sound. Their faces drawn, eyes sunken. Starving. They looked up at him with the hollow patience of those who had buried hope like seed in barren ground.

Gideon stepped aside. Turned to the councilors in the chamber.

"Go," he said. "See what you have made."

They did not move at first. Then slowly, as if their bones had grown brittle in the night, they rose. One by one. No words passed between them. They walked with the gait of men who already bore their judgment.

They filed past him and out into the ashlight.

Outside, the people did not cheer. They did not cry out. They only watched. The air was still. The sound of breath held too long, waiting to be let go.

The chairman stopped beside Gideon. His eyes were wet. "What happens now?"

Gideon looked at him. "Now you live with it."

The chairman nodded as if this was a sentence he had expected. He joined the others on the steps.

Gideon remained in the doorway. He watched as the councilors stood before the crowd, their robes bright against the gray. No one spoke. The banners above them hung limp, their symbols meaningless.

A boy in the crowd called out. "What do we do now?"

No answer came.

Gideon stepped down into the square. The people parted for him, silent, their faces pale with fear or hope—he could not tell which.

He walked to the center of the square, followed by Malgoth and his men. He turned, facing the courthouse, the councilors, the banners.

He spoke, his voice carrying in the stillness.

"You are free from those in the chamber. There will be new leaders here."

No one moved. The words hung in the air, heavy as stones.

A woman stepped forward. Her hands shook. "New? Who?"

Gideon looked at her. The lines of her face were deep, her eyes rimmed with red. "Elections will still come. On time. With bunting and song," he said. "But choose wisely, my friends. Choose wisely."

She shook her head. "We don't understand."

Gideon nodded. "You will. Very soon."

He turned away, walked through the crowd. The people made way, their eyes following him.

Behind him, the councilors stood on the steps, uncertain, their authority stripped away. The banners fluttered in a sudden breeze.

A man called out from the crowd. "Will you lead us?"

Gideon did not turn. He did not respond.

He kept walking. The city stretched before him, silent and waiting.

The people watched him go. Some wept. Others knelt in the mud, pressing their faces to the earth.

The councilors stood on the steps, their hands empty.

The sky brightened, just a little. The rain began again, soft and steady, washing the blood and dust from the stones.

The bells began to ring. Not in celebration, but in mourning.

Gideon walked on, his figure growing small in the rain.

The city watched, waiting for someone to speak, for someone to tell them what came next.

But there was only silence, and the sound of water running in the streets.

Gideon did not look back.

***

In another town, one which Gideon had already visited, the hall was cold. Light slanted in through high windows, pale and without warmth. The banners hung limp from the rafters, their colors faded, their emblems worn smooth by years of dust and indifference. Rows of men sat in silence, their faces turned forward, hands folded in their laps or resting on the polished wood of the benches. The air was heavy with the scent of old paper and the faint, sour tang of fear.

A man entered, his steps echoing on the stone floor. He wore a suit, dark and pressed, the lapels sharp as razors. His hair was combed flat against his skull. He moved with the certainty of one who knows the outcome before the first word is spoken.

He stopped at the front, beneath the largest banner. He took out some papers and placed them on a table. He looked out at the men, his eyes sweeping the room. No one met his gaze.

"Gentlemen," he said. His voice was soft, yet it carried. "We are gathered."

A shuffling, a cough. The scrape of a chair leg.

He waited. The silence thickened.

"Today we confirm the will of the people," he said. "As we have done. As we will do."

An old man in the second row, his hair gone white, raised his hand. It trembled.

The man at the front pointed to the old man. "Yes, Councilor?" he said.

The councilor cleared his throat. "Will there be—" He faltered. "Will there be discussion?"

The man at the front smiled. It was a careful smile, measured and without warmth. "There is always discussion," he said. "But the people have spoken. We are here to affirm."

The councilor lowered his hand. He looked at his lap.

A younger man, his face drawn and pale, leaned forward. "If the people have spoken," he said, "why are we here?"

The man at the front turned to him. "We are here because it is the law. The process must be observed."

The young man's mouth twisted. "A process is not a choice."

The man at the front's smile did not waver. "You are free to abstain," he said. "But the outcome is assured."

The young man looked away. His fingers drummed on the bench.

A bell rang, somewhere distant. The men shifted, their bodies restless in the hard seats.

The men stirred in their seats. Shoulders shifting. Boots scraping the floor. A cough swallowed into a sleeve. The wood beneath them old and unforgiving.

The man at the front raised his hand. His face was hard and pale in the lampglow.

"Let us proceed," he said. "Regarding the issue of food rations. They will be distributed as decreed by Gideon. All in favor."

Hands rose. Some quickly, some slowly. Some hung in the air like leaves caught on a branch, uncertain whether to fall.

The man at the front counted. He nodded.

"All opposed?" he said.

No hands.

He waited. Still no hands.

"Good," he said. "It is done. Food rations will be distributed as decreed by Gideon."

The silence was thicker than before. No one moved.

Outside, the street was empty. The windows rattled in the wind. Somewhere, a dog barked, sharp and lonely.

The man at the front gathered his papers. He looked at the men. "You have served well," he said. "You may go."

They stood, moving with the slow, heavy grace of men underwater. Their eyes were dull, their faces slack. They filed out, one by one, their footsteps muffled on the worn carpet.

In the hall, the banners hung still. The dust settled in the shafts of light.

The young man lingered at the door. He looked back at the empty benches, at the man at the front.

"Does it matter?" he said. His voice was low.

The man at the front looked up. "What?"

"Any of it," the young man said. "Does it matter?"

The man at the front studied him. "It matters that you ask," he said.

The young man shook his head. "That's not enough."

The man at the front smiled again, the same careful smile. "It is what we have now."

The young man left. The door closed behind him with a soft click.

The man at the front stood alone. He looked at the empty room, at the banners, at the dust. He smoothed his papers, straightened his tie.

On the screens in the shop windows, Gideon's face flickered. Smiling. Nodding. Promising.

In the square, a woman swept the pavement. Her broom scratched at the stones. She paused, looked up at the banners, then bent to her work.

A boy watched from the shadows. He held a folded paper in his hands, the ink smudged, the words blurred. He read the headline, lips moving in silence.

The man at the front stepped outside. He looked at the sky, pale and empty. He listened to the wind.

The city waited. The banners hung. The silence deepened.

A bell rang, far away. The day moved on.

***

Outside, the city moved in slow circles.

Ash fell in the gutters like gray snow. The sky was dull and low. No birds flew. No sirens wailed. The roads held no honking, no rush. Only the slow cough of idling trucks long since silenced, their tanks empty or their drivers vanished. A man could walk three blocks and not hear another soul. The wind moved the trash. The city, once full of mouths, had gone dumb.

The press trucks sat cold and idle at the curb. Their paint peeling. Tires flat. Names scrawled on the sides like gravestones for papers already dead. The windows of the newspaper office were dark, the big iron press inside still as a tomb. Dust on the linotypes. Dust on the desk where headlines once shouted. Dust on the floor where a reporter named Krell had fallen last Tuesday, with his throat torn out.

In the shop windows, the screens still flickered. Power routed in from some deep, unseen hand. Gideon's face smiled across a thousand displays. His voice warm. His eyes knowing. He nodded slow. He promised them peace.

Inside one of the holding sites—an old theater converted with bars and bolt-guns and wire—men and women sat on the bare floor. Gaunt, silent, their lips cracked. Some had teeth missing from the beatings. Some had old ink stains on their fingers still, like they'd been caught stealing light. One man lay with his eyes open and his mouth closed forever. No one moved him.

A soldier came down the aisle between the broken seats.

"You," he said. "Up."

The man he pointed to rose without a word. His shirt hung from him like it belonged to a scarecrow. His name had once been Felix. He'd reported on the canals going dry and the ration grain full of sawdust. He stepped out, his head bowed. The soldier kicked him hard in the back and he went down like a sack. He did not cry out.

"Take him," the soldier said.

Two more came. Lifted him by the arms. Dragged him toward the back, past the old velvet curtains now mildewed and flaked. The smell of rot hung in the air like the aftertaste of a dream.

A woman in the third row watched with wide eyes.

"Where are they taking him?" she whispered.

An old man beside her shook his head. "Don't matter."

"They'll kill him," she said.

He looked at her. "There's nothing left to kill."

Somewhere up above, past the plaster ceiling, a speaker crackled. A voice came through. Smooth. Warm as velvet soaked in vinegar.

"You are not forgotten," it said. "You are not our enemies. You are confused. Misled. You will learn. You will return to purpose."

The woman turned her face toward the ceiling. "Liar," she whispered.

The man beside her said nothing. He watched the aisle. The shadows. His eyes never blinked.

***

In the southern quarter, just past the charred university, an office hummed like a beehive from hell. Black trucks came and went. No license plates. Windows blackened. No one ever climbed out.

Inside, Gideon stood at the tall window with his hands behind his back. He looked down over the square, where a group of arrested reporters and others associated with the press knelt in a line. Their hands were zip-tied. Their heads shaved. Their names and publications read aloud by a man with a scroll and a soft voice.

"They'll be gone by morning," said the man behind Gideon. A bureaucrat with slick hair and a hollow face.

Gideon didn't answer. His eyes were fixed on one of the kneeling men. A red-haired kid. Young. Still had fire in him. Still thought this was some mistake. Some misunderstanding. Gideon saw him tremble when the second man in the line was shot in the head.

"Tell me," Gideon said finally, "do they still write when they get to the mines?"

The bureaucrat blinked. "Sir?"

"In the salt pits. In the blackstone mines. Do they still try? Carve their names into the walls with stones? Ink things in the dirt with blood?"

"I . . . I imagine they try, sir."

Gideon nodded slowly.

"Good," he said.

"Sir?"

"If a man still tries to write while dying in the dark, it means we haven't killed the soul yet. Only the voice."

He turned from the window.

"It must be deeper. No printing presses without my consent. No broadcasts without review. No electronic media. Detain all editors. Anyone with a byline in the last two years gets the mark. No food allotment without clearance."

The bureaucrat scribbled notes, eyes darting.

"And if they try to run?"

Gideon smiled. It was a smile that remembered knives.

"We find them," he said. "And we teach them silence."

***

In a corridor under the city, far from any light, a man named Baird sat in a locked room with a microphone. He was thin and shaking and had not eaten in three days. Before that, he had read the evening news for a pirate station on the old FM band. Just facts. Weather. Names of the dead.

Now the mic hissed.

A red light came on.

The door clicked open.

A figure stepped in, boots scraping on the concrete.

"You will read," the figure said.

Baird looked up. His voice was raw. "What's the story?"

The figure dropped a paper on the desk.

Baird read. His hands trembled.

"This is fiction," he whispered.

The figure didn't move.

"It's all lies."

"Truth is what the survivors say," the figure said. "Read it."

"I won't."

There was a long pause.

Then the red light blinked off.

The room went dark again.

When the lights came back alive an hour later, Baird had not moved. His hands still rested on the script. His breath was shallow. His mouth was dry. His eyes swollen and dull. A thin line of blood tracked down from his temple, dark against the skin.

The lights above hummed. The paper beneath his hands was damp with sweat and something else. The blood kept on.

He read from the paper. Every word.

***

Time passed. Too much time. Mara walked to Central Holding. She brought no lawyer, no plea, only a bag of clean clothes and a book he used to read aloud at night.

They met her at the gate.

"No visits," the guard said.

"I brought these for him," she said.

The guard looked into the bag, pulled out the book.

"He won't be needing this," he said.

She stared at him.

"You killed him."

He shook his head. "He's not dead."

"Then where is he?"

"He's no longer under review."

"What does that mean?"

"It means he's serving the Authority in a more fitting role."

"What role?"

The guard smiled like a man told to.

"Silence."

He handed her back the empty bag.

She walked home as the Echoers filled the streets. They had constructed more large screens. Put them on buildings along the streets. With outstretched arms, they began their nightly broadcast, Gideon's voice rolling over the hills like a sermon.

"Tonight, remember," he said. "We are strong because we are united. We are united because the old world is gone. And those who served it must serve us now."

In the dark house, Mara sat at the table where Abram had once read the laws aloud. She opened the book he never got. She tore out the pages one by one and fed them to the stove, the fire hungrily eating the words he once believed would save them.

She did not cry. The children would wake soon. There would be no more broth. The shelves were growing bare.

Outside, the drones watched. The lights never turned off.

***

They met where the ruins touched the edge of the old world.

The halls here were long since swallowed by the earth, walls scabbed with lichen and soot. No lights save for what flickered from broken vents. No witnesses but the rusted eyes of ancient machines. A place forgotten even by those who had built it, left to drown in silence.

Gideon came alone. No security. His boots struck the stone like iron against bone. The cape trailed behind him, black as the deepest pit, the red lining spilling out like blood uncoiled. Beneath the collar, his throat was bare and pale, scarred by something done long ago and not spoken of. His gloved hand moved to the door and it opened not by code but by will.

Inside the sanctum, she was already kneeling.

Her robes pooled around her like milk poured upon ash. Hair like silver thread cascaded down her back. Her hands were bare. Her staff set beside her. The crystal atop it pulsed with a rhythm not unlike a heartbeat. She did not look up when he entered. She waited.

He crossed the room without sound. The cape stirred the dust. He removed the gloves and laid them on the stone table. The monocle followed. He did not speak until he stood above her.

"Oracle."

Her voice came soft, a breath exhaled in reverence.

"My Sovereign. My Light."

He studied her. The hollows of her eyes. The way the white of her garment caught the dim glow and turned it ghostlike. She was kneeling in truth, not in form alone. She had surrendered her voice, her name, her will.

He said, "Are we unseen?"

"All eyes are blind but mine," she said. "And I see only you."

He turned his gaze toward the walls. They were carved with forgotten sigils, long faded. He raised one hand and traced a line in the air. The glyphs lit faintly. He smiled.

"This ground once belonged to kings," he said.

"It belongs to you now," she said.

He circled her, the cape whispering across stone. Her body shifted to follow his movement, but she did not rise. Her spine curved like a bow strung tight. The back of her neck was bared. He looked upon her skin like one looks at territory.

"You and your people have told them I was sent," he said.

"More than sent. You are the end and the beginning. The hand and the flame."

"And they believe it?"

She nodded.

"They believe as I do. As I must."

He crouched behind her and unfastened the clasp at her shoulder. The robes fell from her like water poured over stone. Beneath, she wore nothing. Her body, pale and still, bore the runes of his dominion in ink and scar alike. He touched them with a reverence that did not reach his eyes.

"You have always belonged to me," he said.

She turned her face slightly. Her breath had slowed.

"Yes, my Sovereign."

"And you will kneel until I say otherwise."

"Yes."

Outside, the world burned. Smoke rolled down from the forges and lay thick upon the upper tiers where the sky once showed. The people that remained built monuments from the bones of the old world. They sang the Oracle's hymns in cracked voices. They sifted through ash for relics. They gave up their children. Elsewhere, the cities burned not by accident but by will. A cleansing fire. Dissent set to flame.

Inside, there was only him. And her. And the stone.

He moved over her like nightfall, slow, unstoppable. Her limbs did not resist. They bent as commanded. She trembled but did not speak. Her hair spread across the floor like something spilled. He spoke not of love, for he did not believe in it, nor of worship, for he found it beneath him.

"You were made for this," he said.

"I was made for you."

He took her with the same certainty he had taken everything else—the cities, the nations. The same patience. The same hunger. She gave herself freely. Entirely. He did not thank her.

After, they lay in silence. The room had gone darker, the light reduced to a breath. Her head rested against his chest. His hand curled in her hair.

"I dreamed of this place," she said.

He said nothing.

"I dreamed the earth split open and from it you rose. Clad in fire. Eyes full of war."

He looked down at her.

"I do not rise," he said. "I am always above."

She smiled. Not with joy. With conviction.

"They will try to stop you," she said.

"They will try."

"They will come with relics. With ghosts. With children born of rebellion."

"I know."

She pressed her face against his chest. Gave it a soft kiss.

"You will burn them all."

He closed his eyes.

"I already have."

The silence was deep and holy. It wrapped around them like the womb of something godless. The old machines ticked in sleep. Somewhere beneath the stone, a tremor passed, faint and slow, like the earth remembering its shape.

When she spoke again, her voice was thin.

"May I speak freely?"

"You may."

"There are whispers among some of the Echoers. Doubt woven through the choir."

He did not move.

"Then you will cut them out."

"I have begun."

"And if it spreads?"

She hesitated.

"Then I will burn them. One by one. Until only devotion remains."

"Good. Everything must be pure. We must sing with one voice."

He nodded once. The weight of that nod was enough to seal nations.

"You are my voice," he said. "And my hand when I am not present. Do not fail me."

"I will not."

He rose then. Gathered his gloves, his monocle. Fastened the belt. The cape flowed behind him like smoke from a pyre. She remained where she was. Naked upon the stone. Her body bore no shame. Only service.

At the threshold, he turned back.

"Speak no word of this," he said.

"I will not."

"Not even in your prayers."

"No."

He left her there in the dark, among the ghosts of empires. His boots again upon the stone. The shadows swallowed him.

She lay back upon the stone, alone, the cold rising through her spine like a memory half-buried. Pain and pleasure were not separate things to her now but one thing, indivisible. A truth carved into her like script into the hide of a beast. Her hand moved to her belly slow as moonfall. As if the flesh might speak back. As if something beneath it stirred already. The floor was cold, and the air stank of wax and old prayers left to rot in the rafters. She stood after a time, bare in the candlelight, pale as salt, and thought of the seed set in her. Quiet. Unnamed. A thing meant to grow in dark before ever it met the world.

In time, she would rise. She would cloak herself in white and gold. She would walk among the faithful, her steps measured and unhurried, the hem of her garment whispering against the bones of the world. She would speak of visions and fire, her voice a low thunder in the hollow of the cathedrals built from steel and bone. She would chant the name of Gideon, and the echo would carry through the marrow of the earth.

And they would listen.

Because when the Sovereign speaks, the earth answers.

And when the Oracle kneels, the world bows with her.

4 A Knelt World

Still, fires burned in many cities. Still, some fought for old flags or new names. But it was quieter. The gunshots came further apart. The screams fewer. The world no longer barked or bargained. It knelt.

One day, a woman came alone out of the east. She was striking, almost otherworldly beauty with pale skin, raven-black hair, and bright, almost hypnotic blue eyes. She carried a canvas sack slung over one shoulder and wore an old airman's jacket gone soft with age. A wedding ring hung at her neck, threaded through with wire like some relic fished from the ruins. The world shifted around her as if it too had paused to see what she might do. Gideon felt the shift.

He stood watching her come up the rise. The guards looked to him and he gave a nod.

She stepped through the gate like she'd been there before.

"You Gideon?" she asked.

"I am," he told her.

"I come from the edge of the Eastern Reach. Past the breakers. Past the ashline."

"That's far," he said.

"Further now. We buried half the convoy in the dunes."

He looked at her, at the wire around her neck, the ring strung through it, dulled by time and grit.

"Husband?" he said.

"Dead," she said. "Starved. Made sure I didn't."

Gideon squinted into the wind like it had spoken. He did not offer sorrow. There wasn't any left.

"Hard times press hard choices," he said. "Folks been making them since the first fire went out."

"What do you bring?" he asked.

She stepped forward, chin high despite the dust in her eyes and the blood on her sleeve.

"I'm not here to beg," she said. "I want to be part of it. Whatever it is you're building."

He watched her a long moment, boots quiet in the sand. The wind picked up and carried the smell of burned things.

"You know what I'm building?"

"I think so."

"You sure you about this?"

"I'm not looking for handouts, for shelter," she said. "I want to work."

He studied her face. The lines etched there. The ring swinging on its thread.

"There's seed to be sorted. Numbers to run."

She nodded. Turned to go.

"Your name," he said.

"Elarlu. Elarlu Voss."

"You'll answer to it here."

"I always have."

"Your background?"

"Media and psychology. University. Never put it to much use."

Gideon nodded. The corners of his mouth turned, but only just.

The fields lay beyond the compound wall, past the burnt-out husks of old machines and a line of scorched pylons that hummed though the wires were dead. Elarlu walked, her boots sinking into the gray loam. The air carried the stench of rotting compost and the sweet reek of engineered growths no one trusted but everyone ate. Rows stretched out like scars across the land. Bent figures moved between them—silent, sunburned, their faces wrapped in cloth. No greetings. No one looked up.

A man with a copper whistle around his neck pointed. "Set the sack down. That row there. Weed out the bad ones. Gloves in the bin. Mind the rootmice."

Elarlu did not speak. She swung the sack from her shoulders and let it fall. Slipped her hands into the stiff gloves. The earth was cold beneath the rubber. She dropped to her knees.

After some time, the man passed again. "You don't speak much."

"No one asked me to."

He chewed that over like gristle. "You from the cities?"

"Used to be."

"Then you know what broke them?"

She looked up. "Too much talking. Too little work."

The man barked a dry laugh and moved on. "I think I'm gonna like you, girlie."

Elarlu dug. The crop was spiny and red-veined, hard to pull. Even with gloves it tore the skin from her knuckles. But she didn't stop. The sky turned slow and colorless above her. Shadows crawled across the earth. Somewhere far off a whistle called.

When she finally stood, her back screamed. Dirt clung to her like a second skin.

A boy not more than sixteen. Thin in the way of someone never built for labor. He handed her a tin cup. The water inside sloshed.

He said, "You think we're gonna last?"

She drank. Ran the back of her hand across her mouth.

"I am," she said. "Not sure about you, though."

***

That night there was a council of advisors. Not of equals. There were no equals anymore. Power had ground the notion to dust. They gathered under the vaulted dark where the stars blinked like dying embers. The fire was low and mean. It gave no warmth and asked none.

Gideon stood among them. He did not sit. He spoke plain and without ceremony. His words dropped like stones in the silence. The fire behind him cast his shadow long against the ruin wall. He did not gesture. His voice held no tremble of doubt. The others feasted in silence, their knives whispering against tin. They ate fish pulled from stagnant waters. Game hunted in silence with snares and sharp wire. Vegetables grown in browned fields with soil scrubbed clean of ash. They fed themselves and listened and did not interrupt.

"Today, we took in seven more. Tomorrow there'll be more than that. You've seen how they come. Burned. Broke. Full of promises and thin with lies. You'll listen, but you won't believe. You'll weigh their hands, not their words. They'll tell you about what they had, what they lost, what they deserve."

He looked from face to face, his eyes settling on a tall and gaunt man with piercing gray eyes that seemed to see through people. His sharp features and thin, scarred lips give him a perpetually sinister look. Gideon nodded.

"But none of that matters," said the man, his name Victor Morgar. "Not here. Not now. What they plant, they eat. What they break, they fix. What they kill, they bury. We simply want everything they have."

Morgar was perhaps one of few Gideon trusted, and even that trust was a thing measured like rations. Cold of eye and hard of thought. He made plans the way a butcher maps a carcass, one cut at a time. Tall, long-limbed, his coat like a shroud. The black cloth trimmed in red and silver, not for decoration but to mark him—so the others knew what he was. The high collar stiff against his neck, the epaulets broad like shoulders that never bent. He wore gloves, always. Even in heat. Even in the company of ghosts.

His face was long and pale, the lips drawn tight and thin like scars that never healed. The eyes gray and empty and knowing. He looked at men the way a knife looks at flesh.

Gideon weighed in. "And if they don't follow the rules?"

Morgan didn't pause. "They'll go where the dogs went. Where the kings went. Where every last goddamned general went when the harvest failed."

There was silence. The kind that swallowed breath. The wind moved in the grass beyond the walls, a low sifting whisper like something being buried alive. A knife slipped from a hand and rang against stone. Sharp. Hollow. Final. Heads turned. Eyes held open too long. Nobody spoke.

"The old world had its chance," Gideon said. His voice carried like judgment across the kindling hush. "We're not rebuilding it. We're burying it. What grows here grows different."

They nodded. One by one, their heads dipped like wheat before the reaper's blade. No cheer. No prayer. Only breath and the creak of old bones in the wind.

Gideon looked skyward. The stars were faint, sickly things behind the soot. Ash veils dragged across them like memory. "Let them come," he said. "Let them crawl on rusted knees. If they bring our truth, we'll give them bread. If they bring the old tongue, they'll leave with nothing and face darkness."

He sat. Firelight danced on the ledger beside him. And outside the walls, across the scabbed earth, the caravans moaned like beasts. Wagons pulled by silent men. Bones in sacks. Wheels turning over stone and dust. They came without song. Without banners. Only hunger in their bellies and hope clutched like old nails in their fists.

***

Later that night, Gideon sat alone in the dark at the top of the tower. Wind threaded the broken glass like fingers through harpwire. The city below lay drowned in ash and silence. No stars. No moon. Just the slow drift of smoke across a dead sky. He did not move. Hadn't moved in hours. Just sat there looking over a map. The fire in the grate had long since guttered and the coals gone black. The light gone out of the world and him with it.

He heard the sound on the stairs. A faint tread. Careful. Hesitant. Dust shifted. Then the door opened and the boy came in. He stood there in the threshold, silhouetted, framed by shadow. Said nothing.

Gideon looked up.

He knew the boy. Knew his blood. Victor Morgar's son. Couldn't have been twelve years old. Thin and straight like a cut reed. Eyes too large for his face. Boots black and clean like they'd never known dirt. His hands opened and closed at his sides like he was weighing air, like he was trying to know what a man should do and couldn't quite decide.

"You can come in," said Gideon.

The boy stepped forward.

"And what is your name?" said Gideon.

"Blaise," the boy said, and he smiled when he said it.

Gideon stood and lowered himself to one knee, slow, careful.

"That's a good name," he said. "So. Tell me. What brings you here?"

"My father sends a message," said the boy. "Three shipments were attacked. One near Veracruz. One in the Eastern Reach. The third didn't arrive."

"Who took them?"

"Don't know. Father said might've been rebels. Might've been just been . . . people."

Gideon nodded. Looked past the boy. Looked at the wall like it held some truth.

The boy stood there. Still. Waiting.

"And what should we do about that, Blaise?"

"Father says we should hurt the ones who did this."

"And tell me. What do you think we should do?' Gideon asked.

The boy did not blink. His voice came low and plain, like something carved from wood.

"I think we should make them remember."

Gideon watched him. The boy's fists were clenched at his sides. His shadow trembled, though he did not.

"Not just once," the boy said. "Every day. Until their names are ash in their own mouths. Until there ain't nothing left to crawl home to."

He looked up at Gideon, the fire long gone from the hearth but burning now behind his eyes.

"They took everything. So we take everything back."

Gideon studied him. "You are wise," he said. "You have learned what matters. Tell your father I said so. And tell him I agree with you."

The boy nodded. He turned as if to go, paused.

"Why do we do this?" he said.

The silence that followed had no answer. Not one that could be spoken.

Gideon looked out the window. The lights of the city were faint now, but they were there.

"Because someone has to," he said.

The boy stood over the map, its paper dry and creased like old skin. He traced a line with one finger, then looked up.

"You ever think about just . . . stopping?"

Gideon turned.

"If I did," he said, "the first man in line would take it all for himself. And the second would die. Is that what you want? Men killing men for the taste of something not theirs? We can't have that. No."

The boy watched him, eyes wide. Something inside him pulled tight.

"Go to your parents," Gideon said.

***

Time passed. Days folded into months. Maybe a year. Likely more. Two. Three. The counting slipped away like water through fingers.

The world changed.

Quickly. Unkindly.

Men vanished. Roads cracked. Unrepaired. The lights that once burned through the night guttered out one by one and no hand came to relight them. The old markets became bone-littered squares. The silence grew fat and contented, settled into the bones of things. The air smelled of rust and old ash.

The sky did not soften. The sun hung low and merciless, and the rains came late, if they came at all. But in some places, in the valleys, the people built. Not of concrete or glass but of timber and rusted nails. They dug the ground with tools handed down and whetted dull against stone. They kept goats. Grew beans. Learned again how to make fire from nothing and bread from less. At dusk, they sang. No longer in the tongue of empire, but in the hard vowels of survival. Songs without harmony. But with truth.

The cities still loomed. Vast bones of a world gone. Glass teeth punched out. Towers black and hollow. But the fires no longer burned in them every night. The rage had passed. Some were left to the wind. Others were taken. Walled in. Used for shelter. Or silence.

"They're like carcasses," a man told a woman.

She nodded. "Still standing. Just not alive. Dead."

"Nothing left in 'em but echoes and rot."

"That's enough for some."

There was food. Not much. Enough. The soil churned by hands like roots dug up and reburied. Fields sown without song. The old machines clanked in silence. Out past the wire, the factories hissed and bled their protein cakes, pale and bitter as old ash. You could chew them. You could swallow. And you'd stand, though not for long and not for love. All provided to those who yielded to Gideon's truth.

Not all. But some.

Where madness once reaped its tithe from hunger, now the famine taught the shape of waiting. Men knelt in the dirt and spoke to it like kin. They watched for green like prophets read signs in the dust. The sky their scripture. Their hunger. Their gospel.

And the names of old powers vanished. Flags curled in smoke. No anthem sung. No crest borne. Just wind and ruin and ash.

But one name remained. Gideon Stark.

Not a god. No altar bore his image. No temple his name. No grave was marked with reverence. A man only. A man with science. A man with maps. A man with ledgers. A man with food. A man who remembered.

And still there were those who would not kneel. The last strongholds. The bitter edges. They came from the wastes with iron and powder. They came with guns.

One such nation on the Southern Edge lined their borders—what borders meant anymore. Steel hulls and ragged uniforms. Machines dragged from underground bunkers, sparked to life with the last breath of dying cities. They came not to speak. Not to trade. But to take.

Their leader, a man named Borodin, massed twenty thousand. Marching in columns, boots that cracked the stone. Painted armor and flags that meant nothing. Tanks that trembled the earth.

"They won't talk," said the scout over a commlink. "They won't kneel. They mean to cut through and take the fields that were just planted."

Malgoth sat by the fire. Listening. He peeled a root with a small knife. The edge was notched from long use.

"Let them come," he said.

The scout frowned. "We can't hold them."

Malgoth looked up. "Not with rifles."

The scout waited.

"We hold them with the land."

And they did.

They flooded the low pass with water pulled from broken cisterns. They burned the bridges they'd once built. They laid down thorn and iron, shattered glass in the soil. The goats were led away. The fields salted at the edge.

When Borodin's army arrived, there was nothing to take. They stood beneath a red sky and looked upon a valley they could not eat. Men died from thirst before the first shot. Machines seized. Boots split. Guns jammed with dust.

Borodin sent a messenger.

Malgoth met him at the road. "What do you want?"

The man's voice cracked with dust. "We want food. Safe passage. The promise of land."

"You had that," Malgoth said. "Before you sent the tanks."

The man swallowed. "You can't blame us. People are starving."

"I know," said Malgoth. "We were starving when we planted the first seed."

The man opened his mouth. Closed it. "What will you do?"

Malgoth handed him a small sack. It was rough burlap, the shape of it caved by dried beans shifting inside.

"Take this," he said. "Tell Borodin to plant it. Or eat it. It makes no difference to me. But there will be no place for his people here."

When Borodin received the sack, he turned it over in his hand like it was some old riddle handed down by a god who no longer answered. Then he walked into the dust and did not speak.

That night he burned. Whether it was the fields that caught first or the hands of his own men, no one can say. The fire was already dying by dawn as the men ate the beans.

Others tried.

A fleet came from the drowned coast, sails in tatters, engines sputtering black like the last breath of a dying god. They loosed one volley at Stark's land and struck nothing but air and regret. The sea rose up then. Took them without a word.

Later, a column marched from the north in the dead of winter. They reached the second hill and no farther. The wind there does not bend. It breaks.

And still, the people of Gideon's truth built.

With hands cracked by frost, they cut furrows into the hardpan with stone. Stacked walls from the bones of old cars. They sang songs with no beginning and no end. They laughed like they had always known how.

And when they spoke his name . . . Gideon . . . it was with reverence and the plainness of truth. Without fear.

"Do you think he'll die one day?" a child asked.

"Yes," his mother said. She was grinding grain with a flat stone, and the muscles in her arms moved like ropes drawn tight. "He's only a man."

"Then what will we do?"

The woman looked up. The sun sat in the sky like a watchful eye. "Plant," she said. "Dig. Sing."

Each morning Gideon walked the fields. The ones nearest his compound. He studied the frost. The green shoots pushing up through old ruin. Sometimes he knelt. Pressed his palm into the dirt like he was trying to hear something beneath it.

He never prayed.

He remembered.

***

Gideon had swallowed most of the world. The great northern sprawl of Asia was under the seal of the Amalgam, its languages scrubbed, its names sunk like anchors. Europe, Eastern Reach, buckled. Africa, the Southern Edge, bled. The Americas fractured and yielded, one splinter at a time. What passed for civilization had folded itself into the dark cloak of Gideon Stark, the man with the food, the map, the memory.

But across the sea, far from the reach of his roads and drones and slow iron tractors, there was a land not taken.

The Silent Land, the Last Free, as it was called—Australia.

It was not a land of abundance. The heart of it lay split and white and lifeless. Salted earth and silence. The coasts smothered under ash, the seas warm as blood. But there were places yet unspoiled. Green and stubborn. They'd held on. They had not forgotten what it was to stand alone. What it was to endure.

A teenage boy stood on a cliff above the sea. With him was a woman named Merrow. The wind came cold and fast, whipping grit against their skin. Below, the waves battered old naval wreckage half-submerged in coral.

"There he is," Merrow said. She passed the scope to the boy.

He raised it to his eye. A grainy image swam into view. Two drones, squat and bulbous, hovered like bloated flies over the sea.

They bore no flag. They needed none. Only one man had eyes that far and hands that still reached.

"Stark," the boy said. His voice was thin and dry.

"Not him," said Merrow. "His eye. He won't come himself. Doesn't have the guts. But he watches."

The boy lowered the scope. "Do we shoot it down?"

Merrow shook her head. "Not yet."

"Why not?"

"Because we're not ready."

Inland, past the black ridges and fire-scarred gums, the city of Werrung sat quietly. Not a city by old measure. No towers. No factories. Just a ring of solar stills, water farms, and the burnt skeletons of what came before. They used what they could. They buried what they couldn't.

At the center stood a long hall of iron and eucalyptus wood, scorched and hammered clean. Inside, they gathered. Farmers. Mechanics. Soldiers with rust on their boots.

He sat at the far end of the table. A man named Reza. He'd once worn the insignia of the Royal Navy before it cracked off in a storm and he forgot what it meant. His face was lined with years of sand and gunpowder. One arm was gone from the elbow. The sleeve pinned neat and tight. He'd lost it a long time ago in a battle outside of Varkesh, and the cloth was stiff from dust and old blood.

"They're watching again," said Merrow as she entered. "North coast. Two drones this time. Low altitude. Still probing."

Reza nodded.

A wiry man named Dunlow was with them. A narrow man. Lips thin as a thread. Older. Much older. The kind of man who'd once broken the neck of a scavenger for opening a ration crate too early. Reza didn't care much for him. Too emotional. Too quick with actions. But he needed him. Same as he needed the mines and the guns and the hundred other traps they'd dragged across the earth of this land like bones left for wolves.

Dunlow spat into a cup. "Why wait? Let's send a signal. Drop one of 'em in the drink."

"They want a reason," Reza said. "Don't give them one."

"They already took Papua. New Zealand is next. What makes you think they'll wait for a reason?"

Reza looked across the table. "Because they're not gods. They've got mouths to feed. Same as us. They'll try fear first. Then famine. Then fire."

Dunlow stared. "So, we just sit?"

Reza leaned forward. His voice low and slow.

"No. We build. We prepare. And when the fire comes, we burn the road behind it."

That night, Reza stood alone at the edge of the paddocks, listening to the goats stir in their pens. He lit a thin roll of gumleaf tobacco and smoked without looking up.

Merrow came again. Her hair was pulled back in a tight coil, eyes dark from years of salt wind and watching.

"You believe he'll come?" she asked.

"I believe he won't stop."

She nodded. "We don't have enough guns."

"No."

"Not enough food."

"No."

"Then what do we have?"

He tapped the ashes from his smoke. "Land. And memory."

"Stark has memory, too."

He looked at her. "No. Stark has regret. That's different."

She said nothing for a long while. The moon was rising slow. Orange. Like a scar.

"My son," she said. "He's sixteen next month. Thinks it's going to be him that shoots the first drone."

Reza smiled faintly. "Let him dream."

"And when the dreaming ends?"

Reza looked out across the dry fields.

"Then we plant."

She laughed once, short and bitter. "You think there's hope in this?"

"No," he said. "I think there's us. And I think that's enough."

At dawn, a ship came. Silent. Sleek. Gray as sharkskin. It hovered just offshore, the water beneath it steaming.

Reza stood on the beach with Dunlow and Merrow and a half-dozen others. No weapons drawn. Just eyes.

A voice crackled from the ship's speaker. Tinny. Cold.

"This is the Amalgam. We offer food. Supplies. We ask only for cooperation. The guarantees come at the end."

Merrow huffed. "Guarantees my ass."

Reza stepped forward.

"You got beans in that ship?" he asked.

A pause.

"Yes."

"Then eat 'em," Reza said. "We got enough memory here to grow our own."

The ship hovered a moment longer. Then it turned. And vanished into mist.

Not the last ship.

Not the last message.

But they stood.

And the name of Gideon Stark remained.

Outside.

5 The Instruments

The Spire rose like the rib of some ancient god, black against the pale wash of the sky. It had no adornment, no grace. It was a thing made for dominion. At its crown stood Gideon. He looked out upon the city that had birthed him and which he had remade in his image. Below, the streets coiled like veins through a body long since bled.

The structure had not come in a day. It rose slow and sure from the wreckage of the old world, built not with stone alone but with blood and bone and the long quiet left by those who'd gone missing and never returned. It stood now like some monument unearthed, its arches high and solemn, the air within like the breath of old cathedrals, cold and hollow and waiting. Within it—a war room. The walls bore red banners faded at the seams, the mark of the Dominion sewn in black and gold thread.

The Dominion.

That was the name he had given his movement. His reign. The word he set atop the ashes of the world.

He stood at the head of the table, his shadow long in the morning light. He listened to the silence, to the hush that came before command, and he thought of all that had been lost to bring him here. The banners hung heavy, their colors dark as dried blood, and the arches above seemed to bend beneath the burden of his will.

Light slanted through narrow windows high above, falling in thin, pale columns across the flagstones, dust motes drifting in the silence. The room was vast and empty but for the long table of ironwood at its heart, battered and scorched, its surface scarred by maps and the weight of men's hands. The banners stirred in the draft, and the stone beneath his feet seemed to hum with the memory of voices, of orders given and lives spent, and the slow, grinding calculus of conquest.

He turned and looked out over the city from the high windows, the sprawl of it lost in the haze, the roads like veins through the body of the world. He watched it a moment longer and then turned back. His hand came to rest on the table. Fingers spread wide. The wood cold beneath his skin. He looked down at a screen. Then, he stood at its edge, hands clasped behind his back, as the screen came alive. It showed the shifting land, a projection of provinces and prefectures, each one bending closer to obedience—or rebellion.

He said, "The world breaks and folds like paper. Some creases will hold. Some will tear."

His reflection shimmered across the table, fragmented, almost spectral. He saw it. Smiled.

That's when it came.

Noise.

Shuffling of feet.

They came as dusk bleeds into dusk. One by one. Not as people but as tools. Instruments. Each a made thing honed to a single task, cruel and deliberate. They entered without announcement. Without ceremony.

The first was Victor Morgar.

Gideon watched the air distort around him like heat rising off steel. Morgar moved as if through a world that shifted to make room for him. His coat hung close to him, black and silver, the trim a dull red like something dried and forgotten. He bowed.

"My friend of many strategies, you bend to no man," Gideon said.

Morgan looked up. His face was smooth as stone, but his eyes held famine. "I bend to outcomes," he said. His voice was quiet, low as a sermon given in a ruined chapel. "And to the things that grow in the dark when outcomes are left to rot. Men worship ideas until those ideas turn to chains. You know this. You've worn them. You've broken them. I follow no man, Gideon. I follow the end of things."

Gideon said nothing.

Morgan straightened. "Tell me what you would have burned, and I will bring the flame."

His eyes were slate. No reflection. No bottom.

Next was Nyx Gorgrath. The Shadow Enforcer. That was the name they gave her in whispers, the ones who'd seen her work or felt the chill of it nearby. She walked in silence and was followed by silence. She of the Droppers, for it was said they dropped people from rooftops like coins into wishing wells. She wore the dark like it had claimed her once and never let go. A long coat black as midnight and thick with secrets. Her hat was wide-brimmed and low, the face beneath it all sharpness and famine—hollow cheeks, a sneer carved permanent as if God Himself had forgotten to finish her.

"They still whisper your name in Rilvar," Gideon said.

She looked at him. Her eyes were cinders that remembered fire.

"They should," she said. "I never left."

Then she stepped closer and the air seemed to go with her. "I put one-hundred men in the river there. Two-hundred in the earth. Several hundred I left hanging so the wind could talk to him. Let them whisper. It keeps their mouths from lying. Rilvar belongs to the silence I left behind. And it belongs to you."

She pulled her coat tighter against her ribs. "You called me here. Speak what needs speaking. Or let me go back to the dark."

There was Sienna Malachar. They called her the Technomancer, though there were older names in darker tongues. She was the mind behind the humming heart of the Dominion, the circuitry that fed its hungers and lit its watchfires. The farms, the foundries, the fences—they all bore the shape of her will.

What she wore clung to her like the husk of something shed only once and never again. Dark, seamless, veined in pulses of blue that moved without pity or pause.

She walked the research halls alone. The others came after. Men who read her diagrams like gospel and whispered her formulas like prayers in the dim hours. She spoke little. When she did, it was not for questions. Gideon had remembered her from the university. Thought her a crazed professor who knew too little about a lot of things. He knew she would be needed. An important part of his plans.

But she was different now. Not all flesh. No. Gideon had changed her. Changed her in a way that suited him.

Tall. Skeletal in the way a tower is. Built rather than born. She moved like a clock's hand—measured, inevitable. The light that touched her skin seemed to lose something in the doing. She gave nothing back. Her face shimmered pale like the hide of some drowned god risen from the ocean's floor. Not living. Not dead.

Her hair was the color of scoured steel. Cropped to angles. There was no vanity in her. Only design.

The body was all corners and calculations. Her hips sharp as geometry. Her shoulders drawn like schematics. Her mouth a line that did not yield. Beneath her skin ran the cold signature of machines, metal threaded in meat. You could peel her down to bone and still not find where she ended.

And maybe there was no end.

She did not breathe.

The machines did it for her.

She turned to Gideon, her eyes twin shards of something long frozen and never thawed.

"Food is control," he said.

"Surveillance is faith," she replied.

Then she stepped closer. Her voice was quiet, but the silence that followed it had edges.

"You think words are prophecy. Perhaps. You think naming mechanisms tames free will. Maybe. You think control is the lever. No. It is only the illusion of choice between levers. And faith . . ." Her jaw shifted. Something clicked faintly beneath it. "Faith is what remains when you have nothing else left to sell a man but obedience. The system does not believe. It does not hope. It does not fear. It sees."

She leaned in, her face inches from his.

"And I am what it sees."

Gideon did not reply.

She had already turned away.

Dorian Malgoth came in. The Iron Fist. He'd stood with Gideon when the world still smoked and the earth was broken. He knew the early blood, the hunger that bit at bone, the nights without fire. He bore those days like brands across the soul and never once looked away.

He led the Silencers and carried silence the way a grave carries its dead. He walked like something made to end things. You could hear the armor before you saw him. That drag and clank like chains pulled across stone. He wore the helmet sometimes when the crowd needed reminding. When a face wasn't enough.

A big man. Broad across the shoulders. Wrought like ruin. His head shaved clean, always. His face held the kind of scars that don't mend. Eyes like dead soil. Burned out. He breathed blood. Carried the stink of ash and iron. Like he'd crawled from a furnace and never left. A creature made of gunmetal and what follows after.

"I see war hasn't killed you yet," Gideon said.

"War wouldn't dare," Malgoth said. His voice like boots on frozen mud. "She's an old bitch, but she knows me. We shared fires. Shared meat. I taught her where to sleep and when to rise. She'll outlive us all, but she'll still answer when I whistle. She never forgets. Never forgets forget who holds the leash." He stepped closer, the armor speaking in rusted tones. "Tell me what dogs you've loosed. Tell me what fields you want cleared. And I'll sow them with bones, same as always."

Then there was Lydia Zexus. The Widow. A name spoken soft and far from light. She of the hidden wires and rooms that remember voices. She moved like breath on glass, leaving no mark but fog and doubt. Her dress clung black and tight and glimmered with silver thread sewn in the shape of spiders, their legs reaching. Rings crowned each finger, eyes without faces. At her throat a silver band coiled, no clasp, no break. Her hair rose in blades. Her eyes were half shut, not from sleep but from seeing things one ought not.

She turned to the others, their voices a rising tide of shallow certainty.

"You're all too loud," she said. Her voice was wind through a hollow place. "Truth dies screaming. But lies ... lies walk quiet."

Gideon gave a small smile, tired at the edges. "I fear you've been busy."

She looked at him. Long. Still. "Always," she said. Her lips barely moved. "Especially when no one sees."

She moved her shadow knotted to her feet. "Busy watching the ones who pretend they do not move. Busy listening to the silence between your words. You speak of futures like they are maps drawn in ink. But ink runs. And your hands are wet. I've seen what you plan. I've seen the shape of it in the files they tried to burn, in the cameras that blink too fast. I see it now in your face. In the faces of those here today. You want a new, clean world.

There's no such thing. There's only blood and who scrubs it, and who steps over the stains."

She looked around the chamber, her voice lowering like ash on fire. "So go on. Speak your plans. Draw your diagrams. Measure the burn. But know this. I'll be there when the ash settles. And I'll know who lit the match."

Evelyn Oyra Aldiss stepped through the threshold. The Voice. Minister of Law. She was tall and angular, and her hair was the color of unpolished iron. The face she wore was hewn from something harder than flesh. She moved like a verdict already passed. Her robe was black and bled crimson at the seams, and from her shoulders hung the chain of her station, thick and old and cold as anything dug from the depths of the earth. At her breast gleamed a brooch wrought in the shape of the scales of justice, the pans uneven, the balance broken. It did not symbolize justice. It named the condemned.

"You come as justice?" said Gideon.

"I come as memory," the Voice said.

She looked past him, past the walls, past the years.

"I am what they forgot," she said. "When they bartered truth for comfort and called it peace. I am the names they scratched from the ledgers. The screams turned to numbers. The ash shoveled beneath clean stone. Justice. It was never some bright thing born new. It was old when the world was young. Bent and broke and blind. They dressed it up in light, but it never saw. And now. Now it has no need for eyes."

A pause.

"It has teeth," Gideon said.

The Voice raised an eyebrow. "It bears the new truth. It will not ask. It will not wait. It comes walking, and it will not turn aside. We've sowed order. Process. And the harvest is fire."

Then Jonas Grix. The Reaper. Thin as smoke and just as hard to hold. He had taken the Amalgam and spooned it out like gruel to the starving, made it law and ledger, shaped whole cities on paper and numbers, and made men believe it was justice. He stood in the doorway like something dug up, a ragged silhouette with his cloak trailing like sump oil spilled in a black rain, the hem gone to threads from roads too cruel to name. Beneath it he wore the garb of purpose and finality—black canvas stitched with loops and slits and slung pouches, each home to some blade or cipher or keyed shard of ruin. A man who'd tally your worth in inches of wire and clean your name from the registry, same as grease from a plate.

His eyes were shadowed, sunk deep in a face dry and slack like parchment left out in a flood. Hair hung in ropes, streaked gray and brittle. His fingers moved without rest, slow and twitching, like they meant to count all the sins that ever lived.

"Grix," someone said, soft as breath.

He said nothing. Never had much use for speech.

His fingers kept moving. Tallying debts. Rations. Kill orders. Sand through the neck of the hourglass.

"Still counting bones?" Gideon said, a half-smile under his words.

A chuckle from the dark.

Grix looked up slow, like it cost him.

"Only the useful ones," he said. "Bones speak. You hold 'em in your hand long enough and they'll tell you where the rot starts. Where the break was clean. Where the marrow dried up. I keep 'em close. Like notes in a ledger. Like maps. The world's full of men who never listened."

He paused.

"And now they're part of the count."

Then he smiled. Or something like it. Something crooked and without warmth.

Felix Kul'gath stepped in with a smile like a knife too clean. The Viper. The diplomat. He wore a suit black as the bottom of the river and a tie the color of arterial blood. His hair slicked back like wet ink. The silver cane he carried tapped the floor once, twice, again, like it was counting down to something no one wanted to hear. Silver tip. Sharp as his tongue. His eyes moved like searchlights in a prison yard. Calculating. Cold. Patient. Looking for the crack. The weakness. The leverage. He bowed lower than the others. Always lower. Like a man who'd studied subservience long enough to weaponize it.

"You bring honey or poison?" Gideon said.

"They taste the same at first," the Viper said. He smiled again and took a long step forward, the cane swinging out, tapping like a clock whose hour had finally come. "You'd be surprised what a man will swallow, so long as it's sweet enough. Mercy. Compromise. A little slow death." He looked at Gideon. The smile never touched his eyes. "The difference comes later, when your teeth fall out and the fever sets in. When your children don't wake up." He turned his hand as if weighing two invisible stones. "But by then, the taste is memory. And memory—well. That's a currency too, isn't it?"

Another.

She did not enter. She arrived.

No footfall marked her passing. The air did not shift for her. Still, they knew. Still, they felt her. A presence like drought. Like the stillness before the locusts rise.

The Oracle.

Someone spoke it low, but the name had already died on their tongue. Echoed once and was gone.

The Keeper. The old blood. High voice of the Echoers. She stood in the place where there was no place. Where the world gave way.

Light touched all things but her. It bent its head and turned its face. Her skin pale as stripped bark. As old marble left to sun and weather. Her hair like wire. Unspooled from the void. Silver and still moving. The robe drifted about her with no wind to blame. It carried signs written in a hand older than bone. Glyphs that twisted behind the eyes. That rung the earth like a bell with no sound.

She bore her blade like prophecy. Black wound drawn long and narrow from the chest of some buried star. Its edge carried smoke that never burned out. The gem at the hilt moved like the lungs of a thing long asleep. It did not shine. It remembered.

And hidden beneath her garment, deep in the hush of her body, she bore a truth only the two of them knew. She held his seed. No words had been spoken. No witness called. But the deed had passed and in the silence it endured.

No one breathed. No one dared.

Her eyes passed over them like cloud over graveyard. The things she saw, she kept.

Gideon stepped forward. The breath in him hard as iron.

"You see the end?" he said.

Her voice came not from her throat but from behind the bones of the world.

"I see the thing that comes after it," she said. "When the ashes have cooled. When your machines are rust and your names forgotten. I see those unborn with fire for eyes. I see the world turned inside out and worn like a skin. And I see you there, with blood on your hands and silence in your mouth, asking again what you already know."

Her gaze passed through him. Through them all.

And still she had not blinked.

And as the room held them all. Gideon watched. Fingers steepled. Behind his eyes, the machine turned, slow and inevitable.

A thought and a smile.

He knew then the gods had already chosen sides.

"Let us begin," he said.

Morgar was studying the map, looking over the borders of the Istaran Republic. "They've begun aligning with Varnak," he murmured. "A joint sanction of our grain convoys. If they cut the River, trade—"

"They won't," Malgoth interrupted, arms folded across his armor. "We'll raze the Istaran ports before they dare interfere. Let them starve for a change."

Gorgrath, half-swathed in the folds of her coat, drifted closer, her eyes narrowed. "Razing is a statement, not a strategy," she said. "Fear is a language. The problem is, they've stopped listening."

The room fell quiet.

Gideon lifted his eyes from the map. "They've stopped listening," he echoed, then turned his gaze on her. "Because we've grown complacent. We rely on strength, yes. On scarcity. On control. But our voice—the voice they hear—is fragmented. Cold."

"You want poetry?" Malgoth scoffed. "Let the Oracle sing them lullabies and pray they bow."

"No," Gideon said calmly. "I want a scalpel. A mind that cuts without spilling blood."

Morgar tilted his head. "Are you proposing a new seat?"

"I am. A Minister of Influence."

Silence again. Lydia Zexus, eyes glinting under the webwork embroidery of her dress, spoke next.

"Your network is already saturated," she said. "Echoers, Droppers, Silencers—we choke the very air the people breathe. What more could a . . . Minister of Influence . . . do that our existing structures don't?"

"Unify the message," Gideon replied. "Breathe warmth into obedience. Make the Dominion desirable. Not just feared."

"And who do you propose?" asked Sienna, her voice modulated by implants along her jaw.

"I don't propose anyone," said Gideon. "I want you to."

Gorgrath stirred. "You're asking us to select your instrument of persuasion?"

"I'm asking you to test them. Vet them. Destroy them if they prove unworthy."

"Very well," said Zexus, turning toward the others. "Then we begin with profiles. There are candidates from the Echelon schools—trained, polished, compliant."

"Too polished," the Viper interjected with a flick of his cane. "We need a voice that can charm the masses and the barons. Someone who believes in the message they help invent."

"I've read reports from the reclamation zones," Grix muttered, fingering the worn ring of keys at his belt. "There's a woman in Sector 9. Young. Taken from the fields who helped turn a starving population into a loyal commune without a gun to their heads."

"She used theater," the Oracle murmured with quiet amusement. "I've seen the tapes. Rituals cloaked as rallies. She wrapped Gideon in myth without ever invoking his name."

He raised an eyebrow. "Subtle."

"Dangerously so," Morgar warned. "Too independent. We don't want someone clever enough to believe they're above the Throne."

"No one is," Gideon said, and his voice turned to iron. "But I will speak with her."

"You would risk an audience?" Malgoth asked, frowning.

"I risk more by leaving the Dominion voiceless," Gideon replied. "What is her name?"

"Elarlu Voss," the Oracle said.

Gideon's smile came slow. He remembered the name.

"But they call her something else," the Oracle said.

He nodded once. "And what is that?"

"The Siren."

Gideon smiled again. Not joy. Something else. Something older.

***

Elarlu Voss was brought in under cover of night. Blindfolded. Her wrists bound by silk rope rather than steel. She was led into a chamber, not unlike a sanctum—black walls, a single throne-like chair that faced hers across a low table of transparent crystal. She sat quietly, upright, blindfold removed, hands now unbound but resting still in her lap.

Gideon entered without escort. He wore no armor, no crown. Only a simple black coat and gloves, his presence all the more striking for its restraint. He took the seat across from her and looked at her.

He remembered her. A beautiful thing. Skin like bone and hair black as pitch. Eyes blue and bright. They held the light and did not move, did not flicker.

"Your eyes fix on you," Gideon said. "You do not look away. Ever."

"You remember my eyes," she said. "Good. Let them follow you."

She leaned in, slow and easy. The silk hung from her wrists like the remnants of something half-forgotten. She made no effort to cover the bruising. The skin wore it like truth.

"You come without a crown. Without a blade. But the hunger's the same. I know it. I've seen it in every face that ever claimed peace. It's the need to name what won't be named. To hold it down. To lock it up. And when it's locked away, to call the new reality salvation."

"I remember you," Gideon said. "You came from beyond the breakers, beyond the ashline. You wanted to be part of what we were building. I hear you've made yourself useful. That your voice carries weight."

She tilted her head. Her hair hung loose over her shoulders, dark and tangled.

"But your voice is loudest," she said. "When it's spoken."

"Sometimes, I've no need."

She smiled. Barely. Like something that hurt to remember. "And this . . . I suppose this isn't an interrogation."

"No," he said. "It's a proposition."

Elarlu leaned back, the faintest creak of leather beneath her. "I'm listening."

"You built loyalty without the lash," he said. "No need for breadlines. No need for blood. You made the people sing of suffering like it was some kind of grace. I need that. Not in one corner of the world. Everywhere."

She looked at him and arched an eyebrow.

"You want rallies the size of the earth?" she said.

"I want belief," he said. "Not the kind bought with rations. Not the kind won with fear. Something quieter. Like a melody they hum and don't know why."

"You can't hum a decree," she said softly. "You want art."

"I want you."

Elarlu's gaze held his. "If I say no?"

"You will not be harmed," he replied. "But your commune will be erased. Not in fire. In silence. They will forget your name in weeks. Your legacy will become ash in the archives."

She stared at him, and for a moment, Gideon saw the cold gears turning in her eyes. Not fear. Not rage. Just the spark of something old and buried. Hunger maybe. Or the scent of blood in the air.

"You won't gag me?" she asked.

"No."

"You won't script me?"

"I will give you parameters. And you will speak in your own voice."

She leaned in close. Her breath warm against the stillness.

"What name will I wear?" she said.

He looked at her lips as if they held something sacred or profane. "You will be the voice of the Dominion, its . . . Minister of Influence."

She let the title sit between them.

"Then I accept," she said at last. "But I want direct access to the one called the Voice. The Oracle. And I choose my own scribes."

"You'll have them," he replied. "But know this—your influence will end where my word begins."

Elarlu nodded. "So long as I can speak it first in my mind."

He regarded her a moment longer, stood, then turned and walked away. The sound of his boots on the steel grated like judgment. The sun through the Spire's high panes caught in the red lining of his cape and cast a long wound of color behind him.

She watched him go. Did not call to him. Did not follow.

It was the last time he would see her as she was. The last before she changed.

Power alters everything. It reshapes the face, hollows the voice. Turns the soft to sharp, the honest to strange. He would remember her smile as it had been before it knew the currency of conquest.

And she—she would speak his words first in her mind, as promised. And speak long after.

Even in silence, she would be heard.

***

He came back to the war room long after dark. The lights were dimmed to a dull jaundice and the walls seemed to breathe.

Machines blinked. Steel muttered to itself. Gorgrath sat before a pale screen that flickered like candlelight in wind. Morgar stood near the far wall, arms folded, his shadow taller than him.

"She's accepted," Gideon said.

Gorgrath did not lift her eyes. "Then we'll begin to transition messaging protocols."

"Assign her a liaison," he said. "Smart. Pliant. Someone who believes in things."

"She'll be dangerous," Gorgrath said. Her fingers tapped the keys without rhythm. "Not for rebellion. They will hunger for her every word."

Gideon stepped to the table and placed both hands flat upon it. He studied the map, its trembling lights, borderlines like old scars. "Good," he said. "We've bled. We've starved. We've silenced. Now we seduce."

Morgar smiled without warmth. "The Dominion will speak with a new tongue."

"No," Gideon said. He didn't turn. The map blinked back at him like a dying thing. "It will sing."

The hum of servers rose in the quiet like insects in the dark.

***

The air in the chamber was close and sour. It pressed on the skin like heat from the inside out, though no fire burned. Along the walls, something unseen gave off a low and ceaseless hum, like breath from a dying throat. Elarlu sat at the table. Her hands were knotted together, the fingers twisted and white at the knuckles as if bound. Across from her stood the Voice. Tall and still as carved stone. His eyes were sharp and cold. They did not offer kindness and did not need to.

Beside her sat the Oracle. She who had looked through the veil and called what she saw by its true name. Not vision. Wound.

Her hands rested lightly on her knees. Her eyes were shut. Though Elarlu knew, the Oracle did not sleep. Not anymore.

"Gideon is worried," Elarlu said, voice low, carrying the kind of weight that hung in the air like smoke. "He knows what he has, but it isn't enough. He sees what's missing. Without it, everything comes apart. Fractures. Breaks."

The Voice's lips twisted, a half-smile that had no warmth in it, stretched tight across a face that had looked at too much for too long. "The full weight of what he's done . . . it's not something easy to grasp."

Elarlu shifted. The cloak on her shoulders rustled like a whisper trying to get out. "Yes," she said. "I just have to make sure he thinks I can see it all. Everything that's coming."

The Oracle's eyes fluttered open then, and where there should've been light, there was nothing but shadow. "Your path . . . it is not so simple," she said, voice soft, but it was heavy. Heavier than any words should be. "He has plans for you. Be careful. If the wrong moment comes, he won't hesitate. He'll burn you to get what he wants."

Elarlu didn't flinch. She didn't even blink. She looked at the Oracle, steady, firmly. "That's not going to happen," she said. "Not if I make him think I'm irreplaceable."

The Voice tilted her head a fraction. Not much, just enough to show that calculation was working, gears turning behind eyes that had seen too much. "Irreplaceable? How?"

Elarlu leaned close, elbows planted on the scarred wood. Eyes shone, a light, sharp and edged, something cracked behind it. "A story," he said. "I'll give him a story. Make them think he's a god. And when they think that, he'll see me as a weapon. A weapon he can wield. And then he'll trust me. He'll need me."

The Oracle's eyes closed again as if seeing something in the distance, something she didn't want to see. "You play with fire, Elarlu," she murmured, her voice little more than a breath. "Vanity is madness . . . it devours everything close to it. You would do well to remember that."

Elarlu smiled, but it was all teeth. All edge. No warmth. "I know. I'll be careful. Always have been."

The Voice moved then, her shadow stretching across the floor like it was made of something darker than the room could handle. She spoke, her voice soft, but each word pressed down the air. "You think to hold him. Control him. Draw him to your hand. But you forget. He walks ahead. Ten paces gone. The game is his. He has played it long before you."

Elarlu's gaze was unyielding. "Then I will make it five."

The Oracle's lips twisted, maybe a smile, maybe a warning. It was hard to tell. "You are not the only one who knows how to weave webs. Be careful. You might find yourself caught in the one you are building."

Elarlu stood then, slow and fluid as if her body had learned to move with the shadows that filled the room. "I'm counting on it," she said, voice sharp like glass. "The web is just the start. The real work begins when they think they've caught me."

The Voice said nothing. Her lips barely parted, and when they did, it was like a whisper from a place that shouldn't exist. "You think you can deceive him so easily? Make him dance to your tune like some fool?"

Elarlu turned to a map on the far wall. It flickered, lights blinking, marking fractures in the empire, all the places where things were about to go wrong. Her finger traced the lines, slow and deliberate, like a conductor drawing the first breath before the orchestra played. "He won't know. I'll make him believe it's his heart that's leading him. And when he believes that, he'll be mine."

The Oracle stood, slow, her movements deliberate. "The road you walk . . . it is lined with fire. You will be unable to outrun it."

Elarlu turned to her, cold as stone. "Then I'll burn with it," she said, her voice as sharp as broken glass. "But not before I've had my fill of the ashes."

The Voice stepped back, her shadow receding. The tension in the room did not fade, but it settled. The air was still heavy, but quieter now. She watched Elarlu for a long moment like she was weighing something, measuring the cost of what was about to unfold.

Then, she spoke again, her voice a low murmur, barely more than a breath. "You want to play with madness, then go ahead . . . play. But remember, Elarlu . . . you are not the only one who knows how to dance with that creature. When everything around you falls apart, when everything comes crashing down, you might find the ground beneath was just sand."

Elarlu smiled again. It was cold. It always was. "I will make sure the sand turns to glass before it all shatters."

She turned back to the map, her mind already churning, already weaving the plan that would tie Gideon to her. She didn't need to pull the strings herself. She only needed him to believe that she was the one holding the reins.

***

They sat in the hush of the chamber. A low sound moved through the air like breath through the lungs of some old thing not yet dead. The walls drew close. As if the place had grown weary of what it knew and meant to tell it. The Oracle sat in the corner, as she always did, her hands folded, her eyes closed, though there was no mistaking that she saw everything. And the Voice stood by the table, her tall form cutting a sharp silhouette in the dim light.

Elarlu was gone. The thread that had pulled her into their game had slipped away, leaving only the quiet aftermath of her decisions.

The Oracle's voice broke the silence, soft but insistent. "She is playing a dangerous game. The walls will close in and she does not see it. Do you fear it?"

The Voice did not answer at once. She only moved, the soft sound of her footsteps against the floor barely perceptible. "She thinks she can control the chaos," she said at last, her tone clipped. "She cannot. She does not understand that he has already seen every move she will make before she makes it."

The Oracle's lips parted, but only for a moment. "And yet, she believes she can manipulate him. Her arrogance will be her undoing."

The Voice's eyes were cold, their intensity burning through the still air between them. "Yet, it is that arrogance that is her greatest asset. It is her weapon. She knows it." She leaned closer, her voice dropping to a low murmur. "Gideon is no fool. He is so far ahead of her. She can never catch up."

The Oracle's gaze slid across the shadows, her face unreadable. "No one can question what he has done with her," she said slowly. "Hmmm . . . but I wonder if perhaps we are too quick to underestimate her. The threads she wishes to weave . . . they are sharp, and I believe she knows how to use them."

There was a brief, tense silence between them as if both were contemplating the same question: Was she truly a threat?

The Voice broke it, her words cutting through the quiet. "She will think she is in control. And when she does, she will make her move. But the moment she steps too far, she will be burned." Her lips twitched. "And then she will have nowhere to run."

The Oracle rose. Her movements slow. She set her hand on the table, fingers trailing the wood. Her words hung there between them. "Perhaps. But when everything burns, what is left? What will she leave behind?"

The Voice stepped back, her shadow stretching along the floor like the tip of a blade, dark and consuming. She watched the

Oracle for a moment, her gaze unwavering. "A world in ruin," she said softly. "A broken empire. Nothing but the bare ground."

"And you?" the Oracle asked, turning to face her. "What will you do when the world burns? What happens when there is nothing left to control?"

The Voice's smile was a thin line. "Rebuild it." Her voice was quiet, but the promise hung heavy in the air like a stone waiting to fall. "From the ashes, we will rise again."

The Oracle's eyes closed, her face a mask of quiet contemplation. "You think she is the only one with ambition?" she asked. "You think she is the only one who can play the game? You forget who you are dealing with."

The Voice's smile deepened, but there was no humor in it. "I know exactly who I am dealing with."

And then, the Oracle's voice was softer still, barely a whisper as if the words themselves were reluctant to be spoken. "Be careful. In the end, you may find that even fire cannot cleanse everything."

The Voice did not answer. She did not need to.

The Oracle stood a moment longer, her hands clasped together, and for the briefest of seconds, the two women stood in silence as if they were measuring something invisible in the dark.

Finally, the Voice spoke. "It begins now."

The Oracle's eyes fluttered open, and for a moment, there was nothing in them but an endless stretch of shadow. "So, it does," she murmured.

And they both knew—that no matter how the game played out, there would be no winners. Only those who survived.

The Voice moved toward the door, her shadow melting into the dark. "She plays a very dangerous game. We must make sure she does not finish it."

The Oracle remained still. "And if we come to that point where we find that she has already won?"

The Voice's lips parted, but there was no response. Only silence.

And then, the sound of footsteps fading into the distance.

***

In days, Elarlu had it. A plan set in her mind like stone. Fixed and ready. Clean and cold. And she meant to share it with him. To tell him. To show him.

She walked alone. Through corridors of humming steel. Where the sun never reached. Past the checkpoints, past the watching eyes, through gates and doors where no one passed uncalled. The guards stood aside. No words spoken. Her name was writ into the marrow of the Dominion. And when the lift took her, she rose like a stone flung heavenward.

The Spire rose from the Dominion like some vast blade buried halfway to the hilt. Its sides, dark and seamless, caught no sun. Windows stretched along its surface like eyes cut into obsidian. Beneath it, fields sprawled in rigid squares—green, gold, and umber—shapes too precise to be natural. Great machines, wheels of metal and iron, crawled between the rows like beetles, never stopping. Beyond the fields, the edge of the megalopolis shimmered under the weight of the heat. Towers climbed from the dust like teeth.

He watched it all.

Gideon.

He stood at the edge of the terrace, hands behind his back. The wind curled around him, lifting the edge of his coat.

There came a shift. He heard the steps before he turned. Not hurried. Not cautious.

She emerged from the shadows of the corridor like something conjured. Her flowing robes of deep crimson, embroidered with gold patterns that resemble serpents and eyes, cut to her shape like a poured mold. Her eyes found him.

"It's time," she said.

He turned to face her. "It is."

She gestured, and from behind her, a tall cabinet opened by unseen hands. The uniform hung within. Black and sharp as razors, it looked like it had been skinned from some machine. Polished gold epaulets flanked the shoulders, and a single broad belt cinched the middle in shining silver. The cape hung behind, heavy with presence. Its outer face shimmered like coal, the inner lining blood red.

"You'll wear this," she said. "From now on."

He stepped toward it. The gloves rested beside the boots. The insignia of the Dominion—gear and laurel fused—shone on the breast.

"It's . . . theatrical," he said.

"It must be," she said. "Men do not kneel to a man. They kneel to a symbol."

He turned to look at her. She stood motionless, like some ancient mark carved deep in the earth. Her face was pale in the Spire's shadow. Drained of heat. The color of ash left after clean fire. The light caught on the fine angles of her jaw and cheekbone and cast long hollows in her eyes. There was something wrong about that. As if the world had mislaid some truth about her and left only the image behind, a ghost of intention dressed in flesh. Something that should not be, standing where it should not stand.

"You've changed," he said.

"How so?" The makings of a smile.

"You were once real," he said. "But now you're less so."

Her smile hardened like cooled slag. "Reality is a currency spent by the desperate. I have no need of it anymore."

"I've made you into something," he said. "Haven't I?"

He reached for the uniform. The fabric hissed against his fingers, cold as coiled steel. The gloves fit too perfectly, the leather supple yet unyielding. When he fastened the belt, the silver buckle clicked like a rifle's safety disengaging. The cape dragged at his shoulders—a dead thing clinging.

"Walk," she said.

He took three paces. The boots struck the floor with the finality of gallows steps. The epaulets caught the Spire's pallid light, glinting like animal eyes in a pit.

"They'll see the armor," he said. "Not the man."

"Precisely."

"And when they realize there's nothing inside?"

Elarlu tilted her head. The gold serpents on her robes seemed to writhe in the low light. "They've spent lifetimes worshipping hollow things. Kings. Flags. The brittle promises of weaker men. This?" She flicked the cape's edge. "This they will believe."

He turned toward the arched window. The glass reflected his new silhouette: a blade sheathed in shadow, the insignia burning gold above his heart.

"You hesitate," she said.

He watched his reflection's mouth move. "Do I?"

"All choices are made. Only the . . . theater remains."

She stepped closer. Her scent was ozone and myrrh. "After, they will kneel. Not to you. To the idea of you. The idea will consume the world."

He adjusted the cape, felt its weight settle.

"Let them see their symbol." Elarlu's hand brushed his arm. A touch colder than the uniform. "Remember—the mask is the man now."

He looked down at her. Deep in her eyes.

"Yes," she said. "You've changed me."

"How?"

"Made me see the truth."

He said nothing.

"The world leans," she said. "It lists to ruin."

"And what am I?"

"You are the storm."

His face still. Her face pale in the dim light. "Then let it all break."

Below them, the drones spun their slow courses over the fields. The irrigation towers hissed steam like breathing things. No people could be seen, but he knew they were there. Kept in squares and wards. Fed from trucks marked with his name.

"The food is power," she said. "You control it. You control their blood."

"They're starving in Quarter Three."

"Because they need to," she said. "Because it reminds the others that peace is conditional."

He stepped back. The wind pushed again. It made the cape shift slightly on its hook.

"And this Dominion," she said. "It's a lie. They just don't know it."

"Anything ever built has been a lie. But our . . . our lie runs true."

He looked at her again. He could see she was holding something back. "Say it. Say what it is you believe."

She tilted her head. Her eyes were not cruel, only unshakable.

"Lies mean nothing when you are Gideon. You are Rex. You are rule. Because you must. Because there is only one way. The Gideon Way. That's all that's left. The path forward."

She stepped toward the ledge. Her voice was calm. Not raised, not hushed.

"Supremacy of the issue," she said. "Invent what they fear. Something buried in them. An instinct they don't understand.

Breed it like a fire. Tell them it's coming. Then say you alone can stop it."

He said nothing.

"Surrogation of reality," she went on. "They'll believe anything if you say it often enough. It doesn't matter what. Rewrite what was. They won't check. They'll be grateful not to."

He turned his eyes from the cape, from her, to the fields again. Great machines carved their paths. The crops swayed as if nodding.

"Supplication of the masses," she said. "No peace. No stillness. Keep them angry. Keep them watching. Tell them who to blame. Never step back. Never explain. The fire must be fed."

He took a breath.

"You believe this is the way."

She looked at him then, not with malice, but with the silence of the inevitable.

"Yes."

The cape caught the light again. The red lining glimmered like something slick. The gloves were folded over the boots like a body laid in state. The insignia stared back.

He turned to her fully. "What happens when they see through it."

"They won't," she said. "But if they do . . . it will be too late."

He stepped forward and took the gloves.

The fabric clung to his hands like skin. Cool. Impossibly thin.

He picked up the monocle. Set it over his eye. The lens flickered. Numbers bloomed in the glass.

"And what if I become what they fear."

She stepped back into the dark.

"That's the point," she said.

The wind rose. The cape swung.

He reached for it.

The sky beyond the Spire had begun to bleed. Evening settled over the Dominion. Lights in the far districts blinked on like slow stars. Far below, one of the fields flared white. A fire, or a trial.

He fastened the cape at the shoulder. It settled over him like the fall of night.

He stood there a long time before he spoke.

"Supremacy of the issue. Surrogation of reality. Supplication of the masses."

She smiled. "The Gideon Way."

"They will follow."

"They already do," she said.

The sun dipped and vanished behind the steel rim of the horizon.

And Gideon was gone.

6 *The Road Laid Ahead*

The sky over what had once been Washington, D.C. hung low and sullen, a flat plate of hammered lead. Heat pressed through the gray and held fast to the bones. The sun behind it was a pale smear and did not move. The streets lay scabbed and cracked and blackened where even weeds had quit their work. Ash clung to the corners of old buildings like the residue of some long funeral pyre. The ruins of monuments, once gleaming, now stood in silhouette, eroded by time and neglect. The air held a thick stench, a blend of decay and forgotten promises, choking the silence.

They stood unmoving. Hundreds. Thousands. Thousands upon thousands. Black-clad and ordered in rows that ran the length of the plaza. Men and women. Old. Young. Children with wide eyes peering over the shoulders of their fathers. The silence was complete. No voice among them. No whisper. They stared forward at the platform where the Dominion's seal burned, high above the dais. A silver ring, half-buried in flame. The light of it cast no warmth.

Behind a door of polyglass, thick and dark, Gidcon watched. His face was partly shrouded, his jaw set, the curve of his cheek lit in ghost glow. The cape draped over him hung with the weight of night. His gloved hands lay still at his sides, and when he flexed them, the old leather sighed.

Beside him, Elarlu stood. Her robe of crimson, stitched with gold that coiled like serpents, eyes that gleamed faint as the light of some long-forgotten god. She lifted a hand to her ear, the motion slow, deliberate. The air thick with something unsaid. A blink of green above the doorframe, a flicker of old things watching from the dark.

She nodded.

Gideon stepped forward.

The door opened without a sound. He passed through it. The wind took his cloak and tugged at its edges, its whisper like the last breath of a dying thing. His boots hit the concrete, the thud sharp and final. All around the dead world, the broadcast fed through walls and screens, through metal and stone. Crowds gathered. Thousands upon thousands. Millions upon millions. Drawn to the pulse of it. The drones above caught his image and stitched it across the sky. The ocean rigs stopped their drills. The great wheels went idle in the fields. Men stood from their bowls. The world leaned forward.

He ascended the steps, the cold stone biting at his heels, and stood among them. Below, the people pressed together in silent knots. Behind him, enormous screens hummed, flashing his likeness across the broken air.

The crowd did not shift. A sea of faces bleached pale by hunger. Their cheeks drawn. Eyes dry and solemn as if sleep had been outlawed. Some had markings across their brows, inked in lines and circles, signs of allegiance or punishment, or both. But all in black. Some held cloths over their mouths as if still the air might poison them. The children watched with eyes too old, their fingers curled into the backs of the ones before them. No breath came loud. The silence was not merely absence but observance, a thing built and maintained like a structure, held together by dread and hope alike.

He waited. She told him to do this.

The silence was not stillness. It was pressure. Like the hush before a hammer falls. The air held the tension of something terrible kept barely at bay.

He looked out across them all. Then he spoke.

"I remember what this place was," he said. "Before the end. Before the fields went dry. Before the streets filled with bones and the sky forgot how to rain."

The voice was his but not his. It came from nowhere and everywhere. The architecture spoke it. The very stone carried it.

"I remember the fires. I remember the sirens. I remember watching from the hills when the old buildings fell and the last of the smoke took the sun. I remember the silence that followed. I remember what it took to crawl from that grave."

The people stood as stone. Each man adrift in the quiet wreck of his own mind. The thoughts they bore were loud things, ragged and sharp, clawing in the dark like animals caged. They knew who had done this. Who had dragged them through fire and famine and left them standing in the husk of the world. They knew it was him. They knew it as sure as they knew the taste of ash or the sound of weeping. And still, they buried it. Pressed it down into some deep place where reason no longer stirred. For knowing would not feed them. And it would not save them.

Above him, a drone dipped and circled slow. Its lens gleaming like the eye of some forgotten god. His cloak shifted in the wind, the red lining flashing once like a warning.

"You know," he said. "You know the ash. Dust. Roads broken like old bones. Wells run dry. Mothers burying children with their bare hands. Dogs gone feral. Guns traded for rice. The sun a stranger. But you remember what once was."

The screens changed. Wheat in tight lines. Barns squared and painted. Great wheels of metal harvesting under a regulated sky. Children with round cheeks. Steam rising from dinner tables. Bread cut clean.

"I built this," he said. "We built this. With hands scarred from the fire. With backs bent. With blood."

They shifted. A few nodded. None spoke.

He lifted one hand. The fingers curled slightly. The gesture was old and simple.

"Not all are fed. Not all believe. Some whisper in the shadows. Some pine for ruin. They speak of freedom, but they mean anarchy. They speak of the old days, but they forget the bodies."

He stepped forward. The wind took the cape. The sound of his boots fell sharp.

"There are enemies," he said. "Not of me. Not even of the Dominion. Enemies of this."

The screens shifted again. Cornfields. A boy with a bandaged knee. A mother laughing. A jug of milk on a table. A man lighting a cigarette, grease black under his nails.

"Enemies of peace," he said. "Enemies of order."

He turned slow. His gaze passing over them like some shepherd counting a herd.

"They will call me monster. Tyrant. They will curse my name behind closed doors. Let them."

He paused.

"I never promised freedom," he said. "I promised food. I promised warmth. I promised your children would live to see gray in your hair."

He breathed in. The air was dry. His voice had grown quieter but not weaker.

"My way is not easy. It asks. It takes. It leaves behind nothing unnecessary. But it works. And none before me ever made it work."

He stood tall. The insignia at his chest gleamed.

"Peace is not given. It is demanded. And the price is belief."

Elarlu stepped from behind the wall. The crowd saw her. Her robe was red as a cardinal in snow. Her eyes held gold that had not been mined.

"You have known hunger," she said. "You have known fear. You will never know them again. If you believe."

Gideon's eyes fixed on Elarlu, his lips curling into something between a smile and a grimace.

"You see," he said, his voice quiet, cutting through the stillness like a knife. "There's a line we all walk. Between hunger and fear. Between order and madness. They don't always look the same. Sometimes they don't even feel the same. But they are the same. And when you stand here, in front of me, waiting for your reckoning, remember that there is no turning back. Kneel, and you give up something."

He turned, boots heavy on the concrete, each step a mark on the dust of a thousand dead lives. The drone above him wheeled again, its shadow passing like the sweep of a long-forgotten clock.

"You think they don't know what comes after? You think they don't see the bodies piled high in the streets, the blood running cold in the gutters? They know. They've always known. They've watched their own homes burn, watched their families scatter. They've seen the price of rebellion. And they'll pay it again, just like they always have."

He paused, his gaze heavy, dragging the weight of years with it.

"I'm asking that you believe," he continued. "Believe in me. Believe in my works. Believe in the future I will grow . . . we will grow . . . together. It's not a choice. Not really. It's a truth. And if you can't see that, well . . . then you don't deserve the food . . . the warmth . . . gray hair."

A long silence followed, and in that silence, something in his eyes shifted. Something older. Something darker.

Gideon raised one hand in a fist.

"I do not ask for worship," he said. "I do not need your love. I ask one thing only. Do you want the world to live?"

A voice answered.

Then another. Then ten, then a hundred. Then all, a rising tide of voices, the sound stretching out like an old wound opening across the dead earth. It came from everywhere, from the long-forgotten places, the barren corners of the world where the sun had forgotten to rise.

"Yes!"

He lowered the hand.

"Then believe."

The screens went dark. A silence followed. Then it broke.

The crowd turned their eyes to Elarlu. She raised her hand and they followed. Right arms drawn across their chests. Fists clenched. Hands over hearts. It was no soldier's salute. Nor the posture of prayer. Something made in the middle. Something older.

They cried out as one.

"Salve Rex!"

The sound rolled like thunder across the plaza and deep into the city's bones.

"Salve Rex! Salve Rex! Salve Rex!"

Then the chant changed.

"Gideon Rex! Gideon Rex! Gideon Rex!"

He saluted in return. Then turned from the dais.

Elarlu followed without sound.

Behind them, the chant rose again. It echoed through the ruins and the alleys and up the empty towers where no birds had nested in years.

***

The walk back to the chamber behind the stage was long and without sound save for the muted cadence of her heels on the polished floor. The shadows clung to the walls like mold. Overhead, the old lights flickered where the motion sensors failed, catching him in flashes, leaving him again in grayness. She followed a step behind, her robe drawing along the floor like a wound.

"They believed you," she said.

He did not look at her. His voice came low. "They believed in the food."

"Same thing."

They passed through the aperture, the automated doors hissing open and then shutting behind them like breath. The corridor beyond sloped downward. The lights dimmed. Somewhere in the walls, machines stirred, ancient servos coming awake only to sleep again.

"What now?" he asked.

"Now," she said, "we prepare for the uprisings."

He stopped. Turned. His face still. Pale beneath the overheads. "Where?"

She gave a slow shrug. Her mouth tilted slightly. "Wherever we make them. Give those who don't believe a reason to rise. Then we cull them."

He understood and smiled, sharp and without joy. "Let them rise, then."

"We will," she said. "And then you will put them down. Publicly."

He nodded once. "I will give them martyrs."

"No," she said. "You will give them consequences."

The lift waited behind glass like a relic. They entered. The door sealed with a hush. It rose without tremor. No cables. No sound save the faint current of air along the seams.

"How long can we do this?" he said.

She watched him. Her eyes caught no light at all. A depthless thing. Not cruel. Not kind.

"As long as we need to," she said. "As long as we want them to believe."

He turned then and looked out. The city lay beneath him like a map drawn in fire. Roads stitched through the dark like arteries. Headlamps slid along them, slow as blood. The throngs moved, nameless and many.

"They will believe in me."

"They already do."

He said no more. The silence reclaimed them.

The lift climbed. Slow and smooth. Somewhere in the black fields beyond the perimeter, the fire still burned.

***

The lights in the main chamber were dimmed to a dull ochre hue. Above, thick ribs of alloyed carbon arched like the bones of some vast creature buried beneath the earth, pulsing with the ambient heartbeat of the facility. Dust hung in the low light like spores.

Victor Morgar entered without ceremony. His boots clicked on the polished obsidian floor, and the sound echoed into the void. He moved like a knife—precise, deliberate, indifferent. His gloved hands folded behind his back, and his pale face carried no trace of age save the twin scars that bracketed his mouth like parentheses. The table, black glass, oblong, already bore the sigils of those in attendance.

Elarlu was already seated. Her fingers moved idly through a smoke-dense hologram of shifting serpents. Her eyes did not track Morgar's entrance, but her mouth curled in the faintest arc.

"Victor," she said. Her voice was as smooth as wet silk. "How did you sleep?"

"Didn't," he replied. "Never do."

The hum deepened. The door sighed open like something tired of keeping secrets. Sienna Malachar stepped through. Her entrance carried the dry snap of an electrical storm. Blue light pulsed along her suit in jagged paths, winding through the dark like veins beneath glass. It caught and flared in the gleam of her skull—those titanium-plated temples flashing cold and clean beneath the overheads.

"System integrity at ninety-seven point eight," she said. Her voice was clipped, untouched by courtesy. She spoke into the air, into some unseen circuit. Likely a lab rat on the other end. "No intrusions detected? Perfect. That is what we look for."

She moved to the table and lowered herself into a chair, her limbs folding like she'd rehearsed it. Then she looked up and saw them—finally—and her eyes, lit faintly from within, narrowed.

Morgar stepped to the head of the table. He did not sit. He remained standing, his long frame stiff as iron, his face turned to them like a man counting not colleagues but corpses. His eyes swept the room, pausing on each face without kindness.

"We convene to assess the progression of Mors Annona," he said.

The words did not echo. They settled into the silence like ash.

No one moved. No one spoke.

He lowered one gloved hand and pressed it to the surface of the table. The glass came alive beneath him. A pale shimmer. Then fire. Then famine. Images unfurled across the tabletop—grainy aerials of blasted farmland, soil turned to bone-dust, fields gone to ruin. Rows of stalks bent and brittle snapped like dead limbs. Leaves curled in on themselves, black at the edges, knotted like the hands of starving children who had forgotten how to beg.

"This was one field in Iowa. Three weeks ago."

Another image. Rice paddies in Guangdong gone black and brittle.

"And here, in the Red Valley. Wheat rendered to ash in situ."

Elarlu leaned forward. Her voice, nearly a whisper. "Do farmers suspect?"

Malachar's eyes flickered. "They suspect many things. But not us. Not yet. Their analysts remain fixated on fungal mutation. Some obscure strain. Perhaps climate-linked. Doesn't matter. They'll be unable to identify it."

Morgar turned to her. "And the gene silencing sequences?"

"Stable," Malachar said. "As stable as they can be. The Annona-RNA template maintains fidelity long enough to initiate cascade failure. Once misfolding begins, propagation requires no further input. The host becomes the vector."

"Like laughter," said Elarlu. "Contagious. Untraceable."

Morgar said nothing. His finger moved again across the interface. A diagram appeared—concentric rings expanding outward from a single red dot. Europe. Africa. The Americas.

"Twenty-three percent of global arable output can be quickly compromised," he said. "Projections suggest forty-eight by year's end if we want it."

Elarlu turned her head slightly. "Mors Annona is the fulcrum. Chaos is the lever."

Silence. Then Elarlu stood. Her crimson robe stirred around her ankles like blood in water. She moved to the window and looked out across the facility: vast towers wrapped in antennae and turbines, thousands of feet above the cracked soil of the outer wastes. Below, even the wind was regulated.

"What about variants?" she asked.

Malachar's jaw tightened.

Morgar turned to her. "Well?"

"As expected, it adapted," she said. "Faster than we modeled. There is . . . a drift. In some hosts, the capsid incorporates anomalous proteins. We've seen limited mammalian interaction."

Morgar stepped forward. "Mammalian?"

"Rootmice. Squirrels. Deer. One badger."

Elarlu laughed softly. "Our apocalypse arrives through the belly of a badger."

Malachar shook her head. "It will not cross over. The compatibility rate is functionally zero. But the environment . . . the persistence is greater than expected."

Morgar's hands curled at his sides. "Define greater."

"Projected dormancy: fourteen days. Actual: thirty-eight. Possibly longer in low-UV zones."

Morgar paced. The room seemed to grow smaller with each measured step. Finally, he stopped.

"You assured me it would burn out."

Malachar met his gaze. "It was meant to. It seems evolution had other plans."

Elarlu turned. Her voice was now solemn.

"And the antidote?"

"There is none," Malachar said. A long silence. Then, "Yet."

Morgar's eyes shut like iron gates drawn against a rising tide. When they opened again, there was something gone from them, something left behind in the dark. He did not look at his companions so much as past them, as though they were already part of what had been lost.

"So, do we proceed?" he said.

He turned to Elarlu, her crimson sleeves still as blood in snow.

She smirked. "Malgoth and Gorgrath assure me they have names. Entire sectors, regions, marked. They know who eats and who shouldn't."

"Your plan?" said Malachar.

Elarlu moved to the map. It glowed faintly beneath her fingers. A broken earth drawn in veins of light.

"To balance," she said. "Through necessity. We starve the machine that starved the earth. Then we blame the famine on those who would not kneel. And from that, we build a reason to punish."

Malachar's voice came low, a mutter shaped by steel. "And if this turns back on us?"

Elarlu smiled. It came slow. It came wrong. Like a wire pulled too tight across a bone fence. Something mean in it. Something sure.

"It won't," she said, "We must teach the world how much it needs our protection."

No one spoke again. The lights dimmed. The map blinked out and vanished. In the silence, they sat as figures etched in coal, unmoving, untouched by the cold that gathered like a tide outside the walls.

The wind rose out of the plains and passed like a hand over the broken land. It bore no seed. No water. No sound of life.

Only the hush of old machinery and the promise of a hunger that would not stop.

***

In the darkness before dawn, a man in Calabria walked into a field of barley with a black case under his arm. The field whispered against his boots. He knelt, unsnapped the case, and opened it to reveal a small sphere, no larger than a child's toy. He pressed a switch, and it came alive with a red light, slow and pulsing like a dying star. He left it in the furrows and walked away without looking back.

Three thousand miles west, a woman stood waist-deep in sugarcane near the banks of the Magdalena. Her face was hidden beneath a cloth band. Her hands raw from travel. She worked the soil open with a dull spade and buried the same device like a priest interring some blasphemous relic. The earth took it in silence. When she rose, she crossed herself, not for salvation but remembrance.

And in Kansas, beneath the colorless sky of late spring, an old man drove his pickup into a field he no longer owned. He parked, left the door open, and walked in among the cornstalks with a heavy bag slung over one shoulder. The bag held a cylinder of frosted alloy. He placed it in the irrigation runoff, unscrewed the top, and watched the vapor hiss into the air like a ghost freed from an urn.

By noon, others had done the same in Ukraine. In the Sudan. In Western Europe and the rice flats of the Mekong. They moved like shadows across the farms of the earth, these agents without insignia, without name. They walked into fields and walked out again, and nothing was seen but the tracks they left in the loam.

One of them, a thin man with a burned face, sat alone on a freight train crossing the Rhone Valley. His suitcase rested on his lap, sealed in a biometric lock. When the train slowed near the vineyards, he opened a window and threw the device into the wind. The wind took it. It spun like a seed. It cracked open among the vines, and the air grew still.

In a town outside Agadir, a child helped her mother carry a crate into a terraced plot of fig trees. The mother told her not to ask what was inside. When they opened it, a device within whirred and a mist poured out, silver and slow, and the birds in the trees fell silent. But the child did ask, and the mother said only, "It is for the world. Not for us."

In Alaska, a man in a faded ranger's uniform walked to a clearing of root crops. He placed the device between the rows and covered it again with stone. He did not stay to see if it would work. He had been told it would.

The release of Mors Annona was not broadcast. It needed no announcement. It came in silence, like mold in a cellar or blood beneath a door. It did not roar. It did not scream. It whispered.

In Nigeria, the cassava plants went first. Leaves sagged without reason. Tubers shriveled in the soil. The villagers blamed the sun.

In Bavaria, the hops browned before harvest. The brewers cursed the weather and the pollen and the moon.

In Utah, the barley twisted in its stems and turned to ash beneath the surface. Farmers held it in their hands and found nothing left to save.

And the great harvesters—those mighty wheels of metal stood in the fields where once they had groaned and thundered and wept oil onto the furrowed earth. Their teeth clotted with dry soil. Their engines quiet. Their shadows long and unmoving beneath a bleached and stupid sky. No birds flew above them. No hands reached to start them. The world held its breath, but there was no breath left to hold. What had fed it had died. And what had killed it was gone, leaving no name and no sound. Only stillness. Only the fields. Only the end.

The agents returned to where they had come from. Or they did not. Some walked into cities, into crowds, into the fog of anonymity. Others went into rooms and locked the doors and never emerged. They had no allegiance but to silence. They believed not in the act but in the necessity of it.

In a motel outside of Marrakesh, two men sat across from each other with a terminal between them. The older man, bald and red-eyed, smoked a cigarette to the filter.

"It's done," said the younger. "All sectors confirm."

The older man nodded.

"You think they'll trace it?"

"To what? A drought? A fungus? The cruelty of nature? No. They'll rage against the rain and build temples to luck."

He stubbed the cigarette out on the tile floor and stood. His knees popped like branches in the cold.

"Did they give a number?" he asked.

"Seventeen percent failure in the first wave. Thirty-two by month's end. The rest . . . who knows."

"Good," the old man said. "Then it begins."

In Tokyo, an analyst stared at her screen and frowned. She ran the numbers again. And again. Her supervisor dismissed it as a data inconsistency. She did not sleep that night. In her dream, she walked through a field of rice that turned to glass beneath her feet.

In Montana, the sky turned copper at dusk. A boy stood with his father at the edge of a field gone gray. The stalks hung limp, half-grown and dying.

The boy looked up.

"Did we do something wrong?" he asked.

The father didn't answer. He watched the wind move across the field without touching it. He took off his hat and held it to his chest.

Somewhere beneath the crust of land and law, in bunkers and cold rooms across the world, those monitoring the famine leaned over maps and spoke without raising their voices. They moved pieces. Adjusted graphs. They watched as the numbers climbed—not fast, not loud, but certain. Like water rising in a well.

In the cities, food prices ticked upward like blood pressure before a stroke. Shelves emptied in neighborhoods where the lights always buzzed too loudly. Localities issued reports. Experts contradicted one another. Some said it was genetic collapse. Others said it was soil fatigue. One man on television swore it was biblical. He held up a dead ear of corn as proof.

Across the world, people waited for rain. It did not come.

The fields stood hollow and mute.

And the silence, at last, began to spread.

***

The city of Kairon rose from the desert like a black flower, its towers stark against the embers of the dying sun. Screens vast as churches burned cold light across the faces of stone and glass, casting their glow on every crossing, every stair, every hollowed square. The people came unbidden. They came quiet as dust on the wind. The crowd swelled beyond counting, a multitude pressed shoulder to shoulder, their number stretching into the avenues and alleys, filling the city's bones. From the rooftops to the streets below, they gathered, a silent tide, endless and unyielding, beneath the watchful glare of the city's electric gods.

On the high stage where the flames leaped white and straight into the dusk, Gideon stood. He did not move. At his side, Elarlu, quiet as cut stone. Her face pale and cold and perfect. Eyes a sharp blue. Hair black as pitch. Bound tight behind her like the blade of a sword. She wore long robes the color of dried blood, stitched with gold in shapes like serpents and watching eyes. The sleeves hung like banners. The collar rose to her jaw like a wall. Gideon lifted his hand, gloved in black leather, and all things stopped.

"People of this earth," he said. The voice a slow and grinding thing, borne not from the throat but conjured. As if it had waited in the stone a thousand years to be spoken. As if it were the voice of the earth itself. "You have seen the fields. You have eaten what was left. You have knelt in the ash and known it. The enemy is no longer beyond. He is among us."

Below the stage, the crowd lay packed in silence. Not a gathering. A presence. Shoulder to shoulder in endless ranks, their mouths slack, their hands at their sides. Faces turned upward like corpses lying wrong in the grave. Not the light of reason in their eyes but the stillness of those watching a thing too large to name.

"They call themselves liberationists," he said. "Revolutionaries. Makers of a new dawn. But what they have made is nothing. What they have done is to unmake. To desecrate."

The screen behind him shifted. Grainy flights over land that might once have been fertile, now sunblasted and cracked. Soil blown away in sheets, the bone of the world laid bare. No mark of origin. No time. Just ruin. Crops curled like dead tongues. A dry vein where once ran water. Nothing left for the wind but dust.

"They have loosed a scourge upon the earth. A sickness without root or name or mercy. There is no flag to it. No nation. No song. It eats and is not filled. It has entered the ground beneath our homes and struck the seed dead in the womb. They have salted the future and smiled while they did it."

Elarlu moved not at all. Her gaze swept the rows of faces as if they were not men or women but something else. A great carcass still breathing. She did not blink. She did not look away.

"But we are not helpless," he said, and his voice was not the voice from before but something quieter, something more terrible. The hush did not break but deepened, like a thing with weight. "Even now, my scientists—your scientists—work through the nights without sleep. They peel back the layers of this blight with hands blistered from labor and eyes red with truth. We will find it. The pathogen. The rot. And we will grind it beneath our heel. We will pull its makers from their holes in the ground and string them from the gallows of the old world where no prayer will reach."

A sound came out of the stillness. One man, maybe two, crying out from the mass. Then it broke. A splinter. A shatter. The voices rising like the dead from graves, each louder than the last, until the whole of the plain was filled with a roar that had no end and no source.

"At times like these," he said, "who will save you?"

The voices answered as one as if they had always known. "Gideon Rex!"

Again, louder.

"Who is your shield?"

"Gideon Rex!"

He lifted his hand, fingers curled as if to close around the very air, and again they went quiet. The silence returned like a god reclaiming its place.

"You must be watchful," he said. "You must be without mercy. If your neighbor's crops stand tall where others wither, you ask why. If your kin speaks of rebellion, you cut out the tongue. If a voice comes to you in the hush and speaks of another way, do not listen. There is no other way. That voice is death in the skin of truth, and it will wear your face if you let it."

He stood and watched the mass of them. The horizon bent with their number. They did not move. The wind passed over them like a hand. The torches along the rise guttered in the draft and swung on their poles like deadweights on the gallows, slow, measured, counting out the final seconds of a world grown thin and bitter with its own memory. There was no sky above them. Only a lid of black smoke turning in place.

From the salt flats of São Paulo to the rust-slick piers of Vladivostok, the image of Gideon was broadcast with perfect clarity. His voice poured from the heavens and from speakers nailed to the walls of tenements and slaughterhouses. In the streets of Lagos, soldiers moved among the butchers and hawkers with radios on their hips tuned to the feed, and his voice rang out over the blood-wet floors of the meat markets like gospel. In Seoul, the children sat in their little chairs with their small hands folded and watched him speak from panes of cold glass, their mouths slack, their lunches untouched. In the open-air cafes of Marrakesh, the people sat beneath the awnings and the dust, and they listened. In the narrow halls of Philadelphia's old brick tenements, in the glass towers of Miami where the sea pressed close, in the frostbitten warrens of Yakutsk where the windows shone with hoarfrost, they listened. They heard him.

The multitude was beyond reckoning. They spilled from doorways and crowded the streets, filling the world's cities with their silent congregation. In every quarter, every alley and avenue, the people gathered, a vast host drawn by a voice that moved across continents, unbroken and unyielding, until it seemed the earth itself had come to listen.

"I told you," he said. "They will call me a tyrant."

He smiled. The grin of a man with no shadow left in him.

"I am," he said. "To tyrants."

Behind him, the image changed. Soldiers in black armor standing in lines without end, their masks dull and featureless. No insignia, no nation. Just figures. Figures with rifles. Tanks crouched like animals on heat-shimmered roads. Scientists moved through corridors with verdant light sliding across their faceplates. A laboratory or a mausoleum. It made no difference.

"We do not seek vengeance," he said. "We seek to endure. If the cost of that is fury, then so be it. Let the world tear itself loose for our sake. Let it break. You think we have not counted the cost. You think we have not seen the end of all things. I tell you now, there is no turning back. No forgiveness in the earth for what is coming. Let them remember who brought the fire. Let them remember who stood at the gate and did not turn away."

And then they chanted.

"Gideon Rex! Gideon Rex! Gideon Rex!"

He let it rise. Let it stretch out and curl through the rafters of heaven. A sound without origin or destination. The sound of something ancient clawing its way back into the light. He turned, arms lifted not to bless but to claim. Turned to Elarlu. Took her hand like a man taking up a blade.

"This is not the end," he said, his voice low, close as breath. "This is the threshing floor. The fire before the bloom. And we, together, shall plant a new world. There is no turning from it now. The old order is ash beneath our feet. What we sow here will outlast us, will rise in the morning when we are gone. Do you see it? The shape of what waits beyond the fire. We will walk through it together."

Across the globe, men dropped to their knees without command or understanding. As if something ancient in the marrow had stirred. Screens flared in the dark with the faces of the dead and the dying. With symbols none could read. The crops curled in their beds, blackened, bowed. The wells gave up nothing but silt. And yet in the cities, high among the towers of glass and wire, they looked up. They whispered his name. They sang it. Like prayer. Like blood song.

Out where the earth lay bare and the rusted great wheels listed in the fields, nothing moved. The wind went on without sound. Without resistance. The silence did not ask to be broken.

7 The Scourge

The sun hung over the town like a dead man's watch. Time held and would not pass. Shadows lay where they'd been placed and dared no movement. Children played in silence with dust in their hair and nails worn to the quick. The air was dry and sharp and carried the taste of rust. Out in the fields, the soil was cracked open like old bone, and the stalks that rose from it rose only to die. The banners of the Dominion hung slack on their poles. The wind was gone. Pride without breath. From the sides of buildings, the screens blinked to life with no ceremony. Gideon's face rose again in that monochrome flame.

No one spoke. All turned. All watched. All listened.

A woman named Maree stood in the doorway with a rag in her hand that bore no resemblance to clean. She wiped her fingers across it anyway. Her stomach growled. Hunger. The wind came up from the dry flats and pulled at her skirts. Across the path, the neighbor's window stared like an eye that had not blinked in days. No curtain moved there. No smoke. She had not seen the old man. Not once.

She had heard the talk. Low voices. Rumors like rot in the walls. That he had said the words. The wrong ones.

A boy came by with a mule in tow. The beast's eyes were clouded and old and did not suit its flesh.

"Go to the outpost," she called. "Tell the Silencers there's one here needs lookin' at."

The boy did not speak. He gave a short nod and moved on. The mule brayed once. Long and thin like grief remembered.

That night they came.

They came in a truck with the lights dark and the engine made dumb. They did not knock. They did not call. The doors opened like mouths and the men stepped out. Not men truly. Dressed in black. Masks covering their faces. No mark nor name upon them. One held a clipboard. One carried rope.

Maree stood behind the curtain with her hands gathered at her chest as if in prayer. But there was no god here. They broke the old man's door with the boot. The sound of furniture shunted aside. A chair dragged like something being punished.

They brought him out slowly.

He did not cry out.

He looked once to the stars above him.

"You spoke against him," the one with the clipboard said.

"I spoke what I knew," said the old man. "That the rains failed before the rebels ever came. That the Lord would not have us bow to a cracked vessel."

"Do you deny questioning his word?"

"I deny nothing," said the man. "But I'll not kneel for lies. Not for fear neither."

The Silencer said nothing. He made a mark on the paper. Stepped back. The one with the rope came forward.

The old man lowered his head.

"I remember you," he said. "Your eyes. You were a boy once."

But there was no boy now. Only the black cloth of the mask.

They hanged him from the pole where the old market banner had once flown and left him to turn in the wind.

In the morning, the people came. Quiet. Children at their sides. Some looked up. Most did not.

Maree stood beside her daughter. The girl small and silent. Her hair still matted with sleep. Maree raised her voice so they'd hear it plain.

"He brought it here," she said. "He sowed rebellion and it come back to him. Came back to us. All of us. This is what comes."

A woman nearby lowered her eyes and gave a slow nod. A man made the sign of the cross, though his fingers shook and he held no faith.

That night, more came. Quiet at first. Then not.

They gathered in the square, surrounded by the flickering screens. The wind low and dry like a breath held too long. They gave names. Names of wives and of husbands. Names of cousins and kin. They gave them like offerings. Like coins dropped into a bowl. They did not stammer. Did not pause.

"My older sister," one said. A boy with hollow cheeks. "She asked where the wheat had gone. Asked why her boy's belly swelled with nothing in it. Said someone ought to answer . . ." He let the sentence trail off. The name did not need speaking. It had already been written.

"My neighbor," said another. An old man in a patched coat. "He's got a book. From before. About the old ways. He reads it when the lights go out. I seen him with it."

"A teacher," said a third. A woman holding her wrist where a bracelet used to be. "Told the young ones stories. Stories not from the screen. Said they could choose."

Each name taken. Logged. Ink on the page. After every name, a silence that seemed heavier than the name itself.

The Silencer stood at the edge of the firelight, the ledger in his hands. He turned the pages slowly. He did not look at the faces. He had no need.

"Truth," he said, voice low and without color, "ain't a thing with voices. It's a root. And you dug it out."

He shut the book. The screens playing. He walked out into the dark and did not look back. The square stayed quiet. The people lingered awhile and then slipped off, one by one. Shadows in their own town.

From the next village, a man came riding hard through the last of the night. His horse was foam-laced and hollow-eyed, and the bit hung blood-wet in its mouth. The rider wore no mark. His coat was torn at the sleeve. There was ash on his boots. He rode past the body hanging in the square, slow on the rope. The man did not look up. The banner lay in strips where it had caught on the ironwork. It twitched in the dust.

He said nothing. Not to the dead nor the silence.

He tied the horse to the rusted rail and stepped to the door where the old posthouse stood. The wood blackened with smoke. Bullet holes in the eaves. He knocked twice.

A slot opened, then the door itself. The man inside was lean and tall and wore no insignia. Just a coat dark as coal. Gloves that had not been removed in days. His face had the stillness of a thing carved from driftwood.

"I have names," said the rider.

The man in the doorway said, "Come in. There's always room here for the brave."

They sat at the table beneath the oil lamp. The door was bolted behind them. The Silencer poured tea from a dented tin pot, steam curling through the cold.

"You come fast," he said.

"I rode through the fireline. They're moving east. Digging in by the canals."

"How many?"

"Four units. Maybe five. The talk is they've found the strain. The reason for it. Talk of how it came from science."

"And the names?"

The rider drew a strip of paper from inside his coat. Laid it flat on the table. The Silencer read each one aloud, slow and toneless.

"You sure of these?"

The rider nodded.

"You know what this means."

"I do."

"You give them up."

"They gave themselves up when they planted that seed."

The Silencer looked at the paper again and then folded it once and put it in his pocket.

"There's no taking this back."

"I didn't come to take it back. I came to finish it."

Outside, the wind had turned. Cold and high and dry as powdered glass. The lamplight guttered.

"You'll stay here tonight," said the Silencer. "Rooms in back. You'll go out under false color come morning."

"And the names?"

"They'll be ghosts by midday."

The rider looked down at his hands.

"Does it ever trouble you?"

The Silencer smiled, if it could be called that.

"You want it to trouble me."

"I want it to matter."

"It matters. Not to you. Not to me. But to the wind. To the world when it turns again. That's enough."

And then the dawn came. Slow and hard and gray as iron dragged through sand. The wind moved again through the streets, rattling doors and lifting old ash. The screens flickered to life. And Gideon's face, vast and serene, filled the sky.

And the people, one by one, lifted their eyes.

***

In another place, they came before dawn. No trumpet. No warning. A black procession of trucks without flags or markings crept along the avenues like something old returned. The engines rumbled low and deliberate, not fast, not slow, the sound of judgment made flesh. Not one brake light flared. The windows were mirrored dark and deep, like lakes where no one came back. Inside, nothing stirred. No faces in the glass. No voices. No horns. Above them, the sky was thick with watchers—drones, silent and unwavering, red-lit eyes scanning every window, every roofline, their movements precise and without fatigue. A single buzz echoed as one dipped low and hovered over a cat who froze in the alley, then darted under a car and vanished.

The city gates had closed sometime in the dark, somewhere between midnight and the bad hour. Those who tried them found the locks fused. Welded maybe. Wired from the inside. There was no sound of sirens. No barking orders. Just the trucks rolling in like they'd always been there.

East of the center, where the factories once belched out copper stink and heat haze, the streets were lined with the dead. Hung one by one from the old electric poles, strung up with cord and steel wire. Each body a page in the new gospel. Men and women both. Some still young. Their feet bare, swinging above the gutter water. No names. No signs. Just the long faces swollen, tongues out, eyes grayed over and half-lidded like they'd grown bored of watching.

They'd been stripped of their shoes. Every last one of them. As if something sacred had been taken. Or returned. Their clothes were common, work jackets and faded dresses. One man still wore an apron smeared with flour. One girl's braid blew sideways in the breeze. The wind came up the boulevard slow. Uncertain. Lifting their limbs. Turning them gently. They spun like coins before the drop.

The street smelled of rain and metal and something under it all like rot in a field of flowers. A boy named Callen rode up on a bicycle and stopped. He put his foot down. Said nothing. Just stared. A woman came out behind him. His mother.

"Oh God," she said. She brought her hand to her mouth.

The drone above turned. Its lens locked and watched them.

Callen stood beside her in the yellow light of morning come too soon, his fingers threaded into hers, small and hard with fear. He was six and wore a nightshirt still beneath the coat she'd thrown over his shoulders. The cold pressed up from the gutters and whispered through the stones, the air brittle and sharp with the silence of the dead.

He watched as the bodies moved slow in the wind, like things underwater. One was the baker's girl. The one who used to give him honey biscuits when his mother wasn't looking. Another was a man who'd sat all day on a folding chair outside the tramline, selling bootlaces in every color.

"Mama," Callen said. "Why are they up there?"

His mother said nothing. Her face was still. Wind passed over them, smelling of iron and dust.

"Are they sleeping?"

She looked down at him. Her voice came low.

"No."

He squinted up again. The bodies turned slightly, limp and dreamless, their shadows long on the pavement.

"They look like they're flying."

"They're not," she said.

He nodded. His jaw tightened like he was deciding something and didn't know what it was. He looked up again and did not blink for a long while.

Further up the street stood a Silencer. Black coat opened at the hem where the armor showed like scales. His helmet hung from one hand. No mask. Felt he didn't need one. His face was pale and smooth as uncut stone, and his mouth was set like a line drawn with a ruler. He stood still in the middle of the avenue as if he were the axis on which the morning turned.

His eyes moved slow over the buildings. Over the windows. Over the people. They did not flicker. As though the world were a tally and he meant to finish the count before the sun reached its height.

There was blood on his collar. A single blot like a thumb pressed to cloth. Dried and brown at the edges. He did not reach for it. Did not flinch beneath the heat or the stares. He stood as a man carved from iron and ash, boots sunk into the dust, breath slow and certain as the coming of night.

Behind him, the others waited. Silencers in black. Tall and grim beneath their helms. Some bore rifles fitted with scopes that drank in the light. Others held chains pulled taut, the dogs at their ends slavering, their eyes fever-bright. The hounds twitched with the scent of fear and turned their jaws toward the homes like they understood the weight of doors.

A voice cracked from the truck's black mouth. Metallic. Flat.

"Begin the extraction. Name lists one through six. Confirm with drone."

The Silencer turned his head slightly. He gave a single nod, slow and deliberate. Not a gesture of obedience but of permission. As if this had been foretold, and he was only there to see it through.

From the alley came the Droppers. Men and women in coats black as burned paper. Faces pale. Eyes dull as coins buried too long. They did not speak. They did not knock. They moved like fog and vanished into the rowhouses. Doors opened without a sound and closed the same way. In one window, a child watched them pass. In another, a curtain moved once and stilled forever.

A scream rose up from somewhere inside one of the homes. It was quick, stifled. Like a man who'd bitten his tongue too deep. And then nothing.

By midday, the people had stopped running. There was no point. The plaza filled with bodies drawn like filings to a magnet. Old women in shawls. Mothers with children in their arms. Men with knuckles clenched white. They gathered because they knew the silence would not save them.

In the center of the square, the Echoers unfurled their towers. Black screens that unrolled like monoliths from the soil. Petals of obsidian, wide and high, rising against the sun. The speakers hissed. Cracked. A low moan of static washed across the crowd.

Then firelight. Then the sigil.

The Dominion's sigil burned across the screens—a gear, a laurel wreath—shifting gold, endless red. An emblem that had no beginning and no center. The people stared as though hypnotized.

Then his face.

Gideon.

That terrible grin. Wide and bloodless. The cheeks unmoving. The eyes, two dead suns. He did not blink. He never had.

At the dais stood a woman. If she could be called that. Her robes shimmered like glass dipped in oil. Threads of gold pulsed faintly in the weave. Her mouth was a speaker.

Elarlu.

"You have been chosen," she said. Her voice rang out like metal on stone, amplified and hollow. "You are the stewards of a new era. Through loyalty comes peace. Through order, life. Gideon watches. Gideon rewards."

Her hands did not move. Her eyes never wavered.

The crowd trembled.

A few knelt. As if by instinct. Others followed, slower. One man clutched his chest. A girl sobbed into her shawl. Somewhere, a boy turned his head and vomited onto his shoes.

No one spoke. No one rose. And Gideon's face remained, smiling still, stretched wide across the sky.

A man rose from where he crouched near the edge of the square, slow and stiff like something broken coming upright. He wore no badge. His jacket was canvas and oil-soaked, a tear at the elbow, the cuffs black with labor. His hands were thick, palms grimed with engine grease that never quite washed out. He looked like a man who'd fixed things once, back when things were still meant to run.

He lifted one fist.

"You murdered my wife," he said.

His voice was rough and ruined. Like it had been unused for days. The Echoer standing at the dais turned her head, a glimmer of mesh catching the light across her cheek. She tilted her head like a bird hearing a sound that did not belong.

"You murdered my wife," the man said again, louder now. His eyes swept the Silencers like flame over stone. "You dragged her out in the dark. Made the kids watch. That was your mercy, wasn't it?"

The Echoer said nothing. The screen behind her rippled once, the image of Gideon flickering, then resolving again into that godless smile.

A Silencer broke from the line. Black coat brushing his knees. A rifle across his back, untouched. His steps were unhurried. Careful. He stopped three feet from the man.

The man squared his boots and stared.

"I ain't kneelin'," he said. "You can string me up next to the rest of 'em, but I won't beg. I won't bend. And I sure as hell won't kiss your goddamn boots."

The Silencer looked at him. No expression. Just wind cutting through the square and dust lifting at their feet.

Then he reached into his coat and pulled out a pistol. It was long-barreled. Heavy in the hand. The kind of weapon that bucked like a living thing. He brought it to the man's chest and pulled the trigger.

The sound was flat, brutal, and final. The man crumpled inward like scaffolding collapsing. He hit the ground hard. A wrench fell from his belt and spun twice before stopping.

Two Droppers stepped from the shade of a truck. They lifted him without sound. One took the legs, one the arms. His hands were still fists when they carried him off.

A child in the crowd began to cry. A high, narrow sound. Lost against the wind and the hum of drones above.

Two streets over and a block down, in a house with plastic over the broken windows, a girl named Nessa crouched in the dark. She was nine. Her knees pressed to her chest. Her brother was with her. Five years old. His nose bleeding down into his lip where he'd smashed it on the crawl inside.

He was shaking.

"I heard them, Nessa," he whispered.

She didn't answer. His whisper was too loud.

"They said Mama's name."

She turned and clamped her hand over his mouth. Held it there.

Outside, boots passed the cracked stoop. One pair. Then three. Shadows slid past the curtain like smoke.

A drone dropped low above the porch, its red light pulsing against the glass.

"Open," it said. "Identification required."

Nessa didn't move. Her hand trembled against her brother's face. He was crying now. Soundless.

"Open. Identification required. Final notice."

The drone hovered another breath, then rose. The boots passed on.

Nessa exhaled. A shudder more than breath. Her brother clung to her and didn't speak again.

The silence that followed was not peaceful. It was not a thing given. It was a mercy stolen and hidden, barely alive, crouched in the dark with them.

Back in the square, Callen and his mother watched. Another Echoer stood on the dais, and his voice poured from the black speakers mounted to the stone.

"You are afraid," he said. "That is natural. Fear is the seed of understanding. Through the mercy of Gideon, you are given purpose. You are given place."

The voice drifted down over the gathered like ash. Some looked up. Most did not.

A Dropper moved up the scaffold with the rope coiled over one shoulder. He worked with the calm of repetition. Hands like claws. The knot slipped through his fingers and cinched down on the neck of the next. The children in the front were told to look away, but they did not. Their eyes were wide and dry. They watched as if watching television. Something distant and unreal.

Callen tugged his mother's coat. "I don't understand," he said, and then again asked. "Why are they up there, Mama?"

She did not answer at first. She stared at the scaffold, the legs of the condemned kicking in a final rhythm before the rope took them still. Then she said, "They're showing the rest of us what not to be."

Callen looked at her. "And what are we?"

She said nothing, looking down the rows of black cloaks, the black masks like voids punched through daylight. The smell of ozone and melted plastic hung in the air. The tang of spent wire. Everything scorched. Ash drifted soft and slow across the stones like a season come wrong.

Above them, the flags sagged from the poles. Their edges frayed. The emblem stamped in foil still caught the sun—a gear, centered, teeth perfect, ringed in laurel, set against a black field that took in all light and gave nothing back.

High overhead, the drones circled. They made no sound. They had no wings and no rotors. They moved as if held by wire across the sky, smooth and eternal. Watching. Always watching.

A man near Callen's mother spoke.

"You ever seen a bird fly like that?"

She said nothing.

"They don't eat," said another. "They just swing. Nice like. With the wind."

"Like angels," said the first. "Only colder."

She raised her eyes. One drone passed low, and its red eye flashed once. Then it was gone, swallowed by the sun like a stone tossed into fire.

A Silencer walked by. He wore matte armor, and the rifle on his back was longer than a man's leg. He stopped. Looked at Callen.

"What's your name, boy?"

Callen turned his face up. "Callen."

The Silencer studied him.

"You remember today, Callen. You remember who gave you the sun and the food and the safety. You remember Gideon."

"I will," the boy said.

The Silencer smiled, a motion barely there. Then he walked on, boots silent on the ash-covered stone.

By nightfall, the poles were full. The lights of the city came on in staggered sequence and burned white and pitiless. The screens mounted to the walls flickered with Gideon's message. Again and again. Sacrifice. Unity. Obedience. The voice flat. Tireless.

At the western checkpoint, a woman ran. She held something bundled in her arms. They shouted and when she did not stop they shot her in the leg. She fell in the dust and did not scream until they came to drag her back. The bundle unwrapped itself into a child who watched in silence, mouth open, eyes locked on hers as she bled across the concrete.

A truck passed loaded with bodies. She was thrown in along with the child. The tires left black streaks. No one turned to watch it go. Out to the fields beyond the checkpoints where the pits had been dug and the fuel poured. There would be nothing to bury. Nothing to mark.

Inside a house, lit only by the failing glow of a streetlamp across the glass, Nessa sat cross-legged on the floor with her brother in her lap. She smoothed his hair with a hand still shaking.

"One day the sky will crack," she told him. "And something brighter will come through. And Gideon won't be able to see it. And it won't need drones or poles or rope. It'll drop from the sky."

The boy looked at her. His lip was split. Dried blood under his nose.

"What will it say?"

"It won't say anything."

"Why?"

"Because it won't have to."

He blinked slow. His head leaned against her shoulder. She could feel the hitch in his breath before it smoothed out into sleep.

Outside, the wind came again, low and quiet and full of dust. The bodies turned on their ropes. Steel creaked. The flags rippled in the breath of that dark wind. And the city—silent now, no screens, no voice—listened. As if waiting for something. Or forgetting what it was meant to remember.

***

The chamber was stone and still, ringed with dark basalt veined through with old circuitry, some of it live and some of it dead. The lights overhead buzzed in their dying, casting a dim pallor. In the center sat a round table of black metal, the edge strung with faint blue light, alive with the buzz of a security field meant to kill anything that tried to leave. They were already seated when Gideon came through the steel door. None stood. None spoke.

He moved to his place at the head of the table, leather coat dragging ash and soil behind him. Dust clung to the folds. His face was leaner now, his eyes washed pale, worn to the color of bone. The purge had taken more than blood. It had taken time and sleep and part of his name.

"How many?" he said.

Morgar leaned forward. His fingers pressed together like a man praying. The bones in his hand moved like sticks in a fire.

"Initial estimates," he said, the words dry and sharp as iron filings, "were fifteen million. Revised projections say sixty. Could be more."

No one spoke. The silence was not reverent. It was waiting. Gideon's eyes didn't flicker. He did not move.

"Millions upon millions," said Malachar. Her voice came filtered through the synthplate bolted into her throat, a cold hiss, almost digital. "And climbing."

Elarlu leaned forward in her chair, the folds of her crimson silk robe rustling like dry leaves across stone. Her hair was coiled high, the color of wet rust, and her skin gleamed with the sheen of ritual oil. She turned her face toward Gideon, her mouth curving, her eyes wide as coins held to the sun.

"And yet," she said, "through all this . . . you are loved."

Her voice was low and sure and strangely gentle. Reverent. She studied him as if reading some ancient mark beneath his skin.

"You are seen as the hand that purged the sickness," she said. "The shepherd who culled the herd."

"Shepherd," Gideon repeated.

"Worshipped," whispered The Oracle, her white-robed form near stillness.

Gideon turned to the science cluster, where Malachar sat flanked by Nyx Gorgrath and Lydia Zexus. "When does the antidote begin distribution?"

A glance passed between Malachar and Gorgrath. Then to Zexus. No one answered.

"Speak," Gideon said. "Silence is an enemy."

The machines blinked behind them, soft and useless.

Then Malachar sighed. A tremor, or a glitch.

"Mors Annona has . . . shifted," she said.

"Mutated," Gorgrath corrected. "Multiple times."

"We no longer possess a stable protein map," said Zexus. "The original strain is gone. What's in the air now is . . . mosaic. Viral chimera."

Gideon watched them all. One by one.

Malachar hesitated. "Livestock. Contagion has crossed. Into ruminants. Possibly avians. Swine."

Morgar stirred. "Symptoms?"

"Unclear," Malachar responded. "The data is murky. But behavior alterations have been observed. Aggression. Madness. Neurological decay."

Gideon sat there with his hands folded like prayer. His voice came low, cracked. Barely a thing at all. "So then," he said, "what have we done?"

No one answered.

He rose. The leather coat hung off him like a hide, creaking when he moved. No one spoke. He walked the length of the table, boots tapping like a clock running down. His hands were folded one over the other, calm as a corpse's. He stopped.

"We acted to cleanse," he said.

His voice was quiet, flat. Like scripture remembered too long.

"To purify. To prepare the Dominion for the century to come."

No one spoke. The words hung there. Heavy things.

They watched him. Unmoving. The room held still like a carcass cooling on stone.

"We used a tool," he said. His voice flat. Without plea or pride. "And the tool turned. Turned on us. Uncontrolled."

He turned slow as if his joints remembered something the rest of him had forgotten. The wall lights, soft and blue, cast lines across his face like chalk on cracked earth. His eyes sunk back in the skull, dark and unreadable.

"How do we stop it?" he asked. "How do we gain control?"

The room offered no reply. Circuitry buzzed low through the stone bones of the place, a sound like insects dying in a wall. A coolant valve somewhere let off a hiss, then shut itself quiet. Still nothing. The silence long. Sour.

The Oracle rose without sound. The folds of her robe slipped from the arm of her chair and hung like dead skin. Her eyes did not see the room. They stared into a place none of them could name. When she spoke, her voice was not her own. It dragged up from the pit of some older place, dry and blind and knowing.

"The serpent bites its own tail," she said. "And the poison cycles."

Elarlu stood slowly. Her palms pressed together just above the beltline of her gown as if holding in some wound.

"We did what we must," she said. "The undesirables—"

"The weak," Morgar said. He didn't look up. His fingers tapped once on the metal table, a dull tick like a counting device.

"The corrupted," said the Voice, her tone even as always, as though reading a verdict long since decided. "The unclean."

"The unnecessary," Malgoth rumbled in a low voice.

"They were removed," Elarlu said. "The Mors Annona was a brushfire in tall grass. Now all that remains is fertile ground."

"Fertile," Gideon said. "And salted."

Her smile tightened. Pulled flat across her teeth like an animal tasting something it did not trust.

Then a voice came. Female.

Not a voice carried by air or made by any mouth. It came through the stone itself. High. Brittle. Like glass flexing.

"You have erred, Siren."

Another coolant valve hissed. Lights trembled in their sockets. Dimmed and flared.

"You brought rot into the sanctum," said the voice.

Elarlu turned. She had gone pale.

"Oracle," she said. "What is this? What words do you now speak?"

The Oracle's eyes were wide. "Not I," she said. "Not my tongue. Not my will. You are hearing things."

Then another voice. Low and rasped. Male, or something like it. Not one Elarlu knew.

"Dominion dies from within."

Elarlu backed away from the table. Her chair scraped and toppled.

"Who speaks?" she said. Her voice sharp now, knifed by fear.

"You made of propaganda a crown," said the first voice. "And of lies a foundation."

"Your hands are steeped," said the second. "And still you reach."

"You know nothing," Elarlu shouted. "Nothing of sacrifice."

The others looked at her, worried, frightened.

"You offered them to the wind," said the first. "And the wind turned back upon you."

Gideon raised his hand. His palm open, fingers spread. Silence returned. The voices faded like smoke pulled through a keyhole.

Elarlu breathed in, deep and ragged. Sweat clung to her lip. Her face was wet with it.

The room was cold as a grave.

Gideon looked down at the black of the table. He saw his own face staring up at him. A stranger's face. Creased. Old. The corner of one eye twitched without permission.

"We must contain the mutations," he said.

"We can't," said Malachar. "At least, not now."

"Then kill the infected herds," Malgoth said.

"Which ones?" said Grix. "The mark is invisible. Until we see it."

Morgar let out a breath through his nose. "Then burn them all."

Grix was angry. "The food reserves will fall below threshold. That's just damned foolishness."

"Let them starve," said the Malgoth. "Starvation breeds loyalty. We know this."

"No," said Gideon.

They turned to him.

"We repair what we have broken."

He moved around the table. Slow. His steps echoed against the stone. Every face turned toward him. Watching.

He stopped before Elarlu.

"You told them I was their savior."

"You are," she said. A whisper, dry as dust.

"Then I must act like one."

She looked up at him. Her face cracked around the edges, like something fired and cooled too fast.

He turned back to the room.

"We do not retreat," he said. "We do not unravel. There is order. There is a plan."

A quiet voice, the Oracle's. No longer trembling.

"And there is judgment."

Gideon nodded once.

"Then let it come."

The group bowed their heads.

"Salve Rex," they whispered.

8 *Ashes of the Sacred*

The room was sealed.

A smooth curve of polished black stone closed behind two figures like a vault door. No guards. No scribes. No torchbearers. Only the low whine of the kinetic lock resealing in their wake, and the waiting silence that followed. In the center of the room, a single iron table. Cold, unwelcome. Its edges sharp. Untouched by time. On it rested nothing. Not yet.

The Oracle found her way to one side of the chamber, her face aglow in the half-light, like something drawn from a tomb wall. Her white robes moved faintly with her breath, the fine gold sigils along her sleeves catching what little radiance there was. Her eyes—silver, unfocused—watched the space as if something else lived just beneath the stone.

The Voice stood at the opposite, stiff-backed in her judicial garb, hands folded in front of her like a blade sheathed in discipline. She did not sit. She did not remove her chain of office. Even in the dark, the weight of justice must be visible.

"You waited long enough," she said.

"I pray in silence," the Oracle answered. "The gods speak softly."

The Voice grunted. "Then they have poor timing."

They stared at one another. Not with hostility, but with the recognition of power. Each a pillar of Dominion. One clothed in faith. The other in law. Bound by the throne but not bent by it.

"She is unraveling," the Voice said. "Even her own people murmur it now. I hear them whispering when the halls go still. They know. Her voice breaks. She shudders during briefings. And the rumors—"

She paused.

"—they say she hears voices."

"She is hearing voices," the Oracle said. Her tone made no argument of it. "You saw it."

"We all did," said the Voice.

"She came to me three nights before. Hands trembling like a novice. Said she heard whispering when she closed her eyes. Saw figures in mirrors. That the dead had learned to speak her name."

The Oracle exhaled slowly through her nose. "And you didn't report this?"

"I did," the Voice said. She turned slightly, gazing past the Oracle. "I told Gideon. Said this was a problem. But he still listens to her."

"That's why we're here."

A silence passed. Heavy, patient. The air had the tang of old smoke.

The Voice took a step forward. Her heels echoed like verdicts.

"You've seen the damage," she said. "Sector nine. What's left of it. Villages turned to corpses, heaps of decay. Livestock twisting in their own hides like something trying to crawl out. Spores still settling in the air. Still feeding."

"It was not supposed to persist," the Oracle whispered. "Mors Annona was designed to burn fast. Burn clean. Elarlu insisted the vectors were isolated. That it would die in the first generation."

The Voice's mouth flattened. "It didn't."

"No," the Oracle said. Her voice dropped lower. "It grows. Wild now. Faithless."

They were quiet again.

"She's lost control," the Voice said. "And now she pretends she never had it."

"She even asks for more resources," the Oracle said. "She asks for more bodies. For blind faith from the Echoers. For permission to cull whole regions. I told her no. I would not support such a thing. I said we cannot martyr every dissenter."

"You said it to her face?"

"I did."

"Brave."

"Necessary."

The Voice nodded. "You and I, we differ. But we are alike in this."

"In what way?"

"We protect Gideon," the Voice said. She touched the chain around her neck, heavy with its own history, forged for judgment, not ornament. "From poor counsel. From those who'd wear the throne like a skin and call it theirs."

"And Elarlu has begun to believe the crown suits her."

"She wears it in her sleep."

The Oracle drifted closer to the table. Her robes whispered against the stone.

"You remember the creed," she said. "Three pillars. Voice, Oracle, Hand. The Hand trembles. Gideon bears the title but has no shield. Only us."

"And Elarlu," the Voice said, "dresses herself in armor he never gave her."

They looked at each other then. Saw the same conclusion mapped behind the eyes.

"I watched her once," the Voice said, her voice low. "In a tribunal. She smiled while a boy burned. A child of six. Claimed he'd been fed propaganda. He wept for his mother. She told him the wind had already taken her."

"And Gideon trusts her."

"He doesn't see her anymore," the Voice said. "Only the promise she offers. Victory. Salvation. He built that lie. Now it wears a dress."

The Oracle reached into her sleeve.

"She speaks of rot," she said. "Yet it grows in her skull."

She reached within her robe and brought forth a vial, pale as bone, glinting white as gloom, stoppered with wax dark as dried blood. She set it between them on the stone table.

The Voice's eyes narrowed.

"What is that?"

The Oracle smiled.

"My own Mors Annona."

"You're joking."

"I do not joke."

The Voice stepped closer, the tip of her boot almost brushing the Oracle's hem. "You've synthesized it?"

"I adapted it. Refined it. Unlike her filth, mine obeys."

"To what end?"

"To remind her," the Oracle said, her voice lilting, "that the gods choose whom they bless. And whom they curse."

The Voice considered this. Then, to the Oracle's surprise, she laughed. Just once. Dry and brittle as parchment.

"She hears voices," the Voice said. Her tone was dry as old earth, untouched by rain. "But not like you or I. She hears only herself. And she calls that noise prophecy."

The Oracle's eyes did not blink. Pale as smoke. She spoke low.

"It is said she chants to the wall. Naked. Smeared in ash. She thinks the dead speak back to her. Perhaps they do."

"Or perhaps she's only the first to fall."

"Perhaps," said the Oracle. "But if she continues to drag ruin down upon Gideon, if she continues to taint his reign like rot beneath a harvest, I'll unseal this vial. Another dose she will get."

"Another dose?"

The Oracle smiled. She continued. "I'll name her in the old tongue, the one meant for crows and gravefire. And I will watch her bones remember how to kneel."

The Voice looked at the vial without leaning. Her eyes held it. Quiet. Steady. Then:

"Would you truly do it? Another dose?"

"If she makes me. If she makes us."

The Voice raised a gloved hand and touched the vial with a single finger. Turned it. The powder inside clung a moment to the glass, then sank slowly like snow on windless ground.

"And the fallout?"

"Localized," the Oracle said. "If timed correctly. She will seep into madness. Pass like wind through a barren room."

"You've thought this through."

"I've had to."

The Voice straightened. Her robe caught the light, red thread gleaming like veinwork. She ran her palm down the fabric and let it rest again at her side. Her gaze was hard and flat and long.

"You should have told me."

"You would have objected."

"I still might."

"But now," the Oracle said. "You understand."

The silence that followed held like a dry field under a dead sky. No candles burned. No scent of sanctity. Only the stone and the cold. And the promise of fire to come.

"I need your word," she said.

"For what?"

"That if she fails him again," the Oracle said, her voice rough and low, like the breath of something buried deep, "you will not stand in my way."

The Voice did not speak. She studied her across the dead air between them, the way a judge weighs silence against guilt. Then her gaze dropped to the vial. The powder within like snow sifted from bone. She watched it shift in its glass prison. Watched it settle like ash upon the world. She lifted her eyes again, and they were iron.

"You have it," she said.

There was no hand offered. No pact sealed in blood or skin. Only the stillness of the thing unspoken between them. The Oracle stepped back, her robes whispering like old paper, and the shadows took her in. Her eyes held what little light remained. Pale and lidless. Like moons sunk in black water.

"The gods are watching," she said.

The Voice turned. Her boots struck the stone floor with the finality of a verdict. One. Two. A reckoning set to rhythm.

"Let them," she said.

***

The lab was a furnace. No windows. No wind. Heat curled up off the polymer slabs and settled thick on the skin like grime. The stink in the air was a thing born and bred. Sweat and ozone. Acid rot. Old reagents gone sour in the belly of the place. Lights jittered overhead, pale tubes humming in seizure. The kind of light that shows the truth of faces. Makes corpses out of the living. Men moved like ghosts through it, their eyes rimmed red, hands cracked from solvents, too tired to blink. A centrifuge howled in the back like a dying dog. No one looked at it.

Gorgrath hunched at the console, fingers bent and stiff as if she held fire in her palms. Her coat was plastered to her back.

Her jaw shone with sweat. Zexus stood beside her, dry-eyed, arms folded. She stared through the screen like it owed her something. Nearby, Malachar crouched like a penitent, her tablet bleeding red warnings into her lap. None of them spoke for a time. No one moved.

"It seems nothing holds," Zexus said. "Each strain eats itself before it binds. The chimera chew through their own tails."

Malachar didn't lift her head. "We use cobalt vectors. Go retrograde. Anchor the tail to the head. Close the loop. We'll force it to anchor."

"They slipped the last tether clean," Zexus said. "It's difficult. Each cycle it comes back meaner, growing fangs."

The doors split with a hiss, and he stepped through. Gideon. No guards flanking, no sound save the slow pulse of the ventilators and the rough report of boot on steel. He carried with him a stench that was not of the place. Smoke and wet cinders. The charred remnants of some wilderness thing left to rot under rain. A funeral stink. Ancient and unsummoned.

He came to a halt before a vat and fixed his eyes on the thing inside. It drifted, slow as molasses, blacker than pitch, thinking its unthought thoughts. A slur of matter that moved with the idle conviction of intelligence but bore no mark of knowing. It turned to him, though it had no face, no eyes, no form to aim. Watching all the same.

"Report," he said.

Malachar rose like something dragged from sleep. She flattened the front of her coat with fingers that would not still. Each breath a negotiation.

"No synthesis," she said. "It's broken. Split itself and took root in the ruin of what it consumed. Mors Annona is hunger made flesh."

He said nothing. Turned instead to the screen on the wall—oceans, land masses, continents. Many of the land formations glowed red where the infection bled. It flowered outward. Slow. Patient. No fanfare. No center. Just spread. Like blood leeching into an old bandage, unstoppable. No edge to trim. No center to strike. No salvation.

"I was told you have an agent. Something to fix it all. What about it?"

"We do," she said, "If we drop it now, we might hold ten percent. Livestock. Not humans."

He did not answer.

The silence opened between them like a door onto some room too dark to gauge.

She licked her teeth. A dry scrape.

He looked down. There was blood on the decking. Not fresh. Dull and brown, dried to a shadow. Shaped like a footstep. Heading away from the vat and toward no place known.

He turned and left.

Malachar leaned in toward the screen. Her face lit faint by the tank's glow. The pathogen drifted, forming new strands, loops inside loops. Not chaos.

It was thinking.

She stopped breathing.

The chain folded in on itself. Drew a mark. A circle. Inside it, a crude slit. Watching.

Gorgrath behind her now. Still.

"What does it mean?"

She didn't look at her.

"It means it knows. It remembers. It needs. "

***

Down the corridor, Gideon went. Boots sounding like hooves on stone. The tail of his coat brushing the floor behind him. Heavy with dust and dried blood. Doors shrieked open as he passed, metal mouths yanked wide by unseen hands. Not so much welcoming him as fleeing his approach. He did not slow. He did not look back. The lights overhead buzzed like flies.

He stepped into the room and closed the door behind him.

Elarlu stood alone in the dark. The walls breathed faintly with old circuits, humming like the last threads of a dying dream. Before her, the window rose, a pane of black glass as tall as ten men laid head to toe, smooth and cold as polished obsidian. Beyond it, the Dominion sprawled in silence. Cities like grave markers. Towers jagged as broken bones rising out of the gloom. "Look at it," she said. Her voice flat. "Like a god laid down and forgot to die." The lights along the spires guttered low, thin, and sick as candleflame in a house no longer lived in.

He stepped in behind her. She did not turn. He said nothing.

"We are at the edge," she said. "The storehouses are empty. What fields we had are salted or sick. The aquifers are fouled."

He nodded. A slow gesture, like something sinking.

"How long do you think we have?"

"Ten months," she said. "Maybe twelve. We can hold the inner sectors. The rest . . ."

She broke off. Turned to face him. Her face thin. Drawn. He did not look at her.

"You need a new enemy," she said.

"I need a solution."

"A new enemy is one."

He watched her in the glass. Her reflection a pale stain in the blackness. She did not turn.

He said, "You hear them. Voices."

She was silent. The lights on the towers flickered and died and came again.

He said, "Do they speak to you now?"

She pressed her palm to the glass. Her breath left a dim crescent.

"They come and go," she said. "Like the wind. Like the sea in dreams."

He said, "There is no wind here."

She turned to him then. Her eyes were hollowed. Black with the night behind her.

"You think I am mad," she said.

"I think you hear things that are not meant to be heard."

She looked past him as if the voices gathered in the corners of the room. She said, "Perhaps they are meant. Perhaps they are sent."

He said, "By whom?"

She shrugged. Her hands trembled at her sides. "By God," she said. "Or something like him. Something older."

He watched her. The silence in the room like a third presence.

He said, "There is no God here."

She smiled, thin and cold. "Then what do you call the thing that speaks when all else is silent."

He said nothing.

She said, "I have tried to quiet them. I have prayed. I have cursed. Still, they come."

He said, "What do they say?"

She shook her head. "They speak in riddles. In tongues I do not know. Sometimes I think they are only echoes of my own fears."

He stepped closer. His shadow fell across her.

He said, "If they are only echoes of your own fear, why do you tremble?"

She looked at him then. The lights in the towers guttered and failed. She said, "Because sometimes I think they are not. They are something worse."

He did not answer. He watched her as one might watch a beast in a snare, uncertain if it would bite or beg.

She said, "Perhaps they are a warning."

He said, "Or a curse."

She turned back to the glass. The city lay below, vast and ruined. She said, "We are all cursed, Gideon. Some of us just hear it more clearly.

She reached under the robe and drew forth a curl of fiberplastic, unrolled it on the table. The map blinked alive, flickering low in the dead light. The shape of the Silent Land came forth like a bruise on skin. Green along the coast where the rain had clawed its way back. Gold inland where wheat still stood, half-charred and stubborn.

"They've sealed themselves off," she said. "Walled themselves up like old kings. Clean places. Untouched by fire."

"They'll fight."

"They'll fall."

He said nothing.

She stepped toward him. Her breath close now. The gleam in her eyes like oil over dark water.

"Let them see you burn the air," she said. "Let them see your hand. Not just as the knife. As the bread."

He turned from the window. His coat brushed ash behind him like the tail of some hunted thing. The black concrete floor gave back nothing.

"How many will die?"

She smiled. It had no soul.

"The better question is . . . how many must live?"

He stared at her a long moment.

"You talk like a prophet."

"I talk like a woman who wants to survive."

He crossed the chamber slow, boots heavy. Looked down through the slats in the steel floor. Figures moved beneath—men in white. Machines carrying black bags like coffins. The heat rose like something punished. The air stank of bleach and blood.

He closed his eyes.

"What would you have me do?"

"Go to the people and tell the truth," she said.

"What truth?"

"Your truth. Our truth."

"And what is that?"

"That we know what's behind the sickness that plagues their fields. Those of the Silent Land. That action is needed. You will create men loyal enough to kill and not ask what for."

He opened his eyes.

"And when we win?"

"Then we eat," she said. "Then we live."

He moved to her like a man stepping into flame. No haste in it. No fear either. She did not flinch when he laid a hand to her face, and her skin beneath was cold and dry as ash bark. The lights above them hummed and guttered. The map still pulsed behind her, casting up soft green against the bones of her cheek.

"We will kill to see it done," he said. "Burn what's left."

"Nothing left to spare."

He let the silence close around them again. It settled like dust in a house long abandoned. She reached for the clasp at his throat and undid it with a touch. The coat fell with a thud behind him. It lay there like something dead.

She said, "You want mercy."

"I want to forget."

She leaned into him. Her mouth to his ear. "Then let the world end a little more."

And he did.

She sank to the floor. The concrete held the heat of what was buried, what never cooled. She took hold of him. Her fingers hard. Corded.

"Come down," she said.

He did. There was no gentleness in her. Just the raw grip of need, old as hunger, older than names. She pulled him against her.

Their mouths met. Not in love. In closure. As if some wound had opened in both and this was the stitching. She tore at his shirt. Buttons scattered like teeth on stone.

"Take it off," she said.

He pulled what was left from her hips. Their skin found each other. Their breath filled the silence. Beneath them machines turned. Mindless. Below all reckoning. A distant siren gave a weak cry and fell quiet. Somewhere behind the walls, something gave way.

She arched beneath him, head back, hands at his shoulders, and for a moment she laughed—not out of joy but out of defiance. A sound like bones knocked in a jar.

"There is still time," she said.

"Time for what?"

"For this."

His body against hers, sharp-edged and gaunt. The sinews of war and hunger. The architecture of survival. He entered her and the silence broke, a cry between them not pain and not pleasure, but something old as dust, something deeper than grief.

Their rhythm was slow and without grace. It did not need it. She wrapped her legs around him and bit his shoulder. He did not stop her. His breath against her throat like prayer.

When they finished, they lay tangled on the floor, slick with sweat, the heat rising from the vents below them like the breath of some unseen furnace. The map blinked behind them. A flicker. A pause. Then darkness.

He spoke first.

"I never believed," he said.

She turned her face to him. "In what?"

"In any of it. God. Redemption. Justice."

"Then believe in this . . . in us . . . what we have."

He nodded. The ceiling above them cracked with old strain. She lay against his chest, her fingers tracing the ridge of his ribs.

"They will follow you," she said.

"Then they are lost."

"They were already lost."

He said, "You know what they'll call us."

"I don't care."

"Monsters. They'll call us monsters."

She looked up. Her eyes were calm. "Then let us be monsters."

He closed his eyes. She watched him, unmoving.

Outside the glass, the towers guttered and finally failed. The Dominion gone black. City swallowed by its own night. No stars. No moon. Just the breathless dark.

She said, "We should go soon."

He said, "Not yet."

"No."

She ran her fingers through his hair. His face older than it had been. The lines of it harder now. He looked like stone carved for memory.

"We'll be hunted," he said.

"Then we will run to a place where we cannot be found."

They rose after a time. Dressed in silence. Her robes straightened. His coat shrugged over his bare shoulders. No buttons. No armor. The bloodstain still across the back from when he'd knelt to the man in the corridor. A clean shot. The kind that ends everything.

She stood before him and smoothed the collar. Looked into his face.

She touched his lips once. "Thank you."

He nodded. And the lights around them died.

Outside, thunder rolled dry and empty, like bones in a drum. He turned to her. His face had gone hard. Like stone meant for carving.

The door hissed open. The corridor stretched beyond, long and dim. Dust in the corners like old bones.

They walked out together.

"Tell the others of the plan," he said.

She bowed her head. Just so. A gesture older than language, older than fire. The neck bent not in reverence but in recognition. As one might to an old god, long dead but still feared.

"Salve Rex."

The door shut behind them. Not a slam. Not a click. A sound like breath escaping a broken chest. As if the chamber itself had exhaled one last time and would never again.

Far down the corridor, past where light failed and the stones grew colder the deeper they sank into the world, there were eyes. Unmoving. Unblinking. Not beast eyes nor man's. They did not glint. They did not shine. They waited. The Oracle stood among the dark like a root grown out of time, robes fallen still around her. She had not moved. She did not need to. She had seen it all. Heard it all. And deep within her, the rage was not new, only waiting.

***

The chamber sat in silence long before she entered it. The hush was not the absence of sound but the presence of something old and waiting, a silence that pressed against the stone like a tide. Columns rose from the floor, black and veined, petrified trees in a forest that had forgotten the sun. The stone beneath their feet was polished to a mirror, and the scent of ash and ozone lingered in the rafters, faint as the memory of rain.

They had come one by one, their footsteps echoing in the vastness, each bearing their own silence and suspicion. Morgar stood by the far wall, his high-collared coat swallowing his neck, his eyes cold and bright as cut steel. Gorgrath lingered in the shadow, her face half-hidden, her hands folded into the sleeves of her robe. Malgoth was armored, plates of black metal etched with runes, a war idol carved from the bones of old gods. The Viper paced before the great map, his boots tracing the borders of continents lost and won. The Oracle stood with her eyes closed, her white robes unmoving, her lips parted as if she listened for something that did not speak in words. The Voice sat rigid, hands folded on the table before her, fingers entwined like the inscription on a tomb.

Elarlu crossed the threshold. The doors shut behind her with a sound like the world ending. The echo died slowly. She stood a moment in the hush, her eyes sweeping the room.

"Gideon has decided," she said.

They turned to her, not as one body, but as many minds fracturing around a single question. The light from the high windows fell in bars across the table, dust motes drifting through it like the ghosts of harvests past.

"He will strike at the Silent Land," she said. "The green belt remains fertile. Their waters run clean. The pathogen in our fields—Gideon will tell the people it came from them. That their silence, their isolation, was treachery."

No one moved. No one spoke. The air was thick with the weight of what would come.

Then Morgar, his voice the scrape of a blade across stone. "Another enemy."

"Precisely," Elarlu said.

Morgar's mouth curled in something like a smile. "They will believe it. The people are hungry. They are angry. Give them someone to blame and they will march barefoot over salt."

"It is tactically challenging," Malgoth said. His voice was deep, hollow in the helmet. "The terrain is highly defensible. But if we strike hard, hold the ports, while dropping troops behind the defenses—we can take the farms."

The Viper smiled, slow and slithering. "And when the harvest comes, who will remember the lie? The world is dying. Let them curse us with full stomachs."

The Voice leaned forward, her hands still folded. Her eyes were dark, unreadable. "You intend to justify conquest with fiction," she said. "And feed an army with promises. Promises don't feed men. And lies have no loyalty."

Gorgrath scoffed, her voice low. "Lies have won more wars than truth. This is no different."

"It is different," came the voice of the Oracle. She did not open her eyes. Her words drifted across the table like smoke. "It is different because it ends not with victory but with dominion over rot."

Malgoth tapped something on the glowing strip along her wrist. "The data supports logistical feasibility if the operation is swift. If we stall, we starve."

"And if they resist?" asked Grix from beneath his hood, his voice a rasp. "If those of the Silent Land dig in, burn the crops, poison the wells—what then? What do we rule? Ash? We already have plenty of that."

Morgar turned to Elarlu. "What did Gideon say of the risks?"

Elarlu's face did not move. Her voice was even, but something in it seemed to slow the room. "He did not speak of risk. Only of necessity. He believes the people must see strength, not scarcity. Unity, not fracture."

"And what does he believe of the gods?" the Oracle asked.

The silence grew. It was not a pause but a gulf, a space into which nothing dared fall.

She stepped forward, the hem of her robe whispering on the stone. "There is a thin line between a savior and a butcher. He walks it blind."

Gorgrath shifted, her hands tightening in her sleeves. "Spare us the riddles, Oracle."

"I speak only what I see. You think the Silent Land is a solution. I see only that it becomes a wound. You will open it, and it will not heal. We will rule over bones, and crown ourselves kings of famine."

The Voice nodded slowly as if the movement cost her. "Even if we win, we will lose. The cost of feeding our army may exceed the yield. And the story, once told, cannot be untold. When the lie fails—"

"It will not," Morgar said, his voice flat.

"—when the lie fails," the Voice repeated, "what then? Shall we lie again, and again, until there is no truth left to twist?"

"The people do not care for truth," said the Viper. "They care for certainty. Rage. Bread."

"And we are running out of all three," muttered Grix.

Elarlu watched them. Their faces. The fire in some, the doubt in others. The room was a crucible, and she felt the heat rising.

"Gideon has decided," she said again. "I brought you here not for consensus. Only clarity."

She turned to the Oracle. The others watched, waiting for the old woman's words.

"Speak it plainly. Will the gods forsake us for this?"

The Oracle's eyes opened, pale moons sunk in bone, the folds of her robe unmoved by breath. Her hand stirred beneath the cloth. The small glass vial turned between her fingers.

"They already have," she said.

No one spoke again for a long while. The silence returned, heavier than before. Outside, the wind scoured the stone walls with dust that had once been harvests, and the world beyond the glass seemed to draw away as if it too had heard the words and wished to forget them.

When they stood, they did so slowly. Like men rising from prayer. Or graves. The doors opened and the light fell across the floor. Thin. Cold. Elarlu lingered a moment, her hand on the stone, feeling the tremor of something vast and unseen moving beneath the surface of things. She thought of Gideon, of the voices that came in the night, of the hunger that could not be named.

She left them there, the council of the damned, each lost in their own reckonings. The chamber emptied, but the silence remained, a witness to what had been spoken, and to what would come.

9 Fire

The night pressed close against the Spire, a darkness thick with the memory of fires long dead and the hush of secrets yet to be spoken. The air beyond the council chamber was cold, the stone corridors lit only by the faintest glow from the city's ruined towers, their lights flickering like the last embers of a world set to ash. The Voice moved through these corridors as one born to silence, her steps measured, her breath shallow, the hem of her coat whispering over the floor. She turned down a stairwell, stone worn smooth, and entered a gallery where the shadows pooled deepest.

The Oracle waited there, her white robes pale as bone, her hands folded within the sleeves. She stood by a narrow window, the glass black as a blind eye, and did not turn when the Voice entered. The wind outside moaned in the stones, and the scent of dust and distant rain drifted in.

"You came," the Oracle said.

The Voice stood a moment, watching the woman's back, the way her head bowed as if in prayer. "You summoned me," she replied.

The Oracle's hand emerged from her sleeve, holding the small glass vial. The powder within was white, fine as sifted flour, and it caught the faint light with a dull shimmer. She turned it between her fingers, slow and deliberate.

"You know what this is," the Oracle said.

"We talked about it," the Voice answered. "I know what it is. What it does."

The Oracle smiled. Thin. Without warmth. "Not all know. Not all wish to know."

The Voice stepped closer, her own hands folded, her eyes fixed on the vial. "We discussed a solution."

The Oracle's fingers tightened around the glass. "A higher dose," she said. "That is all it takes. She will hear them louder, the voices. More insistent. They will come for her in the daylight, in the waking hours, not just in dreams. She will not be able to hide them. Not from herself. Not from Gideon. Not from the others."

The Voice's breath caught, a small sound in the dark. "Will it kill her?"

"In time. The powder eats at the brain. It hollows out the cells. Leaves only echoes. But before that, it will drive her to the edge. She will see things that are not there. Hear words that are not spoken. She will speak to shadows, and the others will see her for what she is becoming."

"Madness," the Voice said.

"Madness," the Oracle echoed. She held the vial up, the powder swirling within. "They already whisper it, some of them. Gorgrath. Malgoth. Even Morgar, for all his coldness. They see the cracks. They smell the fear on her."

The Voice looked away, her face drawn. "She is clever. Too clever. She weaves the stories. Bends the people to her will. People follow her. Don't know why. Gideon trusts her. That's the worst of it. He always was blind to ambition when it smiled sweet."

The Oracle's eyes narrowed. "Gideon trusts what he can see. What he can use. When she begins to unravel, he will have no choice. He cannot afford weakness. Not now."

The Voice's voice was low, almost a whisper. "He will not thank us."

"No," the Oracle said. "He will not. But he will understand. In time."

They stood without speaking. The wind moved across the broken city, and the tall glass sang low in its casing. Far off, a bell rang. A single note lost in the sprawl. It came again and again, and then not at all.

"How will you do it?" the Voice said.

The Oracle turned the vial slow in her hand. The powder inside drifted like ash in a storm jar. "She takes tea in the mornings," she said. "Thinks she's alone. But she is not. There are her servants. They answer to me. One in particular. Just a pinch. No more than that. In the cup. Then what comes will come."

The Voice nodded, her eyes on the floor. "And when it begins?"

"It will begin as it always does," the Oracle said. "A tremor in the hand. Slight. A shadow in the corner of the eye. Gray. Then the voices. Delicate. At first, she will try to hide it. She will think herself strong enough. But the powder is patient. It will wear her down. She will speak out of turn. Argue with phantoms. All will see. Gideon will see."

The Voice let out a long breath, her shoulders sagging. "She was not always this way. There was a time she was . . ."

"Brilliant," the Oracle finished. "But brilliance burns fast. And the world is not kind to those who burn too bright."

The Voice looked at the Oracle, her eyes searching. "And you? You feel nothing for this?"

The Oracle's face was stone. "I feel what must be felt. Cold. Nothing more."

They stood together in the gloom, two shadows among many. The city below was quiet, the wind carrying with it the scent of rain and decay.

"Will she know?" the Voice said. "Will she suspect?"

The Oracle did not look up. Outside, wind moved through the broken place like breath through a dying throat.

"She will suspect everyone," she said. "That's the nature of the powder. It seeds doubt like weeds in tilled earth. Paranoia follows. She'll see enemies in every face. Even Gideon's. She won't sleep. She'll turn the knife in her hand a hundred times before choosing where to place it. The eyes that loved her once will narrow and know her not. That is the price of the powder. That is its gift."

The Voice closed her eyes, pressing her fingers to her brow. "And when she is gone?"

"Then we will be free of her. Gideon will grieve, perhaps. Or perhaps he will not. He is not a man given to sentiment."

The Voice's voice was bitter. "He will turn to you. Or to Morgan. Or to me."

The Oracle smiled again, that thin, bloodless smile. "Perhaps. Or perhaps he will turn to the darkness, as all men do in the end."

They fell silent, the only sound the wind and the distant, ceaseless hum of the city's dying heart.

"Do it," the Voice said at last. "But do it clean. No spectacle. No dance."

The Oracle inclined her head. "It will be as if she faded. As if the world simply wore her away."

The Voice turned to leave, her steps slow as if she carried a weight too great to bear. At the threshold, she paused, her hand on the cold stone.

"If she dies," she said, "let it be quick. Let her not suffer more than she must."

The Oracle's voice was soft, almost kind. "She will not suffer long. The powder is merciful, in its way. Of sorts. But pain will come."

"How?"

"She will be there, but buried deep. Caged in her mind. Watching it all come undone. She will try to pull at the seams of her awareness. To crawl back to reality. Screaming without a mouth to scream. Knowing. Powerless."

"Horrible."

"Unfortunate," the Oracle said. "But a price must always be paid, I suppose.

The Voice stood a moment longer, her hands at her sides, the silence broken only by her sigh. Then she said, "So be it," and turned, the folds of her robe trailing the dust. The stone drank her down. And the room was empty but for the echo of what she had spoken.

The Oracle stood alone in the cold blue hush of the room, the vial cupped in her hand like some dead thing. The powder inside was fine as sifted ash, and it trembled in its glass chamber with every gust that clawed at the windowpanes. She stared down into it as if the answer to every grief were buried in the whiteness. The wind moaned and shook the glass, and for a breath of a moment she heard voices. Soft and worn. Like rain sliding down the bones of old stone. She shut her eyes. Listened. Nothing. Only the great silence, wide as death, deep as the pit, waiting like a mouth to be spoken into. She smiled.

"In the morning," she whispered, "they'll hear it. They'll see it. The start of her demise. It will be there for all to witness. Tomorrow. At the rally. The start of Elarlu's fall."

***

The Oracle moved through the stone corridors like a shadow unspooled. No torches burned there. Only the faint breath of the outer winds pressing in through narrow slits in the walls, the sound of them like voices too far to name. At the far end, a handmaid waited. A young woman wrapped in gray, face half turned, eyes lowered.

The Oracle pressed the vial into the woman's hand. Her fingers were thin as twigs, cold as bone.

"Do you know what this is?" the Oracle asked.

The young woman nodded. Once. Her face unreadable. A quiet thing shaped by obedience.

"It will taste of nothing," the Oracle said. "She will drink and not know. Not till it's already begun."

The young woman took the vial. Her hand closed round it like closing a grave.

"Begin when you return to her chambers," the Oracle told her. "Tonight. In her tea."

"How much?" the young woman asked.

"Just enough," the Oracle told her. "Not too much. Not too little. You'll know."

The Oracle made her way back through the darkened halls. The stone beneath her feet cold. Unyielding. In her chamber, the silence held fast. A fire had long since died in the grate, leaving only the scent of old ash and scorched wood. She stood before the mirror. Her hands pulled loose the clasp at her throat, and the robes slipped from her shoulders like falling leaves. She ran her palms over the slight swell of her belly, the skin taut and pale as parchment stretched over the promise of blood and bone. Her hair hung loose, strands of it catching the faint light. She touched her cheek. She looked into her own eyes and saw the last of the girl she once had been.

Then came the pounding.

Fists at the door, sudden and sharp. Then voices—raised, uncertain. The sound of fear trying to wear the mask of command. She turned her head slowly, robe still fallen to her waist, her hand still pressed against the place where youth had once lived. The shouts grew louder. She did not move. Not yet. Only listened. And waited.

***

The sky had gone orange with dust, and the wind from the north carried the breath of dead rivers. In the basin east of the ruin, they gathered, where the stadium had risen anew from the bones of its ancestor. What had once been concrete ribs jutting from the earth now stood as a crown of steel and glass, a marvel of cunning hands and fevered will. The bowl was vast enough to swallow the city's clamor and return it as thunder, its roof a thing of petals wrought in steel that could close against the storm or open to the sky, each moved by engines whose power was measured in the weight of mountains.

The terraces swept down in long arcs, each row a ribbon of stone and light, and the field below lay black and perfect, ringed by the glow of screens that circled the bowl like a halo. The sound in that place was not of the old world but of the new machines and voices and the low hum of power running through the veins of the structure. The old ruin had been a memory of loss, its terraces haunted by the ghosts of games no one remembered. Now the stadium stood as testament and promise, a cathedral of industry and will. It rose against the sky, a beacon, and a challenge, and the dust that blew down from the north swirled around its base and was lost in the shadows of its walls.

They came on foot. In trucks with tires chewed to the wire. Some came wrapped in plastic. Some naked to the waist, their skin the shade of old leather, scarred with the signs of famine and fire. Children clung to their mothers. The old men squinted into the sun as if it bore meaning. They filled the place, not only spectators but participants, their faces cast up on the great board above, their every breath and movement tracked and measured and fed back in numbers and light.

Overhead, the sky rippled with signal. Drones hovered like carrion birds, blinking red and gold. Across the planet, screens blinked to life in metal halls and clay homes, and long-haunted subway hollows. They watched from the oilfields of the northern reach, from the flooded highlands, from the towers of glass and bone that still scraped the edges of heaven. The number of eyes was uncounted. A hunger behind every gaze.

The floor thudded with heavy doors rolling back. From the darkness came Gideon. He walked without fear or flourish, wearing a coat of black scale and ash, the insignia on his chest bright. His beard had gone to silver. The lines in his face cut sharp as old script. He looked once across the people. Then up. The sky had begun to cloud with smoke that was not from any fire.

Elarlu followed. Her robe hung loose. The wind lifted her hair and it swirled like ink in water. Her eyes were far. The crowd stirred at her presence. She did not speak. She didn't need to. She heard the voices again.

"He speaks for the earth," a voice inside her said. "He is the knife. You are the hunger."

A screech of metal followed, and the hush deepened.

They wheeled her out. The Oracle.

Strapped upright to a device of angles, seething metal, and rusted bolts. Naked, her body a ruin. Blood carved down her sides like river lines on alabaster. Her hair hung in mats, her mouth open, chewing at words that never fully came. Eyes rolled to white, but still, she moaned, gibbering into the air.

"I loved you," she said, but her tongue moved wrong. "I protected . . . you . . . the seed . . ." Then laughter, sudden and strangled. "He grows within me. In the dark! He is there! In me! You know he is—"

The crowd didn't cheer. They watched.

Another followed. The handmaid in the same rigging. Slighter. Her body less ruined. But her eyes vacant. One of Elarlu's handmaids. The woman the Oracle met in the darkened hallway. She did not speak. Only blinked slowly as if it pained her.

And then came the Voice.

Unbound. Smiling. Gallant.

She strode forward like a stone given breath, her robe shining with edges of crimson thread. Her face was clear, untouched, her hands folded before her. She bowed only once— to Gideon—and took her place among the others.

Gideon raised his arms.

The microphone clicked. The sound was a breath across a million speakers. His breath. He did not raise his voice.

"This," he said, voice raw like smoke off coals, "is the price of betrayal."

The crowd inhaled. The air trembled.

"There will be no quarter for those who poison the blood of the Dominion. No forgiveness for liars who wear the robes of the sacred."

He turned toward the Oracle. She was shivering. Her mouth twitched.

"The powder you fed to Elarlu," he said, voice cold as iron, "was meant to hollow her. To shatter her. To make her tremble under the weight of psychosis. But you were wrong."

He reached into his coat and drew out a vial, small and heavy with white powder that shimmered like crushed glass. He held it high. All the screens across the world showed the glint.

"It is not poison. No. It is a blessing. It does not unmake her. It opens her. The voices you feared—they guide us now."

He dipped a finger into the vial. Turned to Elarlu.

"Come, my Siren."

She stepped forward, robes trailing through the dust like the dead leaves of a burned forest. For a long moment, she hesitated, eyes dark and wild with something like fear or maybe desire. She looked at him—looked deep, searching for something she could not name.

Then she took the powder from his finger, slow and trembling, pressed it to her lips, and licked it away. Her eyes never left his. The smile that came was slow, terrible, and full of ruin. The crowd held their breath as the world seemed to shift beneath their feet.

"She hears them," Gideon said. "Voices from beyond the veil of what we call the world. Not the madness of what once was. Not the sickness. No. These whispers, unknown to her and to all of us, speak in the tongue of the divine. They do not lie. They do not comfort. They instruct. They command. And she, in her agony, is their vessel. Their chosen one."

He turned to the Oracle.

She whimpered low in her throat and shook her head, strands of blood-matted hair clinging to her cheeks like wet silk. Her lips moved, but no words came, only a soft animal keening. Her body sagged against the metal braces that held her upright, trembling with each breath.

At her feet lay a blade. Ceremonial. Ancient. Its edge dulled by time, but not mercy. He knelt and took it up, the hilt worn smooth, wrapped in cracked black leather gone soft from years of ritual and sweat. He turned it in his hand, the blade catching the light, the blood on the concrete reflecting back the faces of the damned.

The Oracle's eyes, milky with pain and loss, found him. Found his face. Something in her stilled. The last of her mind clawed its way to the surface like a drowning child. Her lips parted.

"Please," she whispered. "I only wanted to protect you. Something grows. Inside. It wasn't . . . for me. It was for you. I was chosen. Chosen to do this."

She hung there on the cold frame, arms strapped above her head, legs trembling beneath the slack weight of her body. Her skin was streaked with blood, fresh and dried, like old brushstrokes on pale stone. Her eyes, milk-glazed and roving, tried to find him in the light.

Gideon stood still. The blade in his hand did not shake.

He stepped forward and drove the steel into her belly, slow, deliberate. A wet sound, like fruit splitting. She gasped once, lips parted, teeth flecked red. Her body jerked, then sagged against the iron bracing. He twisted the knife, felt the resistance give way. Heat spilled over his hands, steaming in the air.

He pulled the blade free. Took a step back. Turned. The handmaid did not scream. He set the blade into her the same. Deep and true. His breath came hard through his teeth. The light above them flickered once.

"The Oracle is dead," he said turning to the crowd. His voice flat. Unadorned. "As is the demon child within her. Let it be known—the false prophet is silenced. The Siren is now keeper of the Echoers. And of all that is divine."

The Voice smiled. A smile that was not joy but something colder. A thing shaped by calculation. Beneath her, the world held its breath. Then it came. The roar. Not a sound but a force. A violence born of fervor. It rose like a furnace blaze catching dry grass, a bellow from the belly of the earth itself, millions of voices torn from their chests in unison.

"Gideon Rex! Gideon Rex! Gideon Rex!"

The cry beat the air like wings, shook steel and stone, rolled over oceans, and into the hearts of children who did not yet know the name they cried. And high above the coliseum, where the lights burned white and unblinking, did drones begin to stir. Hundreds. Thousands. They circled once, then again, small silver cruciforms in the sky, and with a sudden shudder, they fired their flares—red as blood, red as the Dominion's seal—screaming upward into the heavens like prayers set on fire.

"Gideon Rex! Gideon Rex! Gideon Rex!"

And Gideon stood there with Elarlu at his side. Arms folded across his chest like a man carved out of some older stone. He did not move.

"Let them howl," she whispered to him. "Let them tremble beneath the sound of their own worship."

He stepped back from the microphone, slow, deliberate, his boots ringing hollow on the stone dais. The light fell hard on his shoulders. His shadow stretched long behind him like something living. The crowd rose as one body, arms lifted, mouths open wide in a cry that was less praise than hunger. A need to be filled with him. He turned his head slightly, not to see them but to let them see the line of his jaw, the stillness of his gaze. They screamed louder. He let it build.

"Let it crest," another whisper.

He lifted one hand, then lowered it again.

"Not yet. Let them burn. Let them reach out with everything they were."

When he spoke, they would fall to their knees not from fear but from want. And still, he did not speak.

Until.

"Now, my love," came the whisper. "Now."

"You have wondered why your children go hungry," he said, his voice cutting across the air like the blade of something long buried. "Why the wheat dies in the field, black as tar before the scythe can touch it. Why the rains pass you by and the earth splits beneath your feet like old bone."

Murmurs in the crowd, low at first. Faces turned. Some shouted. Others only stared, their mouths half open, their hands curled at their sides like they'd forgotten how to pray.

"You have turned on each other," he said. "Called out your neighbors. Even your kin. Those who whispered dark things. You cursed the names of your elders and the gods you once knew by heart. You have bled for answers. Dug graves looking for truth. Cleansed the land of those who could not see the truth."

He stepped forward. His voice grew. Hardened.

"But hear," he said. "What we now face is not your fault. The rot is not in you. The sickness comes from them. Those across the seas. From the ones who crawl in the shadows. Disbelievers. Those who would rather watch the world burn than see it strong. They have friends. Some that walk among you. Smiling. Whispering. And they have dared—" his voice cracked, rose, broke again into a bellow, "they have dared to send a traitor into my own house."

He struck his chest with a closed fist.

"My own house!" he yelled.

The crowd fell into a hush. A kind of reverent dread. The silence of prey before the strike. Not even the children stirred. Above them, the sound of drones swept low over the heads of the gathered like swarms of mechanized locusts, their wings screaming, the air torn by their passage. Then the screen behind the dais flared to life. On it burned the continent. The shape of Australia ringed in fire. Flickering like a prophecy. The flames danced in their eyes.

"While we suffer," he said, his voice dry as sand and just as patient, "they build their sanctuaries across the seas . . . in the Silent Land. Their fortress-cities behind glass and steel. They feast while your bones dry out and snap like old kindling. Their skies run blue and their fields go untouched by the ash. You bury your dead beneath dust and they grow orchards."

The image on the great screen shifted. Rows of green unbroken by blight. Trees heavy with fruit. Children with full faces and teeth white as pearls. Livestock fat and dumb in the shade, tails flicking in lazy rhythm. A gasp moved through the crowd like wind through a canyon. Some began to sob, the kind of sound that comes when memory and hunger mix.

Elarlu stood unmoving, but she heard it again. The whisper coiled in the hollows of her mind, cold and clear.

"Let them feed on hope," it told her. "Just enough to kill the shame."

Gideon turned slow. No flourish. Just the movement of a man who carried no need for haste.

"We now know the source," he said. "The plague—it is no work of God. No curse from the old world. It was made by hand. Shaped in labs in the Silent Land. Meant to seek out what does not belong to them. It spares their soil. It knows the blood."

A rustle passed through the crowd like wind in bone-dry wheat, a sound not born of movement alone but of something deeper, ancestral, the murmur of a species remembering its own end. A woman brought her hand to her lips and stared as if she'd forgotten what a mouth was for. A man buckled at the knees. Another caught him without looking, eyes still fixed forward, unblinking. The air hung thick, not just with heat but with the heat of bodies pressed in judgment, the breath of thousands thick with fear and something more—fury fed on fear, a hunger turned inward.

"They did this to us," Gideon said. His voice low and flat as hammered iron. "They. The non-believers from across the waters."

Then came the scream. High and wild and cleaved clean of language. A scream not made but born. It split the sky and seemed to find no end, the kind of sound that lives inside a person long before they ever give it voice. Not pain. Not protest. Just the raw, wordless shape of what truth sounds like when it can no longer hide.

"They poisoned our harvests," he said. His voice low. Certain. "They stole our children's futures. And they would have us die quietly. Unseen. Forgotten like dust beneath their boots."

He paused. The silence stretched. Even the wind held its breath.

"No more," he said.

The crowd erupted. A thunder born of blood and fire and years of swallowed rage. The sound rolled over the stone like the sea come inland. A voice older than language. Rising and crashing against the walls of the world.

"No more," Gideon said again. "We will not fade into the ash while they dance in green meadows. While they sing their songs beneath broad trees and let the wind comb their hair like children untouched by war. While they drink from clean rivers and plant seeds in soil we bled to save."

He stood still. The others watched him.

"They think us gone," he said. "Ghosts in the earth. But we are not gone. We've only been waiting. Let them sing. We'll cut the song from their mouths. Let them dance. We'll show them the steps that end in flame. Let them drink their water. We'll hold them under until their breath stops. We will not fade into the ash! We will not fade into the ash!"

He lifted his hand.

"The Dominion must rise. We will take what they have stolen. Not for conquest. For survival!"

The ground shook with the chant.

"Gideon Rex! Gideon Rex! Gideon Rex!"

Elarlu's fingers curled in upon themselves like claws grasping at something just out of reach. Her breath came shallow. The voices had grown louder. No longer whispers thread through the marrow of her skull but howls—screams laced in melody, shrill with prophecy. They rose in a choir of agony and splendor, each note a blade, each chord a wound.

"Blood for soil," they cried inside her. "Fire for food. You are the mouth of the storm."

She did not flinch. Her eyes burned, the whites gone to silver. Her lips parted slightly as if to answer.

The crowd roared. A great thrashing sound, wild and full of hunger. It swept over the stone tiering like water breaking free from the high places. Dust lifted from the ground. Men wept. Women shouted until their throats bled. All of it crashing like judgment at the feet of their gods.

Gideon stepped forward into the wind that rose off the plain like breath drawn from the earth itself. His coat flared behind him, heavy with dust. He stood at the edge of the platform, beneath the dead sun, and looked out upon the sea of upturned faces.

"I call upon every man who has held a rifle," he said, his voice cold and carried far. "Every woman who has buried a child in soil too thin to keep it. Every youth who has never tasted the sweetness of fruit nor seen a tree whose branches bore anything but ash."

The words fell into silence.

"I call you to war," he said. "War!"

He let it hang there, wind catching the hem of his coat. No one moved.

"And when we take the Silent Land," he said, "we will plant it new. We will salt their altars and burn their false temples to the bedrock. We will lay their dead in furrows and seed the ground with their blood. And from that earth will grow a world without chains."

He looked to Elarlu.

She stood still beside him, her hands clasped before her, lips moving in silent prayer. Her eyes wide as if beholding something just beyond the veil. A shape. A promise. A warning.

Gideon leaned into the microphone again, the wind stealing some of the sound.

"We will not go quietly," he said. "We will not starve while they sing."

He raised both hands then, fingers spread, palms upward.

"The Dominion rises!" he screamed.

The crowd surged like a tide breaking its levee. Across the hemispheres, the screens flickered and crackled, carrying fire and noise into markets and hovels and bunkers underground. In some cities, the power failed. In others, the sound was doubled, trebled, turned to a roar of static and breathless awe.

"Gideon Rex! Gideon Rex! Gideon Rex!"

Elarlu swayed.

"They hear you," she said. Her voice was thin. But no one heard her.

Gideon turned his head. The wind stirred his hair.

"What?"

Her pupils vanished a moment, eyes white as stones. Then they came back, black and deep.

"They hear you," she said again. "They want what you have promised."

The sky cracked with a sound like old bone breaking. No rain came. Drones scattered like insects from a fire. The sun flickered once in its long dying. Then it was still.

"Gideon Rex! Gideon Rex! Gideon Rex!"

The chant rose again like some old liturgy dredged from the pit of man's first hunger, low at first and then louder, swelling in dreadful cadence.

"Gideon Rex! Gideon Rex! Gideon Rex!"

A sound not born of hope but of need, of fury, of the desperate. They stamped their feet and clutched at one another, mouths wide, faces raw with dust and spit, the chant warping into something not quite human. Mothers held infants aloft like offerings. Old men wept and screamed. The sick fell to their knees and kissed the black iron ground.

"Gideon Rex! Gideon Rex! Gideon Rex!"

It echoed through the broken towers and sang from the cracked teeth of loudspeakers. It was not praise. It was a possession.

Deep beneath the Spire, past the metal lifts and blackstone corridors and the soundless hush of the lower labs where the lights hummed and the air itself tasted of copper and ozone, Malachar stood before the screen. Watching as the latest variant, that thing that would not die, pulsed. A slow pulse. A quiet living. Like the throb of something that ought not live but did.

"It knows what we do and counters it," she said.

Her voice no more than air moved in the throat. It faded into the cold.

Behind her stood a figure. Gorgrath. A shape hewn from silence. The cloak hung black, untouched by light, as if it drank it. She did not move. She did not speak. She watched. Her eyes were on the screen.

In the coliseum above, ash drifted. It spiraled downward from the broken ribs of the dome. Gideon stood alone on the shattered stone, his coat cut by the wind. He turned his face to the east. The sun there was a pale disc, smothered by the rising smoke. It looked like something drowned.

Elarlu placed her hand on his arm. She said nothing for a long moment.

"They will come," she told him. "Those of the Silent Land. And others. They will come for you. There will be green flame."

He looked at her. His eyes were red from the wind, from the fire, from the waiting.

"Come for us?" he asked.

She did not respond.

Somewhere across the vast sea in a room scrubbed sterile of sound and conscience, a man removed his headset and laid it down like something dead. He turned to the window and watched the green hills standing dumb beyond the glass. He pressed the button.

"It's begun," he whispered. "They'll soon be here."

And though no shot had yet been fired, war was already loose across the Dominion.

10 *The Burning Choir*

The chamber lay in darkness. What light there was came from pale globes strung on wire, their hum low and uncertain as if the things had no wish to see what the room had borne witness to. Smoke drifted through the stillness. Not from fire. From incense long burned down to its bones. The stench of it sharp. A holiness soured to something near profane.

They came without word. No messengers sent. No bells rung. Called and come. The ones he trusted. The ones who knew. Each of them silent. Each of them watchful. Not one among them late. Not one with the gall to ask why.

Gideon stood before the long table of stone. Behind him, the Dominion's banner, black with the silver and gold gear emblem surrounded by a laurel wreath. His hands were folded. His eyes wandered the room like a hunter deciding which beast must next be culled.

He said, "The traitor is dead. Let it be known among you— this is the fate of those who forsake the path."

"Salve Rex," a few whispered.

No one moved. A slow shifting of breath passed between them, low as sand across stone. Morgar stared with eyes like chisels at the hollow where the Oracle had once sat, a place now stained dark with what had been inside her.

"She bore the mark," Morgar said. His voice like wind through sand. "You made her. Shaped her in your image. The people will speak. The words they choose may not favor you."

"The people speak the words I place in their mouths," Gideon said. "Remember that. And when there are no words to give them, they'll only remember one thing. Fear. That will be enough."

"Salve Rex," came the whisper once more.

A stir among the gathered. Elarlu. The Siren. She stood. Tall. Her crimson robes whispering against the stone floor like serpents in sand.

"Some here may have known what she was up to," she told the others. "The darkness in her soul. She tried to take my life. She was not loyal. She was misguided. And the seed—that which she carried. It was not hers to carry."

Malgoth, his great shoulders bent like iron under strain, looked to her with something near grief.

"I wonder if the seed inside of her turned her against us," he said, his eyes growing small. "On the platform, she wept as she fell from this life. She said it. Herself. She believed she was chosen."

Elarlu's eyes found him, cold and unblinking as stones in a riverbed. The hush in the chamber was absolute. Her voice, when it came, was low and edged with scorn.

"Belief is cheap, Malgoth. Even the rats in the gutters believe in bread. She believed, yes. She believed herself above the order. Above the Dominion. Above me." She let the words hang, her gaze sweeping the silent hall. "Faith without obedience is nothing. You know this. Do not forget."

She sat down, the red hem of her robe trailing like a wound. Her shadow fell across him. "So, she wept as she fell from this life. Good. Let her tears be a lesson to any who would covet what is not theirs. That seed she clutched was a cursed thing. It unmade her."

Her mouth twisted, disdainful. "Do you mourn for her, Malgoth? If so, then mourn also for your own blindness. Let this be a warning. To everyone here. The next to betray me will not find the fire so merciful."

She turned from him, her voice rising so all could hear: "Let none mistake mercy for weakness. Let none mistake their own hunger for destiny. The Dominion endures because of our actions. The messages we send. Remember that."

The silence that followed was like a blade pressed to every throat.

"She was not chosen," said the Voice, folding her robed arms like the wings of a carrion bird. "Her mind told her she was. But she was not."

They turned then to the Voice. Not Elarlu. But the Voice. The enforcer of law. Her eyes glittered like flint.

"She tried to poison one of us," the Voice said. "Remember that. She knew exactly what she was doing. Treason is not always with blade or gun. It hides in the womb, waiting."

"Voice, you're telling us that thing inside her—that's what turned her? Malgoth asked.

The Voice's gaze did not waver. Stillness lay over the chamber, absolute, the air thick with the memory of accusation and the promise of violence. She let the silence remain, let it coil around their hearts.

"The thing—that seed within her was only a vessel," the Voice said. Her words dropped into the silence and did not come back. "Treason is not born of flesh alone. It is born of hunger. Of want. Of the emptiness that festers when faith is gone."

She moved forward in her chair, her shadow stretching long across the stone floor. "She carried that emptiness. Nursed it. Fed it until it grew teeth and turned on one of us. The Oracle saw the rot. Chose to embrace it."

Malgoth's mouth worked, but no words came.

The Voice's eyes were cold as winter rain. "You ask if the seed made her a traitor. I tell you, Malgoth, the seed is nothing. The will is everything. She chose her path. She chose to betray. And now she is dust."

She looked to the others, her voice low and final. "Treason is not a thing of blood or birth. It is a thing of choice. And choice is the only law that matters."

The silence that followed was not broken but deepened as if the world itself had turned away. Even the machines that hummed in the walls seemed to still. Malachar, her eyes glowing faint blue, tilted her head as though listening to something outside their range.

"This meeting is not to rehash what was done," Gideon said. "This is not judgment. Judgment has passed. This is about what comes next."

"Salve Rex," a few whispered.

But there came a voice from the far end. Grix. His fingers trembled at the table's edge. "Then speak it plain," he said. "The Silent Land."

Gideon nodded. "The Green Womb of the world. The last wild Eden. It will fall. We will make it ours."

"Salve Rex," the whispers louder.

"It is untouched," Grix said. "Fed by rains that know no cloud machine. Their soil does not sleep under plastics."

"Then it is wasted," said Morgan.

"Wasted?" said Zexus. Her voice was smooth as oil and twice as cold. "No. Not wasted. It is hidden. And what is hidden must be brought into the light or it festers."

Morgan turned to her. "So, you agree then. You counsel war?"

"I counsel inevitability."

Gorgrath had been silent until now. The faint light, her coat swallowing her form like shadow incarnate.

"We must be careful," she said. Her eyes on Elarlu. "She believed the child she carried was the Rex come again. She believed it with the whole of her mind and the ruin of her soul. That none but she could shield the child from the Siren. From us."

She paused. The silence drawn out like thread from a carcass. Her gaze held. Cold.

"But I speak a warning. Dire. Before we drop a fist upon the Silent Land, we must turn it inward. The Oracle has been speaking. Not with voice. With signal. She sent her words on frequencies unsanctioned. Scripture that isn't scripture. Love cloaked in madness. "I fear she's infected the Echoers. Their thoughts not their own."

Elarlu did not flinch. She watched Gorgrath like a flame watches dry kindling.

"She prayed for chaos," Gorgrath went on. "And the Echoers . . . too many of them listened. Something needs to be done."

"Should we dispose of one of the priestesses?" said Kul'gath. His voice low. Almost kind. Like a man offering mercy he didn't possess. "A warning to the others?" He paused. The smile that came was twisted, without joy. "Problem is, you burn a priestess, you risk lighting the whole damn temple."

"I do not burn to warn," said Gideon. "I burn to cleanse."

The light played strange across his face, carving it from the dark like some idol half-remembered. The others watched. No one spoke.

"The Echoers will be dealt with," he said. He looked to Elarlu. "A new voice leads. Let the voice speak. Let it sing. If the Siren sees rot, there'll be cleansing. She'll see to it. She'll not ask. She'll not wait."

There was quiet. Then, the whispers. "Salve Rex."

Elarlu spoke again. Her voice was clear, hypnotic. As though no blood had ever stained her robes.

"The Oracle is dead. The people watched her die. Let fear run its course. Let them bury their questions and rot with them.

The future waits. The Silent Land waits. This room must look forward."

A beat passed. Then another.

Kul'gath ran a finger down the silver tip of his cane.

"We've removed the Oracle, the soul from the faith," he said. "And we replace it with what? Strategy? Steel? A campaign?"

"We replace it," said Elarlu. "With an heir."

The silence that followed was near to stillness. A hush that settled not from peace but from the things it threatened to wake.

They turned then. All of them. Toward Elarlu.

She laid her hand upon her belly. There was no rise there. No shape. Only the thought of shape. The promise of it yet to come.

"You expect them to believe," said Grix, "After all this? In an unborn child?"

"They will believe," said Gideon. "They simply need hunger. And fear. And the absence of choice."

"You would have us rule continue to rule by scarcity?" Grix's eyes gleamed with something between defiance and exhaustion.

"I would have us rule," said Gideon, "by whatever means necessary."

A silence settled then, thick as pitch until the whispers sounded. "Salve Rex."

Gideon stood. He walked slowly, his boots echoing across the stone. He paused before the empty chair left by the Oracle.

"She said she loved me," he said.

No one answered.

"She said she heard my voice in the dark. That she'd carry me into light."

He turned then, and there was no softness in him.

"I will not be carried. I will not be worshipped as a god in white robes. I am not myth. I am war. And this world, this broken husk, will be born anew in fire."

"Salve Rex."

His voice rose but did not waver.

"We will take the Silent Land. We will tear their roots from the soil and plant our own. Those who follow will eat. Those who resist will bleed. There is no other path. Do any here disagree?"

He looked among them.

None spoke.

But within them, some of them at least, something shifted. A stone rolled deeper into the pit. A crack appeared across the monolith. They did not show it. Not yet. But the fire had burned through more than just the Oracle.

Gideon turned to the door. His voice was low, unhurried.

"Prepare the fleets," he said. "We will call on our best. I want deployment plans by week's end. We strike before the new moon."

He looked to Elarlu, his eyes unreadable.

"Cleanse the Echoers as you see fit," he said.

"Yes, my Rex."

"And give the people what they crave."

She turned, that smile slow as dusk, something old behind it. "And what is that?"

"You," he said. "You, my Siren."

They all stood. Heads bent. "Salve Rex."

And he was gone then, the door closing behind him with a hush like falling ash.

The room remained.

Elarlu was first to move. She adjusted her sleeves, the gesture as deliberate as it was performative.

"We are the future," she said. "Not her. Not the dead. What was done—let it die. Tomorrow belongs to us."

Gorgrath tilted her head again. "If tomorrow listens."

Elarlu did not respond.

The circle broke then, one by one. They slipped into the dark like ghosts leaving a grave.

Morgar stayed behind. He traced a fingertip along the edge of the table, eyes fixed on the Oracle's chair.

"You chose spectacle," he murmured.

His voice was lost to stone.

Then he, too, was gone.

And the chamber, bereft of gods and monsters, stood empty.

Only empty chairs remained.

***

The room stank of scorched wire and the bitter sting of white powder. Elarlu sat at the head of the iron table. Her fingers moved along the rusted channels cut deep into the metal where blood once ran and dried. A silver vial lay on its side beside her, empty.

Across the chamber, several Echoers hung in chains. Their eyes were hollow. Their faces broken like pottery under heel.

She dipped her thumb into the powder and rubbed it along her gums. It was her food. Sustenance.

The powder bit down like fire. The world came into focus. The walls hummed. The air drew in tight.

"Speak your lies," she said.

The first Echoer—a woman with a shorn scalp and eyes that refused to blink—lifted her chin. "The Oracle spoke truth. The child was the Rex reborn. You feared him. You feared the light he'd—"

Elarlu rose. Her crimson robes whispered against the stone as she crossed the room. She backhanded the woman. The crack echoed. A tooth skittered across the floor.

"Truth," Elarlu said, "is a blade that cuts both ways. Yours has dulled."

She turned to a group of Enforcers and nodded once. They dragged the woman to the center of the chamber, where a grate in the floor yawned black. The Echoer did not struggle. Her lips moved in silent prayer as they forced her to her knees.

"You think your faith to her shields you," Elarlu said. She scooped a pinch of powder from the vial and let it fall into the dark. "It doesn't. Faith is a currency. And you . . . you are bankrupt."

The Enforcers shoved the woman's face toward the grate. Elarlu crouched, her robes pooling around her like spilled wine. "Breathe deep," she whispered.

The woman inhaled. A sound like dry leaves followed. Then screaming. She writhed, her fingers clawing at her throat as the powder burned through her. Elarlu watched until the movements ceased.

"Next," she said.

A boy—no older than sixteen—was thrust forward. His hands trembled. The chain between his wrists chimed like a dead bell.

"Please," he said. "I only repeated her words. I didn't know—"

Elarlu tilted her head. "Words are weapons. Yours have been turned against me." She dipped two fingers into the vial and pressed them to the boy's lips. "Eat."

He gagged but swallowed. His eyes widened as the powder took hold. Blood trickled from his nose.

"What do you believe in?" Elarlu asked.

"I don't know," he stammered in fear. "I only followed what she said—"

"She said nothing. She was nothing." Elarlu gripped his jaw. "You cling to ghosts. And ghosts . . ." She released him. ". . . burn in flame."

The boy collapsed, convulsing. His screams merged with the clank of chains as the remaining Echoers strained against their bonds. Elarlu turned to them.

"Every rebellion needs a martyr," she said. "But martyrs die. And the living forget." She lifted the vial. The powder glinted like crushed bone. "Who among you wishes to be forgotten?"

Silence.

She laughed—a sound like wire drawn taut. "What? No volunteers? How . . . pragmatic."

An Enforcer stepped forward, dragging a man with a scarred face and hollow cheeks. The man spat at Elarlu's feet.

"You're poison," he hissed. "The child was to rise. The Rex—"

Elarlu struck him. The powder on her knuckles seared his skin. He howled.

"What she carried was a lie," she said. "A lie for fools." She grabbed his hair and forced his head back. "And you . . . you're too foolish to know the truth."

She emptied the vial into his mouth. He choked. Thrashed. Fell.

The remaining Echoers began to shout—a cacophony of pleas and curses. Elarlu let the noise wash over her. She closed her eyes and saw the child inside of her. Small. Silent. Waiting.

When she opened them, the Enforcers were staring.

"Clean this up," she said.

They obeyed.

Alone, Elarlu leaned against the iron table. Her hands shook. She fumbled in her robes for another vial but found none. The world blurred at the edges. Shadows writhed.

A voice—Gideon's—slithered through her mind. "You burn too bright. You'll consume yourself."

She smiled. Let him watch. Let them all watch.

The door swung inward on rusted hinges. Morgar stood in the threshold, the dim light behind him stretching his shadow across the stone. His eyes moved slow over the walls. The blood thick. Fresh. Running down like rain drawn wrong.

"Efficient," he said.

Elarlu did not turn. "You disapprove?"

"Disapproval is a luxury. One I cannot afford."

She laughed. The sound echoed, hollow. "Nor can any of us."

He stepped closer. "The powder," he said. "Be careful. It's too sweet. It'll kill you. Death doesn't take kindly to being called."

"Death?" She faced him. Her eyes were black pools. "We're all dead, Morgar. Some of us just haven't finished dying."

He left without another word.

Elarlu sank into her chair. The chamber spun. The shadows whispered. She pressed her palms to the table and waited for the world to still.

It did not.

But the child waited.

The weeks unspooled like a bloodied thread. Elarlu's crusade carved through the Echoers, their ranks thinned to whispers. The white powder sang in her veins, sharpening her sight to a predator's gleam. She moved through the ash-choked corridors of power like a blade through smoke, Enforcers at her heels—loyal now, or near enough, their resolve tempered by vials of that same pale dust. New converts knelt where rebels once stood, their eyes hollowed by hunger and the powder's cold fire. They spoke her words back to her as liturgy.

"Balance through purge. Strength through surrender."

The chambers reeked of scorched flesh and the metallic tang of devotion. Morgar watched from the shadows, his silence a language she no longer cared to parse. At night, the child haunted her—a flicker in the static, small hands pressed to the mucous membrane of her womb. Eyes wide open. Gideon's voice hissed a warning. She smothered with another pinch of powder.

"You are the flame," he whispered. "You are the wick."

She laughed, her gums raw, her tongue stained ghost-white. The dead piled high, but the living bowed lower. And always, beneath the hum of surrender, the child waited. Unseen. A splinter in the meat of the world.

***

In the shadowed wings of the city square, Elarlu uncorked a small glass vial. The powder within was white as bone, fine as sifted ash. She dipped a trembling finger and raised it to her lips. Licking it slow. Her eyes closing. The gesture was hungry, obscene, as if she'd not eaten in days. The taste made her shudder. She pressed the empty vial to her breast and walked into the light.

The silence in the square was raw. It pressed upon the crowd, thick and suffocating as if the world itself had drawn a breath and would not let it go. The Voice watched her from the shadows. Her own face hooded. Unreadable. Nearby, Malachar.

Elarlu stood on the stage. Body trembling. Her mouth open in a rictus that might have been joy or pain. The crowd's awe began to curdle into fear. Somewhere in the mass of bodies, a child began to cry, the sound thin and lost in the vastness.

The sky hung down like a weight. Swollen and dark. Meant to crush the earth beneath it. The screens behind Elarlu twitched in their frames, as did all the thousands of others from around the world. That golden light guttered and choked. Elarlu's face blinked in and out, her features smeared to noise, and when she came back, she was worse. Like something half-remembered and wrong.

Malachar's hand went to the knife. The one on her belt. The one always there. Her eyes stayed fixed on the dais.

"They're waiting for a sign," she said.

"She'll give it," the Voice said. "Patience."

Her gaze was fixed on Elarlu. She saw the sweat on her brow, the way her fingers curled against the wood. She remembered her before the powder, before the hunger, when she had been only a woman, not yet a god.

In the crowd, Zexus slipped about, her steps careful, her head bowed within a black cloak. She reached the edge of the square and ducked into a narrow alley. The city's heart beat slow and sickly here. The walls slick with old rain and the stink of rot. She crouched in the shadow of a broken archway and opened her notebook.

Her hand shook as she wrote.

The symptoms have worsened. Hallucinations, insomnia, paranoia. She speaks of visions—the Silent Land, the sea, the burning gates. The powder is doing its job. I fear she will not last.

She tore the page free, folded it twice, and slipped it into the lining of her coat. She would pass it to the courier tonight if the city's patrols allowed. She listened for footsteps, for the scrape of boots on stone, but heard only the distant roar of the crowd.

She thought of the Silent Land. The last free place, some said. She had never seen it, but she dreamed of it often: a land of red earth and endless sky, where the Dominion's reach could not follow. She wondered if it was real, or only another vision, another lie.

Back in the square, Elarlu stirred. She pushed herself upright, her limbs trembling. The crowd gasped. She raised her hands, palms open, as if to bless them or curse them.

"Children of the Dominion," she said. "I bring you the Benediction of Hunger."

"That's it," the Voice said. "The sign."

The crowd shuddered as one. Some wept. Some fell to their knees. The Voice watched her with a face carved from stone. Malachar stood arms crossed, eyes narrowed. Zexus down the alleyway now, her notebook pressed to her chest, her gaze darting about the shadows and the men who crawled about within the darkness.

Even in the distance, she could hear Elarlu's words spilling out, wild and uneven. "We are chosen. We are the fire that will burn away the world's rot. Take the Silent Land." She stopped. Her breath ragged. "You have known suffering. You have known want. But I tell you now—sacrifice is the path to salvation. The flesh must be offered. The soul must be emptied. Only then will the gates open."

The crowd murmured, a thousand voices rising and falling like the tide. She raised her arms.

"I have seen it," she said. "I have seen the new world. I have seen the gates open. I have seen the sea burn and the sky split and the land beyond—"

Her voice broke. She staggered, caught herself on the podium. The screen flickered, her image shuddering. She laughed, high and thin.

"You doubt me," she hissed. "You think I am mad. But I am the mouth of God. I am the knife at your throat. I am the hunger that will save you."

The crowd howled. Some tore at their clothes. Some beat their breasts.

"You have seen me fall," she said. "You have seen me rise. I am the fire that will not be quenched. I am the hunger that will not be sated."

A voice called out from the throng, hoarse and desperate. "What must we do?"

Elarlu's head snapped toward the sound. Her eyes glittered. "You must give. You must offer. You must empty yourselves, as I have emptied myself. Only then will the gates open. Only then will the world be made new."

The crowd surged, a tide of bodies pressing closer to the stage. Some reached for her, their fingers clawing at the air. Others fell to their knees, their faces pressed to the filthy stone.

"I have seen the gates open," she cried. "I have seen the land beyond. The Silent Land. The last refuge. I have seen it burn. Green flame."

They wept and writhed in the dust, the broken and the mad, the hollow-eyed faithful and the lost alike. Some tore their garments. Some their skin. Their voices rose not in unison but in a chaos of pleading and praise, a sound without beginning or end. Children clung to their mothers. Old men beat their chests. The air stank of sweat and blood and old hunger. They pressed toward her as if she were a hole in the world through which something terrible and holy might emerge. No one turned away. Not a soul. They knelt or crawled or stood stunned, and in their eyes, there was no doubt, only fire.

Malachar leaned close to the Voice. "If she asks for blood, they'll give it."

She nodded once, slow and grave. "An easy ask."

A memory flickered behind her eyes: the first days of the Dominion, the promises, the hunger. She had seen men die for less.

Elarlu's voice rose, thin and sharp as a blade. "You are the chosen! You are the sacrifice! The gates will open and the world will burn. And from the ashes, we will rise!"

She began to laugh, a sound that rattled through the square like broken glass. The crowd echoed her, their voices wild and unmoored.

Zexus pressed her back to the wall, her breath coming fast. She heard the laughter, the cries, the madness. She closed her eyes and saw the faces of the Silent Land's agents: grim, determined, afraid. She wondered if her warnings would reach them in time.

The Voice and Malachar watched the chaos. The city stretched out around them, a labyrinth of ruin and hope.

Malachar spoke first. "We can't hold this much longer."

The Voice said nothing at first, then turned to Malachar, her face hard. "If she dies, they'll tear us apart. And, if she lives, she'll tear us apart." Her eyes held nothing. "We made her. No choice in the matter. The Oracle carried his child. We couldn't allow that."

"You mean you couldn't allow that."

"It should be me who carries his seed."

Malachar watched her. "You love him?"

The Voice turned her face. That small turning told her all.

"And you knew nothing of the Siren," Malachar said. "Of what's in her now."

She shook her head, her mouth bent like something gone bad. "If I had, I would've ended them both."

Malachar looked at her. "Now, you made a weapon, and it's slipped the leash."

She nodded. "Yes. But there's still the powder."

Malachar shrugged. "Indeed. But it's working. It's working—too well. They listen to her every breath."

They watched as Elarlu staggered around the stage, her followers reaching for her, their hands slick with sweat and tears.

The Voice's words were slow and heavy. "If the Silent Land falls, there will be nothing left."

Malachar's gaze was cold. "He will have everything."

The crowd began to chant. The words were strange, guttural, half-remembered prayers from a time before the Dominion.

Elarlu staggered near to the edge of the dais, her arms outstretched. The gold light flickered, casting her shadow long and monstrous across the square.

"I have seen the gates open," she cried. "I have seen the land beyond. I have seen the end."

The crowd answered her, their voices rising in a single, terrible note.

***

Zexus slipped from the square with her coat drawn tight and her notebook clutched to her ribs like a relic. Her heart beat hard in her chest, a frantic thing. The city stretched before her like something wounded. Alleys narrow and crooked as scars, walls pitted and stained, doors bowed by the years and the rain. The gutters choked with trash and old paper and the stink of rot. Hunger lived in the air. A thing you could smell. A thing with teeth.

She passed them, crouched in the doorways. The lost. The thinned. Their faces drawn tight over bone. Eyes that gleamed not with hope but the memory of it. Children who watched her with the gaze of men too long gone to dream. The hunger was everywhere. It sat on their shoulders. It turned their prayers to whispers. The air itself remembered bread and wept for it.

She thought of the powder. The ash-white stuff on Elarlu's tongue. She thought of the thirst it brought and how it hollowed the belly and turned want into gospel. The world had shrunk down to a single ache, and the ache was a weapon now. Bent and honed and fed to the masses.

Near the end of the alleyway, she paused beneath a broken lamp. The sun was setting, the sky bruised and swollen, clouds dragging their bellies across the rooftops. There was a small, ramshackle house. She knocked at the warped door. Once. Twice.

Three times. The sound was small, but in the hush of the dying day, it carried.

A voice whispered from the darkness beyond. "Who comes?"

Zexus drew a breath. "The wind from the south."

The door opened a crack, yellow light bleeding out. The man who stood there was little more than a shadow, his face lost in the gloom. She saw the glint of a knife at his hip, the careful way he watched her hands.

"I have information," she said. "Bring him here."

He looked at her.

"All this madness," she said. Her voice was quiet. Certain. "It has to end. We have to go back. Before the ruin. Before the hunger became holy. Mankind wasn't meant to live like this."

He looked at her. Nodded once. The gesture was curt and final. "It will take some time. But he will come."

He vanished down the alleyway, his footfalls swallowed by the city's endless hunger.

Zexus closed the door behind him. She leaned against the wall, eyes shut, listening to the city's heartbeat—slow, ragged, the sound of something dying and too proud to say so.

From the square, Elarlu's voice rose, ragged and triumphant, echoing off stone. The crowd answered, their cries flung skyward, praise or protest, it no longer mattered.

The world turned, grinding its slow and terrible course. The gates waited, silent and hungry. And far to the south, across the black and boiling sea, the Silent Land prepared. Iron moved beneath the sands.

***

The room was dark. Bare but for the table. Rough stone walls blotched with the smoke of old fires. Time had stained them. You could see it. If you looked.

But there were eyes.

Small ones. Set into the walls like seeds in clay. No one ever saw them. Not really. But they were there. Watching. Everything.

A lamp hung down from the ceiling, casting its light in a sickly yellow ring that reached no further than it had to.

The wind muttered beyond the walls. A sound like something lost and gone on.

Gideon stood at the table's head, both hands flat on the wood. His face was a ledger of all that had passed and all that would. Worn by cold and loss. Scarred by what men must choose when there is no choice. Across from him sat Morgar, his eyes sharp as knives, his mind able to cut deeper than any sword. Beside Morgar was Malgoth, shoulders like a mountain, a voice that could shatter stone. And at the far end, in the shadows, sat Gorgrath, her presence as silent and deadly as the night itself.

Gideon looked around the table, his gaze settling on each in turn. "We stand on the edge of the world," he said. "The Silent Land lies before us. Untouched. Unbroken. A fortress of earth and sky. They think themselves safe. But they are not."

Morgar leaned forward, his fingers steepled. "Their defenses are strong, but not impenetrable." But even as he said that, he hesitated. Gideon would not want to hear the truth. "The sea is their shield, but it is also their cage. We will break it."

"Our land machines. Our harvesters," Malgoth grunted. "We've turned them into war machines. Great wheels of iron and fire. They will crush the earth beneath them and the bones of any who stand in their path."

"The drones will swarm like locusts." Gorgrath's voice was low, almost a whisper. "Eyes in the sky. Death from above and below. They will find their prey and leave nothing behind."

Gideon nodded.

"The plan is simple, then," he said. "We strike by sea and air. The great ships will carry the machines and the men. The drones will clear the skies and the shores. The land machines will follow, unstoppable. We will bring the Dominion's hunger to their last refuge."

Victor's eyes gleamed. "And the people? The defenders?"

"They will break," Malgoth said. "They have no hope. No choice. No weapons to match ours. We will show them the futility of resistance."

Gorgrath's smile was thin and sharp. "And those who flee will find no sanctuary. The Wraith moves in shadows. We will hunt them to the ends of the earth."

"This is not just a conquest," Gideon said. His voice dropped. An eyebrow lifted. "It is a reckoning. The Silent Land will fall. And with it, the last light of freedom."

They sat in silence then, for just a moment, listening to the sea as it whispered still, patient, and unyielding.

The map lay sprawled across the table, a vast canvas of ochre and green, edged with the endless blue of the ocean. Pins and markers dotted its surface, each a promise of fire and steel.

Morgar traced a finger along the coast. "Here. The northern beaches. Sparse defenses. The dunes are shallow. We land the first wave under cover of darkness. Drones will blind their watchers."

"Once the machines roll ashore, nothing will stand," Malgoth sneered. "Our reforged harvesters of death will roll across the land. Their blades will cut through earth and bone alike."

Gorgrath leaned close to the map, her eyes cold and calculating. "The defenders will scatter. The cities will fall one by one. We will pick them off like rats."

Gideon's hand hovered over the map. "The great port at Sydney. The heart of their resistance. We take it last. When they are broken and desperate."

Morgar nodded. "Their leaders will hide there. We will flush them out."

"And when they come to fight," Malgoth growled, "they will find only death."

In the shadows, eyes flicked. "The Wraith will see to that," Gorgrath said.

The room grew colder as the night deepened. Those around the table spoke little now, each lost in the grim certainty of what was to come.

Gideon's voice broke the silence. "We move. Have ships ready. Have the machines fueled. Have the men in place. Before the new moon"

Morgar's smile was a blade's edge. "They await our orders. The Silent Land will burn."

"Let them try to stand against the Iron Fist." Malgoth's laugh was a thunderclap.

Gorgrath rose, her form slipping into the darkness like smoke. "And when the shadows fall," she said, "the Wraith will be there."

The others watched her. Said nothing. Fearful each time she named herself that way.

Gideon stood, his eyes on the map and beyond it, to the horizon where the Silent Land waited, vast and wild.

"We bring the Dominion's hunger," he said. "And with it, the end."

The sea outside whispered still, patient, and eternal.

11 Splinterglass

Reza stood above the harbor, and he watched. The gray light was broken on the sea like metal worked by an old smith's hand, rough and certain. Below him, the ships rocked in their moorings like beasts with bridled fury. The morning had not yet broken open, but the sky was ash and the rain was coming. The air tasted of rust and brine and of something older. The end of something, maybe. Or the start.

They had waited a long time.

Men moved below, men he had known since the old uprisings in Jakarta and the red days of Manila. Men who had burned their old names like ships set to fire behind them. In the town, there were no banners. No colors. The color had been wrung from them long ago. They were beyond such things.

Reza's eyes tracked the coast, a ragged edge of stone and ruin. The towers loomed there, black iron and plated steel, grim and unyielding. They rose not from any dream of beauty but from the hard bone of terror.

They weren't built to be seen, he thought. They were built to be feared.

They marched for miles, a rusted spine stitched along the shore. Broad at the base like roots sunk in ash, narrowing as they climbed, vanishing into the low and endless sky. Their skins were layered plates, flaked with salt, streaked with soot, like something pulled from a furnace and never meant to cool.

The lower reaches, hulking bulwarks against the ocean's fury. They were made to take the sea's hammering. To take anything. Above the crash and roar, a skein of conduits, raw power humming through their veins. Gaps in the plating, dark openings to what lay within. A glimpse of inner workings, alien and cold. No ornament. Only function.

Higher up, weapon emplacements scarred their flanks. Railgun barrels, long and black, shifted on their mounts, searching the empty horizon. Between them, small apertures, countless, for the laser grids and kinetic systems. To burn the air clean of anything that flew.

At the summit, a reinforced deck. A pulsating crimson light. Sensing the restless waters, the gray and endless sky. They were not merely walls. They were the fist of the regime. Iron and steel. A declaration. Nothing entered. Nothing left. The air around them thrummed. A low, constant thrum. Power held close. The vast and terrible silence of it.

Behind him came footsteps. He did not turn.

"You've seen the patrols," Reza said.

A man halted beside him, breathing heavily from the climb. "They passed at first light. We kept low."

"Airborne?"

"Two drones. Small. Recon only. No strikes."

Reza nodded.

He had not shaved in some time. The beard grew in patches along his jaw. He watched the sea, that open mouth.

"They'll come soon," the other man said.

"We'll be ready."

Below, the harbor town clung to the rock, and the wind moaned against the corrugated roofs. Strips of plastic and old cloth fluttered from broken windows and makeshift lines. Children moved in silence. They had learned the silence better than their elders. Their elders had once known a world of music and screens and pleasure. The children knew only the waiting.

Reza turned from the cliff and walked down the rough path cut into the stone. A goat bleated in a distant yard. A dog barked once and then was silent. The village was not large. It had never needed to be. Its strength lay elsewhere. In the hills above. In the caves and the bunkers and the old military hardpoints long since scrubbed from the Dominion's maps.

He passed two of the guards at the checkpoint. Young men. Black scarves around their necks. Rusted rifles held tight to their chests like holy relics.

"You see anything?" Reza asked them.

One of them shook his head. The other spat.

"We'll know when they come," the second one said. "Smoke first. Always smoke."

Inside the command hall, if such a broken place could still bear the name, he met with the captains. They stood around an old projection table that no longer worked, its surface dead and cold. They used pencils, stubs of graphite, and torn strips of tape, arguing over layered paper maps like priests arguing over broken scripture, each crease a forgotten boundary. Their faces were creased and weathered, scored by wind and hardship, by the unending dust. One man had no left hand, gone in the steaming jungles of Sumatra. Another walked with a brace, a clanking thing of leather and metal, and kept a rosary made of teeth, clicking them in the dim light. They were all that remained of a fighting force, remnants of a world that had once known order. A world that had once known greatness.

The Silent Land. They had marched its breadth. Watched its cities rise like promises and fall like ash. They'd seen the towers lit with fireless light, felt the thrum of machines beneath the stone. It had been mighty once. A land of purpose. Of hunger well-fed. Then came the wars. The Amalgam and the others. Great powers colliding like gods in the sky. After that, the silence. Trade died first. Then the food. They remembered the ration lines stretching across the avenues, remembered the children crying, the hollow faces. Remembered the cold calculus of who would eat and who would not.

And still they marched. The great engines failed. The roads cracked. The power dimmed and never returned. Cities went black and never woke. They bore it in their bones, these captains. Hunger had outlived the nations. A wound. A wound that never closes.

Reza looked at his captains. They straightened.

He pointed to the sea.

"They will come by sea and air," he said. "They will come with fire. We will meet them here."

The captains nodded. Not out of duty, but because the truth required no argument.

"They will bomb the waterline," said one. "Come in with helos, larger drones, to sweep the cliffs."

Reza nodded. "We have the electromagnetic netting ready and launchers placed."

"Do we trust the netting to hold?"

"We don't trust anything," said Reza. "We act. That's all." He looked over the maps. "And the fusion pellets?"

"Hundreds. No. Thousands of them placed. No machine will pass."

"Some are stitched together?"

"Yes. As you commanded."

The men fell quiet. One lit a cigarette. The smoke curled through the room like some pale spirit.

A child came running from the stairs and said nothing. Just wide-eyed and breathless. Reza turned and followed him.

Outside, a crowd had formed in the square. A hundred people, maybe more. They circled the woman in the center like animals watching one of their own fall into madness.

She stood barefoot on the stones, her long gray hair wild in the wind, her eyes blank with vision. She had been a teacher once. A scientist. Now she spoke with voices not her own.

"I have seen the gates open," she cried, her hands outstretched. "I have seen our land. The last refuge. I have seen it burn."

The wind cut through the square like a blade. Her voice hung there like a curse.

Some turned away. Others stood still. A child wept quietly. A man crossed himself.

Reza moved through the crowd. He stood before her and looked into her eyes. He saw nothing of the woman he had known. Only fire. Only loss.

"You've seen this?"

She nodded slow. Like something ruined. Still bound by memory. Her head moved not by will but by some old compulsion. As if the truth itself had taken hold of her spine and worked it like a lever.

"They come," she said, her voice frayed thin as a whisper through gauze. "They come from the black sky."

Reza did not move. The air between them still as judgment.

"I see machines," she went on. "Great wheels. Vast and terrible. Teeth like gods. They tear the land. They tear bone and flesh. I see them feeding. And I see nothing left behind but red earth and silence."

Reza said nothing.

He turned to the crowd. Raised one hand.

"This is not prophecy," he said. "It is memory. It is what they have done to every free city, every free nation on this world. But this is the last. The final land. Bring them. They will taste our ash."

And the crowd answered in silence.

That night, the rain came. It fell hard and cold. In the dark, they moved weapons under tarps. Set charges in the cliffs and more fusion pellets across the land. Checked fuel levels. Reinforced the old perimeter wire. In the caves above the cliffs, men and women readied mortars and sealed crates of ammunition with wax and cloth.

Reza sat with his rifle by the radio. Static whispered like ghosts through the speakers. He thought of the old world. The cities. The noise. The lies. He thought of the long years on the run. The drowned cities. The burned ones.

In the morning, the wind shifted.

A boy came running barefoot and breathless and pointed east with a hand blackened from ash.

Reza took the scope from its mount and peered downrange.

Dark shapes. Fast. Riding low on the water. No flag nor flame.

"More recon drones," he said.

The word went down the cliffs like fire set to tinder. Horns sounded. Men ran shadowlong down the escarpments with weapons in their arms and no words in their mouths.

In the square below, the old bell swung once and again, its sound cold and high and hollow.

"Do not meet them with fear," said Reza. "Meet them with silence."

And the people did.

The first drone came in fast and low, kissed the saltwind off the sea, and lifted into the air like a gull before it was taken by a column of flame that cast black smoke skyward like a curse. Reza stood. He lifted the long rifle to his shoulder. He watched the horizon. He did not speak.

The sea burned in strips. The sky cracked open. More drones came. More scouts.

Steel and fire and thunder.

Still, none knelt.

And from the charred bones of the eastern ruins came the answer the old ones had prayed might never come.

Not surrender.

Fire.

***

The war room was cut from the Spire's bone. Square and tall-ceilinged. The stink of men and lampgas hung in the air like something slaughtered and left to rot. The walls were bare rock, slick with a slow sweat. Red banners hung limp and rotting, the black and gold of the Dominion near faded out. Their seams frayed. Their thread dulled by soot and smoke. They looked like skins flayed and nailed for memory. Dried blood in the shape of pride.

The arches overhead were not wrought of stone but of will. His will. Gideon's. Light slanted down through narrow slits cut high in the wall, a pale blade through the dust. It fell upon the room. Barely. But there was more light. Light from dull glass hung on chains in the rafters. Yellow fire guttered in them. The glow spilled oily across the ironwood black table set at the center of the room. Its surface carved and burned, a ledger of dead men and dying ground. And beneath it all, a floor. Flagstones worn smooth by boots and blood. It whispered. Ghosts. Orders spoken and never taken back. The slow grind of conquest. All of it still here. Still waiting.

A ring of black coats stood about it like penitents or mourners. Their breath steamed in the cold air and turned slow above them and vanished. Gideon sat unmoving at the head of the table. His face smooth as slate. His eyes lit by nothing.

"One more review," he said. "Another look."

"Salve Rex," said General Lorr, his voice grating like boots on sand.

General Lorr stood among the black coats, a lean shape in the chill of the war room. His face was a map of old battles, cut deep with lines time had not softened. His eyes held no light from the sputtering lamps, only the distant shine of wars fought too long and perhaps already lost. When he spoke, it was a rough sound. Gravel and bone. A voice worn down by years of command and hard news. His shoulders stooped not from age but from what he bore. A man who'd watched too many horizons burn away. He was part of the stone now. Forged in fire, left to cool in ash.

He continued. "You'll see here, this inlet, to the northwest, allows for a natural disembarkation. Fewer towers here. Their defenses. If the tides hold, we'll land armor and material within a few hours of first contact. No resistance. Not a soul on that edge for two hundred miles inland."

He pressed a thick finger to the coast. Gideon looked down at the photographs strewn beside the maps. Grainy, half-lit. Empty shores. Broad eucalyptus forests swaying like they were asleep. Grasslands caught mid-turn in the lens like a body startled from dreaming.

"What about their water beasts?" Gideon said. "Those metal things. The ones that swim."

Lorr smiled. His teeth were yellow and few. "We'll take our losses," he said. "But most will burn. Most will go down."

Gideon gave a nod. He did not look up.

"The Silent Land sleeps," said Lorr. "Commander Ralke confirms. No sound. It's as it was left. Since the Exodus."

"Verdant Cross," Gideon said.

"A promise," said Lorr.

The others nodded. Men not agreeing but remembering something already theirs. Nods like graves being tamped flat.

A sound.

The wind. It was not air but something ancestral, something from a place before breath. Soldiers at the entrance reached for their sidearms but stopped.

She stood there. At the threshold.

Elarlu.

Coat open. Feet bare. Hair damp against her face like she had come from beneath the earth. White powder along her lips. Eyes of glass. She walked in like she had been here before, and the room had only forgotten.

"How long have you been there, my Siren?" Gideon asked.

"Since the start of it all," she said. "You dream of locusts."

Her voice was not a sound so much as a rhythm your bones already knew. Trance-like.

"Metal beasts crawling across the Silent Land. I fear you will become hollow. Your realm full of engines with no purpose."

Gideon stood. Slow. Like a man drawn upward by hooks.

"Elarlu," he said. "My dearest Siren."

"You do not sleep," she said. "You lie. You watch the dark. You remember my body and what you did." A hand hovered over her belly. "It grows each hour. For you."

She looked to Lorr. But Lorr did not move.

None of them moved.

"You name it Verdant Cross," she said. "You would strip the last green from this world. Drive steel into the soil and call it salvation. Your crucifix of root and bone."

A worried look upon his steel face.

"Why do you say such things?" he asked.

Her face shifted. Saw only him now.

"I saw your words," she whispered. "Clung to the back of your mind like worms in loam. I licked them free."

Gideon lifted a hand. A soldier at the door moved. He opened it. She did not look back. Just turned and stepped into the black outside. The dark took her.

No one rose. No one spoke. The gaslight hissed its slow death at the corners.

Gideon sat.

The maps lay before him like auguries drawn in blood. Red lines crawling outward, slow and sure, like veins in stone. Old wounds. The kind that never close. The room held its breath. Nothing stirred but the hiss of the gaslamps. Steady. Pale.

He looked at the place where she had stood. The door shut. The dark behind it absolute. He did not speak. Not yet.

He feared what she knew. His Siren. What she'd heard. Seen. What was in her mind. The powder had hollowed her out and left something watching from inside her. Like she had been emptied for a voice not her own.

She had spoken in riddles. Spoken of ruin like it had already come and gone. Like they were only waiting for its echo. He wondered if perhaps she knew the future.

He looked again at the map. The red lines bled still.

"The new moon," he said. "I said we would strike before the new moon."

His voice low. Distant. Not for them. Not really.

He stared at the lines. His hand resting light on the parchment as if it might burn him.

"I want caution. More drones. Send them again. And again. I want to see the flares of their defense. I want their silence tested."

Lorr stirred beside him. "But—"

"No."

The word cut the air. Flat. Final.

"It does not feel right," Gideon said. "There is something wrong. I cannot name it. We wait. More time."

He did not tell them what he feared. That she somehow had seen too much. That she had spoken the end aloud. That the dust had opened her eyes in a way no man's ever should. That this plan, these lines, all of it—it would come to nothing.

He thought maybe it was an omen. Her voice like wind in a tomb. The powder eating her from the inside. Her eyes like mirrors to a place none of them would survive.

They did not know these things. Not yet.

The others sat in silence. The air thick with the press of delay, of hope, curdled into dread.

Then they said it, together. The words like iron.

"Salve Rex."

***

"She in there?" Zexus said.

The two soldiers at the door looked at her. Boys, near enough. Faces still smooth. Eyes gone hollow, just the same. They said nothing. Only nodded. One reached back and pulled the door open.

It shut behind her like iron dragged through ruin. The sound of old things dying slow.

Zexus stood there, her hands gloved, her eyes unreadable.

"Elarlu," she said.

The woman lay curled on a cot of iron and burlap, clinging to a blanket. Her hair was plastered to her face and throat. Her skin shone like candlewax. Her eyes opened not like waking but like returning. There was powder along her lips. A small bowl sat empty on the floor, cracked.

"You've come late," Elarlu said.

Zexus crossed the room. She knelt by her and removed a vial from her coat. A thin cylinder of smoked glass stoppered in copper. She shook it once. The powder within shimmered like bone-dust.

"I am sorry for my delay," Zexus said. "This is what you require. Am I correct?"

Elarlu blinked. Her teeth were black in places. Her voice crawled.

"I remember the lights on their helmets. I remember the jungle set afire."

Zexus uncorked the vial and tapped it against her gloved fingertip. The powder clung to the leather like frost.

"You'll speak to me of that," she said. "Of your memories. Of what you see."

Elarlu nodded once. Her eyes moved in slow arcs.

Zexus raised her hand. Elarlu reached, but the hand stayed above her, waiting.

"No bowl," Zexus said. "No mess. You'll lick it."

Elarlu leaned in slow. Her eyes fixed on Zexus. "Then give it to me," she said.

Zexus raised her hand. The powder rested on the tip of her finger like pale ash. Elarlu took it in her mouth. Lips parting. Tongue warm and slow as it swept the skin clean. Her gaze never left Zexus, something deeper flickering there. A hunger not yet named.

She leaned back. Her breath came sharp through her nose. Fingers twisted in the blanket, knuckles pale. Like a woman who'd tasted more than she was ready to admit.

"I saw them," she said. "In the Spire's belly. They think it theirs. All theirs."

"Where?" Zexus asked.

"The war room. It lay beneath the tribunal cells, down in the rock where no sound lingered long. Gideon and Lorr stood with the others, hunched beneath the gaslight. Maps sprawled across the table, their edges curled and stained. They pointed with thick fingers. Named coasts and rivers as if dressing a carcass."

Zexus touched the powder again with her fingertip. She held it before Elarlu's eyes.

"More, if you tell me what they plan."

Elarlu's head nodded, but her body shuddered. Her mouth opened again. Zexus fed her the dust.

She swallowed like it hurt her. Then she smiled. A grotesque, gentle thing. The corners of her lips cracked.

"Verdant Cross," Elarlu whispered. "That's what they call it. Their salvation. Their crucifixion."

"What date?" Zexus asked.

"Not sure."

Zexus crouched. Still as sculpture. The vial sat on her knee. She watched the woman unravel.

"They'll come with metal carriers," Elarlu went on. "With drones that eat silence. He wants the soil itself to confess. They'll scorch the edges first. Then send in the feeders."

"What's their entry?" Zexus asked.

"Northwest inlet. A sliver in the coast. Lorr said few towers there. Few watchers. They forget what grows in silence."

Zexus stood. She placed the cork back in the vial.

Elarlu moaned, low. Her hand reached.

"More," she said. "Please."

Zexus stepped back. Her boots left pale prints on the floor.

"You've told me enough."

"I've not told you what I saw after," Elarlu croaked. "I dreamt of roots that screamed. I saw your name written in the green flame above the Silent Land."

Zexus paused by the door.

"I have no interest in dreams."

Elarlu laughed. It was a dry and breaking sound.

"You will," she said. "You all will."

Zexus looked once more at Elarlu. Face peeled back by the powder. Voice fed by something not her own. Something older. Watching.

The room stank of iron and spit and dying skin.

Zexus opened the door. Another nod from the two soldiers. The hallway beyond was long and black. Torches hissed at long intervals like beasts asleep.

She stepped out without another word. Her boots vanished into the dark. The door did not close fully. The wind pulled it slow behind her. It caught at the edge and rocked there.

Inside, Elarlu lay alone. The powder still hummed in her bones. Her fingers twitched. Her eyes fluttered.

She began to hum a tune with no melody. A sound from the bottom of the world.

And then, stillness.

She spoke, though no one was there to hear.

"They think they own time," she whispered. "But time has teeth that bite."

A light went out above her.

She smiled.

And waited.

***

Shadows gathered in the corners of the small house. Zexus struck a match and touched it to the wick. The candle guttered, throwing shadows against the walls. She sat at the table, rough wood beneath her palms, one leg shorter than the rest, so the whole thing rocked if you leaned too hard. Wax bled down in slow rivers, pooling in the scars of the grain.

She opened her notebook. In the back of it, a commlink. She turned it on. Saw the room. Frozen. Then played back the video. One more time. Movement. Voices. Plans.

Her fingers trembled. She reviewed her notes. Read everything she had written by the dim light—names, coordinates, crude sketches of the Dominion's ramparts. Ciphered words, passed from lips now silent beneath the earth.

Outside, dogs howled. Or something like dogs.

She heard the scrape of boots and rose without a sound. She creaked open the door. Two figures at one end of the alleyway. One crouched. The other smoked something bright and orange in the dark. She watched them a long while.

Then footsteps from the other end of the alleyway.

She didn't move.

"Zexus," came a voice, low and hoarse.

She opened the door just wide enough.

"You weren't followed?"

"No."

"You sure?"

"As I can be."

"The others down the alley?"

"With me. Protection."

He came in. Worn boots. Mud on the cuffs of his coat. He closed the door gently and stood by the table.

"There's fires near Durn Hollow," he said. His voice was low, rough. "They're burning the outer towns. Clearing a path for the engines of war. Your master's gathering everything he's got. Every blade and barrel. Every goddamn monster in his stable."

Zexus stood watching him, the creases beneath his eyes like dried creekbeds. The wear in him went down to the bone.

"I've seen reports," she said. Her voice was flat. She didn't look at him. "They'll come through the north gate. Air and sea both. He'll lead with the machines. Built by the Dominion. Modified from great harvesters. Wheels."

She felt the weight of that settle into her chest. Passed her notes to him.

"Thank you," he said. Voice low. "We'll be ready. The Silent Land is moving."

He stood there watching nothing. Night stretched endless and starless beyond the dust-hung pane. His coat hung from him, remembering other owners.

"There are iron riders in the dunes. Engines groaning. Smoke in their mouths. Dust thick as wool, clogging the throat, turning the sun to a blood orange smudge. And in the sea, deep and black as sin, great metal monsters swim. You can't see them. But they're there. Turning slow. Listening. And the towers?"

"Towers?"

He gave a slow nod. Very slow.

"Towers of iron. Rusted like old blood. High as a god's shoulder. They wait. They wait for his drones. They wait for his machines of war."

She turned her face to the wall, and the candle threw her shadow against it like something already buried.

"Not enough," she said.

"Maybe," he said. "Maybe not. We hold the Silent Land or we die in it."

Zexus leaned forward and pinched the wick between her fingers. The flame fought and then died.

"You'll do both," she said.

***

Gideon stood in his chamber with the wind crawling through his coat like some old judgment come to roost. Night lay heavy on the stone, a black weight pressed down from the stars. The lamps had all guttered out. What remained was silence. Silence and the cold. His breath left him in strings. He did not shiver.

From the corridor behind him came the Voice. Not footsteps. Only the change in the air. Tall and spare, wrapped in a tunic, fine and elegant, too plain for a priest. She carried no weapon. Needed none. Her shadow passed the pillars without sound.

"She is unraveling," the Voice said. Her tone bore no joy in being right. Only the cold patience of something long waiting.

Gideon stood with his back to her, watching the dark of the land meet the stars. "I know. She spoke things no one taught her," he said. "She walked in my thoughts like they were corridors she'd laid stone by stone. Like she'd lived there always. I know what you desire. But she is not yours."

"She should be."

The Voice stepped closer, arms bound tight beneath the folds of gray linen, like some prophet unsanctioned by god or creed, and all the more dangerous for it. "You love her still."

"I love what she was," he said.

"And she's not that anymore."

"No," Gideon said. "She's not."

The stars burned above them without warmth, old watchers hung like nails over the earth's shroud. There was no kindness in them. No memory of man. Only witness.

"You'd wager the whole world," said the Voice, "for what's left of her?"

"I'd wager only what I must."

"You'll lose the Silent Land. Maybe everything, if you let this rot spread. The others talk. Their whispers gather like flies."

"Let them talk. I can deal with them. Harshly, if I must."

"She frightens them. She frightens me."

"Then be frightened. Quietly."

"You should let me end it."

He turned. Her face was gaunt, the lines not made by grief but by time's steady claw. Her eyes were rimmed red, dry as salt pans.

"You will not touch her," he said.

The Voice regarded him. Eyes cold and still. He nodded once, slow.

"Then guard her well. And pray she stays silent."

She turned and was gone before the wind could catch his shape. Gideon stood there long after, alone beneath the stars. He thought of her. Not the broken thing curled in her room, but the fire she once carried. He remembered the smell of iron and blood and sweetness. Her voice in the night, naming the dead.

The wind howled through the Spire, and the stones remembered it all.

***

The hallway opened ahead of him like the inside of some beast too long dead to be remembered rightly. Narrow. Damp. Pipes along the walls sweating rust. A kind of sorrow that needed no name. The floor wept in slow beats. The stink of rot and oil and old blood lived in the air. Paint hung in curled ribbons, peeling off like skin shed quiet from the dead.

Gideon walked without sound but not without weight. His boots touched the floor like they knew it well. A man taught by silence. By graves. By nights long enough to forget the names of things.

Soldiers at the door. Two of them. Not men yet. Too young. One with freckles. The other with fear working in his jaw like a bad tooth. They watched him. Still in the way of boys who'd seen nothing but been told plenty. They held their rifles like ropes on a cliff. Not like killers. Like climbers who didn't ask to climb.

He said nothing.

Neither did they.

The barrels followed him as he moved. Not aimed.

Bowed heads.

"Salve Rex," they whispered.

He put a hand to the door. Opened it.

Inside the heat lay heavy, hung close like the breath of something too sick to stand. The air full of wax and wet wool and something else, older. A smell without name. A lamp shivered in the corner, its light a yellow sickness barely alive.

Elarlu lay on the bed with the sheet drawn over like some thing left behind. Her face turned to the wall. Her breath thin. Rare. She might have already gone if not for the way the room still held its breath around her.

He stepped close. Found the cold iron of the bedframe and leaned into it. The groan of it rose slow into the heat. Her bones showed beneath the sheet like twigs under snow. She did not turn.

"Why do you come?"

Her voice cracked. Dry as dust.

"I don't know."

"You think I'm mad."

"No," he said. "Not mad."

She turned her face. Eyes like burnt holes in paper.

"I know your thoughts," she said. "I am the hinge of your mind. The fulcrum. You believe you'll die when I do."

He could smell the powder on her breath.

"I think many things."

"I will not die," she said. "Not yet. I will become what you need me to become."

He sank to one knee beside the bed. Took her hand in his. Brought it to his chest and held it there. Like scripture. Like ruin. Her fingers moved once. Then stilled.

"Sometimes," he said, "you scare me."

"I am yours."

The window trembled. The wind scratched at it like something buried, trying to get back in. A vial slipped from the table, rolled, and came to rest. Did not break.

"You don't belong to anyone," he said. "You never did."

"No," she said. "And neither do you."

He stayed there with her hand against him. The lamp gave one last breath, then went out. The room closed in. Like a grave not yet full. Waiting.

When he left her chamber, the boys at the door did not meet his eyes.

"Salve Rex."

He stepped into the corridor. It was darker than before, or maybe that was only in him. The hallway stretched out in its old silence, and his footsteps were slow. A man leaving behind a thing he could neither carry nor leave whole. He did not look back. The stink of rust and sorrow walked with him.

**

The scream came just before dawn.

It was a horrid sound. One that tore through the Spire like a knife dragged slow through flesh. Gideon sat up in the dark, heart hammering. The bed groaned beneath him. He was still dressed. His rifle leaned against the wall beside him like a dog that never slept. He rose, the wool blanket falling in a heap behind his boots. The air was cold and dry and full of waiting.

He moved through the halls without sound. The old stone sweating damp in the corners. The lamps burned out. The walls slick as tongues. His steps echoed like they did in dream. Where nothing alive could follow. Where nothing dead could rest. Down the hallway, he seemed to float. With the slow gravity of a man moving toward what he already knew.

The corridor outside Elarlu's room was still. The guards lay in a mess on the floor. One crumpled against the wall, legs folded beneath him like a puppet dropped in mid-performance. The other sprawled on his back, mouth agape, his blood spreading like ink across the stone. Rifles discarded. Throats opened clean and deep.

No sign of struggle. Just silence. A shard of glass with blood dripping from it. The weapon.

Gideon knelt beside the closest. A boy. Seventeen at most. His hand still grasped at the air like he might take something back. Gideon touched the boy's shoulder. It was still warm. He rose.

He stepped toward the door. It stood slightly ajar. His hand went to it and slowly pushed. The hinges moaned. He entered.

The room stank of sweat and something worse. A sweetness in the air that didn't belong. Too clean. Like it meant to cover something. The lamp lay broken on the floor. The bed was a mess of tangled sheets and dust. And in the far corner, crouched low like a creature worked from shadow and breath, was Elarlu.

She rocked back and forth. Her mouth worked around words that did not come. Her hair wild. Her eyes unfixed. Her hands red in blood to the wrist. Powder clung to the edges of her lips like frost.

Gideon crossed the room.

"My Siren," he said.

She didn't look up.

He crouched beside her. Took her gently by the wrist.

"My Siren. What happened?"

Her mouth opened. She blinked hard as if waking.

"I . . . I don't know. I heard something. At the door. I called out to them."

She stopped. Swallowed. Her eyes darted to the walls and the ceiling as if some piece of truth might be hiding there.

"When I opened it," she said, "they were there. Their life just running out of them. Like water spilled from a glass."

"Who did this?"

She shook her head. "I don't know. I didn't see. I thought maybe I dreamed it."

Gideon reached into the fold of his coat and drew out a cloth. He wiped at the corner of her mouth. The white powder came away easy on the dark fabric. He looked at it in his hand, silent.

"You're consuming too much."

"No," she said quickly. "I don't mean to. It's just . . . it's just something to keep me calm. I—"

She trailed off. Her hands trembled in her lap. The blood on them fresh.

Gideon stood. Looked down at her.

"You sure you didn't scream . . . a scream of rage, perhaps?"

She didn't answer.

He turned. Walked to the bodies in the hall again. Studied the way they'd fallen. Both rifles down. No shots fired. No signs of struggle.

He came back into the room.

"You didn't hear anything?"

"I told you. Just noises. Scraping. Breathing maybe. I don't know anymore."

"You've heard things before."

"Not like this."

He knelt again, slower this time. His hands on his knees.

"The door automatically locks at night. It's designed to keep you safe. No one goes in. No one goes out. It automatically unlocks in the morning."

"Are you sure?"

"Yes. Did you hear the door lock last night?"

"Maybe. I don't remember. I was asleep. I think I was asleep."

"You're not sure."

She looked at him. Her face pale. Lips blue at the edges.

"I'm not sure of anything anymore."

He stared at her. The blood, the powder, the voice that came out small like a child speaking through a mouth that had swallowed fire.

"You remember screaming?"

She nodded.

"Why?"

She closed her eyes. The tears came now. Silent. Slow.

"I thought I saw something," she said.

"Where?"

"In the mirror."

He stood. The mirror was shattered. Splinterglass everywhere. Just a rim of silver glass around the edge of the frame. A jagged moon hanging on the wall.

"What did you see?"

She didn't speak.

He let the silence stretch. Let it take hold of the room. The wind outside howled. Somewhere in the Spire, a door slammed. Gideon reached out and touched her shoulder.

"You said you'd become what I needed."

Her breathing caught.

"Yes. I did," she said. "You are my world. You are the world."

He stood there a long time. Hand on her shoulder. Eyes not on her but the thing that was no longer a mirror. Just the shape of what had been. A ruin of glass-like teeth around a black mouth.

"Do you know what I need?" he asked.

His voice was low, dry. Like something buried too long in the dust, trying to remember its name.

She didn't answer. She couldn't.

He turned his face to hers. Close enough she could see the dark in his eyes. The tired rage of a man who'd walked through fire and found no god waiting on the other side.

"You say I am your world," he said. "That I am the world. Then help me prepare it to burn."

He moved toward her.

"My Siren. You need to clean yourself. You need rest. Sleep."

She gave a small nod. A breath of a gesture.

"I will help," she said. Her eyes on him. Wide and unsure. "I will speak. To the world. Be your voice."

He smiled then. Reached out and moved a strand of hair from her cheek.

"Thank you, my Siren."

He kissed her forehead.

Then he stepped out into the hall, glanced at the dead soldiers. The boys. The older one had wet himself. His eyes were open. He looked like he'd seen something worth dying over. Or something that could never be unseen.

Gideon crouched beside the younger one. He touched the boy's throat, the way a man might test a blade for sharpness. Then he rose. The wind had picked up. The windows moaned.

He looked once over his shoulder. Elarlu sat there in the dim light, head bowed, hands clutched together like she was praying to something that didn't speak the language of mercy.

He didn't close the door behind him. Just walked back down the hall, slow, careful, like each step might bring the sound of another scream.

He called for them in a voice that brooked no delay. Two men from the night watch. Faces drawn with sleep. Boots scuffing the stone.

"Clean this up," Gideon said, and they nodded, wordless, already stooping to the bloody work.

The bodies would be gone before the sun found them. The blood would be scrubbed from the stone. The rifles gathered. The memory of the thing folded away into the dark ledger of the Spire.

He stood in the doorway and fixed the nearest with his gaze. "One more thing. Send a handmaid to my Siren. She is not to be left alone. She sleeps with her tonight and every night until I say otherwise. No one enters her chamber without my word." His voice was iron. They bowed.

"Salve Rex."

One hurried off, boots echoing down the corridor.

Gideon waited a moment more, watching the shadows stretch and shift in the lamplight.

"No one is to visit her," he told the other one, "without my permission first."

The words hung in the air, final as a death sentence.

He turned then and walked away, boots ringing on the stone, the air at his back cold as judgment. Around him, the Spire held its silence, and the world turned slowly toward another day.

12 The Siren's Wound

The coliseum stood tall, like the ribcage of some ancient beast left to bleach in the sun, a ring of stone and steel fused by men. Banners draped from the rafters, red and white, the colors of blood and bone. There were no shadows in the place, only the pale glare of overhead floods and the flicker of giant screens. The seats were filled, every one. Tens of thousands crammed shoulder to shoulder in rags and uniforms and ceremonial whites. Above them, drones hung in the sky. The wind carried nothing but the cold and the sound of voices.

Screens across the world blinked to life. In the marketplaces of Galatra, in the sunken wards of Typhon, even in the salt-sick cities of the eastern shelf, faces lifted toward the light.

Elarlu stood alone on the dais. The robes hung from her shoulders like a banner forgotten in war. Crimson cloth with gold thread stitched in the forms of serpents and eyes that watched without blinking. The wind moved through it and the people below did not speak. Not one.

Her hands were empty. Her face pale as old stone. She looked out over the crowd and saw what they wanted. Saw what they feared. They waited for her and did not know what they waited for.

Her breath showed in the cold. Little clouds rising from her mouth like the last smoke of a fire gone out. She said nothing. Not at first. The silence stretched thin. The eyes of thousands on her. The wind turned and came again.

When she spoke, the sound rang from hidden columns and concave speakers, a voice made vast by artifice but not softened.

"You have suffered," she said.

The crowd screamed. Some fell to their knees.

"You have suffered because the world is foul. You have suffered because flesh is weakness. Because truth was buried in the fat of kings."

A child began to wail somewhere near the front. A woman sobbed and threw up her arms.

"I have seen the edge of the new dawn," Elarlu said. "I have tasted the hunger that cleanses. I have burned the words of the old liars. And I am made clean."

She stood silent then, the hush drawn tight about her like a shroud. The crowd waited.

"Some may think me mad. No. I was mad before. When I believed in mercy. When I thought the old ways would save us."

They murmured now, low and eager, like hounds before the cry.

"I've given us a beginning," she said. "You just don't know it yet."

She stepped forward. Arms streaked with ash. Eyes dry and hard as salt.

"The world we knew is gone. This is the reckoning. And we will come through it scorched and pure or not at all. Will you burn with me?"

Hands went up like wheat in the wind.

"Will you burn with me?"

"Yes!" they cried.

"Will you starve with me?"

"Yes!"

"Will you bury the false and walk naked into the sun?"

"Yes!"

They were not a crowd. They were zealots and they pressed close to the dais. You could know them by the rags on their backs and the deep grooves cut into their cheeks. Their eyes did not blink when the lights flared. Their skin was pocked and stretched thin over bone. Many had burned the shape of the serpents into their flesh, that old glyph dug from desert ruin. They bled and let it run. No one moved to staunch the flow.

Elarlu raised a hand. Silence fell like a cleaver.

"The world must burn. The books, the poisons, the old songs. Those who do not understand. Refuse to understand. All of it must go. Purity is fire. Faith is famine. And only through these shall we be made new. Gideon knows!"

A roar erupted from the stands.

"Gideon Rex! Gideon Rex! Gideon Rex! . . ."

Out in the crowd, a tongue of flame wavered. Then another. Then a dozen. Hundreds. Thousands. Torches kindled against the night.

"Burn the books," Elarlu said. "Burn those who will not see. Cleanse yourselves through want. Weep no more. The Mouth is closing."

***

Elsewhere, in the cities that sat crooked on the banks of the black rivers, they came by the thousands. They filled the plazas and the broken stone squares where statues had once stood. The books were brought forth. Torn from shelves, unearthed from cellars, pried from hands that would not give them up. They carried them like criminals to be judged.

The titles were old and strange. Books of forbidden science. Of vanished gods. Of histories scrubbed clean from official memory. Poetry that spoke in tongues no longer allowed. Stories where men questioned the order of things, where women remembered the world before the silence. They stacked them high in the center of the square, a funeral pyre of ink and defiance.

A man with a scarred cheek tossed a leather-bound volume onto the flames. He watched the gold letters curl and blacken. A woman beside him pressed her palm to the fire until the skin blistered. She smiled at the pain.

"Let it burn," she said. "Let it all burn."

Another man stared at the fire, eyes empty. "They said the old words made you sick."

"They did," the woman said. "They made you remember."

The children danced at the edge of the fire, soot on their faces, ash in their hair. Barefoot and wild-eyed, they moved like sparks thrown from the blaze itself. An old priest knelt at the curb. His robes gone. Just a collar and a tremble left to him. He held nothing in his hands. Nothing left to hold. The book they'd taken from him, a book of saints and prayers, lay in the fire, its pages curling inward like dying leaves.

"No need for your god," one of them said.

Another laughed. A boy with blood on his knuckles and a ribbon tied around his wrist. The priest said nothing. Only wept, his hands trembling over the stones as if trying to bless what could not be named.

The smoke rose in black towers. It moved slow and unbroken into the sky, drawing lines that did not vanish. The sun, what could be seen of it, hung pale behind the haze, like it had turned its face from the city and would not look back.

In the alleys of Alta Coda, a boy of sixteen collapsed mid-chant. He had not eaten in many days. His ribs showed through his skin like the slats of a broken fence. His mother knelt beside him and kissed his brow. Told him he had been chosen.

"You are blessed," she whispered.

His eyes rolled back. His lips moved in silent prayer. She pressed her hand to his chest and felt the flutter of his heart.

"Do not fear," she said. "You will wake in the new world."

She sat with him as the sun set and the alley filled with shadows. Rats crept from the drains and watched with bright, hungry eyes.

"You are chosen," she whispered again.

She rocked him in her arms, humming a song from her childhood. The rats came closer, bold now.

The city moved on, indifferent.

In the glass quarter of Typhon where the light came down like knives, a girl knelt on the steps of the old library and drew a serpent in ash. Her fingers moved careful across the stone, stained dark to the knuckle. The hem of her dress hung in strips, and the wind tugged at the loose threads like it meant to unmake her.

She struck the match against the stair. The flame leapt small and quick. A living thing. She cupped it to her breast.

"I have no name," she said. "Let this be the last thing they remember."

The fire caught her dress like it had always known it. It screamed through the cloth and onto her skin. Ran up her arms and over her chest, and in the span of a breath she was nothing else.

She did not cry out. The flames rose around her. She stood in them like they were kin. Like she'd been born to burn.

A crowd gathered. No one moved. They watched her burn, her face uplifted, her mouth open in silent song. The flames turned her hair to smoke and her skin to cinder.

A boy stepped forward. Small. Wearing a gray coat. He held a flower gone soft at the stem. He walked through the stillness and laid it at her feet.

"You are not afraid," he said.

Her mouth opened, a furnace behind her lips. She fell.

The smoke rose and the crowd gave way.

The boy stayed where he was. Alone now. The flower crisping in the heat. Curling inward. Turning black.

In another quarter, a man with a red sash poured oil on a pile of books. He turned to the people and raised his arms.

"This is the cleansing," he said. "This is the hunger that will save us."

A woman in the crowd nodded. Her eyes were hollow. She clutched her daughter's hand so tightly that the child whimpered. The child tried to pull free but could not.

"Mother, why are you hurting me?" the girl asked.

The woman didn't answer. Her gaze fixed on the figures ahead, the soundless mouths, the smoke drifting up into the ash-colored sky. Her fingers closed tighter.

"Please," the girl said. "It hurts."

The woman pulled her forward to the fire's edge and forced the small hand into the flame. The girl screamed.

No one turned. No one spoke. No one cared.

"Pain is good for you," she said. Her voice broke with a sharp laugh. "And fire cleanses. Remember that."

The fires burned through the night. Ash drifted through the streets, settling on rooftops and in the mouths of sleeping children. The city was quiet, save for the crackle of burning and the distant sound of chanting.

By morning, the plazas stood hollow and gray beneath a sky that held no light. The stones were blackened and slick with old soot, the rain having come and gone like a thief with nothing worth taking. Ash clung to the corners where gutters had once run, and the air carried the dry sting of burnt paper and something older still—regret, maybe. Or mourning.

They moved through the streets like remnants. Men and women wrapped in threadbare coats and threadbare dreams, their eyes gone to glass, their stomachs speaking in the language of ghosts. Their steps were soundless over stone, not for stealth but for the simple absence of strength.

At the far end of the square where once a statue had stood tall and proud and was now only dust and jagged stone, a beggar knelt in the ash. His body was near to gone. Skin drawn tight across the scaffold of him. He held his hands out, palms up, fingers crooked like dry twigs.

"Mercy," he said. "Only that."

His eyes did not rise. He stared at the ground as if it were speaking to him, telling him old truths no man ought to know.

A woman passed by. Her dress was scorched at the hem. Her face drawn tight. She did not meet his eyes. She dropped a scrap of charred parchment into his hand without slowing.

"Read," she told him.

He turned the fragment over in his fingers. The script was gone, letters turned to shadow. Still, he stared at it as if truth might rise up through the ash. He brought it to his lips, closed his eyes, and wept without sound. No one stopped. The square breathed and did not care. The city moved on.

In the glass quarter, the fires burned low. The library steps were stained with ash and something darker. The flower was gone. The crowd had scattered, but the memory of the burning girl lingered like smoke.

Above the city, the sky was the color of lead. No birds sang. The river moved slow. Black beneath the bridges. Carrying ash to the sea.

***

In a high chamber of the Spire, Gideon sat with his hands clasped, watching the feed curve across the dark glass like a living wound. The chamber was windowless. The walls swallowed sound. A slow pulse of light traced lines across the floor where old blood had dried long ago and been polished into the stone. The air held the hush of sanctified violence.

On the screen, Elarlu stood before a crowd. Her voice rang out, echoing off metal and flesh and ancient flags re-stitched for new wars.

"She has them," Malachar murmured. "Body and soul."

"Fanatics," said the Voice. "Useful, but only until they turn."

Gideon did not answer. He leaned forward, elbows on knees, his breath steady, the kind a man learns to hold in war and never quite lets go of.

Onscreen, Elarlu's cry still thundered over the masses:

"A new age! Of blood! Of fire! Of truth! Of Gideon!"

The crowd answered in thunder.

"Siren! Siren! Siren! Siren!"

He raised one hand. The screen blinked to black. The chamber dimmed. He bowed his head. A flicker of something. A motion small as breath.

A courier approached. His face was drawn, eyes downcast. He held out a tablet.

Gideon took it without a word. The message was brief, written in the old way—like those from the frontier battles long past. Gorgrath's mark at the bottom. Sharp as ice on flesh.

He read it slow. His face did not change. He drew a breath through his nose.

"The plague," he said. "Mors Annona. It has reached the sea."

The words fell in the room like thunder in a hollow canyon. The silence that came after held tight as if even the dark dared not move.

"Saltwater adaptation?" said the Voice.

"Yes."

The Voice leaned back, soundless.

"That will breach the coasts," Malachar said. "It'll ruin the fisheries. The floating farms. Everything."

"The invasion," the Voice whispered.

Gideon looked up. His face was a ruin of old lines and old days, carved not by time but by what time made him carry.

"No. It will proceed," he said.

"But—"

"It will proceed," he said again. "But only when I give the order."

No one spoke after that.

They sat in the quiet, each counting consequences behind their eyes. Outside, the roar of the coliseum swelled through the foundations, distant and rising. A sound like the earth cracking open. Like something old crawling out of the grave and remembering its name.

***

The rain had stopped but the stones still wept. Water ran in thin threads down the old arches, pooled in the joints of the broken walk that circled the lower tiers of the Spire. The city's breath rose in steam through the grates, warm and sour. Malachar waited beneath the overhang of a corroded awning, one hand on the butt of the knife she never went without. The sky above her was gray, pocked with dark shapes drifting between spires like carrion birds who'd grown fond of steel. The wind tasted of oil and iron.

Zexus came quiet. Her boots soft on the stone. Malachar didn't turn.

"You're late," she said.

"I had to loop the signal paths," Zexus answered. "They're watching the priest's lines. Voice units. Cloaked and slow-walking. Those hideous machines. One of them brushed a child's face just to watch her flinch."

"I saw one once. Horrible contraption."

"The priest. He's the last one. Refuses to discard his vestments."

"Why don't they just kill him?"

"They will. When it suits them."

Zexus stepped in beside her. She wore a cloak the color of dry blood and a sash that marked her as maintenance detail, one of the many lies they'd wrapped around themselves. Her eyes were dark, restless.

"He's not going to stop," Zexus said.

"Gideon?"

"Who else."

Malachar tilted her head back, stared up at the Spire's ribs, lost in mist. She closed her eyes.

"He's gone."

"No," Zexus said. "He's still in there. I saw it. When the crowd roared her name instead of his. When the screen blinked out. He flinched. Like a dog struck by its own master."

"You're dreaming," Malachar said. "He flinched because she hadn't gone far enough."

Zexus turned to her.

"You think he wants this? What she's creating?"

"I know he wants it. You don't cling to ruin like that unless you love it. He's dragging everything down just so she'll keep looking at him."

They stood there a long moment, the heat from the grates curling around their boots.

"We can't stay," Zexus said.

"No."

"If we go, it has to be soon."

Malachar nodded.

"Before the plague eats everything."

"It's already in the fish. I heard a man in the kitchens coughing up scales."

"Then it's too late."

"No," Zexus said. "Not yet."

Malachar turned. Met her eyes.

"You want to run."

"Leave."

"They'll burn the roads. Seal the tunnels. Blockade the ports. No one gets out."

"Not if we use the old cipher. The priest's. He'll give it to us. It'll lead to safe passage from all this."

"You trust him?"

"He knows the old ways. I've paved the way."

Malachar crossed her arms. She stared out at the lower wards, the lights like dying stars in the fog.

"And after that?"

"We sow what we can. We take her name and twist it back into the dirt where it belongs."

"Elarlu."

Zexus spat.

"A worm with a poet's tongue."

Malachar breathed through her nose.

"I've seen what she makes them do," she said. "A child in the plaza painted her own eyes white. Said she wanted to be like the goddess. When the blood started, the crowd cheered."

"She's no goddess," Zexus said. "She's a mirror. They see what they want. He sees hope. The crowd sees fire. But it's the same lie."

"Gideon doesn't see hope. He sees her."

Zexus shook her head.

"He was a tactician. Once. He knew every front, every corridor. I watched him draw whole invasions in dust. Now, it's as if he prays before battle. Not to any god. Just her."

"And she answers."

"No," Zexus said. "She feeds. There's a difference."

They walked then. Slow. Taking the long bend of the walk that led down into the engineers' trench. No one spoke. The air smelled of rust and wet stone. Far below, a procession of supply carts groaned toward the furnaces. Overhead, the drones passed in lines like beads on a string.

At the mouth of the trench, Malachar stopped.

"We leave. No other way now."

Zexus didn't turn.

"Leave the city to them?"

"It already belongs to them."

"Not the whole of it."

Silence again. A long wind drew up through the ventways, howling low and strange. Somewhere above, something massive shifted on its moorings, and the steel sang.

Malachar pulled something from her coat. A string.

"You meet with him then?"

Zexus took the string from her. She lifted it and let the wind take it

"Yes. Gave him what they need to know."

"If they burn the relay towers—he won't get word to the Green Womb."

"They haven't," Zexus said. "He can still reach them."

Malachar nodded. Her voice was flat.

"Then he'll send your warning."

"Yes. What about the old lines?"

"I've walked the old lines. I still know how to find the tunnels."

"We might need them."

"Maybe."

The two women looked at each other, the kind of look people share only when they've decided they'd rather die standing than live crawling.

"They'll know you gave it to him," Zexus said. They'll come for us."

"Wouldn't expect anything else."

They turned, walked deeper into the trench. The air changed down there. Cooler. Tighter. Smelled of burned wire and salt. Somewhere deep in the works, something hissed in the dark, a breath too long to be a machine.

Malachar didn't flinch.

"Do you believe in gods?" Zexus asked.

"No."

"Why not?"

"Gods wouldn't allow this."

"Maybe they like the show."

"And what about us. Do we like the show?"

"No. We've seen enough shows. But there's one left. One last show to watch."

"What's that?"

"Watching a false god get taken down."

Zexus smiled. It didn't touch her eyes.

"You're a cruel woman."

"I learned from the best."

The trench swallowed them. The last of the light died behind a curve of old stone, and then there was only the sound of boots and breath and the slow, steady grind of the city's broken heart still beating underground.

***

They came without light. Hooded, cloaked. The wind bent in the alleys like a hunted thing, and the stones underfoot were slick with some oil that never dried. Zexus walked in front, her hand never far from the knife she kept stitched into the side of her coat. Malachar followed, quieter than shadow, and when she walked past the wreckage of the old forum, she did not look at the bones that still lay there.

The old church rose from the broken southern quarter of the city like something unearthed. Its columns half-sunk. Leaning. The gate had long since rotted off its hinges. The wind moved freely through the nave.

Inside, the priest stood. His face was drawn, withered. He wore a cloth of black. A somber shade cut from night. It fell from his shoulders without adornment, a dark curtain drawn against the world. No crease nor wrinkle to speak of comfort. Around his throat, a band of white. A stiff blade of light against the black, cut straight and clean. It closed him in, a stark demarcation. A silent witness to vows kept. Of a religion long lost and forgotten. It was not a garment for softness. But for purpose. For the hard road walked.

"You came," he said.

Zexus stepped forward. "You still remembered how it once was."

"I do."

They stood before him like petitioners before an altar, though the altar had long since been torn down and burned for warmth.

"I know why you are here," the priest said. "There is not much time. The Dominion dies loudly. And it will kill as it dies."

Zexus exhaled. "Then we need to be far from it."

"You need more than distance. You need truth."

The wind swept through the gaps in the walls, bearing the scent of ash. The priest turned and led them through the rubble. Behind the altar was a door, difficult to make out. He opened it. There were stairs, narrow and choked with dust. They descended.

"Only crows remember this path," the priest said.

Below, the world was colder. Shelves of rotted books leaned against the walls. A basin still held water, though no one could say how.

The priest reached into the folds of his robe and produced a small metal disk. It caught the lamplight in the shape of an old crest—mountains, severed chains, a bird with its wings on fire.

Zexus stared. "That's from before."

"It is. It opens what remains. Past the beyond. A gate. Forgotten by maps and memory."

Malachar took the relic in gloved hands. "And it leads where?"

"South. Through the old aqueducts. Beyond the Dominion's claw. It will work. But only once."

Zexus shook her head. "There are others. We need to warn them. The Silent Land. We need—"

"You need to live," the priest said. "Or nothing you carry will matter."

She looked at the relic. Then to Malachar.

Zexus took it.

The priest turned to the stone wall. "When you are ready, strike here." He touched the mortar with one pale hand. "And it will open. But not before."

She wanted to speak. To ask who he had once been. Why he remained.

But the old priest was already walking away. The wind swallowed him whole.

***

The room was small. Brick-lined. Damp. The kind of place built to rot the soul. Water seeped from the mortar in slow veins, gathering in the corners where the rats would not go. The air was sour with old sweat and the copper tang of blood. There was a drain in the center of the floor, crusted with black. The walls bore the marks of old violence—scratches, stains, a patch of hair stuck to the brick where someone's head had been driven hard and left to dry.

A single bulb hung from a wire, its light yellow and weak. Shadows pooled in the corners. The Voice stood beneath it, her gloves red with dust or blood or both. Her coat tailored. Gray as ash. Her eyes catching the light like broken glass. To her right and left stood aides in long black robes.

Before them knelt three prisoners. Elarlists. Followers of her. The Siren. They were shackled and filthy. Their faces drawn. Lips split. Eyes lit with something that would not die. Their wrists were bound behind them, the iron biting through the skin.

The smell of infection thick in the air.

"These are hers," an aide said.

The three said nothing. They just knelt there, watching. Waiting.

"Does he know what we're up to?" another aide asked.

"He does not," the Voice said.

"We've already gone too far," the aide said. "This is too risky."

"Sometimes risks are necessary," the Voice said. "If we can get evidence of malfeasance, then perhaps he'll heed my words at last."

The Voice stepped forward and regarded the prisoners. They were dregs to her. Lesser humans, lost in their own misled ways.

"You're not fanatics," she told the prisoners. Her words were soft, almost gentle. "You're parasites. Latching onto a dream you don't understand."

She moved around them, her boots making no sound on the wet stone. She carried a length of wire in one hand, coiled and slick. She let it drag across the floor, the metal singing a little as it passed over the drain.

The first prisoner lifted his head. His nose was broken, dried blood crusted beneath his nostrils. "You think this dream is yours. It was never yours." He spat blood. "She don't forget her own."

The Voice stopped behind him. She pressed the wire against the back of his neck, not hard enough to break the skin. "You chant her name like she's a god."

"She is," whispered another. This one was young, hair matted with sweat and grime, eyes wide and feverish. "Elarlu sees."

The Voice drew a knife from her belt. She pressed the flat of the blade to the young man's cheek. "She starves," the Voice hissed. "She bleeds and you drink it like wine."

A silence fell. The only sound was the drip of water from the ceiling, the slow, steady breathing of the prisoners. The third spoke then. A woman with half her face burned, the skin puckered and shiny, one eye milky and blind.

"The Mouth of the Silent Land will close tightly."

The Voice stopped. The knife hovered at the young man's throat.

"What did you say?"

The woman repeated it. Word for word. Her eyes did not blink.

The Voice turned to the aides at the door. "Leave us."

They hesitated, glancing at one another, then obeyed. The door shut with a heavy groan. She stood there, alone with the three, and for a moment she did not speak. The wire hung from her fist. The knife gleamed.

"You've changed your tone," she said softly. "Haven't you. No more chants of Gideon. No more fire for the new age."

The first prisoner smiled, lips split and bleeding. "The fire burns differently now. The Siren is the light."

"You're planning something," the Voice said. "A fracture. A turn."

No answer. The prisoners stared at her, unblinking.

She stepped forward and placed her hand on the scorched woman's head. Her glove pressed into the ruined flesh. "I will peel what flesh remains from your skull if I have to."

The woman's voice was low, almost a sigh. "Pitiful. You cannot see what is coming. You're blind then."

The Voice recoiled as if stung. She let the wire fall to the floor, the knife slipping back into her belt.

"You're not afraid to die," she said.

The woman laughed, a dry sound. "Why would I be. She'll be there for me. Arms out."

The Voice shook her head slow. Turned on her heel and walked out. Her shadow stretched long. Knife-thin across the floor. Out the doorway and into the hall. Where dust hung in the air and the echo of her boots faded into nothing.

In the hall beyond, her aides waited, faces pale in the half-light. She did not meet their eyes.

"Begin infiltration of the Elarlist cells," she said. "Full spectrum. Biological and synthetic. I want minds broken open. Every word they whisper, every pause they take—mark it down. Let nothing slip unseen."

One of the aides swallowed hard, their throat working. "And if they fight back?"

"They will," the Voice said. "So break them."

"Are you sure. He—"

The Voice moved, sudden as a shadow, and stood before the aide. The aide's pulse could be seen flickering at her neck. The Voice leaned closer still.

"Do as I say," her voice a low murmur, "or you'll be the next in that room. I've seen men go in there and not come out the same. Not come out at all. The light in there is cold, and the hours are long, and you'll listen to your own voice echo back at you until you forget your name."

She stepped back, leaving the aide standing in a silence that hummed with dread.

***

She had held hundreds of them. Rallies. In the fields, in the ruins, in the towns that still dared a name. She spoke beneath broken spires and dead trees, her voice rising like smoke in the throats of the starving. They gathered to hear her, drawn not by hope but by the hunger in her words. What she promised was not peace. It was fire. And they believed. In the fire. Nothing else. In her. No one else.

Now she lay in the sanctum.

The crowds were gone. The fields silent.

Elarlu stared up at the banners above, the faded cloth moving like dead skin in the torchlight. The air was thick with the scent of melted wax and old incense, the shadows pressed close and heavy. Her hands trembled. Her stomach ached with a gnawing that felt older than hunger. It had been six days since she had last eaten. The flesh on her bones seemed to shrink with every hour, the hollows of her cheeks deepening, her lips cracked and bloodless. She found a vial. The powder within. Fingertip. The taste on her tongue.

The visions came in flashes. A tower of fire rising from the earth. A mouth sewn shut with black thread. The sea swelling red with bodies. She saw these things not with her eyes but with something deeper. A wound in her mind that would not close. Sometimes the visions came with a voice. Sometimes only with a terrible silence.

She tried to stand. Failed. Her legs would not hold her. There was dried blood on her inner thighs. She did not remember from when. Or where. She pressed her palm to her belly. She felt the slow churn of emptiness. The body devouring itself.

"Empty," she whispered. But she wasn't sure.

There was nothing there. Just the slow turn of hunger. The body eating what it could. A hollow churn. A silence where life had once been.

She closed her eyes.

The door swung open without knock or call. They entered as one. Three in number. Faces smeared with ash and ochre, robes torn and hanging in strips, the fabric dragging like the remnants of old flesh. Their eyes were bright with a fire not of this world. Mouths drawn tight with something between awe and dread.

They knelt without word. The youngest among them bowed, pressed his forehead to the floor.

"Oh, our Siren," he said. "We bring you water."

The eldest held out a cup. Rough clay. Chipped at the rim. Water within it trembling. Like it knew it was not enough.

She took the cup. Her fingers trembled.

She drank. The water spilled down her chin, down her neck. Cold. Clean. It tasted of old places, of rusted pipes and earth buried deep.

None of them moved. The room held still around her.

"You must rest," said the last one, a woman with scars on her wrists. "Your flesh is the scripture. Do not let it vanish."

Elarlu tried to laugh. But the sound came out as a cough, dry and ragged.

"You think I am holy," she said. "You think I see more than you."

They nodded, three shadows in the half-light.

"I see too much," she said. "And it means nothing."

The youngest stepped forward. He held out a blade, the handle wrapped in red cloth. It was a crude thing, hammered from scrap, but sharp enough.

"We will carry the pain for you," he said.

She looked at the blade. The edge caught the candlelight, glinting. She remembered the first time she had been cut for the crowd, the way the blood had run, the way they had wept and called her blessed.

"I never asked for any of this," she said.

"Are you sure?" he answered. "Maybe you didn't need to."

She turned her face to the wall. The brick was cool against her cheek. She closed her eyes.

"I was only trying to speak. Only trying to survive. And now . . ."

"Now you lead," said the woman, her voice low and steady. "Now you become."

They lit candles, setting them in a ring around her. The flames flickered, shadows leaping on the walls. They sang a quiet hymn, not one she had taught them, but older, full of sorrow and longing.

The youngest pressed the blade to his forearm and drew it down. Blood welled up, dark and slow. He did not flinch. The woman followed, her hands steady, the blood running in thin lines across her skin. The eldest cut his palm and let the drops fall onto the stones at Elarlu's feet.

They offered her the blade. She took it, her hand closing around the rough handle. The metal was cold. She pressed it to her arm. Felt the cut open. Clean. Bright. The warmth ran down her skin, slow against the chill air of the sanctum.

They watched her, their eyes shining.

"This is not salvation," the woman said.

"No," Elarlu said. "It is remembrance. Of the old pain, and the sorrow that walks with us now. Of nights when the world was dark and we were alone with nothing but our hurt and the promise of dawn that never seemed to come. We remember so we do not forget what we have lost and what we have become. So that when the fire burns low and the wind whispers through the cracks, we remember. Why we are here. What we owe to those who are gone."

Elarlu wept, though she did not know why. The tears ran down her face. Mingling with the blood and sweat. The pain was real. The only thing that felt true.

And far beneath, in the depth of that quiet grief, a new terror stirred. That they might be right. That she was not only the voice but the wound, the vessel for all their suffering. That she could not leave, could not die, could not stop. That the hunger would never end.

In the flickering light, the banners above her seemed to shudder. The hymn faded to silence. The three knelt, heads bowed, waiting for her to speak.

But Elarlu had no words left. Only the ache, the fear, the knowledge that the world outside would not let her rest.

13 Ash and Silence

The chamber was hollowed from black stone, vaulted like a cathedral, lit only by slit windows where the high sun burned white and gave nothing. Men gathered at the long table—military leaders and strategists, their armor quiet but never still, their faces rough with dust and long miles. At the head of the table sat Gideon. He had not spoken in the first hour. He rarely did. He let the talk wear itself thin before he entered it.

Gorgrath stood beside him, unreadable as always. Her cloak bore the dirt of a thousand roads. Her boots still wet from the marshes she'd crossed that morning. The only one who traveled farther than the scouts.

"The southern fleets won't hold," said General Lorr. "If the infection moves through saltwater, every line heading to the Silent Land is at risk. Our food, our chem shipments, our long-range artillery, fuel—all compromised."

"Sir, if I may speak," said Durro, Lorr's Lead Lieutenant.

Lorr nodded.

"They're already compromised This invasion will break what we can't already feed."

Gideon watched them. His eyes held no shadow. He rested his hand on the cold, stone table, where a crack ran the full expanse of the table, a dark fissure in the slab. The air grew cold then. The breath caught in their throats. A stillness fell, like dust in an abandoned house. When he finally spoke, the others stilled. Their movements ceased. No sound escaped them.

"We move forward," he said.

No reaction, just held breath. Then Lorr again, bolder now.

"The soldiers haven't eaten proper in a week. You know this. The plague's reached the ports. Floating farms are done. The granaries are overrun. And if that wind shifts—"

"We move forward," Gideon said again, calmly.

Gorgrath stepped forward now. "There's more than grain and fuel to weigh, Commander. The Elarlists are no longer smoke. They're fire. We saw banners in the hill provinces. The villages follow her."

"Rats follow a torch in the dark," said Lorr.

"They follow because they are hungry," Gorgrath said. "And we have not fed them."

Lorr nodded. "Delay. Two weeks. All I ask. Let the scouts finish their sweep of the coastlines. We try to gather more supplies. Then move."

"We move forward," said Gideon. "No delay." He stood. The light caught the angles of his face, a sculpture half-finished and too long in the making. "If we falter now, we hand the cities to the mob. We give them time to remember they are not afraid. We give them fire."

Gorgrath's jaw was clenched. She did not look at Gideon as she spoke. "The Elarlists no longer speak only of salvation. They speak of justice. Of death and fire."

"I know what they speak," Lorr said.

"They shout it in the markets."

"They shout a great many things," Lorr replied. "Crazy people do that."

"They have shrines. In the valleys. Atop hills. Some carved into mountainsides."

"They worship a woman who burns grain stores and calls it prophecy."

"She gives them something," Gorgrath said. "Something we haven't."

Silence took the room.

Then Lorr laughed, hard and mirthless. "We fear a madwoman with a choir of orphans. She only gives them death."

"Or an idea," Gorgrath said. "And those are harder to kill."

Gideon looked across the table. His voice was low.

"This invasion will proceed. Not for victory. Not for gain. For order. The men must march. The cities must see banners. The world must believe the Dominion moves still. Or it dies."

Gorgrath stared at the table for a long time, then lifted the small device from her belt. She tapped the code. A map flickered up, grainy, patched from half a dozen scout feeds.

"Then see this," she said.

The room dimmed around the light of the display. It showed coastlines, ports, and archipelagos once filled with movement. Now: stillness. No boats. No flare of engines. Just black rot creeping in patterns like veins. And marked in red— quarantine fires, miles wide.

Gideon said nothing. The others stared.

"Supply lines have wasted away," Gorgrath said. "Once we cross the sea, we will not return. And we will not be followed."

Lorr swallowed. "We're marching into a grave."

"No," said Gideon. He stepped into the map's light. His face was hollow there, cut by pixel and shadow. "We are marching into silence. And in silence, we become what they need us to be."

The others stared at him.

Lorr muttered, "May the gods help us."

"There are no gods here," Gideon said. "Only choices."

Lorr closed his eyes. A tear squeezed out.

"Salve Rex," he whispered.

***

Those of the Voice came at dusk. Riders. Dust on their cloaks, eyes veiled in cloth against the ash winds. They spoke little. The villagers watched from behind shuttered doors, cracked walls, drawn knives beneath their skirts and sleeves. The silence in the lanes was the silence of waiting, of fear made patient by hunger.

The lead was named Corvan. He had served in the ice campaigns beyond the great northern seas and come back wrong in the ways men come back wrong when they've seen too much. His face bore the color of old bone. His hands were steady, his gaze unreadable.

They tethered their mounts at the edge of the village and walked. The streets were dirt, old tracks worn to bone. A few dogs. A few faces at windows, eyes like dark stones. The air was thick with the scent of woodsmoke and something older, something sour.

Then they found it. Behind the orchard, where the grass grew thin and the wind never rested.

A shrine.

Cut from shale. Rough and beautiful in the way hunger can be beautiful. The likeness of the Siren. Elarlu. Eyes upturned. Arms out. Mouth parted in song or pain—it was hard to know. Around her: candles guttering in the wind. Bones of birds, strung on wire. Stones dyed red with blood or rust. And people. Kneeling. Thin. Silent. One boy had stitched her name into his arm with fishing wire. The blood had dried in black rivulets down his wrist.

Corvan did not speak. He marked the coordinates. He sent the images. His men circled the shrine, boots scuffing the dust, eyes cold.

"Leave nothing," Corvan said.

They dragged the kneelers from the dirt, one by one. The boy with the stitched arm was first. They bound his wrists with cord and pressed his face to the ground. The others watched, hollow-eyed, lips moving in prayer or madness. The riders worked with quiet efficiency. They carried tools in leather rolls: knives, hooks, a coil of wire, a length of pipe filled with sand.

The boy's breath came quick, sharp. He did not cry out when the first cut was made. The knife traced the letters in his flesh, opening them anew. Blood came. Dark. Slow. Corvan knelt beside him.

"Who built this?" Corvan asked.

The boy's mouth worked. He spat blood and dirt.

"She did," he whispered. "She is the fire that does not burn."

Corvan nodded. He took the pipe and pressed it to the boy's hand, breaking three fingers. The sound was like dry twigs snapping. Crack. Crack. Crack. The riders questioned each kneeler in turn. Some wept. Some sang. The wire bit deep. The hooks found purchase in soft flesh. They asked about the Siren. About the prayers. About the men who came in the night with food and candles.

The villagers watched from their windows. Faces pale as wax. No one moved to help. The screams were muffled by the wind and the thick stone walls.

When the riders finished, they left the kneelers in the dust. Some broken and bleeding. Some dead. The shrine blackened with ash and blood. The candles guttered out. The boy bled quietly into the earth behind the shrine. His eyes fixed on the sky.

Corvan did not look back. He wiped his hands on his cloak and walked away.

The riders left before midnight. No sound. No sign. The villagers said nothing. The wind carried the scent of blood through the lanes, and the dogs howled at the moon.

Three days later, the report reached the Voice.

Corvan's words were few. His images were clear. The Voice studied them in the cold light of her chamber, her fingers drumming the table.

"Burn it all," she said.

And so the order went out.

***

Zexus sat still, hands tight in her lap. On the table, the candle burned low. The flame a guttering tongue. Smoke curled up to the rafters, thin as a dying breath, and danced there like serpents. The room was cold. The air tasted of old wax and fear.

Across from her, Malachar leaned against the wall, arms folded, eyes sunk in the shadow. "The priest," she said. "He's not coming back."

Zexus looked away, her face pale in the flickering light. "I know that. He'll be strung up by morning," she said softly. "All I can think about."

"You have the Cipher?"

The silence came again. It always did. It lived in the walls now, in the hollow footfalls and the brittle glass. It was the silence of waiting, of dread thickening in the marrow.

Zexus nodded.

Somewhere above, in other stone chambers, beneath the bell tower, the priest would be caught. The Dominion's men would drag him from the tunnels, their boots echoing in the dark. They would bind his wrists with wire and strip the robe from his back. They would ask him about the cipher, about the women he met, about the secrets he carried in his old and trembling hands.

He would not answer. They would press his face to the flagstones and grind his teeth into dust. They would break his fingers one by one, slow and careful, the way a farmer tests the ripeness of fruit. They would bring out the iron, red and hissing, and lay it against his skin. They would listen for the music of his pain, the way men listen for the first notes of a funeral bell.

When he fainted, they would wake him with brine. When he screamed, they would cover his mouth. When he wept, they would laugh. And when the dawn came, they would string him up in the square, his body a warning, his silence a monument.

"We shouldn't wait," Malachar said. Her voice was flat, brittle as the glass in the window. "We should go. Now. You've sent your message. It's done. We use the cipher, cross the marshlands. Take the long road east. Disappear into the forests."

"Leave?" Zexus said.

"Yes. We talked about this. Remember?"

Zexus rose. Her body moved as if unmoored, but her face had set to something else entirely. Pale and drawn, but her eyes were lit with a hard clarity. The kind you only earn after you've lost too much.

She looked past Malachar toward the far wall. Toward nothing. The silence there was heavy. She let it stretch between them.

"I remember," she said. "When things were different."

Malachar waited. Said nothing.

Zexus turned then and walked to the table, set her hands upon it. The wood scarred. Worn smooth by years of use. She looked down at the grain like it might speak to her, tell her what she already knew.

"I've been thinking," she said. "Thinking that maybe running is just a way of putting off the reckoning. We make choices. And they make us. That's the trade. I chose Gideon once. I chose the Dominion. Then I chose something else. And now the reckoning comes."

"Zexus—"

"No." Her voice was quiet, cut clean. "We talk about escape like it's freedom. But it's just another cage. This time with trees instead of walls."

She turned to Malachar, eyes sharp and strange. "I betrayed him. I betrayed all of them. And I won't run from what that means. Life's made of the things we do. And the price we pay for doing them."

"If we don't leave, we'll die."

"Maybe. You don't have to stay. I can give you the cipher," Zexus said. "What matters now, to me—what matters—is to change things."

Malachar moved forward. Her shadow stretched across the wall, long and dark like the years she'd carried. "Change things?"

"Turn the tables."

Malachar studied her. A stillness settled in her limbs like stone, her face a quiet ledger of days passed in silence. The air held its breath. The light was gray and dry, the kind that forgets warmth.

She could feel what Zexus meant. That pull toward undoing. Toward something broken made new. She'd sensed it before. In Zexus. In herself. The ache to shift what's there. But the road was long. And cruel. And she knew they were too far in to step aside now.

She let out a breath. "Then I stay too," she said.

She turned then. Slow. The sound of his movement like cloth dragged through ash.

"What is death anyways?" she said. "This life has become burdensome. Like carrying something long past the needing."

She looked at Zexus once more, the ghost of a woman who had walked too far and seen too much.

"We stay, then," she said. "Both of us."

"No. There's no reason for you to die."

"It doesn't matter."

Outside, the bells rang once, far off. Not for time. Not for warning. Just once. Then gone.

They held hands in that lonely chamber. Neither spoke. In the morning, they would separate. One to the east. One into shadow. And the Dominion would not see them coming.

***

The priestess had not eaten in many days. The powder her only food. Her lips were cracked and her eyes milky with fever, the skin drawn tight across her bones so that her face seemed carved from old wax. They found her sprawled in the red dust behind the shrine, muttering to herself, voice thin as wind through dead grass. The birds did not go near her. Nor the dogs. Her followers watched from the edges of the clearing like beasts, unsure if the fallen thing still breathed.

The sky above was hard and colorless, the sun a white coin hammered thin. The shrine to Elarlu was little more than a cairn of stones, blackened by old fire. The dust clung to her hair and to the hem of her dress, and the wind moved it in slow eddies about her feet. She lay there as if abandoned by all things living, and the world seemed to hold its breath.

When she rose, she rose like she had never been broken. Her body shook, but she stood. The followers drew back, uncertain, eyes wide and hungry. There was something in the way she moved, something that did not belong to the world of men. She brushed the dust from her palms and walked among them, her shadow long and wavering in the dying light.

They gathered in the old mill. The walls were black with age, streaked with the soot of a thousand winters. The floor was carved with symbols, circles, and spirals. The shapes the old ones had used before the Dominion came. The air inside was thick with the smell of mold and old grain. Her followers pressed close, their faces pale in the gloom, and waited.

Her voice came low as if from some place beneath the earth. "There is no more Dominion," she said.

A murmur passed through the half-dozen gathered there. There was Flint. Mael. Soreth. And there were others. Others whose names had been burned and taken new ones in her shadow. They shifted on their feet, uncertain.

"No," said Mael, voice rough. "It still lives."

"It dies," Elarlu said. "It does not know it yet. But it dies. Like an ox with its throat cut, stumbling in the yard."

"You've seen it?" asked Flint, his eyes narrow. "You've seen its ruin?"

"I see it now," she said. "It falls. Rot. Rots from within."

They said nothing for a long time. The wind rattled the broken shutters. Her breath rattled too, harsh in the silence. Her hand trembled as she reached toward the wall and drew a circle with her blood, the mark bright against the blackened wood.

"What is it?" asked Soreth, voice barely more than a whisper.

She looked at him, eyes lit like fire behind smoke. "We do not march with Gideon. We do not burn with his torch. Ours is a different fire."

Outside, the wind moaned through the eaves, and the dust shifted in the yard. The world seemed smaller, pressed in by the weight of all that had been lost.

There was silence. Then Flint leaned forward, the light catching on the scars at his jaw. "Are you saying—"

"We are different. Separate."

"You speak of treason," said Mael, his voice trembling.

"It's deliverance," she said.

They looked at her as if seeing her for the first time. The bones beneath her skin. The light that was not light. The breath that should have failed but had not. She seemed to stand at the edge of the world, half in shadow, half in something else.

"It was never his Dominion." She closed her eyes. "It was mine."

For a moment, no one moved. The dust settled, the old mill creaked, and the circle of blood on the wall glistened in the candlelight. The followers watched her, and in their eyes was something like fear, and something like hope.

***

The tower was cold and empty but for the Voice and Gideon. No guards. No clerks. Just the two of them and the wind slipping through the stone like a thing alive. The air was thin. The city lay below them, stretched and flattened, a map scribed in ash and old bone. The walls were slick with condensation. The stones sweating in the night. Somewhere far below, a bell tolled. Its sound lost before it reached the spire.

The Voice stood by the iron table, her figure sharp-edged in the lamplight. She held a small tablet, its surface bruised with fingerprints and old secrets. She tapped it once. The screen flickered, blue and ghostly, and showed footage: a hilltop gathering, candles in a ring, shadows cast long across the grass. Elarlu, pale and wasted, speaking in tongues to the faithful. The wind on the hill whipped her hair, her arms thrown wide. The faces in the crowd were rapt, hungry, their eyes shining with something that was not hope but something older, more dangerous.

"She's moving without you," said the Voice. Her voice was flat, the words falling like stones. "They've built temples in ten provinces. But I'm sure there are more. In your name, she is silent. In her own, she roars."

Gideon sat at the table, his hands resting flat on the cold iron. He watched the footage without blinking, the light from the screen carving hollows in his cheeks.

He said nothing.

"There's a phrase," the Voice went on. She let the silence stretch, let it fill the room like water. "It started in the low quarter. Now even soldiers use it."

Gideon's eyes did not move. "What phrase?"

"She is the fire that does not burn."

Gideon stood, the chair scraping the stone. "Then she is the fire that will be drowned."

The Voice did not flinch. Her eyes were pale, almost colorless, reflecting nothing. "If you drown her, they will make her a saint."

"I am only the saint. She is no saint."

"No," said the Voice. "But she is a symbol. And symbols are harder to kill than flesh."

Gideon turned to the window. The city below looked calm, lights scattered like embers, but it was not calm. It was a city waiting for the match. The wind pressed against the glass, rattling it in the frame. Far below, a patrol moved through the streets, their shadows long and thin.

"You want her dead," he said.

"I want her removed."

"You want her erased."

The Voice said nothing, her silence a kind of assent.

Gideon's reflection wavered in the window, a ghost among ghosts. "She fed the hungry," he said. "I starved them. She gave them words. I gave them walls. She has never claimed the throne."

"She does not need to claim it. They will give it to her."

Gideon stepped away from the window, the lamplight catching the hard lines of his face. "You would see her gone. You would spill blood in the streets."

The Voice's lips barely moved. "There is no bloodless end to this."

Gideon's fists clenched at his sides. "She is not the enemy."

"Perhaps not. But she will unmake you."

The silence grew heavy, thick as oil. The wind found its way through the cracks in the stone, carrying with it the scent of rain and distant fires. Somewhere, a dog barked, the sound sharp and lonely.

Gideon's voice was quiet now, stripped of command. "You fear her more than the plague."

The Voice turned from him, sank into the dark like they were looking for something long buried. The city below waited, restless and hungry, for the storm that would come.

"I fear what she carries," she said. "The way a match fears the dry grass."

At her words, Gideon's eyes widened. His jaw clenched hard and sharp, like a man chewing down on rage to keep from spitting blood.

***

The sickness spread in waves. The fisheries. The river wells. In a matter of days, the lower city drank from rusted tanks and dug ditches in the alleys for the dead. Smoke hung over the tenements, thick as old wool. The guards wore masks now. But they did not work. Mors Annona had changed yet again. It now crept past leather and brass. Found skin. Found breath. Found children.

The bodies were stacked in the gutters. Limbs askew. Eyes open to the gray sky. Women wrapped their faces in rags and poured vinegar on their hands. Boys ran with the carts, calling names, marking doors with chalk. The air was sour with rot. In the night, dogs howled and were answered by nothing.

In a broken house, with its walls split and its roof half gone, a mother knelt by her daughter in a narrow room, the girl's hair plastered to her brow with sweat. The mother pressed a damp cloth to the child's lips and whispered, "Drink, my love. Just a little." The girl did not move. The mother's hands shook. "You'll see the Siren soon," she said. "She'll come for you. Like she promised."

The cry rose again and again from every street. A word older than the city.

"Elarlu."

Sometimes a prayer. Sometimes a curse. Sometimes just a sound, broken and lost.

She had warned of this. All of it. That the water would turn. That the old world would die to make room for the next. And they believed her.

In the square called the Nine Stones, a man dropped to his knees and slit his own palms, crying that he had seen her in the smoke. That she had whispered to him. "The fire that does not burn," he said, blood dripping from his hands onto the cobbles. "She walks in the ash. She walks in the water."

A boy knelt beside him, eyes wide. "Did she speak your name?"

The man nodded, tears streaking his face as his lifeforce faded. "She said we would be remade. That we would be clean."

Across the city, in the district of Gossin, they hanged one of the Dominion's governors from the clock tower. Tied his mouth shut with red cloth and left him swinging while the plague carts rolled beneath. The crowd watched, silent. Dominion guards did not intervene. The man's feet twitched above the cobbles. Then stilled.

A woman in the crowd spat on the ground. "He took bread from my children," she said.

Her neighbor, a thin man with a cough, nodded. "He's answered for it now."

The carts rattled past, wheels slick with filth. The men who pushed them wore no masks. They had nothing left to fear.

In the alleys, the sick lay wrapped in blankets, their eyes bright with fever. Some called for mothers. Some for gods. Some for the Siren. A girl with a shaved head sang old songs until her voice broke. Her brother held her hand and watched the sky.

Above it all, in the high rooms of the Spire, Gideon watched reports come in faster than they could be archived. The screens flickered with numbers. With names. With the red sigils of quarantine.

General Lorr stood at the window, his uniform immaculate, his face gray. "It is no longer a sickness," he said. "It is a storm."

Gideon turned away from the glass, his hands clasped behind his back. "Focus on the Silent Land. That's all you need to worry about."

Lorr hesitated. "The city is coming apart."

"It will hold," Gideon said. "It has to."

Lorr's mouth twisted. "The people are starving. The water is gone. They look to the Siren now. Not to you."

Gideon's eyes narrowed. "Then let them look. When the storm passes, they'll remember who kept the gates."

Lorr shook his head. "If it passes."

Gideon walked to the table and picked up a report. "The plague is a tool, General. It burns away the weak. What survives will be stronger."

"That's if anything survives," Lorr said.

Gideon set the report down. "The Silent Land. That's all that concerns you."

"Salve Rex."

Lorr left, boots echoing down the marble hall. Gideon stood alone, the city sprawling below him, a hive of smoke and ruin. He watched the sun slip behind the towers, the sky bruised and red.

In the streets, the chant rose once more.

"Elarlu."

A single word carried on the wind, thin as breath, sharp as any blade. It drifted upward toward the Spire like something loosed from the throat of a dying god.

In that broken house, in that narrow room, the mother held the body of her daughter in her arms. She rocked her slow, her hands smoothing the hair back from the girl's face, though the girl no longer felt it.

"She'll come for you," the woman said. "She'll come for us all."

The city did not move. Night fell like a curtain drawn too long ago. The plague passed through the alleys and doorways, through parlors and gutters and beds made small with grief. It made no sound. It needed none.

And still the world turned beneath it. Slow. Blind. Unknowing.

***

That night, the wind came down from the north like a curse, and the Spire moaned in its bones. Shadows walked the halls with no feet to cast them, and the fire in the hearth burned low and without comfort. Gideon stood in the chamber where the stones remembered blood and old vows. The Voice was there. She had always been. Without arrival. Without form. Just presence. Cold and knowing.

"You know what must be done," she said.

Gideon's hands hung at his sides. Empty. As if they'd never held blade or pen or child. His face was drawn. Not with age. But with some quiet departure. Something gone from behind the eyes. Something taken.

"If we strike her now," he said, "we make her holy."

"If we do not," the Voice replied, "we lose the cities. All of them."

Gideon turned. Slow. As if movement itself had become a burden. "There is no victory here," he said.

"There is only survival."

He looked at the hearth. The coals pulsed like the hearts of things buried alive. "Whatever survives," said Gideon, "may not be worth the breath it draws."

The Voice said nothing.

They stood. Two figures in a room that had seen kings weep and tyrants pray. Outside, a bell began to ring. High and clear. The sound of plague. Of reckoning. Another followed. And another. The sound climbing a ladder to heaven no one believed in anymore.

Gideon said, "What would you have me do?"

The Voice stepped from shadow into half-light. Eyes like the end of the world.

"Not you," it said. "Me."

***

The wind came low and dry through the foothills. Carried dust and the smoke of cypress burned down to ash. Where once stood a chapel of the old design, now stood only black stone. And around it, they gathered. Barefoot. Eyes ringed in soot. Some had sewn their mouths. Some wore cords of thistle and bone. All watched the fire.

Near the stone plinth stood a man. Dominion bronze on his chest, though the sigil was scored near clean away. He watched the flame. Said nothing. Another stood beside him.

"Who gave the order?" he asked.

A boy looked up at him. Skin the color of old clay, ribs like knuckles beneath parchment. The boy did not answer.

The soldier turned. His name was Keel. He'd been through the canal sieges and the border burns. He'd watched good men drown under black banners stitched with nothing.

He looked down the hill. Another shrine. Stones pulled from the foundation of a local archive, stacked like teeth, crowned with a carved woman whose face they would not let him photograph.

"Three this week," said Lamm, his second.

"Seven, if you count the ones inland," Keel said.

Lamm spat into the dust. "No one's counting anymore."

"They're not hiding it."

"No," Lamm said. "They aren't hiding nothing."

Behind them, one of the children stepped forward. She could not have been more than ten. Her hair was sheared. She held a strip of parchment in her hands and pressed it into Keel's palm.

He opened it. Five words written in red.

We will not eat your grain.

He folded the paper. Said nothing.

A wind moved through the crowd. Some whispered. Some sang. A low, droning sound like insects.

"What do we do?" Lamm asked.

Keel looked up at the smoke, at the empty chapel, at the stone faces staring into sky.

"We report," he said. "That's all that's left."

***

In the southern quarter where the law had withered and gutters ran black with the city's bile, the monastery stood still. A carcass of stone and shadow, walls scorched by fire, rain, and years that gave nothing and took everything. The crucifix inside hung aslant, the Christ upon it charred and eyeless, arms outstretched not in blessing but in surrender. Zexus knelt beneath, her cloak heavy with the city's grief, soaked through from the walk through streets slick with old rain and newer sorrow.

Beside her, a lone candle stammered against the dark. Its flame bent sideways as if recoiling from the cold breath of something unseen. The silence in the monastery was not mere absence but presence—ancient, oppressive, thick as dust and just as suffocating. Behind her, Malachar stood in the doorway, her silhouette split by the storm's gray light. She did not step inside. She listened, eyes narrowed, for any sound that did not belong. Boots. Breath. Betrayal.

"Why her?" she asked. "This place?"

Zexus did not turn. Her voice came low, cracked like old leather. "It's where the Dominion stopped looking. A ruin too sacred for men with clean boots and ledgered sins. The bones of belief still lie here. Quiet. Forgotten. Even silence remembers how to kneel."

A gull screamed outside, its cry sharp as flint. Then came stillness, the kind that curled around your ribs and waited.

"We could still run," Malachar said.

"No."

Malachar did not move, but she saw the tension in Zexus. Her face. The old resolve. Iron rusting but unbroken.

"They'll burn us with the others."

"I know."

"We'll die?"

"We already have," Zexus said.

Malachar stepped closer. The floor creaked beneath boots worn to the sole. "And if they come? If they put knives to us and yank the truth from behind our teeth?"

Zexus looked then, past the crucifix. To the narrow window above. Outside, the streets blushed red with firelight. Not the orange fury of soldiers, but the slow glow of pilgrims. Barefoot. Wrapped in rags. Chanting through bloodied throats. Not marching—staggering. Voices worn to threads by hunger and repetition.

"We tell them Elarlu was never a woman," she said.

"Then what was she?"

"Our god," said Zexus. "She spoke. We obeyed."

Malachar's gaze fixed on the glass. She had seen cities rise like bread in the sun and fall like broken glass. She had seen children die clean. Watched killers crowned and children left to die in silence. Her voice came quiet. Flat.

"You point a finger to her," she said, voice low. The corner of her mouth turned upward, though there was no mirth in it. "And the hand still smells of blood."

Zexus returned the smile. "We change the telling."

"Then we will do it together," Malachar said. "As one. Let them know we remember. Let them know we're not finished."

They said nothing more.

Later, in the quiet before dawn, they took a blade. Shaved their heads clean, the hair falling like dead brush onto the floor. They dipped their fingers in ash made from burnt scripture. From robes and banners. From offerings once left by the devout. With this ash, they anointed their faces. Drew lines that made them look like something no longer human. They carved sigils into their flesh with a dull knife. Elarlist runes. Etched into skin slick with blood. Symbols of devotion. Symbols of penance.

Zexus stood in the candlelight, her eyes fixed on the altar. The Elarlist shrine outside had been torn down and raised up four times now. Each time it rose taller. Each time they said it reached nearer to the heavens. She wondered if it would reach far enough to be seen by the dead.

She opened a shutter. The night breathed smoke and flame. The shrine was burning again. The fire crackled like laughter in a throat too dry to weep.

Down in the street, a man dropped to his knees. He did not move again.

14 The Mouth Will Close

The sun did not rise in the Spire. It only bled through the stone in vague intimations, lightless and cold, as if the world beyond had forgotten this place. The chamber was narrow and long, built with no windows and no grace, the walls black with soot and the years. A single lamp burned on the table where Gideon sat, his fingers laced before him, unmoving.

Lorr entered without announcement. The man walked like his bones were wrapped in iron. He halted before the table and did not sit.

Gideon looked at him.

"Speak."

Lorr reached into his coat and placed a thin device on the table. The screen flickered. A single message glowed there, dim and green. Gideon did not move to read it.

"Intercepted this morning," said Lorr. "Message transmitted from the southern quarter. It pinged off our relay towers but was coded. We cracked it."

Gideon raised his eyes.

"From whom?"

"An infiltrator," he said. "A spy out of the Silent Land. Information on our plans given by Zexus."

A silence. The lamp hissed.

"How do you know it was her?" Gideon asked.

"The spy used a code to access the relays. Hers."

"Could've been anyone used it. Taken from her. Stolen."

Lorr shook his head slow. A smile without joy.

"Doubtful."

"So, what was the message?"

Lorr's jaw moved. A muscle shifted along his cheek like something trapped.

"A warning," he said. "To the Silent Land. The message was brief."

Gideon waited.

"'The Mouth of the Silent Land will close tightly,'" Lorr recited. "'Prepare for famine, for fire, for faith. Prepare for war. They will come at night. Northwest Inlet.'"

Still, Gideon did not move. The words hung there between them like smoke.

"Another traitor," Gideon said.

"She believes she can warn them," said Lorr.

"Surely, they already know. That we are coming."

"They may. But that is not the point."

Gideon leaned forward. The lamplight caught the edge of his face. A cut stone. Smooth and hard.

"Then what is?"

"She gives away our plans while we sit here planning the invasion," Lorr said. "The message came from inside the southern quarter. From our district. She's not hiding. She wants us to know she's still in the game. And that she has put us behind."

Gideon looked down at the device. He touched nothing.

"Is she alone?"

"No," Lorr said. "I am sorry to say that intelligence tells us she is with Malachar."

Gideon's eyes lifted.

"Are you certain?"

"One of our shadows saw them. Together. No attempt to hide. They sleep in the lower stacks near the ash flumes. Not far from the east stair."

Gideon leaned back. His chair creaked like old teeth. For a time, he said nothing. Then he looked toward the corner of the room, where the dark hung thicker.

"Gorgrath," he said.

The shadows stirred and Gorgrath stepped forward. The woman wore no insignia. Her cloak flaring about her, her hands blackened with something old. Her eyes were pale as salt.

"Salve Rex," she said.

"You heard."

"I heard."

"Then bring them here. Zexus. Malachar. I want them beneath this stone before the next moon. I want their words. The truth peeled from them. Do you understand?"

"I do," Gorgrath said. "And if they resist?"

"You know what to do."

Lorr nodded once. Gorgrath turned and left, her boots soundless on the stone. The silence she left in her wake was a thing alive.

Gideon rose from his chair and walked to the wall. He laid his palm on the stone.

"This city is full of ghosts," he said. "Old beliefs. Buried songs. And now a sickness spreading underfoot."

"Zexus was always dangerous," said Lorr.

"No. She was faithful once. Her brother died in the southern fields. She carried his sigil to the tribunal gates. She knelt before me and swore herself to the Dominion. I remember her. Eyes like dry wells. A loyal creature."

"She no longer is."

Gideon's hand fell.

"No."

The lamp guttered. A tremor passed through the wall. Somewhere below, the furnaces stoked themselves. The floor shook with low thunder.

"I should have kept her closer," Gideon said. "Fed her our lies and let her spread them."

Lorr looked at the message again.

"It's too late for that."

Gideon turned.

"What does this mean for our plans?"

"The code was clean," said Lorr. "No trace. It went through. Whatever defense they muster, it will be more than we accounted for."

Gideon walked back to the table. He placed both hands flat upon it.

"Then we adjust."

"How?"

"We burn the coast. Every inlet. Every forest road. No quarter."

Lorr nodded. "And if that fails?"

"Then we make gods of our dead," said Gideon. "So the living fear to follow."

Neither man spoke for a long time. The light dimmed. The air was bitter with steel and oil.

Beyond the thick walls, the city moved in its own slow agony. The sound of the furnaces rising, the distant clangor of hammers, the shouts of men in the loading yards. In the lower stacks, the air was thick with ash and the taste of old smoke. Zexus and Malachar moved through the shadows, their faces drawn and sleepless, their eyes wary of every passing figure.

In the alleys, children played with bones, their laughter thin as wire. Old women watched from doorways, their hands folded in their laps, eyes bright and untrusting. The city's heart beat slow. Hard. Each pulse a reminder of the siege to come.

Gideon turned from the table and stepped toward the narrow stairs behind him.

"Keep the war room sealed," he said.

"Salve Rex." Lorr paused. "If Gorgrath fails—"

"She won't."

"But if she does—"

"Then we never speak their names again."

Gideon descended into the dark.

Lorr stood alone with the flickering device. The words still glowing. The prophecy of a traitor. He touched the message once, then killed the screen. The light died. The room went still.

And somewhere beyond the Spire, in the lower stacks where ash fell like snow, two women moved through the ruins of loyalty. They did not know yet how loud a silence could be.

***

They were taken in a group. Elarlists. All of them. Dragged from the holding cells at dawn. Names confirmed by retinal scan. Each green flicker sealing their fate without word or mercy. Shackles clinked like distant bells in some ruined chapel. Barefoot. Soot-smeared. Streaked with dried blood. Faces gone slack with pain or prayer. It was hard to say which. Eyes not closed in rest, but sunken. Dulled. The way the eyes look when there's nothing left to see.

The guards marched in silence. Iron heels struck the floor in measured time. The corridor stretched long and narrow. Hooded lamps hung high from chains. The flames within burned still as buried fire. Casting no shadow worth the name.

The doors to the chamber were of steel. Scarred from heat and impact. They opened with the sound of old iron splitting. Beyond, a room without windows. Without furnishings. Just the floor gridded with drains and a wall of glass. Dark behind it.

They were thrown to the center of the room.

Zexus coughed. Low and hard. She spat. Red on the floor. Malachar kept her eyes forward. Neither wept.

"On your knees," one of the guards said.

They did not move.

Another stepped forward and kicked Malachar behind the knee. She fell. Zexus followed. Not from force but as if to mark the moment.

The man entered.

Malgoth.

His arms were corded with scars. His chest plated with burnished iron. His face was neither angry nor glad. It was the face of a man who believed in pain the way others believed in light.

He stood above them.

"You gave them our plans," he said. "The enemy."

No answer.

He nodded once.

One of the guards stepped forward and pulled a narrow instrument from the wall. Slender. Metal. Curved at the end like a question left too long unanswered. A hook.

It caught the light and gleamed.

"Speak," Malgoth said. "Or you will be opened."

Zexus lowered her head. Her lip torn at the corner. "You'll do it anyway."

He did not smile. He only looked to the man with the hook.

A scream followed. Long and thin. Like it had been waiting in the stone. Malachar's head tipped back. Her mouth opened. But no sound came from her. Blood ran down her thigh.

Malgoth watched. He did not flinch.

Behind the glass, Gideon stood with his arms folded. An aide by his side. The room beyond was cold and still. No sound reached it. Only the vision of the two women on the floor. Blood pooling like ink beneath them. He did not move.

Zexus raised her head. She was trembling.

"She told us," she said.

Malgoth raised an eyebrow. "Who told you?"

"Elarlu," Zexus said. "She came to us. Covered in powder. Eyes like glass. She said the world would end in green flame. That we had to warn the Silent Land."

Malgoth circled her. "You expect me to believe this?"

"In the war room," Zexus said. "Saw the maps. The red lines. Heard Lorr name the coastlines."

"How did she know this?" he said.

Zexus looked at him. Her eyes fixed. Hollow.

"Because she was there."

She coughed. Dark red threading her lips.

"I told you. In the war room. Told all of us."

Malgoth stepped back. He glanced to the man at the wall. A flick of the wrist. More instruments. More steel.

Malachar coughed more dark red.

Gideon leaned toward the glass. The memory came to him. Elarlu, barefoot in the war room. Powder white on her lips. Her voice like ruin in song. "You dream of locusts," she'd said.

He turned to the aide.

"Where is Gorgrath?" he asked.

"In the barracks."

"Send for her."

"Salve Rex."

Gideon did not watch further. He left the room, the glass at his back filled with shadows and blood and writhing figures.

He passed through the tunnels beneath the Spire. Men stepped aside. His steps made no sound.

He found Gorgrath in the hall where the sentinels trained. Her face was drawn tight. Cheeks hollowed out like old stone. Eyes cold and fixed like they'd never once blinked. The sneer on her mouth looked carved there.

Gideon spoke without preamble.

"Elarlu has become a hole in our perimeter. She speaks things she should not know. Zexus and Malachar named her. You will bring her in. Alive. If she refuses to follow, break her legs. Drag her back here if you must."

Gorgrath stood. Her voice was slow, like stone scraped.

"I thought she belonged to you."

"She did," Gideon said. "But the voices in her now does not."

Gorgrath bowed once and turned away.

Gideon did not watch her go.

Later, when the air had grown still again and the corridors silent, the guards returned to the torture room. Zexus was slumped against the wall. Shallow breaths. Malachar had passed out. The tools lay bloodied. Malgoth stood still. Arms folded. A butcher in a clean apron.

He looked once toward the glass. He knew Gideon no longer watched.

He knelt beside Zexus. Took her jaw in his hand.

"You have given us all we needed," he said. "Now you will be made useful."

Zexus tried to smile. Her teeth were red.

"I've always been useful."

Malgoth stood. He turned to the guards.

"Hang them from the tower," he said. "By their feet. Let them bleed out slow. Make everyone see them. Let the wind take their screams."

One of the men nodded.

They dragged the women out. Limp. Their heads lolling. Blood streaked the floor behind them.

***

The wind cut through the spires like a knife pulled slow through gristle. High above the city, where the stone narrowed and broke like a knuckle punched skyward, they hung. Two bodies. Bare. Bruised. Bound at the ankles with iron cordage. The blood had dried in ropes down their torsos. Black in the light. Black in the dark.

The sky turned. Burned gold to ash. Beneath them, the city sprawled in rot. Smoke wandered between broken arches. The ruins of towers split by shellfire. Fires smoldered where no one lived. The reek of old meat and burning things climbed upward like incense for no god. Wind carried it. The stink. The silence. A charred hymn sung up the Spire.

Zexus opened one eye.

The lids cracked. The lashes matted with blood. Her throat dry. She could feel her shoulders grinding in their sockets. Stretched near out of her skin. The sky was gray now. Or maybe her sight was dimming. She breathed slow through her nose.

"Malachar," she said.

It came out a whisper. More wind than sound. A tremble in the air like something about to be lost.

"Malachar," she said again.

Nothing.

The body beside her swayed in its own rhythm. Ribs sunken. Mouth open. A dark clot at the corner of her lip like a drop of tar. Her eyes were half-lidded. Her body a hollow cage turned to meat and wind. No breath moved there.

Zexus turned her head. Inch by inch. Every nerve a raw thread.

The city had not changed. Not really. No shouting in the streets. No hammering. No machines. Only the wind and the black towers rising like ribs out of a grave.

"She's gone," came a voice.

Zexus turned. To the side, Malgoth. From a window. Uniformed.

"She fought longer than most," he said. "Didn't scream when we peeled her hands open. Not once."

Zexus stared. One eye swollen shut. Her breath a thread.

"Any last words, traitor?" Malgoth asked.

She licked her lips. Tasted rust.

"I dream of a white field," she said.

Malgoth tilted his head.

"I walk across it barefoot," she said. "There are no towers. No cities. Just wind and the sound of something dying out of sight."

"You'll be dead before sundown," Malgoth said. "To let you know." He smiled. A most crooked smile. "I wanted to be here. To see it."

Zexus closed her eyes. The cord about her ankles burned. Her arms had gone numb long ago. Still, she could feel the ache behind her eyes. Something vast. Slow. Old. She saw the message she had sent in her mind. The twist of letters she had sent. A warning. A message into silence.

The wind shifted. A low whimper of air moving through broken glass. Far off, dogs. Or what passed for them now. The city breathed shallow as if ashamed of its own stink.

Zexus coughed. Blood dripped from her mouth. Hit the stone with a sound like rain.

"She believed in you," Malgoth said. "Malachar. Some salvation. All that faith. Wasted."

He spat. Watched it arc and vanish.

"Did what had to be done. For her. For my Siren." Zexus said.

The sky was darker now. A smear of violet bleeding westward.

"You think you'll be remembered?" Malgoth asked. "Some martyr? Some saint?"

"No," she said.

He reached. Touched her shoulder with his hand. Just a little. Enough to make her sway. The cord creaked.

"Then why? Why do this?"

She smiled. Barely.

"Because someone has to begin it."

He tilted his head again. "Begin what?"

"The forgetting," she said.

She didn't explain.

Below, there were footsteps. Others coming. The soft hiss of voices just out of hearing.

Zexus turned her head again. Looked at Malachar's face. Blood had dried across her jaw in a fan. A single fly crawled over her eye. Slow and without fear.

Zexus breathed in.

"The softness," she said.

"What?" said Malgoth.

Zexus didn't answer.

"That white field," she said. "Flowers under your bare feet. Soft. I will always dream."

Malgoth turned from her. The city sprawled below, ash gray and still.

"You're not the first to die here," he said. "You won't be the last."

"Fuck you," she sneered.

The wind coiled around the Spire once more. The bodies swayed in it, slow and solemn. Time kept by blood on stone.

She thought of the old priest. Her message sent beyond the border. A warning to the Silent Land. Famine. Fire. Faith.

She closed her eyes again.

There were no bells. No cries. The sky above the city grew darker still. The last of the sun cut the towers in half. One by one, the lights below flickered. Dim. Yellow. Like memory faltering.

She breathed once.

Twice.

Her body shuddered.

And then stillness.

A sigh escaped her lips. Nothing more.

Malgoth turned and looked.

They hung side by side. Silent now. The cords taut above them. The stone beneath stained dark where the blood had fallen. The wind sang soft between the rafters.

He stared at them a moment longer. Then he turned and walked away. His boots echoed on the stone.

Behind him, the sky broke into stars.

***

Not too far from the city, in a collapsed orchard where the old stone walls had fallen and been swallowed by vines, Gorgrath stood with six men. The trees were broken. Limbs twisted. Bare. The ground beneath a tangle of roots and bones. Wind moved through the branches, carrying the scent of ash and something sweeter. Something rotten. Before them, the ruin of a temple. The door hung from one hinge. Blackened and split. Smoke curled from the rafters though no fire burned. Only the memory of flame.

Inside, Elarlu sat on the floor. Her limbs curled beneath her like a dying dog. Powder lined the rim of her nose. Her belly swelled slightly beneath her robe. The cloth stained. Torn. She looked up when they entered. Her eyes were vast and wrong. The pupils blown wide. The whites jaundiced. Streaked with red. Around her lay the dead bodies of hundreds of followers.

"You came late," she said. Her voice was thin, broke at the edges.

Gorgrath did not reply. She stepped into the temple. Boots crunching on charred wood and scattered glass. Sometimes stepping on the arm or leg of a body. Her cloak swished, heavy with the dust of a thousand roads. The men behind her fanned out. Rifles at the ready. Faces hidden behind masks of cloth and wire.

Elarlu tilted her head, the gesture slow and animal. "The green flame," she said. "It takes root. You cannot kill it. You cannot burn it out. The seeds are already in your skin."

Gorgrath's eyes narrowed. She walked closer. Her shadow falling across the broken altar. The temple was cold. The air thick with the ghosts of prayers never answered. She could hear the men breathing behind her. The scrape of boots. The click of a safety thumbed off.

"You talk in riddles," Gorgrath said. "But the time for riddles is done."

Elarlu smiled. Her lips were cracked and bloody. "You think I am the end," she whispered. "But I am only the beginning."

Gorgrath struck her. The back of her hand cutting across Elarlu's face with a sound like wet leather. Elarlu collapsed to one side. Her robe twisting around her legs. She did not rise. The powder on her nose smeared across her cheek, mingling with blood.

One of the men, Harl, stepped forward. "She's weak," he said. "She'll not make it to the city."

"She'll make it," Gorgrath replied. "Or she'll die on the road. Either way, the Rex will see her."

Gorgrath knelt, her knees grinding into the cold stone. She looped the iron manacles through Elarlu's wrists. The metal biting into the flesh. Elarlu's hands were thin. The veins raised like blue cords beneath the skin.

"You belong to the Rex now," Gorgrath said.

Elarlu smiled again. Her teeth pink with blood. "I always have."

Outside, the wind picked up, rattling the broken shutters. The men shifted. Uneasy. Their eyes darting to the shadows that clung to the corners of the chapel. One of them, Jerrin, spat on the floor.

"Let's be done with it," he muttered.

Gorgrath rose and took hold of her arm. Pulled her to her feet.

She staggered. Her head hung loose on her neck like something broken. She looked about the room. At the altar. Scorched and blackened. The carvings beneath it worn down and buried in moss and old ash.

Her eyes moved to the bodies. The dead sprawled across the floor like cut blossoms. Pools of blood gone dark in the cold.

"They followed me," she said.

Gorgrath said nothing.

"They followed me. And I led them here."

"They were fools."

"You think you can drag me back," she said. "But you cannot drag the river upstream. You cannot unburn the field."

Gorgrath's grip tightened. "You'll walk," she said. "Or you'll be dragged. Doesn't matter to me."

Elarlu laughed, a sound that echoed in the empty chapel. Thin and sharp. "You don't know what's coming," she said. "You don't know what you serve."

Harl and Jerrin moved to her sides, each taking an arm. The other men fell in behind. Rifles raised. Eyes wary.

They led her out of the temple, into the orchard where the grass grew in tangled mats. Where the trees leaned together like old men sharing secrets. The sky was low. The sun hidden behind a wall of cloud. Somewhere, a crow called. Harsh and lonely.

As they walked, Elarlu spoke in a low voice. Words tumbling from her mouth like water from a broken pipe. "The world is ending," she said. "But not as you think. The fire is not the end. It is the seed. The hunger is not death. It is birth."

Gorgrath ignored her. Eyes fixed on the path ahead. The ground squelched beneath their boots. Mud sucking at their heels. The men glanced at one another, uneasy.

"She's mad," Jerrin said.

"Mad or not," Gorgrath replied, "she's the Siren. And the Rex wants her alive."

They reached the edge of the orchard. Where the old stone wall had collapsed into the ditch. Beyond, the road wound east. Back toward the city. Back toward the Spire.

Elarlu stumbled. Her breath coming in ragged gasps. Gorgrath caught her. Holding her upright.

They came into the first ring of the city. The air was foul with the reek of scorched metal and carrion. Smoke without flame. The rot of long-dead things cooked under sunless skies. Elarlists gathered. Stood in ranks along the broken thoroughfares. Barefoot. Robes in tatters. The color of spoiled meat. Their garments steeped in root pulp and bile. Their arms lifted to a god unseen by man or beast. Come with eyes sewn shut with cord black as coal. Their mouths moved at first in silence. Then not silence—a sound like air sucked through a slit in the throat. Slow and bubbling.

Children beat drums made of stretched hide and hammered tin. Their hands raw. Women stood among them and struck sickle to sickle. The ringing clash rising up like voices of buried iron. No eyes turned. Yet as the column passed, the song shifted. Not louder. Only nearer as if the sound itself had taken shape and walked among them. A chant without melody. Without mercy. The breath of the city made flesh. In its hollow heart, Elarlu lifted her face to the sound. Her grin a torn wound. Her lips forming the words though no air stirred them.

"Do you hear them?" Elarlu whispered. "They are singing. They are waiting for me."

Gorgrath looked at her. Eyes cold. "It is a song never to be heard again."

Elarlu smiled. Her eyes bright with fever. "You are wrong. The whole world sings. The world will remember the sound."

They crossed the wall and vanished into the trees. The orchard behind them silent but for the wind and the memory of smoke.

***

. . . it is still her." Gideon's voice strong.

Gorgrath blinked. Slow. Reptilian. The torchlight behind her outlined the rise and fall of her breath. "She appears each morning," she said. "Stares out the window. Still draws her sigils."

"Powder?"

"Devours it. Without it, she would go mad. Perish."

"She does not speak."

"No."

"Not a word?"

"Not a breath."

Gideon's jaw moved. "Then something else speaks through her."

Gorgrath nodded. "Or nothing at all."

He looked past her. The sentinels moved in silence. Wooden dummies shattered beneath their drills. The clang of their rhythm, though distant, bled into him.

"I'll send her to the vaults," Gorgrath said. "Be done with her."

"No," Gideon said. "Bring her to me. I want her eyes to see the Spire's heart. If there's anything left of her, it will scream there."

***

Morning in the Spire was the lie of morning. No sun reached those high corridors. No warmth. Only the ghost of light filtered down through a narrow slit cut long before memory. A wound in the wall where air slipped through laced with coal smoke. The scent of rust. Shadows pooled in the corners like things left behind. Dust hung in the air. Unmoving. Below, the courtyard turned slow as a wheel in a forgotten ritual. Pale figures drifted there. Men in armor. Eyes hollow behind their visors. Blackbirds crouched on the ramparts. Still and watching. Their heads tilted as if they knew what was coming and pitied the world for it.

Gideon stood in the quiet. His hands clasped behind him. He did not move.

Elarlu appeared.

She wore white. A prisoner's robe, frayed at the sleeves. No chains. Her hands moved slowly. Careful motions. Tracing symbols in the air. One after another. She did not speak. Her feet bare on the froststone. Gideon watched as she moved through the lower atrium toward the Hollow. Her guide, as always, was Keeper Hyros—silent and half-crippled, one arm bound in wire. His eyes too wide for his skull.

She passed beneath the threshold. Her steps never faltered.

Gideon followed.

***

The Hollow had no doors. Only descent. They walked single file into its throat. The walls narrowing. The sound of dripping iron echoing from places deeper than the Dominion's maps. No lights. No fire. The stones here glowed of their own accord, a dull corpse-luster from veins long thought dead.

Hyros led. Elarlu followed.

Gideon last.

When they emerged, it was into the round of the Hollow proper—a chamber so vast the ceiling vanished, and so silent no sound dared echo.

Elarlu stopped.

She turned to face the dark. Something there. Or nothing.

Her hands began to move. Not by her will. Fingers twitching. Rising. Dancing strange through the air like broken birds.

"Watcher's grace," Hyros said. His voice low. Afraid. He took a step back. Another.

Gideon came forward. "Elarlu," he said.

No answer came.

She drew a circle in the air. Then another. Then a line. Straight. Hard. Turned it. Inverted it. The shapes hung there like scars cut into the world.

"These ain't sigils," Hyros said. His hands shook. "Not ones I know."

"Leave us," Gideon said.

Hyros didn't wait. He was unnerved. He turned. Walked out. The door shut behind him.

"Salve Rex," said the Keeper with a bow.

When the last of his steps had faded down the hall, Gideon turned.

She stood there.

His dearest. The one who had bent over maps beside him in the firelit dark. Her breath soft against his ear. Naming cities like children not yet born. Whispering omens in the hush between battles. He had not forgotten. God help him, he had tried. She had not changed. Or if she had, the change was not in skin or voice or bearing, but in something deeper. Something time could not name nor undo. The silence between them yawned out wide and old. Not the silence of strangers, but of things unsaid and unforgiven.

He looked at her and something in him came apart. A shatter too quiet to echo. Like glass in snow. His heart, shut like a fist for years, opened of its own accord. No command. No permission. Just the ache of her presence blowing through the hollow places he thought long buried. As if time itself had only been a breath held too long.

"You betrayed us," he said. "You spoke of green flame. Of locusts. You told them things they should not know. Why? You broke the spine of everything we built. Why would you do that?"

She waited. Not to speak, but to let the words pass through her. Like wind through a ruined temple.

"I should hate you," he said. "Should kill you."

She did not flinch. Her eyes never left his.

There was powder on her lips. Pale. Almost silver.

"But I look at you," he said, voice gone rough, "and every wrong thing you have done—it's gone. Blown out like ash in a strong wind. And there's only this. Whatever this is. Whatever we are now."

And in the silence that followed, he felt it yet. The love.

Not gone.

Not gentle either. Nor clean.

A thing feral. Wounded. Still breathing.

Refusing to die.

No answer came. Only the sense of it. Like an animal in the dark. Watching. Waiting.

"I never knew how to let go," he said.

The silence that followed was thick as old blood. He looked at her. She looked back.

"I brought you back," he said.

Still, she was quiet. Then:

"I knew you would," she said.

He stepped closer. "My Siren, you hold life inside of you," he said. "Life I have helped to create. The future. How could I not love you."

Then her eyes. Hollowed out by time. By what she'd seen. Left his. Her hands began to move again. More sigils in the air.

He stepped closer. Watched her eyes. Unfocused. Pale, with a faint shimmer like something cold behind them.

Her hands continued to move uncontrollably.

"You are not mad," he said. "You're listening. To voices. To something I don't know. But it's there. And it's something that is greater than us."

The sigils changed. Faster. A spiral now. Then a descending curve. The air between her hands shimmered faintly. Not with heat but absence as if what she summoned peeled something from the world.

Gideon reached out. Grabbed her wrist.

She stopped. Stiffened. Stone beneath his fingers. Her lips parted, dry and cracked.

She spoke.

But the voice was not hers.

"You dream wrong."

The sound crawled from her mouth like smoke. Layered. Not one voice but three. All saying the same thing.

"You dream of burning trees and call it prophecy. You will lead them into silence and find no one left to kneel. The green flame will consume you."

Gideon let go. Stepped back.

Elarlu blinked once. Then again.

And began to scream.

It was not loud. Not panicked. It was a thin scream, ceaseless, like breath through a slit throat.

She did not stop.

Even when Gorgrath entered from the rear stairs. Knife already in hand.

Even when Gideon turned and said, "Seal her here. Nothing in. Nothing out. Give her the powder."

Even when the Hollow itself seemed to tremble with a sound older than stone.

***

That night, Gideon slept.

Or believed he did.

In the dream, he stood in the war room alone. The maps unrolled. The red lines gone. Only ash now. Drifts of it on the floor. On his hands. On the throne where once he sat.

And across from him sat himself.

But older. Weathered. A scar at the eye. A mouth curled with something like regret.

"What is this?" Gideon asked.

The other Gideon smiled faintly. "This is the end you refused to imagine."

"I have made no errors."

"Not yet. But soon."

The map curled into flame. A green flame.

"No one remembers who lights the match," said the other. "Only who burns."

Gideon reached for his blade.

The other stood.

"You sent her down into the Hollow. You thought you buried something you couldn't let go. You buried a message."

The room turned black. The sound of Elarlu's scream rising again. No longer thin. No longer human.

Just a long, cavernous sound. Like something clawing through stone.

And in the dark, a whisper not from Elarlu, not from any mouth—

"Prepare for famine, for fire, for faith."

Gideon woke with blood in his mouth and no memory of biting his tongue.

15 Fire

They met in the bowels of the Spire. Stone slick with condensation. Pipes overhead bleeding rust. The corridor twisted in on itself like the gut of a dying beast. No guards. No eyes. Only the dripping echo of water that had never seen the sun.

Gorgrath stood in the shadows, motionless. The wide brim of her hat swallowed her face. Her cloak, black and stained from travel, flared at the hem like something molted. She leaned against the wall. Hands in her pockets. One boot resting on the toe of the other. A shape more than a woman.

The Voice came alone.

Her footsteps rang like verdicts passed. She moved with the finality of iron. The robe she wore shimmered with threads of blood. The chain around her neck looked heavy enough to hang a man. Her face was carved from the same stone as the Spire. Hard and bloodless. Her eyes set deep and gray like forged nails.

They stood across from each other, the corridor tight and cold, the walls sweating.

"You summoned me," Gorgrath said.

"I did," said the Voice.

A silence then. As if the walls themselves had gone still to listen.

"I want her subdued," the Voice said. "Not silenced. Not broken. Comatose."

Gorgrath's mouth turned in a way that wasn't quite a smile. "Who?"

"You know who."

"Yes. I know who. But why not kill her?"

The Voice's hands tightened at her sides. "Because the people still listen. They listen even when she sleeps. But a corpse is a relic. A martyr. A banner for the next lunatic. So, I want her quiet. Harmless. Out of sight. I want her dreaming in a room no one visits."

Gorgrath shifted. Her fingers tapped once against the wall behind her. A code or a habit.

"What about Rex?"

"What about him?"

"She's his."

"Love makes fools of us all."

"You're saying Rex is a fool?"

"Doesn't matter what I say. We need to free ourselves from her. For good."

"I take it you want something from me," Gorgrath said.

"A neurotoxin. The best you have."

Gorgrath turned her head. Her eyes glinted under the hat's brim. "I don't keep that sort of thing around for favors."

"You're not being asked for a favor."

"No?" Gorgrath leaned forward. "You going to threaten me, Voice? You going to send your judges in their fine robes and ornamental gallows? I've seen whole cities eaten from the inside. I've seen men boil their children for lack of grain. I've seen the fire burn so slow it starts to hum. From a time when the world was young and cruel. You don't scare me."

The Voice didn't blink. "I don't need to scare you, Gorgrath. I only need you to listen."

More silence.

A pipe hissed above them. Gorgrath reached into her cloak and pulled out a vial the size of a thumbbone. She let it hang between two fingers.

"One drop," she said. "Into any drink. Slows the lungs. Then shuts the mind. She'll sleep like the dead. Maybe forever."

"That's not a no."

"It's not a yes."

The Voice took a step closer. Her voice dropped. "Do it. For the world that's left. For the silence we need. You've seen what she does. What she says. That madness grows roots."

Gorgrath pocketed the vial. "I'll think on it."

"You don't have long."

"Time's a problem, isn't it?"

They parted without a handshake. Gorgrath vanished into the dark like breath through a crack in the wall.

The Voice walked back alone.

She passed through stonework so ancient it bore no seams. The torches here were chemical. Spitting blue flame that smelled of solder and salt. Her boots left prints in the wet. Rats moved in the shadows and didn't run.

Her mind went back. To Elarlu's face lit with firelight. To the murmuring of her followers. The way silence fell when she spoke as if the very air grew still to bear her words. Madness, yes. But with a rhythm. A shape that could seduce.

She thought of Malachar. Of Zexus. Now dead. Their faces blue with blood. Their mouths open in useless protest. Their ends had meant nothing.

And still, some people watched the Spire as if it might answer them.

She passed a door. Didn't open it. She passed a soldier. So young.

At the lift, she paused. Touched the wall. Stone cold on her skin.

She would give the order. She would seal the chamber herself. If Gorgrath did it. Just one drop.

The city had grown quiet. The old quiet. Not peace but aftermath.

The kind of quiet that comes before rot.

She looked up.

And she felt a phantom rope. Around her neck. Not yet tied. Humming with promise.

***

The Voice woke to the sound of wind and wings.

Not the rustle of flight but the steady clatter of claws on stone. The wind up there was thin and mean and full of soot. She opened her eyes. The sky above was pale, neither dawn nor dusk. A flat gray without promise. Her vision swam, and she felt the pull in her shoulders, the weight of her own blood sinking in her skull. She turned her head, but the world did not turn with it. It hung, spinning, wrong side out.

She did not know where she was at first.

Only that she was high. And bound. Her arms lashed behind her. Her legs roped at the ankles. She swayed in the wind like a carcass from a butcher's rack. Beside her, what once had been Zexus. Further still, the remains of Malachar. Neither moved. Their bodies stiff. Flies wove their slow circles around their heads. The skin gone from Zexus' cheek. A socket open to the light. Malachar's ribs torn open like shutters in a storm.

"Help!" she shouted. Her voice cracked in her throat. "Help me!"

The wind answered her. The wind and nothing more. She looked down. The Spire fell away beneath her like the spine of some vast beast. At its base, the city sprawled. Still and silent. Not a soul in the street. No figures in windows. No footsteps. The stones below were ash-colored and empty. Like a map of a dead country.

"Is anyone there?" she screamed.

Zexus swung beside her in the breeze. Lips gone. Teeth bared like a sneer.

The pain began in her feet.

She felt the weight first. The shift of air. Then the pressure. Something light. Something with claws. She looked down. A crow stood on her upturned sole. Head cocked. Watching her with one beady eye. Feathers greasy and black. Its beak touched skin and pulled.

She screamed.

The crow hopped. Flapped. Dug its beak again into the meat just above her heel. A wet sound like fruit torn from rind. Her body jerked and she swung in place. Crashing softly into the shoulder of Zexus. Her body yielded no warmth. Her skin papery. The crow rode her movement. Pecked again. Blood ran down her leg in thin red lines.

"Get off!" she shrieked. "Gods, get off me!"

A second crow landed.

It perched beside the first. Didn't hesitate. Set to its work. They moved methodically. Tearing at the skin. Pulling loose ribbons of flesh. Swallowing them whole. One cocked its head and tore a flap from her arch. Twisting as it went. She cried out. Her voice gone ragged. The sound of it lost in the high air. Her arms burned. Her vision blurred.

"You bastards," she said, weeping now. "You bastards."

No one heard her. The crows perched in silence. Their eyes like coals sunk deep in a pit. One drew back its head and lunged again. A sick sound. Wet. She shuddered. Mouth trembling.

"I'll be free of this," she said. "Do you hear? No more walls. No more chains. No more names passed like coins from hand to bloody hand."

She turned her head to what was left of Zexus and Malachar.

"There will be an undoing," she said. "A great unraveling. The kind that doesn't stop with men or cities. They'll see. All of them. When the sky comes apart like skin and the roots rot black. I'll be watching. Laughing."

Her body swung again. The wind tugged at her robe. At her hair. Zexus' mouth touched her ear as the breeze turned them. The sound of it like whispering. She moaned. Clenched her hands behind her back as if she might pull the ropes apart by force of will alone.

The crows worked.

They hopped and squabbled. One paused to look at her face. Its eyes were empty of pity. It blinked. Then drove its beak into the soft webbing between her toes. She screamed again. She thrashed. It made no difference.

She did not know how long she hung there.

Time came loose. It spilled like oil. The sun moved behind the clouds. The light grew cold. Blood ran from her feet and dried in the wind. Her mouth tasted of salt and iron. Her head felt heavy.

One crow had taken roost on Malachar's ribcage and was tugging at something inside. The other still gnawed at her foot. She did not scream now. Her throat was raw and spent. She watched the bird work. Her mouth open. Breathing in the scent of her own ruin. Flies clung to her face. She blinked them away.

Far below, she saw a movement.

A figure. Small. Cloaked. Moving through the dead square. At the base of the Spire. She tried to move her head. She tried to call out. Only a whisper came.

"Please," she said. "Please."

The figure did not look up. It passed through the square like a ghost. Leaving no mark behind.

She closed her eyes.

The wind carried the smell of ash and under it the sweetness of decay. A bell rang somewhere. Thin and cracked. Not near. Not far. Somewhere in the bones of the city. The crows shifted. One took flight. Its wings slapped her face. The other pecked once more at her heel, then leaped away.

She hung there.

Above the city. Below the gray sky. The silence returned. Not peace. Not death. The silence of things abandoned.

She opened her mouth and laughed.

The sound came out broken. Like glass dropped on stone.

***

The wind rolled down off the high stone and dragged the ash with it. Across the rooftops and parapets. Along the blackened lanes and through the scorched trees that stood like mourners in the courtyards. Above them all rose the Spire, and from its pinnacle, three figures hung.

Gideon stood in the square at its base. Alone. His hands in the pockets of his coat. He looked up. The wind made the ropes creak against the stone. Around the square the fountains dry. No market stalls. No soldiers. Just the flagstones and the dust and the hush of a world waiting for something else.

He did not move until he heard the footsteps behind him.

Gorgrath stepped out from the archway and came to stand beside him. Her cloak was streaked with soot. The blade at her hip glistening. She looked up, too. Her breath shallow in the cold.

"It is done," she said.

Gideon nodded. His face unreadable. A man born to watch such things and remember.

"She scream?"

"She did at the end," said Gorgrath. "Longer than the others. The crows came before she stopped."

He looked at her. "You stayed?"

"I watched. I saw it through. As much as was needed."

The wind shifted. The ropes groaned. A piece of cloth came loose and fell, spiraling down and catching on the spiked railings below. Neither of them moved.

"Change comes fast," Gideon said.

"Always does."

He turned from the bodies and looked toward the far wall where tattered, pale ghosts of banners hung against the stone.

"Faster than we thought," he said. "Or hoped."

Gorgrath's jaw was tight.

"She would not yield quickly. Not even at the end. Spoke of freedom. Of a great undoing."

"There is no such thing as freedom," said Gideon. "Never was."

"How many more do you think will hang here?"

Gideon sighed. "Everyone if necessary."

She looked at him. "What comes now?"

"Now we clean what's left. Burn what we can't carry. Make ready for what follows."

"A new Voice?"

He shook his head. "No more Voices. No more sermons. No more songs. Just men and women and the silence between them."

Gorgrath looked up once more. A crow had returned and clung to the ribcage of the Voice. It pecked methodically. Its beak slick with flesh.

"Kind of pitiful in a way," she said.

"Pitiful," Gideon said.

The word hung in the air like a fly caught in the web of what wasn't there.

"Pitiful," again he said the word. "Pity. Such a true thing. Like dust. The endless dust that settles on everything. The dust of what was. The dust of what might have been. And the dust of what was left. Yes. Pitiful. But who is the pity for? The damned or the saved? And does it matter? The blood still runs. The sun still burns. Pitiful. She knew the word. They all knew the word. And now they carry it. Like a stone. A cold stone in a cold hand. Pitiful."

Gorgrath folded her arms. The sky was turning. A dull crimson behind the smoke. The city around them practically lifeless. She heard something in the wind then—something not wind at all. A cry, maybe. A baby. Or an animal. Far off.

"You hear that?"

He nodded. "Change eventually wakes up everything."

They stood in the square a while longer. Neither spoke. Then he turned and walked toward the tower. She followed. Behind them, the Spire stood like a broken tooth in the sky. The ropes swayed. The bodies danced their slow circle in the wind.

***

The sky was the color of rotted flesh, and the rain came in long sheets that hissed when it hit the ground. It sizzled on the steel of the barricades and left welts where it touched bare skin. A sour stench rose from the mud. Metal and mold and something worse. Like meat gone soft in the sun. The rivers had swallowed their banks. The fields were gone under water dark as tar. Roads buckled. Lanes vanished. What moved across them now did so without ceremony, dragging the world behind it.

At the edge of what passed for the Dominion's northern reach, the checkpoint stood. A box of rusted girders and wire. No banners. No guards. Just the slow drip of rain off steel.

Beyond it, the trees began. Black. Unyielding. The kind of forest that swallowed things. Light. Memory. Names.

The road that led there was swollen with the displaced. Not Elarlists. Just people. Sick. Filthy. Silent. They came with what they could carry and what they could not let go. Sacks and wheelbarrows. Things tied with twine. Children barefoot, their eyes gone strange from seeing too much. Men hunched under warped sheets of plastic. Women dragging the last dry blankets over crying mouths. The rain came and stayed and burned like smoke when it hit the skin. They walked in it as if they knew there'd be no end to the walking.

Sergeant Amlen stood atop the barricade. He was a tall man and narrow through the hips. His coat soaked straight through to his undershirt. The gas mask hung heavy from his neck. He had not put it on in hours. He looked out across the crowd like he had stared too long into a fire and couldn't look away now. His mouth was drawn tight. There was no blood in his knuckles.

Corporal Venn stood below him working the scanner, the small blue screen pulsing like a heartbeat. He turned a knob. It spat static and tried to die. He struck it with the heel of his palm and it flared to life again.

"They're not looking for salvation," Venn said.

"No," said Amlen. "Just a place to fall down."

"Do you think they'll stop?"

"They won't," said Amlen. "Would you?"

A woman broke from the line, clutching a bundle tight to her chest. She staggered through the muck. Hair stuck to her face. Dress torn at the hem. Her voice came broken and rough.

"Please," she said. "My baby—she's sick. And we have no food or water."

Amlen stepped down. Lifted his hand. Palm out. "Ma'am. You need to get back in line."

"She won't make it," the woman cried. "The rain—it's killing her. It's killing everyone, everything."

Venn approached. He held the scanner out over the bundle. It clicked and flashed. He stared at it, then looked at the woman.

"She's infected," he said.

The woman fell to her knees. Her sobs were thick and wet. The bundle did not move. Behind her, the crowd surged a step forward. The sound rose like wind through hollow things. Moaning. Murmuring. Prayers or threats. Hard to tell.

Venn turned to Amlen. "We can't hold them much longer."

"Orders are to contain," Amlen said. "No exceptions."

At the far end of the column, a shout went up, and the crowd shifted again. Someone screamed. Others followed. A young man ran past a cart and was struck down by another man, who dragged him back and threw him into the mud. They came forward then. Shoulder to shoulder. Hands out. Not pleading anymore. Just coming.

"Brace!" Amlen shouted. "Hold the line!"

The soldiers raised their rifles. The muzzles glinted black. The sky wept fire.

"They're not slowing," said Venn.

"We can't shoot them all," said another.

"No," said Amlen. "Then we fall back. Regroup at the secondary mark."

The barricade buckled. Boards cracked underfoot. Men turned and ran. Amlen stood a moment longer. Then he too went down the path they'd marked three days earlier. Through a grove of trees now half-felled by the wind. Behind them, the checkpoint broke apart like something meant to rot. The people poured through and kept going. There was no more order to lose.

In the command tent, Major Dren paced before a battered map tacked to plywood. Red pins dotted the country like wounds. The pins spread every day. His radio buzzed and coughed static.

". . . new strain . . . airborne . . . rainfall altering jet streams . . ."

He muttered a curse and turned to face the tent's flap where Captain Lira Sorn stood.

"They breached," she said.

Dren frowned. "Casualties?"

"Unknown. Venn and Amlen pulled back. They're coming in now."

Dren slammed his fist on the table. The pins jumped.

"Where are the reinforcements?"

"They're not coming," Sorn said. "Capital's under quarantine."

Dren stood there, his hands on the map as if the shape of the world might change beneath them if he stared long enough.

"Thought I was told it wasn't airborne," he said.

"Can't listen to everything they say."

Outside, the wind picked up and the rain slanted sideways. The storm wall was building again. The forest hissed like it had caught fire. From the treeline, the lights of the refugee column glimmered. Bobbing like will-o'-the-wisps in the fog.

Venn and Amlen entered the tent dripping, boots black with filth.

"How bad?" asked Dren.

Amlen shrugged. "They're not dying fast enough to stop coming."

"They were singing," said Venn. "Toward the end. Some of them. Singing."

"Songs?" Lira asked.

"Sounded like it. Might've been coughing."

Dren looked at the map again. He tapped one of the red pins.

"Next rain line cuts through here in thirty-six hours. The wind's shifting. They'll reach us before then."

"No perimeter will hold," Amlen said. "We saw it today."

Dren didn't speak for a long while. Then:

"Pull the supplies. Burn what we can't carry. We move at dusk."

"To where?" asked Venn.

"North," said Dren. "Further than the storm."

"And when it catches us?"

Dren looked up. There was no answer in his eyes. Only the gray of spent ash.

Outside, the rain came harder. It hissed in the trees and on the roofs and on the skin of the world itself. The Dominion had become a place the living passed through on their way to something else. What that was, no one knew. But they went just the same.

***

The Spire rose from the earth like a blade driven into the back of the world. Its shadow lay long across the city. Cold. Even in the bleeding light that leaked through the clouded sky. The stone was the color of old blood. The towers rose in crooked spirals, not made so much as born as if some dark thing had planted them there long ago. Inside, the air was dense with oil and iron. The walls wept with water that never dried. Pipes ran through the corridors like veins beneath skin, clanking and hissing in the silence. They spoke in tongues of pressure and steam. Breathing. Watching. Waiting.

Gideon stood at the window. Hands behind his back. Face pale and grave. His eyes traced the horizon where smoke curled from distant fires. Slow and mournful like something grieving.

Malgoth entered the chamber without a word. His boots echoed on the stones. His armor was etched with sigils too old for memory and too cruel for prayer. He stopped a few paces behind Gideon and waited.

"They still worship her," Gideon said. "The Elarlists. Even though we've removed her from them. They sing in the streets. They still build their shrines. Bone and bark in the gutters. The people listen to her words. Words in their heads. They kneel."

"They believe the Siren speaks for the gods," Malgoth said, his voice like gravel under water. "That she carries their will in her womb. That the child will be more than man."

Gideon turned. His face was carved from ash. "But we've silenced her."

Malgoth nodded once. "But only her. What about them?"

"Them?"

"Her followers. They still talk of her words. They sing her songs. Her voice is in their thoughts. The memory is too embedded."

"What's left of them . . . root them out," Gideon said. "Burn their shrines. Scatter their ashes. Let the city see what becomes of heretics."

Outside, the wind howled through the narrow streets. It carried with it the stench of fire and rot. Underneath it came the sound of voices raised in chant. Elarlists. The only ones who remained in the city. They stood in broken ranks. Robes dyed with pulp and bile. Crusted with filth. Some, their eyes sewn shut with black cord. All with arms raised to a god no man had seen. Children beat on drums made of stretched skin and hammered tin. Women struck sickles edge to edge, the clang rising like voices from a pit.

The soldiers came in silence. Helmets slick with rain. The iron of their boots red with rust. The hymn did not stop. It followed them like a tide.

Malgoth moved through the crowd. His face unreadable, like something carved into a ruined monument. He stopped before a cloaked woman bent in prayer. Her hands shaking.

"Do you believe in her?" he asked.

The woman said nothing. He pulled back her hood. Her eyelids sewn tight. Blood glistened at the threads like dew. She smiled.

"I see her," she whispered. "Hear her. She is everywhere."

Malgoth stepped back. He did not speak. He turned to his men.

"Burn it all!" he shouted.

The fires came. First, the shrines. Then the bodies. Then the silence.

The hymn broke into screams. High and endless. Then guttered like breath from a slit throat. Ash fell like snow. It coated the streets. The soldiers. The walls. It filled the mouths of the dead. Somewhere, a child kept beating a drum until the skin split. The frame cracked and the sound died.

From high in the Spire, he watched the smoke rising. Watched it curl into the pallid sky without a word. His face unmoved. He turned from the glass. The table stretched before him. Long and narrow. Upon it a map. Crosshatched with red. Veins drawn by fire. Every line a name no one dared speak aloud. He placed his hand to it.

"Like laying palm to a grave," he said. "My people will remember this day."

Malgoth stood at the threshold. His cloak caked with soot. Blood on his gauntlets like rust. His eyes sunk and gray.

"Fear will keep those who remain in line," he said.

Gideon nodded once. "For now."

Within the gardens, the orchard was dead. Its walls had fallen long ago. The vines took them like graveclothes. Roots twisted from the soil like limbs trying to escape the earth. Among them, an Elarist priestess sat. Her body curled in the dirt, her hands pressed to her thighs. Her robe stained. Torn. The flesh beneath it moved.

She raised her head to the wind. The scent of ash was strong now. And something else. Sweet and foul. Like rot beneath a summer sun.

"They come," she said.

The twisted trees groaned in the wind. Their limbs blackened. Clawing the sky. A ruined temple stood among them. Smoke curled from its rafters though no fire burned. Only the memory of flame. The stones bore carvings worn smooth by rain. By time. Inside, bones arranged in circles. Candles burned low.

Her teeth dripped with blood. Her lips cracked. Her eyes shone with something terrible and serene.

"They think they can stop us," she whispered. "We are forever."

Behind her, the dead did not stir. Eyes unblinking. Mouths slack in some last word never spoken. They waited as she waited. The wind blew, and the trees swayed. Like penitents in a dream. And from the belly of the city, the hymn began again. Broken. Thin. But alive.

There would be more. And they, too, would have to die.

***

The wind moved inland from the coast in long. Sulfuric breaths. The air thick with smoke. With the dead light of distant fires. Charred birds lay in the surf of the Silent Land. Feathers curled like burnt paper. The sea itself glowed faintly beneath a pall of drifting ash. Where the ocean met land, the towers stood. Thin and black. Sheathed in ceramic skin that shed heat like old snakeskin. Some smoldered. Most did not.

General Lorr stood on a rise above the first shelf of beach. Boots sunk into the powdery ruin of a once-road. His coat flapped at his legs. The mask hung from his neck, unused. He squinted against the brightness and listened to the wind. Behind him, the mechanized ranks waited. Drones stitched across the sky in silence. From time to time, one would fall. Tumbling end over end until it vanished. In a plume of its own unmaking.

"Report," Lorr said.

A man stepped forward. Mott. Face grimed. Hand to his ear. "Firegrid successful. Drones passed the perimeter. Scouting. Few heat signatures on the coast. But the towers. They remain intact. Holding."

"Holding?"

"Yes sir. They're built for fire."

Lorr turned back to the water. "We move. We go inland."

The beach was littered with slag and bone. Vehicles half-submerged in sand. Metal twisted. Windows melted. Whatever had come through here before had done so fast. The only things left were dead or dumb or waiting to be either.

Another soldier came running over the crest. Sand kicked up behind him.

"Sir," he said, breath hitching. "Drones have seen heat signatures. Farther inland."

Lorr didn't turn. "Plot their location for our machines."

"Yes sir."

"They'll die in the interior. No one survives our fist."

The man hesitated. "And the orders for their capital?"

Lorr looked at him then. One sharp glance. "My orders stand. Nothing survives. Nothing remains."

The soldier saluted. Retreated. Boots sliding in the dust.

Mott leaned in. "Sir, the coast's a graveyard. Except for a handful. Most. Those of the Silent Land. They're buried deep. Past the coasts."

"Good," said Lorr. "We'll bring shovels."

He walked down the slope toward the first tower. The wind cut around it with a whine like glass under tension. The structure rose eighty meters at least. Smooth. Silent. No doors visible. Just a single black seam. Running from the base to the peak. Around its base were bodies. Not charred. Not broken. Just laid out in circles. Hands folded. Eyes shut like sleepers.

Lorr stopped.

Mott stared. "They're not burned."

"No."

"What the hell is this place?"

Lorr raised a hand. "Listen."

They did. The wind. The hiss of cooling steel. The distant thunder of drones. And beneath it all. Something else.

A hum.

Low. Constant. Without rhythm. Not mechanical. Not natural. As if the tower itself breathed.

He stepped closer. Mott reached out. "Sir—"

But Lorr was already at the base of the tower. He touched the seam with his gloved hand. It was warm. Not from the fire. Not from the sun. Something else. The material gave slightly. Like flesh.

He pulled back.

"Bring the thermite," he said. "Melt it down."

They moved quickly. Two men ran down with canisters strapped to their backs. The fire spread in a tight circle. Molten metal chewing into the tower's skin. Opening a seam. Spraying white-hot droplets that hissed as they hit the sand. For a moment, it seemed the tower would open. Split like fruit. Then the flame died out. The metal cooled. The seam reformed. Whole.

Mott shook his head. "What are these things made of?"

"Don't know."

"Bring some scientists out here to study one of them."

Mott nodded.

"South," Lorr said. "We move now."

Mott hesitated. "Sir, the men . . . they are tired and hungry."

"Don't care. Time is not our friend."

With a signal, columns of soldiers moved over the dunes. Boots kicking up black sand. The sun hidden now behind smoke and drone shadow. The sky a smudge. The towers shrank behind them. Receding like sentinels unmoved by war. Ahead, the land stretched empty. Vast. Occasionally, the ground cracked beneath them. Craters. Tunnels. Too round to be natural. Too old to be recent. Lorr said nothing of them. Just walked.

They quickly came upon corrugated metal structures warped by heat. Plastic sheeting melted into ribcages. Signs painted with glyphs not found on any map.

A child's doll lay in the dirt. Its face scorched smooth.

Lorr stepped through the ash and looked at the tracks. Not animal. Not human. Something between.

Mott joined him. "What is that?"

"Doesn't matter. We move onward."

A drone returned and hovered above them. Dirt on its surface.

"General," he said, "there's something ahead. You should see."

Lorr called for a viewscreen.

"Show me," he told the drone.

The drone led them around a collapsed wall. Into a pit. At the bottom of it lay a thing. Once a man. But different. Its body was stretched. Ribs split open like wings. Jaw dislocated. Skin peeled back from the skull. On the wall above it, a message burned in soot:

THE FLAME DOES NOT END.

Lorr stared at the viewscreen. He turned to Mott.

"Bio-engineered human. Meant to fight."

"Experiment turned bad?" Mott asked.

"Most likely," Lorr said. "Burn this place."

Mott nodded. "All of it?"

On the viewscreen, Lorr looked into the dark beyond the pit. At the country with few roads. The mountains green with vines and memory.

"All of it. We keep going. Bring the machines."

The fire came again. The drones passed overhead. Dropping their payloads in perfect silence. The ground shook. The sky changed. The men marched.

And the towers watched. Unbroken.

16 The Great Machines

The fireline at the coast had broken again. It spread like oil in a ditch. Black tongues gnawing the low trees. Smoke seething over the high ground where the Dominion's first machines had landed.

Reza stood before the wall of screens in the half-light. The room was carved from the side of a dead hill. Lit only by the cold glow of the viewscreens and a red bulb swinging slowly from a wire. An eye of some patient animal. The floor was dirt. Packed and dry. He'd not spoken in over an hour.

Dunlow stood with arms crossed. That narrow man. The one Reza needed.

"They're burning everything," Dunlow said.

Reza did not look at him.

"That's their plan. To smoke us out. Flush the hills. Standard Dominion way. Fire and smoke. Push to the center. Cut the heart. Let the body rot behind it."

Reza touched a knob on the central console. The view blinked to a long slope of yellowed grass. Smoke moving low. Close to the dirt. In the distance, the sea glinted copper beneath the plume.

"Now?" Dunlow asked.

"Not yet," Reza said slowly.

"You're waiting for them," said Dunlow. "You think they'll send them?"

"They have to."

Dunlow sucked his teeth. He stepped closer to the screen. Pointed with a crooked finger at a group of Dominion soldiers disembarking from an armored crawler. White armor, backlit by flame. They looked like bones walking.

"They're already inside the perimeter," Dunlow said. "Soon, they'll hit the towers."

Reza didn't reply. His left sleeve was pinned up tight where the arm ended at the elbow. His remaining hand still rested on the console like something carved from dark stone.

"They're coming," he said. "The great wheels."

He knew it. Could sense it.

Then the earth gave its answer.

A sound like the oldest thing in the world waking from a long sleep. A long-buried god rolling over in its grave. The ground gave off a tremble that ran through the concrete. Through the soles of their boots. Through the bones. A deep rumble that made the screens quiver in their mounts. One of the drone feeds stuttered. Cracked into snow. Then blinked back to the image of a soldier halfway through turning. His mouth open. Eyes lifted to something the camera didn't catch.

Reza didn't speak. His face had not changed. A long face carved by time. By wind and loss. Dark with sand and oil. He clicked through the feeds one by one. Fingers deliberate. No hurry.

And there they were.

Dunlow stepped backward without thinking.

"Shit."

Over the rise. Great metal beasts. Wheels. Climbed like beasts from the old world. Coated in mesh. Slag. Welded bone. Their size absurd. They stood taller than the grain towers that once fed a world gone dry. Taller than the husks of the old refineries. Taller than the gutted temples that still clawed at the sky in the cities left behind. Their hulls were blackened with soot and ritual.

Daubed in old blood and machine oil. Names of the fallen carved into their sides like scripture.

"Godless things they've made," Dunlow muttered.

The treads beneath them were not of rubber. Not of steel. They were slabs torn from refinery walls, the concrete chipped and pocked, twisted rebar still jutting out like veins. Each link remade with teeth. With blades. Things meant not just to roll forward. But to rend. To chew the world as they passed.

Modified harvesters. Grain-machines turned to war. The irony did not move Reza. He had seen worse turned worse still.

They came in a slow line. No haste in them. Several of them. No fear. The dust peeled off the monsters in tall columns. Spiraling upward as if the sky itself recoiled. Their engines made no scream. Just the low grind of mass in motion. Deaf and inexorable.

Reza leaned forward.

Dunlow said nothing. Then, he asked, "How many?"

Reza did not count. His eyes moved between the machines and the fields. Fire still burning on the coastline. The gulls wheeling over it like scavengers circling some perverse paradise.

He said, "Enough."

"They've breached," Dunlow said.

Reza nodded. His face was worn deep with years of heat and gunpowder. Lines like dry riverbeds ran from the corners of his eyes. Down into his beard. He turned to the radio panel. Flipped the switch.

"All stations," he said. "Condition Red. The wheels have crossed the line. Begin ignition protocols at the towers. Drones to hold back until nets engage."

Dunlow was already moving. Shouting into another commlink. Rattling off codes. Red lights came to life across the room. Somewhere above them, they heard the groan of servo-motors. The electromagnetic nets began to charge. A high, sharp whine building like cicadas in a box.

"You ever seen one of those things up close?" Dunlow asked without looking at him.

Reza didn't answer. Didn't need to. Of course, he had.

"Back in the southern farms," Dunlow said. "One of 'em rolled straight over a group of farmhands. Didn't even notice. They were screaming. Crawling out from under each other. It didn't stop."

Reza said, "They don't stop. Easily."

"Not made to," Dunlow said.

The largest of the machines came into view. Its front chassis bore the Dominion sigil. Antennae coiled above it like the horns of a beast. The thing moved with a terrible grace. Like it was too big to be allowed and knew it. The ground trembled with its coming. Everyone could feel it in their teeth.

Dunlow leaned close to the commlink.

"Cliff helos green. All wings confirm. Ready sweep."

There came a chorus of acknowledgments. Static voices. Men with names that were barely men anymore. Callsigns. Designators. Dogs waiting for a signal.

Reza said, "Send them."

Dunlow relayed the order. The screens began to shift again. One by one, black dragonfly helos rose from crevices in the cliffs. Long rotors. Thin bodies. The wind kicked up dust and old flags alike. Below them, the towers stood. Humming with a pale light. The netting extended outward like silver veins. And beyond all of it, the Dominion wheels pressed onward.

"They're baiting us," Dunlow said.

"Maybe," said Reza.

"Trying to draw out the birds. Expose the towers."

"Doesn't matter now."

"You think this is all they've got?"

"Who knows."

Reza watched as one of the great machines turned toward a tower. Slow. Deliberate. The helos swept toward it, banking low. From their undersides dropped canisters that opened midair and released burning trails. The screen flared. Then dimmed.

When the picture returned, the machine had not stopped.

"Net it," Reza said.

Dunlow punched in the command. The tower arced with lightning. The electromagnetic web flared to life like a god's hand outstretched. It lanced into the side of the great machine. The thing shuddered. Groaned. Sparks flew from its flanks.

Then it did stop.

Smoke poured from beneath the wheel. Panels burst and hung open like flayed skin. For a long moment, it just stood there. Hissing.

"One down," said Dunlow.

"It's not down yet," said Reza.

Sure enough, the thing moved.

Jerked forward once. Then again. As if it was angry. As if the earth itself had grown teeth and decided it would not lie quiet. The wheels spun. Though the treads screamed against the ground. Then it found grip.

"Goddammit," Dunlow whispered.

Reza's face did not change.

"Ready the launchers," he said.

"They're not in range."

"They will be."

The great machine staggered forward, dragging part of its flank. Smoke poured from the venting slits. Around it, Dominion soldiers gathered. Some dragging lines of flame. Others planting exploding rods in the earth. They moved in concert, not like men but like limbs of the same creature.

From the ridge, a second wheel crested the slope.

"Another," Dunlow said.

"Aye."

"Should we fall back?"

"No."

"They'll flatten us."

"Let 'em try."

Reza stepped back from the screens. Walked across the room and opened a steel box against the far wall. Inside were the launch codes. He pulled the thick switch free. Tucked the tag with codes into his breast pocket.

Dunlow was staring. The sweat on his brow catching the red light.

"You really gonna do it?"

"If they reach the heart of the land."

"That'll kill everything from the cliff to the salt fields."

"Everything will already be dead."

Dunlow shook his head. "Were we meant for this war?"

"Yes."

"I didn't come for glory. I joined for the money. For the hate. For the damn rifle."

Reza looked at him. A smile. Raised eyebrows.

"And you'll die for it all, old man."

Dunlow opened his mouth. Then closed it.

A tremor rocked the compound. Dust rained from the ceiling. One of the screens broke into flickering lines. When it steadied, another wheel was climbing the slope. Behind it came the Dominion walkers. Different kinds. Bipedal gun-things. Crab-legged and armored in ribbed steel. More wheels.

The lead wheel reached the first tower.

Reza flipped a switch.

The netting deployed. The wheel touched it. Sparks flew again.

Then the wheel fell. With a crack. Like the world breaking open. The firelight washed everything red.

From the hills, the launchers roared.

Missiles tore across the sky. Fire trailing them like comets loosed from the hand of God. The horizon flared. The other wheels turned. But too slow. They were made for war but not for escape.

It was too late.

They were caught. Half-dead things watching death approach. The impact came hard and final. One. Two. Three. The wheels shuddered. Then fell. Flames rose and took the sky. The screens went white. Then black. Then nothing at all.

Reza stood still. Like a thing carved from the silence.

Dunlow sagged against the wall. His breath came like he'd climbed out of drowning.

"Did we win?" he said.

Reza said nothing.

The last screen flickered. It came to life. Showed the scorched fields. Smoke rising from dead wheels. Fire dancing across the broken sea.

Reza watched. He knew it wasn't the end. More would come. More wheels. More men. More blood.

***

The machine had no name. But the men inside called it the Mule. The word was scratched into its side. On one of its many panels. It was a tower on wheels. Ribbed and riveted and swaying like a thing alive as it crawled across the broken shoreline. Like the others, it was built from the frame of an old harvester. The kind that once tore wheat from the world in long golden waves. There was no wheat now. Only ash and grit and the stink of old oil.

A man riding inside was Corporal Vant. He had once been a mechanic before the wars. Before the soil went black and the skies filled with drones. Now he wore armor that didn't fit. Carried a rifle he didn't know how to clean. His stomach growled in the dim amber light of the control bay. The rations had been thin and old. Something like salted paste wrapped in foil. He'd traded two of his packs for a woman back in the southern barracks. She wasn't worth it.

Now the Mule crawled up the incline toward the cliffs. Its groaning limbs kicking loose scree and burned brambles. The air around it trembling with the hum of its generators.

He scratched at his neck, listened to the breathing of the other men around him. Three in the bay. Two above in the cannon turret. And Lieutenant Grahn in the forward cockpit, silent as a statue. His gloved hands resting on the throttle like they were praying.

"Something stinks," said Brell, the youngest of the crew. He had that twitchy look some men got when they didn't sleep.

"That's just you," Vant muttered.

"No, I mean something's wrong."

"You want to spell that out?"

Brell looked around the bay. Saw the fire on the water. Saw the dead machines. Saw the dead bodies. He said nothing.

There was something. Vant felt it too. The kind of knowing that didn't come from the eyes. Or the ears. But from somewhere lower down. Deep in the guts. The old feeling he used to get right before a fuel tank blew. Or when an axle was about to shear clean off and bury you under it.

"This ain't good," he said.

He shifted in his seat and rubbed his stomach. It growled again. Long and low. He patted it like it was a dog that wouldn't calm down.

Above them, the gunner yelled, "Movement on the cliffs."

The Mule shuddered as it slowed. Brakes screeching like pigs being skinned. The cabin filled with the hot stink of metal and sweat. Outside, the air was full of black fog and ash drifting like insects.

Grahn's voice came down from the cockpit. Low and dry. "Visual?"

"No," said the gunner. "Not clear. Could be a bird. Could be a drone. Hell if I know."

"You shoot it?"

"No sir. Out of range."

In a matter of seconds, the gunner saw it.

A bird.

The Mule resumed its crawl.

Vant looked at the screen before him. Grainy feed from the hull cameras. Scrub and stone. The torn-up remains of another machine. A Mule like theirs burned through the belly. A dark shape stuck to the cliffside, like a shadow that had teeth.

"Shit," Vant said.

Grahn's voice again: "What?"

Then he said nothing more.

"They're everywhere," Vant said. "Dead wheels."

Brell was tapping his boot against the floor now. "They stopped sending scouts up the ridgeline."

"Yeah, because they didn't come back."

Vant said it like he was telling the kid a bedtime story. Something the elders whispered to keep the little ones from wandering.

"You feel it, don't you?" Brell whispered. "Same as me."

Vant nodded. He did. He wouldn't say it. Not loud. Not in front of the others. But it was there. Like a splinter buried too deep to pull out. That crawling itch under the skin. Something waiting. Something watching.

"You know of the nets?" Brell asked.

"Nets?"

"The ones they bury into the land. To catch prey. But they don't catch animals."

"Shut up," said Vant. "You don't know what the hell you're talking about."

"That's what they use. To catch war machines."

The Mule halted again. This time, the brakes didn't squeal. Just a low pneumatic hiss. The sort of noise that meant systems were cycling. Cooling down. Or giving up.

Vant turned to the screen again. Still just stone. Smoke. The black sky broken by the jagged spires of towers.

"Orders?" he said into the comm.

No answer.

"Lieutenant?"

Still nothing.

He looked at the other two men. Brell wide-eyed. The third man, Desco, hadn't spoken once since they rolled out. He was staring at his boots.

Vant unstrapped himself. Climbed the ladder to the cockpit.

Grahn sat stiff in the seat. Hands locked to the throttle like a man steering into judgment. His eyes were open. Fixed. No blink. No breath.

"Lieutenant?"

Silence.

Vant leaned in. Close enough to smell the metal and sweat still clinging to the man's collar. The stillness was absolute.

The chest did not rise.

Gone.

"Heart must've gave out," Vant whispered. Maybe to the dead man. Maybe to himself.

He backed away. Slow at first. Then stumbled down into the cabin below. The silence chasing him like it meant to drag him down too.

"Grahn's dead," he told the others. "No more words from him."

Brell laughed once. Sharp and awful. "He knew," he said. "He knew and got out while he could."

"What killed him?"

Desco looked up. "Same thing that's gonna kill us. Fear."

Outside the Mule, something shifted. The air was thick now. Vant stepped to the hatch. Unsealed it. The wind hit him like a slap. Ozone and iron, and something else. Something like a scorched corpse.

On the ridge above them, lights were blinking.

Not fire. Not flares.

Something watching.

He stepped back inside and bolted the hatch.

"Buckle in," he said.

"For what?" Brell asked.

"For whatever comes next."

And the Mule sat still in the black dust, while the cliffs above began to hum. Then it moved forward. Ever so slowly.

***

The room stank of old sweat and the faint copper tang of blood leached from the stone. Reza stood before the screens. The red bulb continuing its swing on its wire. The dirt walls pulsing slowly with color. Smoke on the monitors. Black tongues licking the ground. The Dominion's machines crawling over the land like beetles upon a dying carcass. Dunlow shifted beside him. Boots creaking. Arms crossed tight against his chest.

Reza's voice was quiet. But it cut through the hum of the bunker. "Switch more power to the netting. All towers."

Dunlow looked at him, eyes narrowed. "You sure? It'll mean little to no power for those inland."

Reza did not look away from the screens. "No choice. Do it."

Dunlow turned, barking orders into the commlink. "Grid command, this is Dunlow. Route all spare capacity to the towers. I want every coil hot. Do it now." His voice echoed down the passageways. Down to the men huddled in the generator rooms. Faces smeared with oil and fear.

The screens flickered. The image shuddering as the power surged. Outside, the towers began to hum, a sound that built in the bones. A keening that set the teeth on edge. The netting stretched between them. Glowed faintly. Blue and cold as winter lightning.

"More?" Dunlow asked.

Reza nodded. "Yes. But we've got a surprise for them."

On the screens, the machines rolled forward. The great wheels. Armored flanks wearing the Dominion sigil. Painted in black and white. The Mule was one of them. A tower on treads. Bristling with antennae and guns. Men moved in its shadow. Rifles slung. Faces hidden behind mirrored masks.

Reza leaned into the console. His one hand steady on the controls. "Hold until they're in the kill zone."

Dunlow wiped sweat from his brow. "They're almost there."

A tremor ran through the floor. In the monitors, dust peeled away from the machines, spiraling into the sky. The Mule's engines growled. The sound of it rolling over stone and bone and the memory of wheat fields.

"Now," Reza said.

Dunlow slammed the switch. "All towers. Full discharge."

Outside, the towers screamed like dying animals. The netting flared and buckled. Lit through with fire. The color of frozen stars. Blue arcs leapt from coil to coil. Ran wild through the mesh. Poured like molten iron across the sky. The ground spat sparks. They climbed the legs of the war machines. Skittering like insects. Licking at the joints and wheels with a hunger that knew no end.

In the Mule, Corporal Vant felt the world go white. The control bay filled with a sound like the sky tearing. Sound tore through it. Raw and high and endless. Like the sky itself had split from crown to root. His hands snapped back on the levers. Blood filled his mouth where his teeth had closed on his tongue. The stink of ozone choked the cabin, and something beneath it. Darker. Plastic. Flesh. Wires.

Brell screamed. A thin sound. Sharp and almost human, before his body seized hard against the straps and went silent. Desco convulsed. Foam at the mouth, eyes rolled to the ceiling. Boots kicking against the floor. No prayer. No curse. Just the silence of a mind drowning in fire.

The hull of the Mule went red. Then white. Then red again. Rivets burst like gunfire. Plates warped. Smoke coiled from the vents and curled around their feet like something alive. The machine shuddered and died on its treads. The gunner's body sagged in the turret. His hands still gripped the firing controls like he hadn't yet understood he was dead.

Outside, the others suffered the same. The lightning net bound them all. Arcs danced across armored hides. Danced inside helmets. Circuitry bloomed into ruin. Dominion soldiers dropped mid-step. Twitching. Glowing. Their armor hissed and smoked as if the heat within had become too much for even metal to bear. Some tried to crawl. None got far.

Dunlow watched the monitors, jaw slack. "God almighty."

Reza's face was stone. "Keep it going."

The power surged again. The towers burned with light. The netting alive with energy. The Mule groaned. Metal screeching. The Dominion sigil blistering. Peeling from its flank. Inside, Vant's body smoked in the harness. Eyes wide and blind. The control panel sparked. Screens shattering. The smell of cooked flesh filling the cabin.

On the ridge, the great machines staggered. Their movements locking. Seizing. One toppled. Crashed into the rocks. Its crew already dead.

Dunlow turned to Reza. "We're going to blow the coils."

Reza shook his head. "We blow them, or we die."

The ground bucked beneath them with the last shudders of the dying machines. The sky above the killing field flared. Blue and white. Split by arcs of energy that danced across the wreckage. Like lightning without thunder. The towers stood silent in the haze. Black. Skeletal. Remnants of an age that had long since eaten its own children. The netting sagged low. Burned through in places. Scorched. Frayed. But still enough of it held. Just enough to finish what had been started.

The Mule's engines sputtered once. Then again. A coughing rattle like something drowning in its own blood. Then silence. The machine sagged forward. Metal groaning. Smoke billowing out in long, choking streams from its seams and joints. Inside, the crew had died without a scream. Armor fused to skin. Eyes gone to steam behind the visors. What had once been men were now meat sealed in tin.

Reza stood at the console, the dim green light of the screens dancing across his face. His hands still. His breath slow. The last machine on the field gave a final twitch, then stilled. Nothing moved but the smoke.

The field lay ruined. Twisted frames. Torn steel. Scattered like bones after a feast. The air was heavy with the stink. Burning oil. Scorched wiring. Something underneath it all that might once have been human.

Dunlow slumped against the wall. Breathing hard. "It's done."

Reza nodded. "For now. Send in the helos. Pick off any who remain."

The sun never quite broke through the smoke. It hung above the field. A dull coin. The air was thick with the stink of scorched oil. The sweet rot of burned flesh. The ground was littered with the dead. The dying Dominion soldiers in white armor. Sprawled in attitudes of agony or surrender. Some crawling, some kneeling. Some simply staring at the sky. Eyes that saw nothing. The machines were still. Hulks of metal and wire. Hulls blackened. Innards leaking steam and blood.

From the cliffs came the sound of rotors. The big helos. Painted in the old colors. They swept low over the field. Their blades beat the air into submission, sending up coils of dust and ash. Doors slid open. Gunners leaned out. Faces hidden behind mirrored visors. Hands steady on the grips of their guns.

The first burst came sudden. Clean. A Dominion soldier in the open. Helmet cracked. Staggered to his feet. He raised one hand. To plead or curse. But the gun spat, and he folded. Arms flung wide. The dust blooming red beneath him. The helo banked. Another burst stitched the ground. Catching two more as they tried to crawl for the cover of a dead machine. They jerked and lay still.

The helos moved in a slow circle. Methodical. Hunting. The gunners picked off anything that moved. A Dominion officer. His cape torn. Burning. Tried to run for the treeline. He made it three steps before the rounds caught him in the back. Spun him around. Dropped him face-first in the black grass. A medic. Helmetless. Wild-eyed. Waved a strip of white cloth. The helo gunner didn't hesitate. It fired. The medic fell. The cloth fluttering down beside him.

Reza watched the feeds in silence. The screens showed the field from a dozen angles. Each one the same. Smoke. Ruin. The slow, deliberate sweep of the helos finishing what the towers had begun.

Dunlow stood at Reza's shoulder. Arms folded. Face pale. "No prisoners," he said.

Reza did not answer. His eyes were fixed on the images. The slow erasure of the enemy. The helos moved on. Their guns never silent. Until there was nothing left but the dead and the silence that followed.

When it was done, the helos circled once more. Then rose into the smoke and were gone. Their shadows passing over the field like the wings of some old and vengeful god. The wind stirred the dust, and the world was quiet again. Save for the crackle of distant fire and the low moan of the wounded, fading into nothing.

Reza turned from the screens. "It's finished."

Dunlow nodded. But his eyes did not leave the field. "For now," he said.

And outside, beneath the ruined sky, the land remembered its dead.

Inside the Mule, the world had become a cage of light. Of pain. Vant's last thought was of wheat fields. Golden. Endless. Before the charge took him. Brell's scream never made it past his teeth. Desco's hands clawed at the air. Then fell still.

The machine sat in the dust. Smoke clawed from its hull. The Dominion sigil was scorched, the paint running in black rivulets. Within, the crew sat silent. Bodies twisted in the harnesses like old rags. Eyes staring at nothing.

On the field, the other machines were still. Some burned. Some simply lay quiet. Their engines dead. The Dominion soldiers who had followed them lay scattered. Armor fused to flesh. Rifles melted in their hands.

Above, the towers still hummed. The netting sagging in the heat. The wind carried the smell of ozone and scorched earth.

Dunlow looked at Reza. "What now?"

Reza stared at the screens. The field of wreckage. The towers standing against the sky. "We wait."

Dunlow nodded. "And if they come again?"

Reza's eyes were dark. "We do it again. And again. And again. Until there is nothing left."

The red bulb swung on its wire. The only light in the room. Outside, the world was quiet. The fireline at the coast still burning. The sea glinting copper beneath the smoke.

Reza stood alone before the screens, his hand resting on the console. The land was dead. The machines were dead. But something in him was not yet spent. He watched the monitors, waiting for the next thing to come crawling out of the smoke.

He did not have to wait long.

On the far edge of the field, a new shape moved. Smaller than the Mule. Quicker. A scout or a drone. It picked its way through the wreckage. Sensors glowing in the twilight.

Reza leaned forward. "Dunlow. Get the birds up."

Dunlow moved to the commlinks, voice sharp. "All wings, scramble. We've got movement on the field."

The screens flickered. The image shifting as the cameras tracked the new machine. It moved like a thing alive. Weaving between the corpses of the larger machines. Pausing to scan the wreckage.

Reza watched in silence. The war was not over. It would never be over. Not while there was breath left in the land. Not while there were men to fight and machines to build.

The towers stood against the sky. Humming with the last of their power. The netting gave off a faint blue light. Cold and dying. The field lay still. Only the wind moved. Somewhere far off, a fire snapped. Hissed.

Reza turned from the screens. His face carved from stone. "Prepare the charges," he said.

Dunlow nodded. "Aye."

They moved through the bunker. Men gathering weapons. Checking charges. Eyes empty with exhaustion. Outside, the wind howled, carrying the promise of another night, another battle.

The field of wreckage glowed in the twilight. The towers standing like sentinels over the dead. The Mule sat in the dust. Its crew silent, its engines cold.

Reza stood at the door of the bunker, looking out over the land. The sky was dark. The fireline still burning. The sea reflecting the last light of the day.

He did not speak. There was nothing left to say.

The war would go on. The land would burn. The towers would stand. Humming with stolen power, waiting for the next assault.

And in the dust, the machines would wait. Silent and dead. Until the earth swallowed them and the world forgot their names.

17 A Tapestry of Ruin

The chamber air was dry and still, a hush that pressed the skin. No windows. Only the ceaseless hum of filtration. The slow, subterranean breath of power in the walls as if the very stone dreamed of old, dark days. General Lorr stood. Boots set on the polished concrete. His uniform, brushed clean, still bore the scalds and black seams of a ruined campaign. Fabric stiff with old ash and memory. Gideon sat behind a desk that rose from the floor, seamless, immovable. His hands steepled, fingers bone-white against the black surface. Eyes fixed and unblinking.

"You have something to report," Gideon said. His voice flat as stone.

Lorr nodded once. "The Silent Land is lost."

Gideon did not move. The silence between them gathered.

"They used fields," Lorr said. "Electromagnetic. Not known to us. Our engines choked. Machines locked. Shields blinked out. The men—"

He stopped. Words caught. A thing remembered too clearly.

"The men died in their armor. Boiled raw."

Gideon's eyes closed. His jaw clamped. Tight as a trap. Then they opened again. His breath came long. Slow. Controlled. As if to shape the air to something less bitter.

"Death is just part of the game," Gideon said. Cold.

Lorr held silent.

"And you retreated," Gideon said.

Lorr looked down. The shade of ruin lay heavy on his shoulders. "We did not retreat. Not as you mean it. Those who lived when the electromagnetic charges collapsed—"

Lorr paused. The words caught like bone in his throat.

Gideon watched. "Yes?" he said. "What happened?"

"They were hunted. Large helos came. No sound. Only wind. They culled the survivors like cattle led to slaughter. Took some. Most were killed."

Lorr's voice held no inflection. Like something long since drained of meaning. Words fell from his mouth. Just drifting about. Behind his eyes, things moved. Old things.

"What of those taken?" the other man said.

"Most likely tortured for information. For anything. For nothing."

"What information could they possibly have?"

"None," Lorr said. "That's the horror of it. The emptiness."

He looked away then. Shook his head. A shadow passed over his face. A fleeting recognition of dread. And was gone.

"They knew what they were getting into," Gideon said. Words flat and dry as dust.

Lorr held his tongue. Swallowed something bitter.

"And the machines?" Gideon asked. His gaze on the empty air.

"Gone. Only dead metal." Lorr said. "Nothing left but wreckage and ash. Wind through the bones."

"Drones?"

"A thousand or so. Few remain to guide them. Starvation runs now. Unchecked." His hands straight at his side.

"Hold the drones back," Gideon said. "They could still be useful."

The silence that followed was not empty. It filled the room, thick. A suffocating garment. Swelled behind Gideon's eyes until they nearly watered. But they did not. He leaned back in the chair. Looked at the ceiling as if it might crack open with something other than truth. The hum of the chamber seemed louder now. A dirge for the fallen.

"Probably cannot mount another assault?"

"We cannot, my Rex."

Gideon nodded. Once. The gesture slow. Final.

"What remains of our forces?"

Lorr did not hesitate. "The few we have are being used to dispose of the Elarlists."

"How many?"

"Not many. Ten thousand, give or take. Scattered through the districts."

Gideon looked at Lorr. Something moved in the older man's gaze that was not surprise. Not regret. Only something fossilized as if the bones of old kings stirred there. The air between them was heavy. Freighted with all that could not be said.

"Change," Gideon said softly, "is sometimes difficult."

Lorr turned. Shoulders taut as if to leave. Then the sirens began. He froze. The wail swelled. Filling the marrow of his bones. A sound ancient as grief. The first shockwave struck. A dull thud that rattled the glass in the pane. Sent dust sifting from the ceiling seams. Outside, the city bloomed in orange and white. Bombs fell in silent arcs before the thunder of their arrival. The ground bucked beneath their boots. Through the glass, city structures shuddered and split. Flame licked skyward. Black smoke writhed in the wind. The world beyond became a furnace. The night alive with the howl and hammer of the Silent Land's wrath. The sky torn open in violence.

"Report!" Lorr shouted into the commlink. His voice was clipped. Hard-edged. Like steel dragged across stone.

The reply came cracked and stammering. Broken by static. Panic.

"Dominion's under attack. Repeat. Dominion's under attack. Silent Land forces in Dominion airspace. Large helos inbound. Multiple strikes. East towers hit. Coastline's breached."

Lorr moved to the black glass on the far wall. Boots rang in the hush. The regions beyond the city a fire pit. The horizon scrawled with flame. Helos swept through the night like sharks breaching water. Dropping payloads of light and heat that tore through the grid. Each blast bloomed and faded in the smog. The air was thick with the reek of burning metal. Somewhere west, a tower fell. It did not shatter. It folded. Sinking into itself with a slow, dreadful grace, as if bowing to an unseen king.

Gideon stood behind him. His shadow long in the red gloom. "Iron ships?"

"Yes," the voice came, thin and distant. "They have landed. On the coast."

"How many?"

"Unknown. Thousands. Men in cloaks. Green. Wearing masks. They make their way here. Two. Maybe three days."

Lorr turned from the glass. His face carved by the flicker of distant fires. "Were I in their place, I would have done the same."

"But you are not," Gideon said. Wry.

Gideon moved slow to the desk. Steps measured. A man walking on broken glass.

He opened a panel low to the floor. Brushed the dust off with the side of his hand. Took out a key. It was old. Black with time. The metal dull. The edges worn near smooth. He turned it over in his palm.

His right hand trembled.

Lorr watched him. "You're shaking," he said.

Gideon said nothing. Brought up his left hand to still the right. The fingers stiff. White at the joints.

He slid the key toward the slot.

The key went in with a hard click. Loud as a shot in the dark.

He turned it.

The walls gave a low sound. Mechanical. Then they moved. Panels slid aside. Light poured out. Screens blinked to life in rows. Lines of code ran like blood down the face of the machine. Maps. Warfront schematics. Energy grids. All blinking in and out of relevance. A tapestry of ruin stitched in light.

Lorr looked at him. Voice low. "What now?"

"We survive," Gideon said.

The helos roared overhead. Their shapes like wasps etched against flame. Men in green cloaks poured in from the coastline. The iron ships groaned, releasing more. The streets filled with the sound of metal on stone. Of voices behind filters. They moved with discipline. Not haste. No rage. Precision. The land's bones trembled beneath their march.

The Dominion burned.

And deep within it, Gideon turned toward the darkness behind the wall. His face unreadable.

"We always knew this was possible," he said.

Lorr stared. Uncertainty flickered in his eyes. "Did we?"

Gideon pressed his thumb to a panel. A hiss. A door opened. Exhaling a cold breath from the black below.

"There are others," he said. "Below. The old units. The ones that never spoke. The ones that were buried."

Lorr narrowed his eyes. Suspicion and memory warring in his gaze. "I thought they were shut down."

"They've been waiting," Gideon said.

The sound of the city now was beyond sirens. It was the scream of metal. The song of war. From the deep, low under the chamber, something began to rise. Ancient and inexorable.

And Gideon smiled without joy.

"Let them see what silence made," he said.

The two men took a lift down deeper into the Spire. And in the streets above, men in green moved like tidewater. But the stone beneath them began to shift. The ground woke.

***

The lift groaned. A shudder. Then dropped them into the bowels of the Spire. Far from the burning city and the howl of sirens that still carried in the stone. The descent held no sound save the cables' mechanical grief and the sour, faint scent of rust. Lorr stood with hands clasped behind his back, eyes fixed on the dull metal of the doors. Gideon watched the floor numbers pass, each a measure of distance from the dying world above.

The lift shuddered again. The doors drew back. Gideon stepped into a dim passage of pipes and conduits. Water wept from the walls. The air lay thick. The odor of cold iron and wet stone. And something else. A damp rot. Like things long buried.

Lorr followed. Each step seemed to tear at the ground as if it might open and take him.

They passed through a succession of gates, each yielding to Gideon's touch. At last, the vault. The doors were great slabs of iron. Pitted with rust. Gideon pressed his hand to the panel. They opened with a grinding sigh.

Inside, the air grew colder still. The vault was vast. Its ceiling lost to shadow. Rows of metal men stood in silence. Their forms dulled by dust and years. A thousand. More. Their faces blank. Eyes dark holes. Limbs stiff at their sides. Some bore the faded mark of the Amalgam. Others were bare. Their plating scarred. Crimped.

Lorr stopped. Just inside the threshold. The sight held him. "Incredible," he whispered. "I'd heard. I never believed them. Automatons from the fields."

Gideon stepped forward. His voice echoed in the space. "This is your new army, General. They do not tire. They do not eat. They do not question. The perfect fighting force."

Lorr moved among the ranks. His boots stirred dust. He reached out. Ran a gloved hand along one outstretched arm. The dust was thick. The metal beneath it was pitted and cold. Scabbed over with old corrosion.

"Dead a long time," he said.

He walked on. The rows rising like rusted gravestones around him.

"Relics, my Rex. Look at them. No oil. No wire in decades. Half of them want limbs. Some have no heads."

"They can be mended."

Lorr turned. His face hard. "By whom? The are no more engineers. The workshops are ruin. You think these things will rise and save the Dominion? They're as dead as the men we lost in the Silent Land."

Gideon's jaw tightened. He moved to a console. Flipped switches. Lights flared overhead. They cast long shadows across the vault. "You do not know their strength. You do not know mine."

"No," Lorr said. His voice climbed. "I don't know their strength. But I do know you, my Rex. Your thoughts. You'd raise the dead if it bought you another day. But these—" He swept a hand at the metal ranks. "These are nothing. They require new wire. New oil. New code. They require hands to fix them and minds to guide them. And there's few left to do all that. Few."

Gideon's right hand shook on the console. "We must try."

Lorr shook his head. "Try what? Fight the Silent Land with ghosts? With rust and faded memory? What is this madness? How many times can a man die?"

Gideon turned from the console. His face pale in the harsh light. "If we do nothing, we are already dead. You saw what remains up there. Ash and ruin. The men in green will spare no one."

Lorr's voice was bitter. "So, you'd send these broken things in our place? Hide below while they march to fire?"

"They are machines," Gideon said. His voice cold. "Tools. Nothing more."

Lorr stared at him. "And what are we?"

Silence fell. Heavy as a shroud. The metal men stood in their ranks. Eyes empty. Waiting. For orders that would not come. Somewhere in the dark, water dripped. Slow. Steady.

Gideon looked away. "I should've used them earlier. I thought I'd keep them hidden. Just in case—"

"Just in case?" Lorr's voice was a low growl, a rasping sound in the cold air of the vault. "Just in case the world ended and you still had a king's toy? Just in case you wanted to still play with armies in the ruins of our own making? There is no 'just in case,' my Rex. There is only now. And now is ash. And these—" he swept a hand across the rows of silent, broken forms, "—these are the forgotten. What you hid, you let die. Like everything else. They are our failures. Not our salvation."

Gideon stood silent. His jaw worked. His right hand shaking. The air in the vault grew colder still. Or perhaps it was only in his own blood. His eyes, fixed on Lorr's face, held no discernible light. A flicker of something. Gone. The words hung in the vast space. A challenge. A judgment. He looked past Lorr. At the ranks of silent metal. The dust lay thick. A breath. Then he spoke. His voice was low. Flat. Carried no echo.

"You are dismissed, General."

Lorr hesitated. Then turned. Strode back to the lift. The doors sighed open and he stepped inside. His shadow long and thin across the vault floor. He looked back once. His eyes found Gideon's.

"My Rex, I hope you find what you're looking for," he said. "But I won't be here to see it. Madness is just a door opening where there was no door before. Or a door closing where there was no wall."

The doors closed with a hiss. The lift began its ascent, carrying Lorr back toward the war-torn surface, leaving Gideon alone in the cold and the dark.

Gideon stood in silence, the weight of the vault pressing in on him. He moved among the metal men. Their faces blank. Their bodies still. He reached out and touched one. The chill of the metal biting through his glove.

He remembered the fields of the Amalgam. The way these machines had once moved through rows of wheat and barley. Their hands gentle. Their steps careful. He remembered the laughter of children. The songs of workers in the dawn. All gone now. All burned away.

He stood before the console. Hands shaking. He keyed in a sequence. Watched as a few lights flickered on the nearest automaton. The eyes glowed faintly, then faded.

"Wake up," Gideon whispered. "Wake up. Just once more. For me."

But the metal men did not move. They stood in silence. Still as a tombstone.

Gideon turned away. Footfalls rang in the deep. He walked the length of the vault. His mind's eye tracing rows of dead men. Silent soldiers. Their forms broken. Their hearts stone. Every fault. Every lost fight. Bore down upon him. A great weight.

He stopped at the far wall. Leaned his head against the cold stone. He closed his eyes and listened to the sound of the city above. The distant thunder of bombs. The roar of the helos. The screams of the dying.

He wondered if Lorr was right. If madness was all that remained. If hope was just another word for delusion.

He opened his eyes. Looked back at the army of metal men. Their ranks stretching into darkness.

"This is what we are," he said softly. "All that's left."

He stood in silence. Alone in the vault. While the world burned above him and the dead waited in the dark.

**

The Spire's bowels. A labyrinth of stone and steel. Corridors swallowed the distant thunder of bombs. Walls wept condensation. Slick. Cold. The air, ancient and close as if the earth itself craved to devour the last remnants of the Dominion. The door hissed open. Gideon walked at the head of a table. Boots clanging on iron grating. His eyes, twin embers, wild and rimmed red in the strobing flicker of emergency light. He smelled the dust of ruin. The metallic tang of fear. The walls seemed to breathe. A slow, decaying breath.

They came. What was left of them. His inner circle. They passed through a blast door that sealed behind them. A sound like a sepulcher's final gasp. The chamber beyond, low-slung, was lined with battered consoles and maps. The table at its heart, scarred by the knives of men long departed. They gathered round. Shadows in the red gloom. Faces pale as chalk. Eyes hollowed by the years. No one spoke. Only the city did. Far off its ruin humming up through the bones of the place like something buried alive.

Morgar stood nearest. Tall and gaunt. His uniform, a gray flag in the despair. Immaculate even now. Gray eyes, calculating as ice shards, flickered. Gorgrath lingered in the deep shadows. Her hat pulled low. Lips thin. A cruel curl. Malgoth's armored form filled half the space. Black and red plates. Streaked with the soot of judgment. Grix, thin as a wraith, hovered at the edge. Hands clasped. Eyes darting from one dark corner to the next. Seeking an escape not yet offered. The air was thick with unspoken words. With the scent of dying hope.

Gideon turned. His breath, a ragged rasp. The bombs above sent tremors through the very rock beneath them. Dust, fine as ash, sifted from the ceiling. He ran a hand through his hair. Fingers trembling. He felt the cold iron in his guts. The weight of his failures. A physical thing.

"All is not lost," Gideon said. His voice, raw, brittle. "The Silent Land rains fire. But we are not yet broken. Not while we draw breath from this tomb."

Morgar's eyes, chips of flint, glinted. "Our lines are gone. The city burns. What remains is this." He made a gesture. A sweep of hand that encompassed the failing chamber. The dwindling light. The end of all things.

Gideon's gaze snapped to him. Fever-bright. "You speak as if defeat is inevitable, Morgar. I do not accept that. We stand. We fight."

A silence. Gorgrath's voice, a hiss from the dark. "The Viper is gone. No word. No trace. Perhaps he saw what was coming. A rat seeking high ground."

Grix coughed. A dry rattle in the throat. "Or perhaps he simply chose the winning side. The side that breathes."

"Cowardice," Malgoth sneered. His armored fists clenched. The steel plates creaked. "He should have stood with us. Died with us."

Gideon pressed his left palm to the scarred table. His shaking right hand down to his side. Head bowed. For a moment, he seemed to shrink. Shrivel into himself. His voice, a whisper. "I killed the Oracle. The Voice. Malachar. Zexus. All loyal. All dead by my word. Was it necessary? Did I believe too much in Elarlu? In her plan for the pathogen? I thought it would save us. I thought—" He broke off. The taste of ash in his mouth.

The others watched him. Silent. The bombs above grew louder. Closer now. The Spire shuddered with every impact. A tremor in the bones of the earth.

Gideon's eyes darted. Unfocused. "Why did I believe her? Why did I think we could control everything? We built so much—" He trailed off. Lost in memory. In regret. A deeper wound than any blade. The ghost of Elarlu's smile in the dust motes.

Morgar's voice, cold and flat. "Regret is for the dead, my Rex. We are not dead yet. Not while we stand."

Gideon looked up. Something feral in his gaze. "No. No, we are not. We are not dead." He straightened. Shoulders squared against the impossible weight. "We will not die here. We will not surrender. I want a plan. I want a way to take the Silent Land. I want it in my hands within twenty-four hours. Or there will be others sitting at this table."

Gorgrath's lips twisted. "You ask for the impossible. The dead cannot rise."

"I ask for loyalty," Gideon said. "I ask for faith. In the end of all things, we choose."

He turned. Cloak swirling in the thin air. Strode from the room. The door hissed shut behind him. A sound of finality. The silence he left was thick. Like blood congealing.

Morgar stared at the closed door. "He is lost," he said softly. His voice barely more than a whisper. "He is gone somewhere we cannot follow. Into the dark."

"Do you see how his hand shakes so," Grix's voice, thin as a dying breath. "He was always mad. Now it shows itself. Like some disease. A malfunction of the body."

"He is our leader," Malgoth shook his head. "We follow him until the end. Into the fire."

Gorgrath stepped from the shadows. Eyes cold as polished stone. "The Viper saw the truth. There is no plan. There is no victory. Only survival. Perhaps we should vanish, as he did. Become ghosts."

Morgar's lips curled in disdain. "You would run? Like a dog?"

"I would live," Gorgrath said. Her eyes met his, unwavering.

Grix hunched his shoulders. "Where would you go? There is nowhere left to run. The city is ash. The Silent Land will soon own the night. All of it."

Malgoth's hand fell to the hilt of his great blade. "We are the last. If we fall, the Dominion falls with us. Into the void."

Morgar turned to the others. "There can be no plan to take the Silent Land," he said. "We have no men. No machines. No hope. We are ghosts in a tomb. Waiting for dawn."

"Then we should try to disappear," Grix's voice, a whisper in the echoing dark. "Fade into the dark. Live to see another dawn. What good is a dead leader?"

"The Viper was right," Gorgrath nodded. "There is nothing left here but death. Only the bones remain."

Malgoth's eyes burned in the gloom. "You can run. But I will not. I cannot. I will not leave him. He is the last of us."

Morgar was silent a long moment. The bombs above grew distant. The city's agony, a constant undertone. The smell of burning.

"He was a great man," Morgar said at last. "Once. Perhaps still. I will not abandon him. Not now. Not at the end. Not when all is lost."

Grix stared at his hands. The ash in his palms. The lines of defeat. He let out a breath. "Nor will I. But where will we go? Those who remain will not look kindly upon us. I stand with him."

Gorgrath's eyes widened. A flicker of something else in them. "All of us then. We are all mad."

Malgoth nodded. "Madness is all that remains. In the face of truth."

They stood in silence. The four of them. As the Spire shuddered and the world above burned itself clean. Somewhere in the deep, Gideon raged against the dying of his dream. The circle was broken. But what remained was bound by something older than loyalty. Older than fear. Older than death.

"We stay," Morgar said. His voice, a final decree. "To the end. To the bitter ash."

The others nodded. One by one. Their faces set.

Above, the bombs continued to fall. The Dominion burned. And in the depths of the Spire, the last of Gideon's circle waited for the end, bound together by ruin and memory. By the echo of a world that would soon be lost to the dust.

***

The chamber was dim. Curtains drawn, though no sun beyond them. Only the iron glow of machines turning in endless silence. A pall hung in the air. A metallic scent of industry and old despair. The guards at the door did not speak when Gideon passed. They did not move. They stood like statues made of burnt wood. Rooted to the floor. Their cloaks were streaked with ash and something darker. Something coagulated and stiff. Like ancient blood. Their eyes, though hidden, seemed to follow him. Or perhaps they saw nothing at all. They were husks.

Gideon stepped through. The door swung shut behind him. It did not close clean. The latch gave a long and mournful groan, drawn from some place buried in the grain. The sound lingered. Like something that knew suffering and would not let it be forgot.

She lay on the bed. Her body a frail shudder in the stale warmth. Candles burned low. Steady. Placed on every sill and every available surface. Their flames small. Trembling hearts in the gloom. Their wax had bled in yellow rivulets. Slow tears to the floor. Hardening into little towers of melted time. Monuments to passing hours. The air in the room was thick. Tasting of salt. A raw tang of the sea. The bitter sweetness of boiled roots A desperate remedy. She was sitting up when he came in. Her hands folded.

Almost protectively, over the distended rise of her belly. Her hair was thin and oily. Plastered back from her skull like wet wire. Showing the contours of her skull. Her skin shone with sweat. A slick, unhealthy sheen. Her eyes, open wide, glowed faintly in the half-dark. Like coins lost in deep water, reflecting some distant, internal light.

"Gideon," she said. Her voice was thin. Almost without body.

He knelt beside her. His coat was stiff, encrusted with the dried ash of what he'd walked through. The grime clinging to the rough fabric of the sleeves. His eyes were sunk deep in their sockets. Ringed with shadow. The color of bruised fruit. He had not slept. Not in days. Not in any real way. Not since the fires began to bloom in the cities. The sleep of men. It had forsaken him.

"My Siren," he whispered, the words ripping in his throat. "I've come."

She touched his face. Her fingers were cold. Cold as bone. Or stone. Despite the heat of the room. "You've been in the fire."

"I live in it," he said. The words tasted of smoke.

She smiled then. A thing without warmth. A stretching of skin. Her teeth were thin and gray. Flakes of shale. Worn down by some unseen grit.

"They tried to pull me back," she said. Her voice held a dry, hollow echo. "The healers. They scraped me clean with their powders and their kindness. Their soft hands. They stitched songs in my ears. Thin melodies of peace and forgetting. But the sea, Gideon. The sea doesn't forget. It carries all things. It brings them back."

He looked at her belly. A small roundness there. Beneath the thin blanket. "You're thinner."

"The child isn't." She rubbed it gently. A slow possessive gesture. "He feeds. On whatever I have left. He takes it all. His hunger, endless."

"They say you don't eat."

"I ate salt from the walls," she said, her voice barely a whisper. "I drank the wax of candles. I sucked the roots of the floor. Pulling what little life was left in them." Her voice broke. A fragile thing that became a true whisper. Barely audible. "I walked across the ocean floor. All of it. There was no light. Only cold."

He sat back on his heels. Watching her. His gaze unwavering. She reached for the bowl beside her bed. Rough. Unglazed ceramic. She took a pinch of powder from it. Fine. White. But did not bring it to her mouth. Only let it fall between her fingers. A slow, drifting cascade.

"They think it's poison," she said. Her eyes fixed on the falling dust. "Your healers. They say it's a disease that hollows the mind. They don't understand. It isn't the powder that does the hollowing. It's the world. The world does the hollowing. It takes and it takes."

He bowed his head. His shoulders slumped beneath the ash-caked coat. The silence settled around them.

"I wanted to see you," he said.

"I know."

"I've been dreaming. The people. The ones we burned. I see them again. But they're not burning now. They're blooming. Like dark flowers. They grow from the ash."

She looked at him. Her eyes unblinking. The faint glow steady.

She laughed. It was a low sound. Wet. Rasping. It made her cough. A dry wracking sound that shook her thin frame.

"You're haunted," she said.

"I hear things."

She looked at him. "What?"

"The Dominion."

She tilted her head, a bird listening for a distant call. "And what does it say?"

He did not answer. The silence held its breath.

"You've changed," she said. Her gaze sharp. "You wear madness like a robe. It suits you."

"I've seen what we've built. What we've burned."

"Yes," she said. "I know. It is clear."

"There are cities made of bone. The dust blows through them. There are children with teeth like glass. They gnaw on the air."

"They were here long before us, Gideon. Long before the fires. They waited. Their death inevitable."

He looked at her. His eyes were red and wet. Unshed tears gathering at the rims. "You said we were chosen."

She smiled. A faint sad curve of her mouth. "We were. We are. But not to conquer. Never to conquer. That was the lie."

He stared. His face a mask of bewilderment. "Then what?"

She looked away. Her gaze fixed on the flickering candles. Small fires. "To remember. To suffer. To carry. The burden of all things."

The candlelight moved in her eyes. Then a reflection like distant fire, like cities burning on a far horizon.

"You said it was ours," he whispered.

"The Silent Land was never going to be ours. It holds its own counsel. It holds its own dead."

He put his hand on her belly. The skin stretched taut beneath his palm. Gideon smiled.

"He's moving. I feel him."

"A simple life. Yours. Mine."

"You still believe in the Dominion? In me?" His voice was edged with disbelief.

"I believe in what is. In the dark. In the bones beneath the fields. In the hunger." She coughed. A dry sound. "And the sea. It always brings its gifts. What rises. What falls. It holds no allegiances." Another cough. "The Dominion is a word. And you? You are flesh. Both, like everything else, will be undone."

He drew back his hand as if burned.

"You know they'll kill you," he said.

"When this is over. They'll scour the land. They'll kill everything."

"They've tried. So many times. They learn nothing."

"They say . . . the healers . . . the others . . . they say you're mad."

"I am," she said, smiling fully now. Her gray teeth showing. "It is the only way to see."

"What should we do?" He looked desperate.

She didn't wait. Didn't think it over. The answer came like it had already been there.

"A feast. Let's have a feast." Her voice was suddenly stronger. A strange cheer in it.

He blinked.

"A feast," she said. "To honor the Dominion. The power. I'll speak the words. I'll set the fire. The people are broken. They don't believe in the war. But they might believe in the scar."

She looked at him then, a smile carved from something old and bitter.

"Scars are real. They always are."

He was silent.

"We'll bring them into our house. The airwaves. The ether. We'll call them home. To see the truth of their brokenness."

"And you'll speak."

"Yes. Like I've always had."

He nodded slowly. A deliberate movement. "You'll give sermons. Each night. From the ashes."

Her smile widened. The teeth gleamed. A shark's maw.

"We'll broadcast it," his voice gaining a grim resolve. "Across the Dominion. Every city. Every settlement. Every dead place."

She laughed again. A sound less wet now. More like dry leaves rattling. "Yes. Let them hear. Let them know what they have done."

"They need something."

"They need to be undone. So they can begin again. Or not."

He rose to his feet. He swayed as he stood. A man still tethered to the burning world. She watched him with eyes that did not blink, the distant fires reflected there.

"I'll tell them," he said. "Tonight. What machines we have left will carry the word."

He stepped away, turning to the door. But she reached for him. Her cold fingers closed on his wrist.

"You came back," she said. "You always do. Like the tides."

"I don't know who I am anymore," his voice hollow.

"You're Gideon. Rex. You're the knife they sent into the fruit. And I'm the rot that blooms from the core. The truth of it. We are the reckoning."

He looked down at her. She was so thin. She seemed to flicker in the dim light. A leaf caught in a draft. A wisp.

"You'll speak to them," he said. "Like you once did. Before all this."

"Yes."

"You'll bring the Dominion back."

"No," her voice filled with a terrible certainty. "I'll push it forward. Into the dark. To its truth."

He left her there. With her bowl of dust and her candles. Her silence. The low moan of the door as he closed it again.

And when the guards saw him, they did not speak. They parted and let him pass. Their burnt wood forms unmoving.

And behind him, in the dark chamber, she began to hum. A slow sound. A sound that had no tune and no end. The same sound she'd made on the ocean floor. In the deep silence before the light. It was the sound of the world ending and beginning.

18 A Feast of Ash

The hall was long and cold. The stone walls stood blackened by the soot of a thousand torches. Banners hung there. Faded. Colors bled by years of smoke. The patient rot of time. The table was a monolith of blackwood. Its surface gouged. Pitted by the knives and cups of men who had once believed in something. It stretched the length of the chamber. A scar splitting the room in two. At its head sat Gideon. Eyes wide. Fever-bright. Hands splayed as if he might hold the world together by will alone. Right hand shaking terribly.

The feast was a lie. Platters of meat. Slick with oil and herbs. Steamed in the torchlight. But the flesh beneath was gray and sour. The bones brittle. Black. The bread was hard as stone. The fruit soft. Weeping. The wine dark. Sharp. Poured in abundance. A mockery. The air was thick with the scent of rot and spice. A perfume meant to mask the truth, but failing at the edges. The servants who brought the dishes were silent. Their eyes hollow. Their faces drawn in the flickering light.

Morgar sat to Gideon's right. His uniform immaculate despite the ruin around him. His gray eyes flickered over the food with the same cold calculation he brought to battlefields. He picked at a slice of meat. Turning it over with his knife. Searching for something untouched by decay. But finding little. He wore black gloves, as always. The red and silver trim of his collar caught the light like a wound.

Gorgrath was a shadow at the far end. Her face half-hidden beneath the brim of her hat. She ate nothing. Her hands folded before her. Eyes moving from face to face. Measuring. Weighing. Her coat seemed to drink the light. The sneer that curled her lips was as much habit as sentiment.

Malgoth, hulking and scarred, tore at a hunk of bread. Jaw working with mechanical fury. His armor creaked with every movement. The spikes catching the light like the teeth of some ancient beast. He chewed and swallowed. His eyes fixed on Gideon. For a moment, he looked like a man who had never known another life.

Grix hunched over his plate. Thin fingers picking through a pile of beans and wilted greens. He sniffed each morsel before eating. Eyes darting to the others. Expecting a rebuke or a blow. His cloak hung from his shoulders like a shroud. The tools at his belt clinked softly when he moved.

Lorr sat near the foot of the table. Shoulders squared. Eyes fixed on Gideon. He did not eat. His plate was untouched. The food cooling in the draft that crept beneath the doors. His uniform bore the burns of a ruined campaign. The lines of exhaustion in his face, deep and unyielding.

Elarlu stood behind Gideon. Her hands folded in the sleeves of her robe. Her hair now mostly white as bone. Her eyes black. Bottomless. She moved with the slow, deliberate grace of a priestess. Her voice a whisper that seemed to echo in the stone.

Gideon raised his cup using his left hand. "To the Dominion," he said. His voice rang in the emptiness, brittle as glass. "To what tomorrow brings."

The others murmured their assent. Some raising their cups. Others only nodding. The wine burned in their throats, and the silence that followed was thick as oil.

Morgar set down his knife. "This is a strange feast, my Rex. The city burns. The stores are empty. And yet here we sit, pretending at plenty."

Gideon smiled, a thin, cracked thing. "Illusion is all we have left, Morgar. Would you rather starve in the dark?"

"I'd rather fight," Malgoth grunted.

"There is nothing left to fight for," Gorgrath sneered. A sound as sharp as knife. "The Silent Land owns most of the streets. Our men are ghosts."

Elarlu's voice slid through the air. "Not all ghosts are powerless. Some linger for a reason."

Grix coughed. A dry rattle. "And what reason is that, Siren?"

Elarlu stepped forward. Her hands came up. "Tonight is not a night for despair," she said. "No. Tonight, we honor what remains. Tonight, we prepare for passage."

She moved around the table, stopping before each of them. From a pouch at her belt, she drew a shard of bone. Blackened by fire. She pressed it to Morgar's forehead. Leaving a charred sigil. He did not flinch.

"To the blade that cuts the path," she said.

She marked Gorgrath next. The sigil stark against her pale skin. "To the shadow that sees all."

Malgoth bowed his head. The bone left its mark. "To the fist that breaks the chains."

Grix trembled as she touched him. But he did not resist. "To the hand that feeds the flame."

She came to Lorr last. Her touch lingering. "To the shield that bears the burden."

Finally, she turned to Gideon. He closed his eyes as she drew the mark. "To the king who walks in darkness."

The room was silent. The torches guttered in the draft. Shadows dancing on the walls. The marks on their foreheads smelled faintly of ash and old marrow.

Elarlu returned to her place by Gideon. "I have a gift," she said. "A sacrament for the passage to come."

Gideon's eyes widened. "What gift, my Siren?"

She smiled, teeth the color of old coins. "An offering," she said. "A thousand souls. Starving. Desperate. We send them out like lambs to whatever gods still bother to watch. The latest Mors Annona strain in their blood now. Deep. When they cross the border, they'll carry death with them like breath. A gift wrapped in skin."

Her gaze swept the chamber. Eyes narrowed to slits.

"They'll be our bombs. Their bodies bursting with plague. Pustules and rot. We'll salt the Silent Land with corpses. There is no place on this earth that shall be free from the Dominion's reach."

The words did not fall. They hung there in the dim. Smoke from a dying fire. No one moved. No one breathed.

The others stared at her. There was horror in them. And something else. "What did you say?" someone whispered.

But she said nothing more.

Gideon stood and laughed. The sound came up ragged and strange. Something that had to be dug out of him with a hook. His eyes glittered in the low light. The veins in his temples stood out like black cord.

"Brilliant," he said, walking over to Lorr. "Why didn't you think of this, General?"

Lorr did not answer at first. His jaw worked. The muscles in his neck stood out in ropes. He turned to the others sitting there in silence. Their faces drawn and hollow as dry wells. Then he looked back at Gideon.

"Because it's madness," he said.

Gideon's smile faded from his face. He stepped forward. The stink off Lorr's collar met him. Sweat and fear. And something older. He took hold of the back of the man's neck with a trembling hand and squeezed.

"Madness," he said. "Is what we live for."

He did not blink. The others stood still as stone.

"Make it happen, General."

Lorr's voice was a ragged thing. It rose from his throat. A sound dredged from the bottom of a well. Each word a broken vessel. Spilling pain into the silence.

"We've got nothing, my Rex. Few men. Few machines. No food. The city's dying."

He waited. The silence lengthened.

"And so are we," said Gideon. His eyes burned like coals buried in ash. "Use what you have. Fix what you can. Make it happen. I do not think you wish to join the bones that hang from the Spire."

He let go.

Lorr rolled his neck. Winced. Rubbed at the skin.

Gideon returned to his place at the head of the table. Stood. Waited.

Morgar leaned forward. "This is not strategy," he said. "This is desperation."

Gorgrath's sneer deepened. "Desperation and madness," came his whisper.

Gideon's eyes passed over them like the wind that stripped the last trees. They were hollow. Worn. Gathering dust. He did not speak. Not right away. His gaze settled on Morgar. Then on Gorgrath. Then back again. The silence between his words was not space. It was blade.

"I've seen cities burn for less than what we've lost," he said. "Seen men eat their own to buy themselves one more quiet night."

He paused. No one dared breathe.

"You call this madness. You call this desperation. So be it."

He turned his head slightly. The light caught the lines carved deep into his brow. He looked old. Terribly so. Like time had not passed over him but through him.

"Did you think it would be poetry? That we'd ride out with brass banners and the world would move aside?"

His voice was low and without anger. Flat as stone.

Malgoth slammed his fist on the table. Plates jumping. "But you ask us to send what few men we have to herd the starving like cattle?"

Elarlu's voice was silk. "They are already dead, Malgoth. Think of this as mercy with a heavy dose of vengeance."

"There will be nothing left," Grix said, shaking his head. "No one to rule. No one to remember."

Gideon gripped the table. "There will be memory. There will be fear. The Silent Land will choke on our dead. Then they will choke on their own."

Lorr rose. Eyes burning. "Utter madness. You would damn us all for spite."

Gideon's voice was a whip. "I would damn them before they damn us."

The room was silent. The only sound was the drip of water from the stones, and from above, the distant thunder of aircraft and bombs.

Elarlu moved to Lorr. Her hand on his arm. "You are the shield. Bear this burden. Lead them to the gates."

Lorr shook her off. "I am no butcher."

"A leader of armies claims he is no butcher!" Gideon laughed. A hollow sound. "Listen to me . . . you are what I say you are."

Morgar's voice was soft. "This is the end, my Rex. There is no victory here."

Gideon stared at him. Eyes wild. "There is always victory. Even in death."

"Then let us die well," Gorgrath said, eyes closed in surrender.

Malgoth stood. Towering over the table. "I will not watch this. I cannot."

Gideon's voice was iron. "You will do as you are told. Everyone here will do as they are told."

Malgoth met his gaze. Unflinching. "I serve the Dominion. Not your madness."

Gideon's hand went to his belt. Fingers brushing against the grip of a pistol.

"Guards!" he called.

Footsteps pounded. The door burst wide. Soldiers spilled in. Rifles raised. Eyes flat and ready.

"Careful, Malgoth," Gideon said. "Loyalty's the last thing left to us."

Malgoth sighed. It was long and low and full of something old and bitter. He sat.

"Loyalty to what?" Grix's voice was a whisper.

Elarlu's smile was cold. "To the end."

The feast continued in silence. The food was untouched. The wine bitter. The shadows grew longer. The torches burning low.

Outside, the city screamed. The Silent Land rained fire on the ruins. The sky alight with the fury of gods and men. The streets were empty, save for the dead and the dying. The wind carried the smell of burning flesh. The wailing of those who had not yet learned to be silent.

Within the hall, the last of the Dominion's lords sat in judgment over a world already lost. Servants cleared the plates in silence. Their faces gray. Drawn. Their eyes fixed on nothing. The banners above them stirred in the draft. The sigils of old victories now little more than stains.

Gideon stared at the table. His eyes were unfixed. The dead gathered there. The Oracle. Malachar. Zexus. The Voice. Their faces like stones laid on his spine.

He paused.

"My Siren is right," he said. "Vengeance. Sweet. Is all there is now."

The marks burned above his brow. The scent of bone. Of ash. It filled his lungs like something final.

Morgar watched him. Gray eyes cold. He saw the madness growing. The cracks in the king. He wondered how long it would be before the last of it crumbled. He picked at the meat. Found a strip that was less gray than the rest. Chewed it slowly as if by force of will he could make it nourishing. The taste was horrible.

Gorgrath slipped from the table. Moving through the shadows. She whispered to herself. Her eyes never leaving Gideon. She wondered if she would live to see another dawn. Her footsteps were silent. Her coat trailing behind her like a shadow that had learned to walk.

Malgoth stood at the door with his arms crossed. The soldiers watched him. Watched every breath he took. Every twitch of his fingers. He didn't look at them. He looked at Lorr. Saw the struggle in his eyes. He wondered if the shield would break. Or if he would bear the burden to the end. His armor creaked as he shifted. The spikes glinting in the dying light.

Grix sat alone. Picking at his food. He counted the days. The rations. The lives. He wondered if there was anything left to save. The numbers ran through his mind like a litany. Each one a measure of what had been lost.

Elarlu stood behind Gideon. Her hands folded. She watched. Her eyes black and bottomless. She wondered if the gods would answer. Or if they too had turned away. Her smile was small and secret. The smile of one who knows the end of the story.

The night wore on. The wine ran out. The torches guttered and died. One by one. Until only the cold remained.

Gideon rose. His voice a whisper. "It is done. Lorr, you have your orders. The rest of you—prepare. The end is coming."

He left the hall. His footsteps echoing in the emptiness.

The others were silent. Each alone with their thoughts. The marks on their foreheads burned. The memory of bone and fire lingering in the air.

Outside, the city burned.

Within, the last of the Dominion royalty waited for the darkness to claim them.

And in the shadows, Elarlu smiled.

***

The square was a pit. The sky above it was the color of lead. The sun, if it lived, was a thing buried and forgotten. Ten thousand souls pressed together behind the wire. Their faces gaunt. Black and hollow. Their eyes sunk in the shadows of their skulls. The wind carried the stink of them. A rot that clung to the stone. The iron. The broken banners that hung limp from the shattered walls.

Lorr stood at the edge of the crowd. His boots half-buried in the black mud. The rain left its mark. Earth churned to gruel. The stink of iron and ash. Soldiers arrayed behind him. They were loyal. Given a few strips of rotted meat. Their uniforms were gray and tattered. The red of the Dominion a memory only. He watched the people. Their hands clutching rags. Their mouths open. Silent. He wondered if they could remember when last they had eaten.

Gideon came down the steps. His cloak trailing behind him. Elarlu at his side. Her eyes black as the pit. Her hands folded in the sleeves of her robe. He looked at Lorr. But Lorr looked away.

"Are they ready?" Gideon said.

Lorr still not looking. Shouted. "No one is ready for this."

Gideon's mouth twisted. Anger.

Elarlu looked at Lorr. Her voice was soft. "Think of it this way . . . you are just sending them on. You are their redeemer."

Lorr's jaw worked. He looked at the crowd. He saw children. Their faces streaked with filth. Their bellies caved. He saw old men. Their eyes glazed with hunger. Women with hair like straw. He saw himself among them.

Gideon raised his hand. The soldiers brought their rifles to bear. The crowd stood still. Silent. Watching with the dumb calm of beasts before the hammer.

"Let it be done," Gideon said.

He dropped his hand.

The rifles cracked in a single volley. A sound like the sky breaking. The front ranks fell. The ones behind stumbled over them. The rifles fired again. And again. And the bodies piled up in the mud. Blood running in black rivulets between the stones. Some screamed. But most were silent. They had no strength left for fear.

When it was done, the square lay still and red as a butcher's pan. Smoke drifted low across the flagstones. Thin as gauze. Catching on the splintered bones of benches and the blackened stalks of banners fallen in ash. The soldiers moved among the dead with their rifles slung low. Their faces pale. Their boots slipping in the gore. One knelt and turned over a boy with the toe of his boot. The boy's eyes were open. His mouth was open. The soldier turned away.

They worked without talk. Knives out. Sleeves up. They split the bodies open like game. Quick. Sure. The meat opened easy. Their hands shook. Didn't matter. The coats they wore were red and stiff and heavy with it.

The blades whispered through sinew and skin.

Steam rose off the dead like breath.

A young soldier vomited.

"Keep cutting," Lorr said. "The organs. Open them up. The lungs first. Everything."

"There's nothing left," a soldier said.

"There's always something left," Lorr responded.

The soldier turned to a woman lying facedown. Drove the blade in at the spine. Dragged it down to the tailbone. Pulled her open like a coat. The smell that came out was sweet and rancid and thick as a curtain.

The drones came down overhead. Many repaired. All coded with coordinates. They made no sound but the hum of their engines. Low and steady. Like something dreaming. Black things shaped like beetles. Seamless. The crucibles beneath them shined dully in the half-light. Ribbed in steel. Their flanks marked with glyphs no living man could read. Not now. Not ever.

They passed over the square and stopped there. Motionless. As if listening.

One opened.

A trickle of gray dust sifted out and turned to nothing in the wind.

Then the limbs came. Long and jointed. Like iron vines.

It lowered itself beside a body facedown.

"What is it doing?" a soldier asked.

No one answered.

The drone curled its metal arms around the corpse and lifted it. Another. Then another. When it could carry no more, it turned skyward. Its frame shuddering with the strain. Then it was gone. To the Silent Land.

Another came. It hovered. Its belly opened like a wound. Took what was left. Did the same.

More followed. No words. No thought. Just machines clearing a gravesite no one would speak of.

"They'll call this a victory," someone said.

Lorr stood over the corpses. "No," he said. "They'll call it something else."

Morgar watched from the steps. His face unreadable. "This is no victory," he said.

Gorgrath stood beside him. Her coat drawn tight. Her eyes on the blood pooling in the gutters. "It's the shape of what's left to us," she said.

One of the drones. Bigger than the rest. Came down slow and low. It began stacking the bodies like cordwood. Careful in its work. Making it easier for the others to lift them. Quicker. Cleaner.

The drones continued to come. Like a swarm. Heavy in the air. Swaying like beasts yoked to a purpose they did not choose. They turned in unison. The holds beneath them brimming with death. No warning. No light. They slipped into the gray sky like ghosts taught to fly.

When the square was clear of the dead, Gideon found Lorr kneeling in the blood.

His arms soaked to the wrist. He made no move to rise.

"You did this, General," Gideon said.

Lorr kept his gaze on the crimson puddling around his knees.

"We both did," he said.

Gideon's voice wavered. "You've done your duty."

Lorr said nothing.

He looked down at his hands.

The blood had gone cold.

Elarlu stood beside Gideon. They watched the drones recede into the gray distance. "Go with vengeance," she whispered. "Go with fire."

Malgoth came from the shadows. His armor dented. Blackened. "They will know what we have done," he said.

Gideon's eyes glittered. "Good. Let them choke on it."

Grix stood apart. His back to the wall. His eyes on the sky. He counted the drones. Lips moving in silent calculation. But he lost count. "There will be nothing left," he said.

Gorgrath laughed. A sound like broken glass. "There is nothing left now."

The wind shifted. It carried the stink of blood and entrails up through the ruined streets. Into the hollowed city. What folk remained pressed themselves behind splintered doors. Behind broken shutters. They watched through the cracks with wide eyes. The city was silent but for the crows.

Gideon turned to Lorr. "You are the shield. You have borne the burden."

Lorr stood. His face was stone. "There is no shield. Only the blade."

Gideon's smile came slow. Narrow as a wound. "Then let us be the blade."

Lorr quickly drew his pistol. For a moment, leveled it true at Gideon's chest. All eyes held fast. The crows watched from the rooftops. Black shapes against the bruised sky. The wind stirred the dust in the empty square.

"Everyone was weak," Lorr said. "Everyone who listened. Who stepped into the snares you left. Who swallowed what you fed them. What you called truth. That was me, too. I was one of them. So, what do you do with the weak, then?"

Gideon shrugged. "You tell me?"

Lorr turned the pistol. No hesitation. The muzzle pressed cold against his own temple. The shot came hard and fast. The sound slapped the buildings and scattered the birds. Lorr crumpled to the blood and mud.

"A pity," Gideon said shaking his head. a man watching the end of something he'd already forgotten.

The crows returned. Black shapes folding out of the gray. A drone came down out of the gray sky. Engines whining like something hurt. It hung there a moment above the body of the Lorr. Then reached with arms of metal and took him up. Turned south. Gone. The crows called after it. The city held its silence.

The square emptied slowly. The soldiers moved away. Their faces pale. Thinking of where they'd find their next meal. The blood dried on the stones. Black and sticky. The sky was unchanged.

Elarlu stood alone in the square with her arms outstretched. She sang in a tongue long buried. Her voice thin as wire and cold as stone. The wind took it. Sent it spinning south over the blackened bones of the city. Across the dead river. Into the empty sky.

Above the Silent Land, the drones split open. They dropped their loads into the clouds. The bodies fell. Struck rock. Struck field. Split open like rotted fruit. The blood was dark. Full of death. The earth took it. The wind carried it. The sickness. Into towns. Into the lungs of the living.

A girl stood in a field where the wheat no longer grew. She looked up at the falling dead. Her hands balled into fists. She did not run. She did not cry. She watched them fall. She knew the old world had died again.

In the ruined square, Gideon watched the sky. "It is done," he said.

Morgar turned away. "It is never done."

The sun did not rise. The city lay in darkness. Waiting. Waiting for the men from the Silent Land. The green masks.

The wind moved through the streets like something lost. It cried against the broken glass and loose tin. The banners hung slack on their poles. No color in them. Only the old threads and the stains of rain.

Crows lined the rooftops. Black and still. They watched the city as if it were already dead.

***

The storm had come in the night. It left the Silent Land scoured and raw. In the east, the sky was a bruise. The sun, if it rose, did so behind a pall of smoke and cloud. Reza stood at the window and watched. He saw the black shapes of the drones as they moved over the borderlands. He saw the bodies spill from their bellies. Tumbling. Breaking open on the rocks. The fields. The water. And he knew it was too late. The wind would carry the sickness. The rivers would bear it to wells. Nothing would be left to save.

Dunlow came into the room. He was pale. His hands shook. He stood beside Reza. They watched the drones vanish into the haze.

"We were too slow," Dunlow said.

Reza did not answer. He watched the wind take the smoke south. He watched the crows rise in black clouds from the trees. He saw the world ending. He saw himself in it. A witness and nothing more.

"They'll pay for this with their lives," Dunlow said.

"Tell me," Reza said. "What's left to take from a man who walks through this world as if he's already crossed over?"

Dunlow turned from the window. In the corner, the radio crackled. Spat static. The men who spoke on it did so in thin voices. Distant. Like they were speaking from the grave.

"Only one thing left," Reza said.

Dunlow looked at him. His eyes rimmed with red. His mouth was a thin line.

"You mean it."

Reza nodded. "There's nothing else."

He looked at his hands. He thought of the fields before the war. The smell of grass and earth. The sound of water running in the ditches. He remembered his father's voice. Low. Steady. Telling him there is always a way back.

He removed the tag from his breast pocket. Read the code. Then typed the sequence into the console. The numbers glowed. Cold. Blue. Outside, the wind howled. The place shuddered.

Dunlow watched him.

When it was done, Reza looked up.

"It's sent," he said.

Dunlow nodded. He closed his eyes. He thought of the city as it had been. The towers. The markets. The children running in the squares. He saw the Spire rising above it all. Black. Unbroken. He saw the end coming, and he did not look away.

***

In the city of the Dominion, Gideon stood atop the Spire with Elarlu. The wind flayed their garments like skins hung to dry. The sky churned with ash. The fire bore no promise. Beneath them, the streets lay barren but for the dead. For the few who moved among them. Silent. Without purpose. As if death had mistaken its count.

Elarlu's hair whipped about her face. She turned to Gideon. He took her in his arms. Held her close.

"It is over," she said.

Gideon shook his head. He placed his hand upon her belly. Smiled.

"No," he said. "There will always be a future."

She looked at him. Her eyes were full of sorrow. Hope. Of all the things that had been lost.

The sky to the west burned with a strange light. Pale and sick with it. It moved like oil across water. Lit from beneath by something the earth had never asked for.

The helo came down from the clouds. Low over the carcass of the city. Its rotors hauling the wind in chains.

Beneath its belly hung the bomb. Black as pitch. Mute. Turning slow where it hung. Like a coin tossed by some blind old god whose hands forgot mercy.

Those who remained looked up. Some fell. Some knelt. A few wept. Though not loudly. Most just stood there. Watching. As if by seeing it, they might change its mind.

Gideon held Elarlu. Close. Her face streaked with dirt and salt. Her hair tangled. Eyes glassy with smoke. She did not speak.

He watched the helo draw nearer. The bomb a shadow crucified beneath it.

"Do you believe in it?" she asked.

"Believe in what?"

"The future?"

"I do," he said. "There was a man. He once told me the future's a hungry thing. Said its appetite shifts with the wind. Feed it what it wants, he said, and maybe it passes you by. But starve it and it'll come for you all the same."

"Did we starve it?"

He shook his head. Slow. Like a man watching smoke rise off something long dead.

"No."

He smiled then. It wasn't joy. Just the shape of the thing stretched thin across a desert of dust. He lifted his arms to the scorched heavens. Palms open to nothing.

"What great fun for a leader that people do not think," he shouted. "What a feast of fools."

The streets did not empty so much as fall silent. No curtains drawn. No doors slammed. Just stillness. A kind the dead might envy. Dogs sniffed at rusted cans. The bones of dinners forgotten. Wind moved through the alleyways. Carrying soot and curled paper. The scent of burnt copper. Ghosts of memory. Untethered. Drifting. Somewhere a child cried out. Once. There was no answer.

Above, the bomb swung on its tether. A pendulum in a clock no man had wound. No countdown. No mercy. It was not god's thing. No. It was man's. A thing made to end.

Then it fell.

No scream. No thunder at its coming. Just the parting of smoke. The slipping of sound. Clean. Without remorse. It passed through what remained of fire. The trailing ash. The empty air scratched by ruin.

The earth did not tremble. Not yet. It waited.

The moment poised. A beat unplayed. The breath not yet exhaled.

And then the sky came open.

Not blue. But green. Unnatural. Holy in its wrongness. Like something made not to be seen. Light flooded down in sheets, and the heavens poured their judgment unspoken. Unanswerable.

The Spire vanished first. Unmade in an instant. And the city folded in on itself. Streets opened like wounds. Stone turned to slag. The green flame moved fast. Where it passed, nothing remained. Flesh turned to ash. Bone to vapor.

Men caught in its wake ignited like tinder. Birds dropped out of the sky like burnt paper. Rivers rose in steam. Forests collapsed inward. Black trunks crumbling to soot.

The Dominion died with no scream. Only fire. Only ruin.

And in that place where the tower once stood, the fire still burned. The sky was dark. The world was hollow. No voice. No sound. Only the wind. And in the wind, the memory of things lost. Carried forever through a world that no longer was alive.

ABOUT THE AUTHOR

Philip Mazza is a novelist with a boundless imagination, captivating readers with the epic fantasy series *The Harrow Saga* and the sci-fi thriller *The Neon Hive*. Born in New York in 1959, he earned a degree in Business from LeMoyne College and an MBA, later holding leadership roles in human resources and operations. Now a professor at the Madden School of Business and Economics, Philip dedicates his time to his students and writing. *Gideon Rex* is his fourteenth literary work. He and his wife enjoy travel and continue to live in upstate New York.